USA Today Bestselling Author

LINDSAY McKENNA

presents the exhilarating story of Captain Maya Stevenson and the man she was born to battle—and destined to love. It's the MORGAN'S MERCENARIES book you've been waiting for!

* * *

"You're not going to give me an inch, are you?"

"Not a chance," Maya replied, her green eyes blazing. "I know you. I suffered under your command. This time, you're the one on the edge of the sword."

Dane held her gaze. "I promise not to let our past get in the way of this mission. Is that enough? Or do you want a pound of my flesh while you're at it?"

"You don't have anything I want," Maya replied, shaking with fury. Why did Dane York have to be such a bastard?

And yet, although she hated to admit it, she was powerfully drawn to the army officer....

* * *

"Lindsay McKenna continues to leave her distinctive mark on the romance genre with...timeless tales about the healing powers of love."
—*Affaire de Coeur*

Also available from

LINDSAY McKENNA

MAN WITH A MISSION
(Silhouette Special Edition #1376)

Coming in April, read the first three stories featuring Morgan Trayhern's team in this special volume containing all three books!

MORGAN'S MERCENARIES: IN THE BEGINNING...
(Silhouette Books)

And if you haven't read the story of Maya's sister, Inca, look for:

MORGAN'S MERCENARIES: HEART OF THE WARRIOR
(Silhouette Books)

Look for more MORGAN'S MERCENARIES, featuring Maya and her team, coming soon!

LINDSAY McKENNA

Morgan's Mercenaries:

Heart of Stone

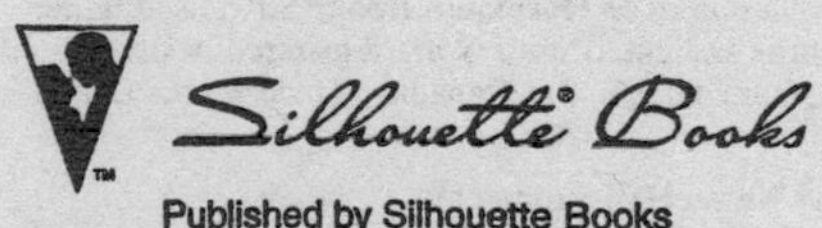

Published by Silhouette Books
America's Publisher of Contemporary Romance

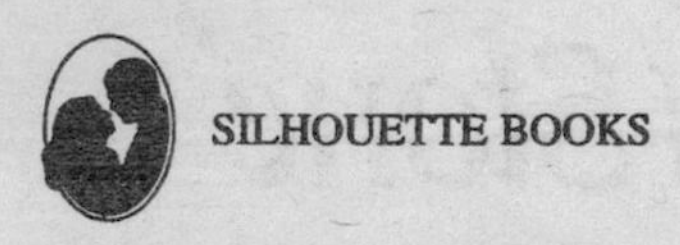

MORGAN'S MERCENARIES: HEART OF STONE

ISBN 0-373-48426-7

This edition published by arrangement with Harlequin Books S.A.

Visit Silhouette at www.eHarlequin.com

Printed in U.S.A.

For Hal Klopper, Boeing public relations,
Todd Brown, Boeing Apache test pilot,
and Phillip Mooney, Boeing aviation expert.

Thank you for your help, your dedication
and your passion for the Apache helicopter.

Chapter 1

"Morgan, I've got to warn you. Captain Maya Stevenson is a modern-day woman warrior," Mike Houston said as he sat down with his boss at a round table beneath a red-and-white-striped umbrella. "She kicks butt and takes names later."

Morgan sipped his fragrant Peruvian coffee, his gaze restless as he looked down the narrow, red tiled walk toward the entranceway of the India Feliz Restaurant, where they were shortly to meet the clandestine and legendary Maya Stevenson. Directly in front of them rose the massive, loaf-shaped dome of Machu Picchu. It was December, summertime, and the landscape was dotted with orchids.

Morgan and Mike had arrived a half hour earlier by helicopter from Cuzco. Agua Caliente was a small, bustling tourist town, the closest community to the archeological wonder that was Machu Picchu.

"She's kind of like a real-life Lara Croft," Mike continued, using the action heroine and the popular video game to describe Maya.

"My son, Jason, is in love with Lara Croft, the female archeologist in his Tomb Raider game." Morgan chuckled. "He's fourteen years old and plays that game every chance he gets." Quirking one eyebrow toward Mike, he said, "A living Lara Croft. That's saying a lot."

Mike, dressed in the typical tourist gear of a Machu Picchu T-shirt, jeans and hiking boots because he didn't want to draw attention to himself, grinned and sipped from his china coffee cup. "You know, for years while we were out here chasin' the bad guys—the drug dealers—my soldiers and I would come busting into the area north of Machu Picchu. We'd fly in with helicopters, then drop down and start raiding. Our goal was to stop shipments from getting into Bolivia. Every once in a while we'd get outnumbered and outgunned, trapped by the druggies, who were trying to take us out. I knew there was no help coming to save our butts. We performed our missions alone, with the government's approval, but they didn't have the money to bankroll us like we needed. So if we got into trouble, we were on our own." Mike's eyes sparkled. "And out of nowhere would come these black Boeing Apache assault helicopters. Two of them. And I mean out of nowhere."

"You've told me about these unmarked black helos coming in and saving your neck from time to time," Morgan acknowledged. "Way back when, we didn't know it was a spec ops—special operations—that was behind them. Now we do." He looked up at the late morning sky, a pale blue with thin white clouds silently wafting overhead. Every now and again a snakelike wisp would coil around the top of one of the towering mountains that literally surrounded Agua Caliente. At six thousand feet in altitude, the small Peruvian town looked to Morgan like a mystical Shangri-la, hidden deep in the mountainous jungle, in the middle of nowhere. The roar of the mighty Urubamba river, less than a half mile away, was clearly audible from the restaurant patio.

Watching the ceaseless flow of tourists passing the India

Feliz, Morgan heard snatches of German, French, Italian, as well as British and American accents. It was a Tower of Babel, quite literally, a baby United Nations.

Morgan had boned up on Machu Picchu and found out that what drew people from around the world was the spiritual nature of this old Incan temple complex. It was said to be the center of feminine energy on the planet, just as the Tibetan Himalayas, on the opposite side of the globe, were considered the masculine center. New Agers came here, from the looks of it—many on some kind of spiritual quest, he supposed.

"This is a very peaceful place," he murmured. "And drop-dead gorgeous. Look at the thousands of orchids clinging to that lava cliff face in front of us. That's pretty astounding."

Mike grimaced. "Yeah, it is. On the surface it's peaceful." He pointed at the hazy, mist-shrouded canyon, where a whole series of mountains nestled shoulder-to-shoulder along the raging, unharnessed Urubamba. The mountains looked like soldiers at attention to him. "Go twenty miles north or east or west, and you're going to meet drug runners trying to get their cocaine crop across the Peruvian border into Bolivia, where they know they won't be pursued by us."

"At least the Peruvian government let Maya come in here with U.S. support. The records suggest she and her squadron of women pilots are slowing the trade out of Peru more than a little. Fifty percent reduction isn't a bad figure considering what she's up against."

Mike nodded and lifted his chin. "Yeah, she's done one helluva job on a shoestring budget. Normally, spec ops get money thrown at them. Millions of dollars, as a matter of fact. But not her program. It was her idea to start an all-women squadron hidden deep in the mountain jungles to take out the bad guys. The only reason the idea took off was because her father's an army general and backed it. If he hadn't been, she wouldn't be here today or done the incredible job she and her band of women rebels have done.'' Mike grinned, respect in his tone.

''My wife, Laura, who is a military archivist and history buff, is very taken with Maya's legend.'' Morgan waved his hand. ''Not that I've told her that much, but Laura is gung ho about what she knows, and glad we'll be supporting Maya's mission now, in place of the CIA.''

Rubbing his jaw, Mike sat back and stretched out his long legs. Two local dogs came up to the table and lay down between them. One was a black-and-white terrier type and the other looked like the descendant of a golden retriever who'd met an ugly mutt in one of the back alleys of Agua Caliente one night. The dogs sat contentedly near their feet, hoping for a few handouts. ''Personally, I think the spooks wanted Maya to fail,'' he stated.

''Of course they did.'' Morgan chuckled as he finished his coffee. ''She's a woman. And she has a band of women doing a 'man's job' better, probably, than any male squadron would do it. Doesn't look good to the Pentagon to have women outshining men in spec ops, you know?'' He smiled across the white-linen-draped table at Mike, who was also grinning like a fox.

''I think she'll be happy to hear that her squadron has been transferred over to you.''

Raising his thick black brows, Morgan said, ''I hope so. You've met her, right?''

''Yes, a number of times.''

''Anything I should know so I don't put my foot into it with her? I'd like to get off to a good start with Maya, since I'm going to be her new boss.''

Mike smiled hugely. ''She doesn't suffer fools gladly or for long. She shoots straight from the hip, doesn't waste words. She was raised an army brat, flew civilian helicopters when she was just a teenager, and went directly into the warrant officer program the army offered. Took her training in Apache combat helicopters at Fort Rucker, Alabama, which is where everyone takes their training to fly an assault helo. When she volunteered for this spook spec ops, she suggested a very provocative idea to the head honchos—let her choose a band of trained women Apache pilots, handpick the crews, and come down here to stop the cocaine drug trade from getting into Bolivia. They promoted her from the warrant ranks and made her a captain because she was going to be C.O.—commanding officer—for this mission. She makes Indiana Jones look like pabulum compared to what she and her women pilots do down here.''

''And why does she have such determination to do this? That's what I don't understand,'' Morgan murmured. ''It's the one piece of her background I can't integrate.'' He gazed over at Mike. ''Do you know why she would scuttle a potentially brilliant army career and go into a spec ops mission like this?''

Mike moved uncomfortably. ''I know *some* of it. The rest, you'll have to ask her.'' He propped his chin on his folded hands and placed his elbows on the table. ''I know you have Maya's personnel records. She was adopted as a baby. General Stevenson was an attaché in São Paulo, Brazil, for the U.S. ambassador. At that time, he was a light colonel. He and his wife hadn't been able to conceive a child. They'd tried everything and nothing worked. One day, a Brazilian Indian woman came to the embassy asking for Eugenia Stevenson. She carried a baby girl no more than two weeks old in her arms. When Mrs. Stevenson came to the back gate to see the Indian woman, she found the baby lying on the walk, alone. That's how Maya was adopted—she was dropped on the U.S. Embassy's doorstep. Eugenia fell in love with her, and they went ahead with formal adoption, giving her the name Maya, which means 'mystery.''' Mike smiled a little. ''No one knows Maya's real origins. I'd say she was part Brazilian Indian and part Portuguese aristocracy, judging from her features and skin color.''

"So, Maya has a stake down here in South America because of her bloodlines?"

"Yes, I'd say so. Just like bloodhounds need to hunt, she needs to be down here with her people, would be my guess."

"That makes sense with what I know. From what I understand, Inca is her fraternal twin sister," Morgan said. "They were born in the Amazon. Somehow, Maya was taken to the city, while Inca was left behind in the jungle to be raised."

"Yes, and Inca didn't know she was a twin until just recently, when you worked with her on that drug mission in the Brazilian Amazon jungle."

"Which is how we learned of Maya and her spec ops," Morgan murmured. "If she'd never shown up that night after Inca got wounded, we'd still been in the dark about her and her mission."

"I think we got lucky," Mike said. "Fate, maybe."

"What else can you tell me about her?"

"I think you know that Inca belongs to a secretive spiritual group known as the Jaguar Clan?"

"Yes. Does Maya, too?"

"Yes and no. She's a member of the Black Jaguar Clan, a branch of the main clan."

"What does that all mean? I know you have Quechua Indian blood running through your veins, and you're more educated about this mystical belief system than I am."

Mike avoided Morgan's incisive gaze. He knew more than a little, but he wasn't willing to bet the farm that Morgan was ready for the bald truth. Mike's wife, Ann, had had enough trouble grasping what it meant to be member of the Jaguar Clan, when she'd learned her husband was one. Mike hedged. "As I understand it, genetically speaking, there's a strong spiritual mission bred into the people who belong to the Jaguar Clan. They're here to help people. To make this a better world to live in. The Black Jaguar Clan is the underbelly, so to speak. They do the dirty work with the ugliness of our world, handle the confrontations in the trenches."

"And you think that's why Maya sacrificed her army career to become a pain in the ass to the drug lords down here in Peru?"

Chuckling, Mike nodded. "Would be my guess."

"She's more like a laser-fired rocket," Morgan murmured. "Almost a zealot or fanatic."

"Isn't that what it takes to be successful at something like this?" Mike questioned. "And aren't you a little bit of a fanatic yourself? Didn't your own background, your unsavory experiences in Vietnam, turn you into a do-gooder for those who couldn't fight and win for themselves?"

Lifting his hands, Morgan said, "Guilty as charged. I'm the pot calling the kettle black."

"Glad you can see that you and Maya have the same jaguar spots." Mike chuckled. "It takes one to know its own kind."

Morgan raised his chin, suddenly alert. "Is that her?"

Mike cocked his head, his eyes narrowing. There, turning into the entrance of the French restaurant, was a woman who stood six foot tall. Her long black hair, slightly curled from the high humidity, swung loosely about her proud shoulders and full breasts. She wore khaki-colored shorts and hiking boots with thick black socks peeking over the tops. Her dark brown T-shirt had a picture of a cream-colored Condor, its wings spread wide, across it. Over her left shoulder hung a fairly large olive-green backpack. A pair of sunglasses on a bright red cord swung between her breasts.

"Yeah, that's her," he told Morgan in a low tone.

Morgan watched Maya with a keen, assessing eye. He knew warriors, and he knew how to size up someone astutely. Captain Maya Stevenson looked like a tourist, plain and simple. She was dressed in what rich travelers from foreign countries wore around here. Only her golden skin and long, rippling black hair suggested that she might be South American. Morgan liked the way she moved; on those firm, long legs of hers—with a bold, confident stride. Maya's eyes were wide and alert. Their emerald depths showed interest, excitement and wariness all at the same time as she pinned her gaze directly on Morgan.

There was no wasted motion about this army aviation officer. Morgan found himself smiling to himself. The energy, the power, the confidence around Maya Stevenson was something to behold. She was at least a hundred feet away from them, yet Morgan could swear he felt her stalwart presence, as if the sun itself was shining directly upon him. No photo did her justice, he thought. She was beautiful and looked very similar to Inca, her fraternal twin sister. But there were dissimilarities, too. Maya was six foot tall and a big-boned woman. She had a slight cleft in her chin, and Inca did not. Her face was oval, cheekbones high, shouting of her Indian heritage. Yet the aristocratic thin nose, flaring nostrils and full mouth were very similar to Inca's features.

Morgan was fascinated with this story of twins separated at birth, one becoming an environmental warrior in the Amazon jungles for the rights of the Indians, and the other a maverick military helicopter pilot. While Inca was calm, proud and quiet there was an edginess to Maya, he noted. Maya wore her brazenness, her strength, without fear. He admired that. Getting to his feet, Morgan was glad he was over six feet tall. Yet as she approached him, he saw Maya's eyes narrow speculatively on him, as if she was using x-ray vision to see right through him. Did she read minds, as Inca was purported to do? Morgan hoped not. If Maya knew that he thought her statuesque and possessing a bold, primal quality few women willingly showed, she'd probably deck him where he stood. This was a woman who brooked no bull from anyone—ever. No, she was an equal and it was obvious in every step she took that she expected to be treated as such.

Mike rose. He moved forward, his hand extended toward Maya.

She glared at him and halted. Glancing back toward the street, she whispered, "Follow me. And don't look so damned obvious, will you?"

Morgan looked at Mike, who lowered his hand, a contrite expression on his features. They both watched as Maya headed into the restaurant. It was 11:00 a.m. and there were few people in the usually popular place.

"Let's go," Morgan murmured, a cockeyed grin tugging at one corner of his mouth.

Mike good-naturedly grinned back and gestured for Morgan to go first.

Inside the restaurant, Morgan saw the owner, Patrick, standing behind the mahogany bar. Maya was leaning up against the counter, speaking to him in fluid French. As they approached, she swung her head in their direction. Her eyes grew slitted.

"Come on. Patrick has a table he reserves for me and my friends when I come into town." She brushed between them and moved up the mahogany stairs, taking the steps two at a time to the second floor.

The restaurant was light and airy, with many green jungle plants and bright red, pink and yellow bromeliads in brightly painted pots here and there. Each table had a starched and pressed white linen cloth across it, and there were fresh flowers on every one. As Morgan climbed the stairs, classical music, soft and haunting, wafted through the restaurant. He shook his head, finding it odd that a five-star French chef would come to Peru and set up a gourmet restaurant in such a little backwater town. He wondered what the man was running from.

Maya was sitting at a rectangular table at the rear of the second floor of the restaurant, her back against the wall. It was a good position, Morgan thought. From her vantage point she could see everyone coming up and down those stairs. She'd put her pack down beside her chair and was speaking in Quechua to the waiter. As they approached, she looked up at them.

"Patrick makes the best mocha lattes in Peru. You two want some?"

"Sounds good," Morgan said, making himself at home across from Maya. "Mike? How about you?"

"Make it three," Mike said in Spanish to the Peruvian waiter, who was a Quechua Indian. The waiter nodded and quickly moved to the bar nearby to make the drinks.

Maya held Morgan's glacial blue gaze. She knew he was sizing her up. Well, she was sizing him up, too, whether he knew it or not. As she folded her long, spare hands on the white linen tablecloth, she said, "Mike said you're my new boss. Is that right?"

Nodding, Morgan said, "I'd prefer to say that you've joined our international team and we're glad to have you on board." He stretched his hand across the table toward her. "I'm Morgan Trayhern. It's nice to meet you." She took his hand. Not surprised by the strength of her grip, he met her cold, flinty eyes. She reminded him of a no-nonsense leader capable of split-second decisions, with a mind that moved at the speed of light, or damn near close to it. Already Morgan was feeling elated that he'd fought to get her spec ops as part of his organization, Perseus.

"Don't bite him, Maya," Mike intoned humorously as they released their mutual grip. "He's the only junkyard dog in town that's friendly to you and your squadron."

Taking the napkin, Maya delicately opened it and spread it across her lap. "It looks like I owe you some thanks, Mr. Trayhern. Mike, here, tells me that my number was up at spook HQ and with the boys over at the Pentagon. You certainly look the part of a white knight. Where's your horse?"

Grinning, Morgan met her humor-filled eyes. Her laughter was husky and low. "I can't ride a horse worth a damn. My daughter, Katy, now, she can," he answered. "I like to watch her, but that's as close as I get to a four-legged animal."

"Got a picture of her?"

Taken off guard, Morgan nodded, moved his hand to the back pocket of his chinos and took out his well-worn, black leather wallet. Opening it on the table, he noted Maya's sudden, intense interest. Her gaze was pinned on the color photos he kept within his wallet. Taking them out, he turned them around for her to look at.

"This is my oldest son, Jason. He's fourteen."

"He looks a lot like you," Maya murmured. "That same dark, handsome face."

Morgan warmed beneath her praise because he could tell already that Maya wasn't one to make small talk or say things just to be polite. "Thanks. This is Katherine Alyssa, my oldest daughter. She's riding her Welsh pony, Fred. And this last one is of my wife, Laura, holding our latest children, fraternal twins...."

Maya picked up the photo, her brows arching with surprise. "So, you have twins...." She studied it with renewed intensity. "You have beautiful children."

"Thanks. My wife and I agree, though we are a little partial toward our children." He said nothing more, realizing that because Maya was a fraternal twin, she would make a positive connection with his children. He liked the fact that despite her being a hardened military veteran, she had a soft heart, too. The more he got to know Maya, the more he liked her.

Handing him back the photos, she looked up. "Ah, here are our lattes. You have no idea how long I've waited for this...." And she reached out to take a cup and saucer from the waiter, thanking him warmly in his own language. He bowed his head and shyly smiled at her.

Mike thanked him also. When the waiter left, he chuckled quietly and sipped his mocha latte. "See? I told you Trayhern wasn't the typical male bastard that you're used to working with."

Wrinkling her nose, Maya again met the solid blue gaze

of her new boss. She sipped the rich coffee with delicious slowness and allowed the sweetness to run delectably across her tongue. Placing the flowered china cup on the saucer, she folded her hands on the table.

"I hope you know what you're getting yourself into, Mr. Trayhern."

"Call me Morgan. I don't stand on ceremony with my people."

"All right," Maya murmured. "Do you know anything about us or did you buy us sight unseen, Morgan? A pig in a poke, maybe?"

Her direct and uncompromising gaze would have been unsettling had Morgan not liked that kind of straight-across-the-board honesty. When she lifted her lips and smiled, it was with a carnivore's grin. She was playing with him, like a jaguar might with its helpless quarry. Houston was right: she shot from the hip. *Good.* "Yes, I saw the bottom line."

"And the fact that I used to have three Boeing Apaches, but because spookdom decided to strangle me slowly by cutting my budget yearly, I had to cannibalize one to keep the other two flying?"

"I saw that."

"And that I've got twelve overworked pilots who need some help and relief?"

"Yes, I saw that, too."

"And that the men don't like us women showing them up?" Her eyes glinted and she leaned forward slightly.

Morgan wasn't intimidated by her low, furious tone or her directness. He met and held her stare. "I saw that, too, Maya." When he used her first name, rolling it gently off his tongue, she recoiled. At first, Morgan wondered if she didn't like his informality with her. And then, intuitively, he figured it out: Maya was expecting a hard-nosed bastard to show up and try to push her around, keep her outside the circle, like other men had before him. The look in her eyes was one of surprise—and then naked suspicion. Morgan knew he was going to have to sell himself to Maya. He would have to prove that, although male, he was trustworthy. That he would fully support her and the hardworking women comprising the secret squadron hidden in the mountains of Peru.

Leaning down, Morgan pulled out several papers from his own backpack. He looked around. The place was deserted. He wanted no other eyes on the material that he was going to lay out before her.

"Don't worry," Maya said. "Patrick knows who we are. He and I are good friends. He protects me and my women when we come into town and need a little R and R. This is our home away from home. He'll make sure no one comes up here during lunch. We've got this place all to ourselves."

"Good." Morgan placed the first sheet of paper in front of Maya. "This is an acquisition form showing that two Boeing Apache Longbow helicopters have just been purchased for your squadron by me." He put a second paper in front of her. "This is a Blackhawk helicopter to replace the Vietnam era Cobra that you're flying." He put a third document in front of her. "Within a week, you will be receiving three I.P.s—instructor pilots—to train you and your team on the new Apache D model, and three enlisted men who will train your crews in software, armaments and mechanics. And lastly—" he put a fourth piece of paper in front of Maya "—here's your new budget. As you look it over, you'll see the financial strangulation your squadron has been experiencing is over."

Maya took all the papers, intently perusing them. Did she dare believe her eyes? Was this really true? She'd gone for three years with so little, watching her people bear the brunt of their financial distress. The task before them had seemed almost impossible, and yet they'd managed to strangle the drug trade to Bolivia by fifty percent, despite the odds, despite the fact that the U.S. government had practically choked off the mission through lack of funding. Looking up, Maya regarded Morgan through her thick, black lashes. He was at ease, almost smiling. She knew the sparkle in his eyes was not there because he was laughing at her. It reflected his pride in the job he'd done getting her the aircraft and help she so desperately needed.

Cutting her gaze to Houston, she growled, "Is this for real, Mike?" After all, Mike was one of her kind, a Jaguar Clan member, and she relied on him heavily at times like this. No clan member would ever lie to another.

"It's for real, Maya. Every word of it. Morgan is your sugar daddy." And he gave her a playful, teasing grin.

Maya grimaced. "What a sexist you are, Houston."

He scratched his head ruefully. "I was teasing you, Maya. Morgan Trayhern runs a first-class operation known as Perseus. You and your squadron are officially moved under his wing and command." Mike tapped the budget paper. "Look at the bottom line. That's money. U.S. funds, not Peruvian soles."

Maya looked at it. Her heart thudded with excitement. "I'm afraid to believe this," she whispered as she looked through the pages again. "We're really going to get two new D models? The ones with radar? I've heard so much about them.... I tried to get them, but they kept telling me they didn't have the budget to let us have the upgraded model."

Morgan tempered his excitement over the joy he saw in Maya's face. This woman was used to running her squadron her way. And he respected that. Still, he needed to be able to gently move her in the direction that he saw her duties down here heading, now and in the future. Maya's plan had been a greenhouse experiment—an all-woman military contingent doing some of the most demanding, most dangerous work in the world. Despite the difficulties of going up against drug runners who flew the Russian Kamov Black Shark assault helicopters, which were nearly equal to an Apache, and flying in this nasty, always changing weather at some of the highest altitudes on the planet, she'd been more than successful. She'd never lost a helicopter or a pilot in the three years since she'd started this operation, and that was a phenomenal record of achievement in Morgan's eyes.

He knew that it was Maya's careful selection of the right women pilots and crews that made this mission successful. Furthermore, she was a charismatic leader, someone people either hated or loved on sight. Morgan understood that, because he had that quality himself. Only Maya was a much younger version of him; she was only twenty-five years old. She had a lot going for her. And he admired her deeply for her commitment to Peru and its people.

"There's just one hitch," Morgan told her quietly. He saw her eyes narrow speculatively on him.

"What?" she growled, putting the papers aside.

Seeing her tense, Morgan said, "I know you have an all-woman squadron. Unfortunately, I couldn't find women IPs to come down here to upgrade you on flying the Apache D models. Do you have a problem with men coming in for six weeks and staying at your base to teach your people?"

"I don't have a problem with men, Mr.—Morgan. *They* have a problem with *me*. If you can guarantee they won't be gender prejudiced, I won't kick and scream about it."

"Good," Morgan said, breathing a sigh of relief. He turned and dug into his pack again, producing a set of orders that had been cut by the army. "Here's the list of men who will be coming in shortly. We haven't been able to tell them they are coming down here yet, but that's a mere formality. I give you my personal guarantee that they are the best. The army's cream of the crop of teachers, to move your people into the D models as rapidly as possible. Because you are so shorthanded, you can't afford to send your pilots back to Fort Rucker for training. Instead, we're bringing the training to you, so it won't interfere with your ongoing missions."

Taking the list of names, Maya frowned as she rapidly perused it. She knew just about everyone in the training field. The Apache team was a small unit within the army as whole—a tight, select family, for better or worse.

Morgan started to lift the cup to his lips when he heard Maya curse richly beneath her breath. She jerked her head up, her green eyes blazing like the hounds from hell. Her glare was aimed directly at him. His cup froze midway to his lips.

"There's no way I'm letting this son of a bitch anywhere near me or my pilots," she hissed, jabbing her finger at the paper she flattened between them. "You can take Major Dane York and shove him where the sun never shines, Mr. Trayhern. That sexist bastard is never going to step foot onto my base. Not *ever!*"

Houston scowled and took the paper. "Major Dane York? Who is he?"

Maya breathed angrily and sat back in the chair, her arms folded across her breasts. "You didn't do your research, Mr. Trayhern. I'm really disappointed in you."

Carefully setting the cup down in the saucer, Morgan allowed a few moments to stretch between them. The anger in her eyes was very real. Her nostrils were flared, her full lips flattened and corners pulled in with pain. Taking the set of orders, he stared at the name.

"Major York is the most accomplished I.P. in the Apache D model instruction unit."

"Yeah, and he could walk on water, too, and it wouldn't mean a damn thing to me."

"You have words with this guy back at Fort Rucker?" Mike asked, a worried look on his face.

"Words?" Maya clenched her teeth as she leaned toward Morgan. "That bastard damn near had me and all the other women going through Apache training five years ago washed out! Why? Because we were *women*. That's the only reason." She jabbed at the paper Mike held. "I'm not letting that Neanderthal anywhere near me or my crews. Over my dead body."

"Hold on," Morgan murmured. "Major York's credentials are impeccable. I wanted the best for you and your pilots, Maya."

"I can't believe this!" Maya suddenly stood up, energy swirling around her. She moved abruptly away from the table and walked over to the row of windows that overlooked the busy street below. Hands on her hips, she said, "He's gender prejudiced. He didn't like me. He didn't like my flying skills. He didn't like anything I did because I was a woman. Well—" Maya turned around and glared at them "—I had the last laugh on him and his not-so-subtle tactics. He didn't know my father was an army general. When York was unable to acknowledge some of the women's superior flying skills and wouldn't grade them accordingly, I got angry. When he did nothing to stop his other instructors from harassing us with innuendos, I called my father."

Morgan frowned. "What happened then?"

Moving slowly toward the table, Maya tried to settle her rapidly beating heart. "You know, York is like a black cloud that follows me around." She laughed sharply. "Here I am in backwater Peru, and he manages to find me anyway. What kind of karma do I have?"

Houston glanced at Morgan and noticed the worry in his boss's eyes. "Maya, what happened?"

"My father had a 'talk' with York's commanding officer. I don't know what was said. I do know that from that day forward, York straightened his act out. He doesn't like women. At least, not military women pilots." Her nostrils quivered. She stood in front of them, her legs slightly apart for good balance and her arms crossed. "He was never fair with any of us. I challenged him. I called him what he was to his face. I'd like to have decked him." She balled her hand into a fist. "Just because we were women, he wanted to fail us."

"But you didn't fail," Morgan said.

With a disgusted snort, Maya moved to her chair, her hands gripping the back of it as she stared malevolently down at him. "Only because I had my father's influence and help. Otherwise, he'd have canned every one of us." Maya jerked a thumb toward the windows where Machu Picchu's black lava sides rose upward. "And you know the funny thing? Every woman in that company volunteered to come down here with me and take this spec ops. They didn't like the odds, the army's obvious gender preference toward males getting all the good orders and bases, while the women got the dregs. Screw 'em. I said to hell with the whole army career ladder and came up with a plan for this base. My father backed it and I got it."

Maya's voice lowered with feeling. "I'm sure the army was glad to see all of us go away. Out of sight, out of mind. Well, that's okay with us, because we have a higher calling than the army. We couldn't care less about our career slots or getting the right bases and orders to advance. We love to fly. All any of us wanted was a chance to fly and do what we love the most. We're linchpins down here, holding the balance between the good people and the bad guys, and we know it. What we do makes a difference."

Morgan stood and placed his napkin on the table. "I'm sorry to hear how tough it was on you and your women friends, Maya. I'm sure the army realizes what assets you are. Your stats speak for themselves." He held her angry green gaze. "But York is the best. You have my personal promise that when he arrives, he will not be the same man you trained under before."

"I will *not* allow him to step foot on my base."

Morgan held her challenging stare. He heard the low, angry vibration in her tone. "You've got to learn to trust me, Maya," he said huskily. "I want only the best for your squadron. You've earned that right. If Major York steps out of line, you call me and I'll take care of it. I promise."

"I don't want him back in my life!"

Her explosion of anger and pain echoed around the room.

"If you don't accept him as your I.P., you forfeit everything on those papers." Morgan pointed to the table where they lay.

Still glaring, Maya looked from him to the papers. She desperately needed those new D models. Her pilots deserved to have the safety the new copters would afford them. And she was dying without the necessary funds for spare parts for her old Apaches. Swallowing hard, she looked slowly back up at Trayhern.

"Very well," she rasped, "authorize the bastard to come down here."

Chapter 2

"Major York, if you don't want to be kicked out of the U.S. Army and asked to resign your commission, I suggest you take this temporary duty assignment."

Dane stood at attention in front of his superior's desk. "Yes, sir!"

"At ease," Colonel Ronald Davidson said, and gestured toward a chair that sat at one side of his huge maple desk. The winter sunshine of December moved through the venetian blinds and painted shadows throughout his large office. Was it an omen of things to come? Dane had a gut feeling it was.

Dressed in his one-piece, olive-green flight suit, Dane took the orders and sat down. Davidson's gray eyes were fixed on him and he knew why. Trying to choke down his fear, he tucked the garrison cap he'd been wearing into the left shoulder epaulet of his flight suit. He sat at attention. The tone in his C.O.'s voice made his heart beat harder. Dane knew he'd screwed up—again—with a woman Apache pilot in training to upgrade to the D model. Was this his death sentence? He tried to concentrate on the neatly typed set of orders before him. Reading rapidly, he felt a little relief began to bleed through him.

"Sir, this is TDY for six weeks down to Peru, to teach some spook ops pilots D model characteristics?" He tried to keep the surprise out of his voice. Dane thought the colonel had called him to this office to tell him to resign his commission because of his latest mistake. Obviously, he'd been wrong, and more of the tension leaked out of him. The last thing he'd expected was an assignment like this.

"That's right," Davidson informed him in a growl. Getting up, his body thin and ramrod straight, he tapped his fingertips lightly on the desk before him. "You'll see I've assigned two other I.P.s and three enlisted men to accompany you down there to train these pilots. You're to head it up—unless you don't want the assignment, Major."

Dane looked up. He got the gist of his commander's warning. Yesterday, Warrant Officer Kathy Juarez had filed a gender complaint against him. Dane had been warned it was coming. Swallowing against his constricted throat, he scowled down at the orders. He'd opened his big mouth without thinking first, and the words had flown out. Dane was trying very hard to think before he spoke after his lesson four years earlier with another student, Chief Warrant Officer Maya Stevenson, and the group of women going through training with her. He'd cleaned up his act quite a bit, but sometimes, when he was dog tired and stressed out from the heavy demands on his shoulders, he'd slip up. And he had.

Davidson was giving him one last chance to shape up. There was no choice and Dane knew it. He either took this TDY or Davidson was going to make sure that this most recent complaint from a female pilot was going in his jacket. And once it got in there, his career was over. He would be better off resigning and saving them the trouble of putting the complaint into his permanent military record. It would be a black mark that would follow him until the day he died, a stain he did not want on his record. The army was on a crusade to make itself genderless. Male and female no longer existed. Just bodies. Just human beings. Well, Dane was having real problems adjusting to that new perspective.

"Just to give you a little background on this spook ops group," Davidson continued in a milder tone, "it's been shifted to Perseus, a Q-clearance organization within the CIA family. They operate on a need-to-know-basis by only a handful of people within the government. Morgan Trayhern is the boss. He's asked the army for the *best* I.P.s we've got. The detachment known as Black Jaguar Base has twelve pilots who need upgrade training. The work they do down there is crucial to stemming the flow of cocaine from Peru into Bolivia. Because they cannot spare their people to come up here to Fort Rucker for training, you're going to go down there and train them, instead."

"I see, sir." Well, Dane really didn't, but that didn't matter, either. What mattered was that his C.O. was yanking him out of this messy and potentially embarrassing situation and tucking him quietly away. Out of sight, out of mind. And out of trouble, as far as he was concerned. Because of Dane's jaded past, Davidson, who was in his fifties, didn't particularly care for him, though he respected his abilities as a teacher and pilot. It was a good thing, for Dane knew his career would have been over with this latest charge set against him.

Not that he didn't deserve it. Warrant Officer Juarez was Hispanic, and he'd made the off-the-cuff remark that no South American could fly as well as a North American one. Stupid, yes, but he'd shot off his mouth to his new class of Apache pilots first without thinking about the consequences. And Davidson wasn't happy about it or he wouldn't be sending him away for a long time to let the situation cool down. Dane's ill-timed comment reflected directly back on the colonel, too. Davidson was protecting his own hind end in this. He was up for general's stars in another month. If this incident took off and the newspapers ran with it, Davidson's stars were down the toilet.

"Sounds interesting, sir." And it did. Dane had never been to South America, although he was born in Del Rio, Texas, a little border town, and grew up bilingual, even though they moved from base to base frequently.

"You're getting the assignment because you speak Spanish, Major," Davidson said heavily. "Everyone chosen is bilingual. This spook ops has Peruvian, and other South American pilots, as well as some on loan from overseas. Mr. Trayhern needed someone who could handle the different languages and get the job done. That is why you're getting this TDY." Davidson glared down at him. He picked up another paper. "And perhaps, while you're gone, Major, I can sweet-talk Warrant Officer Juarez into dropping her legitimate charge against you. I'm *sure* you won't make the same mistake twice, will you? After all, you're going to South America to find out just how good the pilots are down there."

Swallowing hard, Dane said, "Sir, I'll make sure it never happens again."

Scowling, Davidson glared at him. "You're old guard, Major. You're a lot younger than me, but you sound like the army back in World War II. Well, those days are gone and you'd better get with the new program of gender neutrality or your butt is history. You'd best make good on this mission, Major. I'm expecting a glowing report back from the C.O. of that ops about you and your men's white glove behavior. Do you read me loud and clear?"

"Yes, sir, I hear you." Dane stood up at attention beneath the man's drilling, cold look.

"Sit down."

Dane sat. He felt the C.O.'s anger avalanche him.

"I'll be damned lucky if this warrant officer doesn't go to the press with your remarks. Our women pilots are just as good—probably better—than our male pilots. They've distinguished themselves time and again, and you keep working against them. I don't know what your agenda is, Major, but on this TDY, you'd better stuff it and work with the people down there four square."

"Yes, sir, I will."

"You and your contingent are leaving tomorrow at 0800. You're taking a navy helicopter carrier down to Lima, Peru. The capital city sits right on prime beachfront property. You're also taking two D model Apaches and a Blackhawk with you. You've got three I.P.s, one for each aircraft. One of the three enlisted instructors will fly with each of you. The aircraft, once assembled inside the carrier when it arrives at Lima, will be flown off it and you'll rendezvous with elements of Black Jaguar at an agreed-upon time."

"I see, sir." Dane felt a little excitement. He'd never been on spook ops before. His world revolved around teaching pilots about the deadly beauty of the Boeing Apache. He lived to fly. And he was a good teacher, to boot—at least with male pilots.

"We've got an agreement with the Peruvian government, Major. Once those D models are assembled and brought up to the deck of the carrier, you will fly them on specific coordinates that will be preprogrammed into the flight computers. You will not, under any circumstances, be carrying hot ordnance on board. The Peruvian government wants those three aircraft to leave under cover of darkness, just before dawn. They don't want any nosy newspaper reporters to get wind of us coming into their country or the president will have a *lot* of explaining to do.

"You will meet two Black Jaguar Apaches at a specific location deep in the mountains, far from the capital. They will then escort you to their base. As I understand it, it is dangerous where you will be flying. There is a drug lord, Faro Valentino, who has two Russian Kamov Ka-50's assault helicopters that ply the same area. If they see you, they're going to try and blow you out of the sky. It will be up to the

C.O. of the base and their Apaches to protect you and fly shotgun. They will be carrying hot ordnance on board, in case the Kamovs jump you. There's no guarantee they will. But the C.O. has informed us that you should expect attack. You need to review the terrain of the area and be ready to cut and run if that happens. You need to know where the hell you're going and what you're going to do to make sure these new D models aren't downed before they get to their new base."

Frowning, Dane said, "No hot ordnance for us in a dangerous situation? Isn't that stupid, sir?"

Davidson grimaced. "Major, choose your words more carefully, will you? Didn't you just hear me? The Peruvian government will *not* allow you to bring these assault helos over their territory with missiles, bullets or rockets. What if you crash into homes and kill people? They're afraid that if the combat helicopters are seen, word will leak back to their press, and all hell will break loose. Having U.S. military aircraft flying in Peru is a political hot potato, anyway. We're stepping on eggs. There is no way to get where you're going, except by helicopter. The jungle where the drug lords produce their cocaine is wild, dangerous, country."

"But they've got Apaches carrying ordnance." Dane tried to keep the irritation out of his voice. "Why is it all right in one place in Peru, but not another? Why should I open up my crews to possible confrontation with a Kamov and get shot all to pieces?"

"We have a lot of political toes we just can't step on," Davidson said slowly, obviously at the limits of his patience with Dane. "Once you get the D models to the base, you'll be able to train the pilots there. When everyone is up to speed, the D models will join the A models already there, and you can fly with hot ordnance."

"So, we risk three helos and six people trying to get them to this jungle base?" Dane frowned.

"You will have two Apache A's escorting you in, Major.

Just follow the C.O.'s instructions, and things should go well. But as mission commander on this TDY, you need to realize that if the Kamovs attack, you have to have a plan on outrunning and outmaneuvering them because they can outgun you. The only thing standing between you and them will be those two A models rigged for combat."

Unhappily, Dane nodded. "I see, sir."

"Good." Davidson reached for a folder and handed it to him in a brisk manner. "Here's more info. Take a look at it."

Opening the file, Dane nearly choked. The color photo of the C.O. of the Black Jaguar Base stared back at him.

"Problems, Major?"

Heat shot up his neck and into his face. Dane tried to squelch a curse as he sat there, pinned in place by his C.O.'s gaze.

"Sir…" he rasped, half standing, pointing at the photo in the file "….this is impossible…this can't be…. I mean—"

"Captain Maya Stevenson is the C.O. of Black Jaguar Base, Major. And she's *your* commanding officer on this mission."

No! Dane sat down, before his knees buckled beneath him, disbelief thrumming through him. Those cool, half-closed emerald eyes, eyes that reminded him of a jungle cat, stared back at him. Maya Stevenson was the biggest thorn he'd ever had in his side. She'd nearly scuttled his career so many years ago. After she'd graduated into the Apache A model, she'd quite literally disappeared. Not that Dane was unhappy about that. He wasn't. She was the in-your-face kind of woman who made him see red with great regularity. He didn't like her independence. Or her chutzpah. She'd call him out every time he said something wrong—or politically incorrect. There wasn't a day that went by when she was his student that they hadn't flared up and had words, angry words, with one another. Worse, she'd reported him and he'd damn near lost his status as an I.P., had been threatened with losing his army career.

Davidson moved quietly around the desk, trailing his fingers along the highly polished edge of it. All the while, his gaze remained on Dane.

"A word of warning, Major York," he whispered.

Dane looked up. "Sir?"

"Mr. Trayhern of Perseus, and myself, are all too aware of the dog-and-cat fight you got into with Captain Stevenson four years ago. If either of us hear a word from her that you or your crew are not being perfectly behaved down there, then things are really going to hit the fan. Big time. You will be training twelve women pilots, Major. And it's well known you don't get along well with women in the military. The crew you're taking down is going to behave just as you do. So I suggest you clean up your act, accept that women make just as good pilots as men, and get on with your teaching and training down there."

Dane stared down at the photo again, disbelief bolting through him. He felt as if he'd been struck by lightning. Maya was in a black, body-fitting flight suit. There were no insignias on the uniform, nothing to indicate her country of origin or that she was a pilot, much less in the U.S. Army. Her hair, as black as the uniform, was in a chignon at the nape of her slender neck. The look of pride in her raised chin, that confidence he'd always disliked about her, now radiated from the photo. He felt hot and sweaty—an adrenaline reaction. Davidson stood within a few feet of him, and Dane could feel his C.O.'s icy gaze drilling into his back as he looked at the photo.

"I feel like I'm being fed to the lions…sir."

Davidson chuckled. "Maybe you are, Major, but this is going to be your final test to see if you can achieve gender neutral status. You pass this test, and I'm sure your career will continue. If you don't, well…this is your last chance. Do you understand that?"

Bitterness flowed through Dane. He glared up at the colonel, whose gaze was unwavering. "I get the picture, sir. Frankly, this is a no-win situation."

"It doesn't have to be, Major, if you let your prejudice against women in the military dissipate. This can be a real turn-around mission for you. But it's up to you. If you want to keep your caveman mentality about women, that's your choice. Or you can see this as a golden opportunity to drop some old, archaic attitudes and embrace and support women in the military. They pay with their lives just like a man does. They deserve equal treatment and respect. It's that simple."

Sure it is. Dane clenched his teeth, his jaw tightening. *Great. Just great.* Not only would he have a woman C.O. lording over him, it was his nemesis, Maya Stevenson. And her father was still in the army and still a general. Dane felt hemmed in and no way out. Wiping his thinned mouth with the back of his hand, he closed the file abruptly.

"My secretary has everything you need for the trip south, Major. You're to meet your crew at 0800 tomorrow morning at base ops. You'll take a C-130 Hercules flight from here to San Diego. There, you'll board the *USS Gendarme,* one of our navy helicopter carriers. They've already got the two Boeing Apaches and the Blackhawks disassembled and on board. Questions?"

Dane stood. He came to attention. "No, sir."

"Very well, dismissed. Oh, and good luck, Major. I hear that Captain Stevenson has been giving a good account of herself and her women pilots down there. This just might be the eye-opening experience you need to convince you that women can do a job just as well as any man." Davidson's mouth lifted slightly. "And maybe better. But you go down there with an open mind and see for yourself."

"Looks like a right purty city," Chief Warrant Officer Joe Calhoun said in his soft Texas drawl as he stood, his hands resting on his hips. "Never been this far south before."

Dane stood next to the other instructor pilot on the deck of the navy helicopter carrier anchored off the coast near Lima. Because the carrier was so large, it could not go near the shallow coastline. A thick gray blanket of fog had lifted hours earlier, and the sparkling lights of Lima, the largest city and capital of Peru, blinked to welcome them.

"Looks are deceiving at night," he muttered. His stomach was in knots. The last week had been hell on him. Dane hadn't been looking forward to this moment. Below, the mechanics were giving a final check on the Boeing Apaches before they were lifted by elevator to the deck where they stood. Glancing at the watch on his hairy wrist, he saw that in an hour they would be taking off.

Although it was December, it was summer in the southern hemisphere. A slight, humid breeze wafted by them. Around them, navy sailors worked quietly and efficiently, preparing the deck for the forthcoming helicopters. Joe, a Chief Warrant Officer 3, and Craig Barton, a CWO4, were under his command, and would be flying the other two helos. Craig, who had experience flying Blackhawks as well as Apaches, would take the Blackhawk into the base.

"Wonder if the women are as beautiful as they say they are," Craig said, coming up to them and grinning.

Dane scowled. "This isn't a party trip, Mr. Barton."

"Hey," Craig murmured, "I'm only kidding. You've been uptight ever since we came on board, sir."

Warrant officers made up the ranks of most of the army's helicopter pilots. Dane had been a West Point graduate and gone into helicopters aviation as a full-fledged officer, so the other men were beneath him in rank. They stood halfway between enlisted personnel and officers such as himself. They were sharp people with fine skills and had shown their capability to fly these deadly machines. The warrants had a long and proud history.

Dane managed a one-cornered smile. "I'm worried about the Kamovs jumping us."

Joe snickered. "What's there to worry about? We got two Apaches to protect us if things get dicey. From what you said, those lady pilots have had plenty of practice shootin' at the bad guys, so I'm sure they can handle a little action, if need be."

Yeah, like a bunch of women were going to protect them. Dane kept the acid comment to himself. He didn't dare breathe a word of his prejudice to these two warrant officers. He'd worked with them for over a year and neither felt the prejudice against women that he did. Joe was half Commanche, born in Texas and twenty-six and Craig twenty-eight, both single, competitive, type A personalities. So was Dane, but he was twenty-nine and feeling like he was eighty right now. If only Maya Stevenson was not in this equation. Dane was still reeling from the shock of it all. Was she as mouthy and in-your-face as she'd been years ago? God, he hoped not. How was he going to keep his inflammatory words in his mouth?

"Well," Joe said in his Texas drawl, "I, for one, am gonna enjoy this little TDY. I mean, dudes, this is a man's dream come true—an all-ladies base." And he rubbed his large, square hands together, his teeth starkly white in the darkness on the deck of the ship.

Craig grinned. "Roger that." He was tall and lean, almost six feet five inches tall. And when he scrunched his frame into the cockpit of an Apache, Dane often wondered how the man could fly it at all. The cockpit of an Apache was small, the seat adjustable from about five feet three to six feet five inches. Being from Minnesota, from good Swedish stock, Craig was big-boned, even though he was lean. His nickname was Scarecrow. Dane liked his patient nature and softness with students. He was an excellent instructor.

Joe, who was a fellow Texan, was an exceptional instructor because he became so impassioned about the Apache helicopter and passing on that excitement to the trainees. Joe lived, ate and breathed the Apache. Maybe because he was half-Commanche he spoke Apache in his sleep—and made the bachelor officer quarters shake and shudder with his ungodly snoring. Grinning in the darkness, Dane admitted to himself that he had good people around him, and maybe, just maybe, that would make the difference on this nasty little TDY.

The other three crewmen, all sergeants, were experts in the new software, the ordnance and the handling of the 'doughnut' or radar dome that was on the D model Apaches. Those three men, Barry Hartford, Alphonse 'Fonzie' Gianni and Luke Ingmar, would teach the women crew chiefs and mechanics at the base the fine points of the new model. They were all married, so Dane had less to worry about in that respect. However, judging from Joe's gray eyes and the sparkling look of a hunter in Craig's brown ones, Dane would have his hands full with these two lone wolves running around loose in the sheep's pen.

"Well, let's turn and burn," Craig said, as he lifted his hand and started for the hatch that led down to the deck where the helicopters were being prepared.

"Roger that," Joe seconded, following quickly on his heels.

Dane stood alone. He *felt* alone. Watching the last of the fog disperse, he saw the twinkling of stars above him. It struck him that he was seeing the Southern Cross for the first time in his life. It was as famous here as the Big Dipper was in the Northern Hemisphere. Snorting softly, he hung his head and looked down at the highly polished flight boots he wore with his one-piece flight uniform. Alone. Yes, he'd been alone for a long, long time. Ever since his mother had abruptly left him and his father, he'd felt this gnawing ache in his gut and heart. His brows drew downward as memories assailed him. His mother was a red-haired, green-eyed, vital woman who had exuded a confidence he rarely saw in females. She'd had enough of being a "housewife" and had made an ultimatum to his military pilot father to either let her work outside the home or face a divorce.

Only twelve at the time, Dane recalled the fear he'd felt when he'd heard them arguing hotly one night in the living room after he'd gone to bed. His father's shouting had awakened him. Dane had lain on his belly at the top of the stairs, head pressed to the wood, hands wrapped around the banister, as she began screaming back at Dane's father just as loudly. She was tall, athletic, brainy, and had no fear of speaking her mind—ever.

"Damn..." Dane forced himself to look up...up at the Southern Cross, which glimmered like diamond droplets against an ebony sky being edged with the first hint of dawn. His mother had left. She'd tried to explain it to Dane, but at twelve, the message he got was that he wasn't lovable enough for her to stay and be his mother. And from that day onward, he'd felt alone. Well, at twenty-nine, he still felt that way, and nothing would probably ever change it. Or the way he felt about his mother. When he was eighteen, about to graduate from high school and enter West Point, she'd left him forever. His mother had been coming to his graduation, driving from San Antonio, Texas, where she'd settled, and a drunk driver had careened into her car and killed her. Dane would never forget that day. Ever.

He heard the whirring of the elevators that would soon bring the Apaches and the Blackhawk to the deck where he stood. Moving his shoulders as if to rid them of an accumulated weight, Dane turned. As he did so, he saw a bright trail streak across the sky toward the east, where they would be flying shortly. It was a meteorite.

Dane didn't believe in omens. He believed only in what his eyes saw, his hands felt and his ears heard. Scowling deeply, he turned on his heel. *Screw it all.* Did the meteorite foretell of his demise? Would it be because of his mouth? His feelings about women? Or were they going to be jumped by Kamovs? Or left at the mercy of a bunch of renegade

Amazon women warriors who thought they knew how to fight?

"Be my luck that it's the latter," Dane grumbled as he jerked open the hatch door and went below to his fate.

"It's time, Maya...." Dallas Klein poked her head through the opened door of her commanding officer's office. Dallas, who was the executive officer for the base operations, raised her dark brown brows as she looked across the wooden floor at Maya's pitiful excuse for a work area—a dark green metal, military issue desk that was battered from years of use. Maya was pouring over several maps spread across it, her face intense, her hand on her chin as she studied them.

"What? Oh...." Maya looked up. She nodded to Dallas. Glancing down at the watch on her left wrist, she blew a breath of air in consternation. "Yeah, it's time all right."

Dallas moved inside the office and shut the door. She was dressed in the uniform of the day—a black, body-fitting Nomex fire retardent flight suit. Her black flight boots gleamed in the fluorescent light from a fixture above the desk. Running her fingers briskly through her short sable hair, she met Maya's gaze. "Did you sleep at all?"

"What do you think?" Maya grimaced, then straightened and opened her arms, stretching languidly like a large cat. "I've got the nightmare from hell visiting us for six weeks. I couldn't catch a wink." Maya quickly wrapped her loose ebony hair into a chignon at the nape of her neck placing a thick rubber band around her tresses to keep them in place.

"Hmm."

"You aren't upset about York coming?" Maya took her knee board, which she used to write things down if she needed it, and strapped it to her right thigh with Velcro. She reached into a glass sitting on her desk and took out several pens, placing them in the left upper sleeve of her uniform.

"Upset? Yeah. Lose sleep over the guy? Not a chance." She grinned wolfishly.

"You Israelis are one tough lot," Maya grumped. "Has Penny got the coffee on in the mess hall? I desperately need a cup before we take off."

"Yeah, everyone's up and around," Dallas murmured as she opened the door for her C.O. "*Edgy* is the word I'd use...."

Maya grinned tiredly. "Edgy? As in on edge dancing on the edge of a sword? No kidding. Come on, I need my intravenous of java before we blow this joint and meet our male comrades in arms."

Chuckling, Dallas, who at five foot eleven inches was almost as tall as her C.O., followed Maya down the dimly lit hall of the two-story building. Their headquarters sat deep in a cave, well hidden from any prying eyes that might try and find the complex. Maya grabbed her helmet on the way, stuffed her black Nomex gloves into it and then picked up her chicken plate, which was the name for the bullet proof vest they each wore when they flew a mission. Though they were normally called flak jackets, the army slang name was more commonly used.

Maya moved rapidly down the stairs rapidly and out the door. If not for the lights hung far above them on the cave's ceiling, finding their way out of the place would be impossible. Familiar sounds—the clink of tools, the low murmurs of women's voices from the maintenance area—soothed Maya's fractious nervousness. She felt wired—and suspected it was because she would have to meet her worst enemy today.

"You're jumpy," Dallas observed, coming up and matching her long stride. "You sensing something?"

With an explosive laugh, Maya said, "Oh, yeah. Trouble with a capital *T* in the form of Major Dane York. How's that for a mouthful, Klein?"

Chuckling, Dallas opened the door to the Quonset hut structure that housed the mess hall and kitchen facility.

"Mmm, it's more than that. You usually get this way when you smell Kamovs around."

As Maya made her way into the small mess hall which was lined with a series of long picnic tables made of metal and wood, she saw that about half of her crews were up and eating an early breakfast. She called to them, lifting her hand in greeting, and then picked up a metal tray to go through the chow line. The flight crews had been up and working for several hours. There was ordnance to load on the Apaches, fuel to be put on board and a massive amount of software to be checked out to ensure it was working properly before any pilot sat in the cockpit. Today, Maya wanted a full array of Hellfire missiles on the underbelly of each Apache, rockets as well as a good stash of 30-millimeter bullets on board.

Penny, a red-haired army sergeant with lively blue eyes who was the head chef for their base stood behind the line, spoon in hand.

"'Morning, ma'am," she greeted Maya as she heaped dark orange, fluffy scrambled eggs onto her tray.

"'Morning, Penny. You got any of your famous cinnamon rolls?" Maya lifted her nose and sniffed. "I can smell 'em. Any left?"

Penny blushed a bright pink. "Yes, ma'am. I managed to save a couple for you and Ms. Klein." Penny turned to retrieve the rolls, revealing how the white apron she wore over her green fatigues hung to her knees due to her short stature. Sometimes, when she moved too quickly, the apron would become tangled around her short legs and nearly trip her.

"So you didn't let the condors eat them all," Maya said, pleased. She watched as Penny opened the oven and drew out two big cinnamon rolls slathered with white frosting.

"Oh, we've got a buncha buzzards here, no doubt, ma'am," Penny laughed. She placed a roll on each officer's tray. "But I know they're your favorite, so I told my crew to keep their hands off them, threatening that they'd lose their fingers if anyone stole 'em."

Maya grinned. "Thanks, Penny. We appreciate your being a watchdog." Maya poured some coffee from the tall steel canister into a white ceramic mug and then went over to an empty table. She wanted time to talk to Dallas alone before the flight. Every time she thought of Dane York, her gut tightened. And yet there *was* something else troubling her. Maya couldn't shake the feeling...the premonition that Kamovs were around and hunting them. Sometimes they did. Sometimes Faro Valentino, a very rich Colombian drug lord, who had money to burn and could buy the latest in Russian weaponry and aircraft, would deliberately try and hunt them down to kill them. Most of the time he was making cocaine runs over their jungle and mountains. But sometimes...he turned the tables on them. Sometimes the hunted became the hunter. Was today the day?

Dallas sat down opposite her. "You've got that look in your eyes," she said as she eagerly dove into the scrambled eggs. They had Penny to thank for the fresh eggs. A farm girl from Iowa she had long ago bought a bunch of hens in Aqua Caliente, and built them a chicken coop. Penny had her "girls" laying eggs for the entire squadron. Everyone appreciated farm-fresh eggs. They had a much better taste than any store-bought variety, which were sterile in comparison, Dallas thought. Maya always urged her women to be creative, to make this base more a home than a military warehouse. Little touches like Penny's made staying here survivable. Since Lieutenant Ana Luca Contina had married Jake Travers, and Jake had come to stay with her at the base, he had created a huge vegetable garden that yielded wonderful lettuce salads and other hard-to-get items. Jake also took care of supply and Maya was grateful for the ex-Army Ranger's presence on their base. While Ana flew missions, Jake took care of things on the ground. Everyone, including Maya, was happy with the arrangement.

"What look is that?" Even though Maya was far from hungry, she knew today's flight required her to be alert, and that meant feeding her body. Brain cells needed food to work, and in her business of flying the deadly Apache assault aircraft, she needed every iota of intelligence to stay on top of things.

Dallas sipped her coffee after putting a dry creamer into it. "That 'we're gonna get jumped by Kamovs' look."

"Oh."

Dallas set the cup down. "You always have a sixth sense for this stuff. Are you too exhausted to be in touch with it this morning?"

Having known Dallas for the three years that they'd been at the base, Maya trusted the Israeli pilot with her life. On loan to them from her country, Dallas was a tough, no-nonsense warrior who had many times saved Maya's butt when they'd come up against the Black Sharks that would hide and jump them. And Dallas knew her better than anyone at the base. As executive officer—X.O.—she had almost as much responsibility for this base operating as Maya did. And Dallas was someone she could blow off steam to without it getting around. Giving her a narrowed look, she muttered, "Okay, I have a feeling."

Lips curving ruefully, Dallas said lightly, "Couldn't be that Black Jaguar Clan stuff you're connected with?"

Maya didn't often talk about her spiritual heritage or training. Dallas knew more than most, but Maya's affiliation with the Clan wasn't for public consumption. Over the years, Maya's intrepid and loyal pilots and crews had learned there was something "different" about her, but not *what* was different. Of course, Maya didn't have anywhere near the metaphysical talents her sister, Inca, did. No, the only thing she was good at, when in the right space, was teleportation. And in her line of business, Maya was rarely in the right space to use that talent because it required her to be in perfect harmony within herself in order to initiate it. Nope, on any given day, she was painfully human like everyone else. The other talent she had was intuition. She'd get these "feelings" and when she did, she was rarely wrong.

Maya realized Dallas was patiently looking at her with those golden eyes.

"Okay...I got a bad feeling. I think Faro is going to turn the tables on us again. He's going to be the hunter and us the hunted today. Satisfied?"

Pursing her full lips, Dallas said, "Yep, I am. I'm gonna tell my copilot to play heads up then, more than usual. Damn, I wish we could get a radar signature off them."

Maya nodded in agreement. The Russian helicopter was able to somehow dodge their massive radar array and capabilities. Because it could, the Kamov had the ability to sneak up on them and blow them out of the sky—literally. That meant Maya and her pilots had to stay even more alert than usual. They were fighting one of the most deadly helicopter opponents in the world. Their own sensor equipment was useless against the Kamov unless it showed itself, which wasn't often. The mercenary Russian pilots Faro Valentino hired were hardened veterans of many campaigns and knew the ropes of stealth and combat—just like Maya's crew did.

Each Apache had two HUDS, or heads-up displays—small, television-like screens—in each of its two cockpits. Maya's pilots could use IR—or infrared—a television camera or radar. The HUDs had saved the lives of Maya's crew innumerable times, as well as helped them find the heat of bodies beneath the jungle canopy so they could stop drug runners in their tracks as they carried heavy loads of cocaine toward the Bolivian border. In the sky, the Apache's ability to find its target was legendary. Except the Kamovs had their own arsenal of commensurate hardware, and on any given day, a Kamov could jump one of their Apaches without warning. That was when Maya used her sixth sense to the optimum. She'd not lost a helo crew yet, and she wasn't about to start now.

Maya pulled the warm cinnamon roll apart with her long, spare fingers. "This is one of those days I'd just as soon tell the Cosmos I pass on this mission, you know? That's okay, you don't have to answer on the grounds it may incriminate you, Klein.'' She grinned and popped a piece of the soft, sweet bread into her mouth.

''Well,'' Dallas said with a sly look, ''I'm glad I'm not in your boots today, Captain. Whatta choice—Kamovs or Major Dane York.''

''Humph, with our luck, we'll get hit with both.''

Chuckling, Dallas finished her coffee. ''Yeah, that's what I call Black Jaguar luck at its finest.''

That was true, and Maya nodded as she chewed on the roll. ''If we didn't have bad luck, we wouldn't have any at all.''

Dallas's eyes gleamed with laughter. ''And if I'm reading you right, you'd rather face Faro's Kamovs today than York.''

''Bingo.''

''Damned if you do and damned if you don't.'' Dallas rose, picked up her empty tray and said, ''Meet you out on the apron. Time to turn and burn.''

Maya sat there, feeling glum. The soft sounds of women talking and laughing made her feel a little better. The mess hall was always a happy meeting place for her and her hard-working crews. They pulled twelve hours on and twelve off when Faro and his Kamovs decided to take to the sky and make run after run of cocaine to the Bolivian border.

Rubbing her neck ruefully, Maya grimaced. Today was going to be one helluva day, and she wasn't looking forward to any of it.

Chapter 3

Just the act of climbing up the metal rungs that doubled as a ladder, and then onto the black metal fuselage before ducking into the front cockpit of the Boeing Apache, soothed some of Maya's initial anxiousness. Dawn had yet to break in the east. The cockpit canopy opened on the left side, folding upward and back so that both pilots could climb into their respective positions at once. The crew chief was Sergeant Elena Macedo from Peru. Maya could hear her copilot and gunner, Chief Warrant Officer 2 Jessica Merril, settling into her position directly behind her. Jessica hailed from California. Her nickname was Wild Woman. Though she was twenty-six, she had the look of an impish pixie, her blond hair dyed with streaks of red. The splashes of color were Jess's way of donning warpaint and going off to battle, in a sense. Everyone's got a big bang out of Wild Woman's wild "do." She more than symbolized the highly individualized rebel attitude of the base. Maya liked it and approved of it.

The Apache was a big, ugly looking dog with a bulbous nose that housed the infrared, television and radar equipment.

The cockpits rose upward on a metal frame, the front cockpit Plexiglas hardened to take a 30 mm cannon hit as well as bird strikes. The seat felt welcoming to Maya, the space narrow, with the cyclic positioned between her legs, the collective by her left, gloved hand. Between her and her copilot was a blast shield; in case they took a hit and one pilot was killed or wounded, the other would be protected so they could fly the chopper home.

Settling the helmet on her head, Maya lifted her hand and twirled it in a clockwise motion, signaling the ground crew to start up the Apache. The first thing that came on in the assault gunship was the air conditioning, designed to cool the miles of circuitry that were bundled along the sides of the prehistoric-looking craft beneath the black metal fuselage. The blast of air from the ducts in the front panel, along with the high-pitched whine of the air conditioning cranking up, surrounded Maya. She watched all the instruments in front of her start to blink and flicker on. The two HUD's came to life, glowing a pleasant green color that was easy on the eyes and didn't contribute to night blindness. She pressed some buttons, making sure the related systems were operational. Positioning the mouthpiece within an inch of her lips, she tested communications with her copilot.

"Wild Woman, how are you reading me?"

"Loud and clear, Captain."

"Roger."

Looking up, Maya saw the constant wisps of clouds that embraced the ten-thousand foot inactive volcano where their base was located. The two Apaches faced outward, having been pushed into position from beneath the cave's overhang by the crews earlier. The lip of lava extended out a good four hundred feet in front of them and made an excellent landing and takeoff spot for the birds. Squinting above the cockpit console, Maya noted the lava wall that rose directly in front of them a thousand feet high, like a big rock curtain. The only way in and out of this cave complex was through the "eye of the needle," as they called it.

The eye of the needle was a natural geologic wonder—a hole in the lava wall sixty feet high and eighty feet wide, just large enough for an Apache or Cobra to move very carefully through it. The rotor diameter on an Apache was forty-eight feet, so they had very little clearance at any time.

Clouds also helped hide the base from prying eyes. Far below them flowed the mighty Urubamba River, a continual source of moisture rising upward in the tropical heat. As this humid air rolled up the mountainside, it met and mixed with cooler, descending air—exactly where the cave and their base was located, creating a fog that was nearly constant all year-round.

This morning was no exception. They would be required to lift off and fly out on instruments and radar in order to thread the Eye squarely and not take off a chunk of their titanium-edged rotor blades, risking a crash. The operation wasn't for fools or anyone not paying attention to her flying. After logging three hundred miles on a mission, the pilots were often tired coming back, and this obstacle became even more dangerous in their exhausted state.

Glancing down, Maya positioned her chicken plate, the bulletproof vest across her chest and abdomen, so that it rode as comfortably as possible. The radio in her helmet crackled to life.

"Black Jaguar one, this is Two. You read me?" It was Dallas Klein's whiskey-smooth voice.

"Roger, Black Jaguar Two. Read you loud and clear."

"Looks like we got split pea soup out there as usual, Saber."

Maya smiled as she hooked up her harness. Saber was her nickname, given to her upon graduation from army basic aviation school, when she'd gotten her wings. Everyone got a nickname. She'd earned hers because her company said she was like a fine-bladed army ceremonial sword, slicing through any situation with finality. The name Saber had stuck. Maya liked living up to it. "Roger that, Dallas. Nothing new. The boys comin' up from Lima oughta be real impressed if this stuff hangs around the Eye like it usually does," she chuckled darkly. She made sure the knee board on her right thigh was adjusted, in case she needed to jot anything down.

Continuing her checks, Maya felt her left thigh pocket to make sure that her sister's medicine necklace was in there. Inca had given her the protective necklace soon after they'd met, and Maya always kept it on her during a mission. She couldn't wear jewlery, so she tucked it into a side pocket. It felt warm and secure in there and she gave it a pat of affection. In a way, it reminded Maya that now she had a sister to come home to, and to be careful out there in the skies over Peru.

Chuckling, Dallas said, "Oh, I'm sure they're gonna be *real* impressed, anyway."

"We'll see just how tough the good ole boys from Fort Rucker are when they encounter the Eye. I'd give my right arm to see the looks on their faces when they approach it."

"They've been given prior info on it, right?" Wild Woman interjected from the rear cockpit.

Maya nodded. She was ready. They were ready. Excitement thrummed through her. "Roger that, Jess. But looking at it on paper and seeing it in person, and knowing your forty-eight-foot blade has no room for error, despite the winds that are always whipping up from the river, is gonna make it real interesting for those boys."

Laughter filled Maya's earphones. She grinned mirthlessly. Yes, she'd like to see York's face when he came up against the Eye wrapped in thick clouds that were subject to the whim of the winds in this mountainous region. He'd learn to respect Eye real fast. Maya could hardly wait until they returned and she saw the two new Apaches thread it. There wasn't a pilot around that didn't approach it slowly and with a lot of trepidation.

The crew chief moved toward the ladder. "You're ready to go, Captain," she said, and snapped a salute to the two pilots.

Maya snapped off an answering salute. "Thank you, Sergeant Macedo."

Macedo then brought down both canopies and locked them into position, making the cabin of each cockpit secure.

Maya rested her gloved hands in plain sight of the crew below. Until everyone was clear, Maya would not start the massive engines of the helo or endanger her ground crew. As the three of them stepped away, their faces shadowed by the low lighting provided by a nearby generator, Maya lifted her hand and twirled her index finger in a circular motion, which meant she was going to start engines.

"Let's get down to work," she told Wild Woman, her voice turning businesslike. Maya flipped the first switch, which would engage the engine on the starboard, or right side of the fuselage. Instantly, a high whine and shudder worked through the aircraft. Eyes narrowing, Maya watched the engine indicator leap like active thermometers, bobbing up and down. When the engine was activated to a certain level, she thumbed the second engine switch. The gunship was awakening. In some sense Maya always thought of it as an ugly and ungainly looking thing. The image of a Tyrannosaurus rex came to mind: king of the dinosaurs and a mean bastard who ruled its turf—just like the Apache did. She could feel the sleek shudder that ran through it as the gunship gained power.

To Maya, her helicopter was a living being consisting of metal, wire circuitry, software and engine parts. She found her own power in that machinery. Whatever nervousness she'd felt about the coming encounter with Major Dane York was soothed away. When she was in the cockpit, the world and all its troubles dissolved. Her love of flying, of handling this remarkable machine, took over completely.

As the engine indicators leveled out, Maya engaged the main rotor. The four blades began to turn in a counterclockwise motion, slowly at first, then faster and faster as she notched up the power with the cyclic grasped in her fingers. Her entire left forearm rested comfortably on a panel so that her hand wouldn't cramp up and the cyclic became a natural extension of her hand.

"Jess, switch on the radar. I need to thread the needle here in a moment."

"Right… We're up…go for it…."

Maya saw the full sweep of a bright green set of lines on the right HUD. It looked like a slice of pie as the long, green needle of radar swept ceaselessly back and forth, clearly revealing the hole in the wall directly in front of them, despite the cloud cover beyond.

"Let's go over our checklist," Maya ordered.

"Roger," Jess returned, and they began to move through a sequence they had memorized long ago. Maya reached for her knee board, systematically checking off each station as it was called out. There was no room for sloppiness in her squadron. Things were done by the book. It improved their chances of survival.

They were ready. Maya devoured the excitement still throbbing through her. The Apache shook around her, the noise muted to a great degree by her helmet. She tested the yaw pedals beneath her booted feet. Everything was functioning properly. Proud of her hardworking ground crews, Maya lifted her hand to them in farewell as they moved back to watch the two assault helicopters take off, one at a time, to thread the needle.

"Black Jaguar Two. You ready to rock 'n' roll?" Maya asked.

Dallas chuckled indulgently. "Roger that, Saber. My girl

is checked out and we're ready to boogie on down the road with you. I want to dance on a Black Shark's head today."

"Roger. Let's go meet those good ole boys from Fort Rucker first, shall we? They might have the new D models, but us girls have got the guns."

Chuckling, Dallas said, "I don't think Gunslinger is ready for us."

Gunslinger was Dane York's nickname, Maya remembered starkly. He was an aggressive, type A individual who lived to hunt and kill in the air. Of course, so did anyone who got assigned to Apaches. They were a breed apart, bloodhounds in the sky, looking for quarry. Grinning, Maya notched up to takeoff speed and gently lifted the fully armed Apache off the lava lip. Smoothly, she nudged the helo forward into the swirling clouds. Within moments, they were completely embraced by the thick moisture.

"On glide path," Jess called out.

Maya flew by instruments only. Her eyes were narrowed on the HUD, watching the swiftly moving radar that whipped back and forth on the screen to create a picture of the approaching Eye. The winds were erratic at this time of the morning, because when the sun rose, the land heated up and made air currents unpredictable—and dangerous. Raindrops splattered across the windshield of her aircraft, falling from clouds which carried moisture from the humid jungle below. The Apache eased forward, closer and closer to the opening in the lava wall.

"On glide path..."

Compressing her lips, Maya tensed a little, as always. The aircraft was within twenty feet of the Eye. Right now, the wrong wind current, the wrong move with her hands or feet, would crash them into the wall. *Easy...easy...* She moved the aircraft smoothly through the hole and out over the jungle far below. They were at eight thousand feet now, and Maya eased away from the cliff to allow Dallas's aircraft to exit in turn.

"Switching to radar to hunt for the bad guys," Jess called.

"Roger." Maya looked up briefly. She could see nothing but the thick, white mists all around them. It was dark and the Apaches ran with no lights on them. Their instruments were all they had. "Keep a lookout for Kamovs. I got a bad feeling on this one, Jess."

"I thought you might. Scanning beginning now..."

Of course, Maya knew that even with their advanced radar, Kamovs had a certain type of paint on their fuselage that absorbed the Apache's radar signal, so that what little pinged back to the instruments on board was negligible, and therefore unreadable. A Kamov could spot them in fog like this, providing the cloud cover wasn't too thick, and nail them. Plus, their radar could send out a strong signal through thinner clouds and get an equally strong returning signal back from its target. Right now, they were sitting ducks and Maya knew it.

"We're out, Saber," Dallas said.

"Roger," Maya replied. "Let's split up, make less of a target of ourselves. Leave a mile between us and head for the meeting point. Keep your eyes and ears open, ladies."

"Roger that," Dallas said.

Inching up the throttles, Maya felt the Apache growl more deeply as it rose higher and higher. She wanted out of this cloud cover, to get on top of it so her 360-degree radar could detect and protect them from any lurking intruders. The Apache felt good around her. It was sleek and smooth compared to many other helicopters she'd flown. With a full load of ordnance on board, she felt the lethal power of it as well. At a flick of a switch on her collective, the stick between her legs, she could send a fiery hell to earth in a matter of moments.

As they rose to nine thousand feet, they suddenly popped out of the cloud cover. Above, Maya saw the familiar sight of the Southern Cross. She smiled a little at the peaceful looking stars as they glimmered across the ebony arc above them. And yet here they were in a cat-and-mouse game with killers who'd just as soon see them dead as alive. The incongruity of it all struck her.

The helicopter dipped its nose forward as Maya poured in more power, and they swiftly moved along the top of the ever-moving clouds.

"Beautiful out tonight," Wild Woman murmured as she scanned her instruments carefully.

"Yeah, it is," Maya said. "I was just thinking how peaceful it looks up there, above us. And how Faro Valentino probably has his Russian merc pilots in their Kamovs hunting for us right now."

"Ain't life a dichotomy?" Jess chuckled.

Scowling, Maya kept moving her head from side to side and looking above her—"rubbernecking," a term coined by World War II pilots. The Black Sharks were deadly hunters in their own right. When the Soviet Union broke up, Faro Valentino had marched in with his millions, purchased two state-of-the-art Kamovs and hired a cadre of out-of-work Soviet pilots, who liked being paid big bucks to fly cocaine in South America. The pilots were considered mercenaries for hire. And Faro had his pick of the best, waving his drug money under their noses.

Grimly, Maya kept switching her gaze from her instruments to the space around them. Somewhere off to her left was Dallas and the other Apache. Because the gunships were painted black, she could not see them at all. And because of their stealth duties, they ran without outboard lights.

"This time of morning there should be no other aircraft around," Maya said to Jess.

"Roger that. The civilians are still tucked in their beds, sleeping in Cuzco."

Chuckling, Maya returned to her duties. She could fly the Apache blind; she knew each movement and each sensation of this stalwart warrior they flew in. The Apache was a killing machine that responded to the most delicate touch. And had a heart that beat strongly within her. The soothing vibration of the engines moved throughout Maya's body, and to her, it was like a mother holding a child and rocking it; it gave her that sense of completeness and wholeness. The Apache was one of the most marvelous inventions of the air, as far as she was concerned. It had been built by Boeing to protect the pilots, first and foremost, and secondly, to become a sky hunter that had no equal. And it did. The Kamov's ability to sneak up on them was the one Achilles heel of this magnificent machine. And because of the type of flying they did, it was a constant threat. The Russian mercenary pilots were the cream of the crop, and they were hunters just like Maya. They lived to fly, hunt and kill. There was no difference between her and these pilots except that they were on the wrong side of the law, in Maya's eyes. Greed ran those pilots. Morals ran her and her people.

Beneath them, Maya knew, there was thick, continuous jungle. She and her teammates had to constantly fly among precipitous peaks covered in greenery. Most of the mountains were at least ten thousand feet high, some higher. Whatever the altitude, flying was not easy and required intense concentration in order not to crash into one of the unseen obstacles. The radar kept the shapes, elevation and height of the mountains on the HUD in front of Maya so that she could fly around them accordingly.

"Hey, look at that red stripe on the eastern horizon," Jess called out. "Bummer."

Dawn was coming. Maya scanned the bloodred horizon.

"Think it's a sign of things to come?" Jess asked.

Maya took the natural world around her seriously. Maybe it was her background with the Jaguar Clan. Or her innate Indian heritage. It didn't matter. There were signs all around them, all the time. The trick was in reading them correctly. "Damn," she muttered.

"Black Jaguar One, this is Two. Over."

Flicking down the button on the collective, Maya answered, "This is Black Jaguar One. Over."

"See the horizon?"

Mouth quirking, Maya glared at the crimson ribbon. "Yeah, I see it."

"Not a good sign. Over."

"No. Keep your eyes peeled, ladies. I'm betting on more company than was originally invited."

"Roger. Out."

Jess chuckled. "Wouldn't those good ole boys from Fort Rucker die laughing if they heard us looking at a red horizon as a sign of a coming Kamov attack?"

Maya knew that there would be radio silence maintained between them and the new Apaches and Blackhawk coming in to meet them. Only once they met would they all switch to another radio frequency to speak for the first time. Ruthlessly grinning, she said, "Yeah, they're gonna pee in their pants when they start flying with us in those new D models. It will shake up their well-ordered little male world."

Laughing, Jess said, "Speaking of which...here they come. Got three blips on radar and..." she peered closely at her HUD "...yep, it's them. It's showing two Apaches, and a Blackhawk bringing up the rear. What do you know? They can navigate."

Maya laughed. It broke the tension in her cockpit. "Well, we'll give them an A for meeting us at the right time and place. Let's just loiter here until they arrive."

Placing the Apache in a hover at nine thousand feet, Maya watched her HUD with interest. The radar clearly showed the three aircraft speeding toward them. The lead one was flown by Dane York, no doubt. Her mouth compressed. Maya held on to the anger that she still had toward him. Every woman pilot at her base had had the misfortune of being under his training command. That was why, when the idea for this base came about, they had all left with Maya. They wanted no part of the continuing prejudice they knew would be thrown at them. At least down here they were graded on their abilities, not their sex.

The crimson ribbon on the horizon was expanding minute by minute, staining the retreating blackness of the starlit sky and chasing it away like a gaping, bleeding wound. Maya kept looking around. She could feel the Kamovs lurking somewhere near...but where? All she needed was to have three unarmed gunships jumped by fully loaded Kamov Black Sharks, with only two Apaches standing between them. Her mind raced. If the Kamovs were near, just waiting for the right moment to jump them, she wondered how they had found out the meeting location in the first place? Was there a leak in intelligence? How could Faro Valentino have gotten hold of this information? Maya frowned. Her gaze moved ceaselessly now. Her gut was tightening. She smelled Kamovs. *Where? Dammit, where?*

"Black Jaguar One, this is Rocky One. Do you read? Over?"

Maya instantly flinched. It was Dane York's deep, controlling voice rolling in over the headset inside her helmet. Her heart leaped at that moment, beating hard. With fear. Old fear that she had felt at the school so many years ago. Anger quickly snuffed out her reaction. Thumbing the cyclic, she answered, "Rocky One, this is Black Jaguar One. Welcome to our turf." She grinned recklessly because she wanted to let him know from the get-go that he was on *her* turf, *her* base and under *her* command.

There was a brief silence. Then he answered, "Roger, Black Jaguar One. What are your instructions? Over."

Her eyes slitted as she saw the three aircraft coming out of the fleeing darkness. They were all painted the mandatory black, with absolutely no insignias on them. Her lips lifted away from her teeth and she said, "We're worried about Kamovs jumping us. No sign of them yet, but we feel them out there. You know the routine if we're jumped? Over."

"Roger, Black Jaguar One. How do you know there're Kamovs around?"

It was just like York to question her. Maya rolled her eyes. "Major, just accept it as a reality. Over."

"Roger, Black Jaguar One. We know the routine in case we are attacked. Over."

"Roger." At that point Maya, gave them the heading for the base. "Stay above the cloud cover. We'll be flying about a mile on either side of you. Over."

"Roger."

"He hasn't changed one bit," Dallas said over their private frequency. "Maybe you oughta tell him you looked into your crystal ball this morning before you got into the Apache, Maya. Tell him you saw Kamovs in your future." And she giggled.

Maya didn't think it was funny at all. Already York was trying to assert control over her by questioning her authority and ability. "No, I'd rather tell him the truth—that we've got a red sunrise and that means Kamovs are hunting us. Think he'd buy that instead?" Maya heard the other three women laughing hysterically in her headset. The laughter broke the tension among them. They knew from three years of experience that red sunrises were an ominous sign.

The light of day shone dully across the sky. Off to Maya's left, she saw the three new aircraft flying in a loose formation, staying far enough apart that they couldn't be hit as a unit by a missile and destroyed. At least York was smart enough not to fly in a tight formation—she'd give him that. Maya could barely make out Dallas's aircraft, positioned a mile on the other side of the group. They had an hour to go before they reached the base. And an hour would feel like a lifetime when she knew the Kamovs were up and hunting them.

"Break, break!" Dallas called. "We've got a visual on a Kamov at eleven o'clock!"

Instantly, Maya thumbed the radio. "Rocky One, hightail it out of here. We've got company. Over."

"Roger. Over and out."

Maya sucked in a breath and cursed as she saw the long shape of the Black Shark with its coaxial rotors coming down out of the sky toward the fleeing aircraft.

"Damn! Come on, Jess, let's get with it!" She punched fuel into the Apache engines. The aircraft instantly responded, the motors deepening in sound as they flew toward the attacking Kamov, which was trying to get a bead on one of the escaping U.S. aircraft. Right now, Maya thought, York was probably pissing in his pants over this. He was a combat pilot in a combat aircraft with no ammunition. Nada. And he was probably hotter than a two-dollar pistol about it. She didn't blame him.

"*Whoa!*" Jess yelled. "Another Kamov at nine o'clock, starboard!"

That was two of them. Maya thumbed the radio. "Dallas, I'll take the one at nine. You take the one at eleven. Over."

"Roger, you got it. Out." Dallas's voice was tight with tension.

Maya banked the screaming Apache to the right. She spotted the sleek Russian machine trying to go after the escaping Blackhawk below it. The U.S. aircraft had scattered in three different directions like birds that had been shot at. The Blackhawk had dropped quickly in altitude and was making for the cloud cover. The only problem was that once the Blackhawk entered the clouds, the pilot would have to go on instrumentation in an area he didn't know, while being pursued by a Kamov pilot who knew this territory like the back of his hand.

"Damn," Maya whispered. She sent the Apache into a steep dive. The machine screamed and cranked out, the beating pulsations of the rotors thumping through her tense body. Gripping the controls, Maya grimaced, her lips lifting away from her clenched teeth.

"Put a rocket on 'em, Jess."

"Roger. I got a fix!"

"Fire when ready."

They were arcing at a steep, banking dive toward the Kamov, which was closing in on the slower Blackhawk. Maya knew the shot would be wide. She hoped it would be close enough to scare off the Kamov. Or at least make him turn and pick on them instead of an unarmed helicopter.

"Fire!" Jess cried.

There was a flash of light from the starboard wing where the rocket launched. Maya followed the trail of the speeding weapon as it careened toward the Kamov.

"Fire two more!"

"Roger. One sec...firing now!"

Two more rockets left the pod on the right wing of the Apache.

Maya watched as all three streaked toward the Kamov. Satisfaction rose in her as the first one dived in front of its nose. The pilot had seemed so intent on pursuing the Blackhawk that he wasn't aware of them—until now. The problem with the Kamov was that it was a single seater, and the pilot not only had to fly the damn thing, but work all the instruments, as well. That led to attention overload, and Maya was betting the pilot had been so engaged in downing the Blackhawk that he hadn't had time to check who else might be around.

The Kamov suddenly banked sharply to the left. The other two rockets flew harmlessly past it.

Good. Maya sucked air between her teeth as she pushed the diving Apache to the left now, to follow the fleeing Kamov. In her headset, she could hear Dallas and her copilot talking excitedly back and forth to one another as they engaged the other Kamov. It sounded like they had everything under control.

"We're going after this son of a bitch," Maya muttered to Jess. "Hang on."

The Kamov pilot knew it. In a split second, the gunship suddenly moved skyward in an awesome display of power and agility. It was trying to do an inside loop over Maya's Apache so that it would come down behind her "six" or the rear of her machine and put a rocket into her. The Kamov turned a bloodred color as it arced high into the dawn sky, the twin blades a blur as it rose swiftly and then turned over. Maya knew that few helicopter pilots in the world could accomplish an inside loop. But she was one of them. Gripping the controls, she pushed the power on the Apache to the redline. The engines howled. The machine shuddered like a frothing monster, chasing after its quarry. It shot up well above where the Kamov was making its own maneuver. With a deft twist of her hands and feet, Maya brought the Apache into a tight inside loop. All the while she kept her eyes pinned on the Kamov below her.

Within seconds, the Apache was shrieking into a somersault, the pressure pounding against her body. Breathing hard, Maya felt the sweat coursing down the sides of her face beneath her helmet. The Apache was handling well, the gravity rising as she kept the loop tight.

"I'm going to make that bastard's day," she said through gritted teeth. Snapping the Apache out of the loop, she ended up behind the Kamov.

"Jess?" It wasn't truly a question; it was an order. Her copilot knew what to do: arm a missile and fire at the Kamov.

"I'm on it. Firing one, two..."

Eyes gleaming, Maya watched as rockets on either side of the Apache lit up and sped off toward the Kamov, which was now diving for the cloud cover. They were wild shots, but Maya wanted to let the pilot know that she'd pursue him. It was a ruse, of course, because her first duty was to the three unarmed helicopters.

The Kamov dove into the clouds and raced away. The rockets missed their intended target because of the Kamov's rapid response.

"I think he's gone," Jess said, studying the radar.

Maya blew out a breath of air. Looking above her, she rapidly climbed to gain altitude.

"Black Jaguar Two. What's your status? Over."

Dallas came on moments later, her voice tight. "Black Jaguar One, we just routed the second Kamov. He's heading back north. And you? Over."

"Same here. Let's catch up with our unarmed children. Over."

Dallas's laugh was tense and explosive. "Yeah, roger that, One. Out."

Turning the Apache back toward base, Maya didn't for a moment think that the game with the Kamovs was over, but she kept a sharp lookout as they flew homewards. Adrenaline was making her feel shaky now. It was a common reaction after combat. Wiping her face, Maya saw that the bloodred ribbon along the horizon had turned a deep pink color. Now it looked more beautiful than deadly.

"You think our boys peed their pants yet, Captain?"

Maya chuckled over Jess's comment. "Well, if they haven't, they probably thought about it."

"Helluva welcome to the killing fields," Dallas intoned.

"Yeah, well, it will put them on warning that this is a hot area and they can expect this anytime, day or night."

"Probably killed York to have to run. You know how aggressive he is in the air," Dallas said.

Maya laughed fully. "He probably feels like a coward about now. And gee, he had to leave it to four women to protect his behind. *That* is probably eating at him more than anything."

Jess giggled. "Can you imagine his horror that he's still alive and flying and that we didn't drop the ball?"

"Yeah, what's he gonna do," Dallas said, "when he has to stare us in the face and admit we saved his bacon?"

The laughter felt good to Maya. She knew the letdown after a tense combat situation was necessary. Fortunately, they could talk on a private channel between the two Apaches, so that no one else could pick up their banter. She was sure York would have a hemorrhage if he'd heard them just now. No, it was going to be fun to watch the good ole boys from Fort Rucker get a look-see at the Eye of the Needle. It was going to be even more enjoyable to watch them sweat their way through it for the first time. That made any pilot, no matter how experienced, tense up big time.

"Well, ladies, let's go home and see these guys pucker up."

The laughter was raucous.

Chapter 4

Dane York was nervous as he stood aside, watching the all-women crews hurriedly move the three new helicopters into the maw of the huge cave. His heart was still pounding in his chest from barely squeaking through that damned entrance they called the Eye. His other pilots and crew members stood off to one side on the rough rock surface of the lip of the cave, out of the way, tense looks on their faces. Only one person had welcomed them, a woman with short red hair who introduced herself as Chief Warrant Officer Lynn Crown before hurriedly running off to direct the crews as to the placement of the new gunships.

As the clouds around the high lava wall thinned, Dane gazed at the Eye. He heard the approaching Apaches on the other side of it. Wiping his mouth with the back of his hand, he settled his garrison cap on his head and waited. As the morning sun burned off some of the thicker clouds he could see the entrance better. Shaking his head, Dane realized just how tight that aperture really was. How many times a day did Maya fly her Apaches in and out of that thing? What a helluva "needle" to try and thread. Dane wondered how anyone, man or woman, could muster enough brain power and concentration after an exhausting mission to slip through it without nicking the blades of their Apache on the unforgiving lava walls. His admiration for Maya's pilots rose.

Joe and Craig moved to his side. They all watched as another woman, dressed in an olive-green T-shirt and fatigues, trotted out with red-orange flare sticks in her hands and stood at attention opposite the Eye. One of the Apaches was coming through. The crewmember raised her hands above her head to direct the helicopter into a landing spot once it flew through the opening. Dane's eyes narrowed as he watched. Though he and his men had crawled through, literally, this first Apache came through like the pilot was on a Sunday drive!

"I'll be go-to-hell," Joe gasped in amazement. "That's some purty flying. Will ya look at that? Whoever the pilot is, she just flew through that opening like it wasn't there!"

"No kidding," Craig muttered, scowling.

Dane said nothing, his mouth flattening. The first Apache landed opposite where they stood, on the other side of the massive lava lip. Bruising waves of air buffeted them, kicked up by the rotor blast as the gunship landed. The lip was at least four hundred feet wide and about one-quarter of a mile long, from his estimates. The maw of the gigantic cave was simply mindboggling. Inside the shadowy space, crews were running at full tilt as they positioned the three new helicopters in the maintenance area.

The second Apache flew through smoothly in turn, as if the Eye weren't there, either. It landed so close to the first one that Dane held his breath momentarily. The punctuation of the rotors pounded the entire area; the wall across the cave opening acted like an echo chamber of huge proportions, until his eardrums hurt from the reverberations. Wind kicked up by the rotor blades slammed like a boxer's gloves against his body. Still, as Dane watched the two crews hurry toward the Apaches that had just landed, he was critical of everything.

He didn't think Maya Stevenson could run a squadron. However, from the way the crews worked in almost balletlike precision, that prejudice was blown away, too. As the engines were shut down, the high, ear-piercing whine echoing from the wall began to lessen. The rotors began to slow, and finally came to a stop. Instantly, one crew woman ducked beneath the nose of the first Apache and hooked up the device used to pull it inside. He watched as the left-sided canopies were opened to allow the two pilots from each helicopter to exit.

Morning sunlight shot through the Eye in gold streamers that lit up the murky depths of the cave. Dane ignored the surprised murmurs of his I.P.'s, his gaze fastened ruthlessly upon the two flight crews. Maya Stevenson would be there. His heart squeezed a little in anticipation. What was she like now? Even more sure and confident? More mouthy? He scowled. Why did he have to hold such a grudge against her? If the truth be known, and it wasn't something he liked to think about often, from the first time he'd met Maya he'd been powerfully drawn to her. But once he'd come up against her willful nature, he'd instantly rejected the primal attraction.

The wisps of clouds thinned. He saw fragments of the constantly moving mist weave through the Eye, then dissipate beneath the rays of equatorial sunlight that was growing stronger by the minute. Dane saw the legs of the returning women pilots as they gathered close to one another behind the carriage of the last Apache. They were probably talking over their fight with the Kamovs. That would be typical of any group of pilots, male or female. Impatience thrummed through him. He wanted to see her. As repelled as he was by the assignment, there was something in him that ached to see Maya once again. That surprised Dane more than anything else. How could he miss someone who had been such a thorn in his side? Challenging him? Confronting him daily as she'd done at school?

The crews hurriedly took the two Apaches farther into the cave, where they would be unseen from the air. When they'd slowly rolled by, Dane saw the four women pilots, helmets tucked beneath their arms, standing in a circle, talking animatedly. One of them, to his surprise, was a blond with red streaks through her hair. What kind of base did Maya run that she'd let one of her pilots look like that?

The women were all heights and body builds, but it was easy to pick out Maya, because at six foot tall, she stood above all of them. The body-hugging black flight suits they wore had no insignias on them. They were long-sleeved despite the heat and humidity. He knew the suits were styled that way because in the event of a fire in the cockpit, the Nomex material would protect them against burns. He saw that Maya wore knee-high, polished black boots, while the others had on regulation flight boots that fit snugly up to their ankles. Maya looked every inch an Amazon warrior—formidable in her own right.

The drift of women's laughter made him tense. And then he saw Maya lift her head and look directly at him. Dane felt a heated prickle at the base of his neck—a warning—as her eyes settled flatly on him. He was the tallest in his own group, so he would be just as easy to spot as she was. Unconsciously, Dane wrapped his arms across his chest as he locked onto her gaze. At this distance, he couldn't make out her expression. He could feel the coming confrontation, however. And he saw that a number of crew women were casting furtive looks as if to see when, not if, a fight might break out. The tension was thick. Even he could feel it. Joe and Craig moved restlessly, sensing his unease.

Mouth going dry, Dane watched as the women pilots broke from their huddle and walked toward them. Maya strode with her chin up, her black, hair flowing across her proud shoulders, the black helmet beneath her left arm. The other three pilots walked slightly behind her, in a caliper formation. They looked like proud, confident, fierce warriors even though they were women. As they passed through the bright shafts of sunlight, now shining strongly though the Eye, he watched the golden radiance embrace them.

For a moment, Dane thought there was even more light around them. He blinked. Was he seeing things? He must be rattled from being chased by the Kamovs and then having to get through that hole in the wall to land here in the cave. Mouth compressing, he watched as Maya closed the distance between them. There was nothing wasted in her movements. She was tall, graceful and balanced. The chicken plate she wore on her tall, strong body hid most of her attributes. Locking into Maya's assessing emerald green gaze, he rocked internally from the power of her formidable presence.

She was even more stunning than he could recall. In the four years since she'd left the school where he'd been her I.P., she had grown and matured. Her black hair shone with reddish tones as the sunlight embraced her stalwart form. Her skin was a golden color, her cheekbones high, that set of glorious, large green eyes framed with thick, black, arching brows. But it was the slight play of a smile, one corner of her full lips cocked upward, and that slightly dimpled chin and clean jawline, that made him feel momentarily shaky.

The high humidity made her ebony hair curl slightly around her face, neck and shoulders. Still, she could have been a model strutting her elegant beauty down a Paris runway instead of the proficient Apache helicopter pilot she was. The snug-fitting flight suit displayed every inch of her statuesque form. She was big boned and had a lot of firm muscles beneath that material, but there wasn't an ounce of fat anywhere on her that he could see. She seemed all legs, and slightly short waisted as a result. All Thoroughbred. All woman—a powerful, confident woman such as Dane had never known before now. With the sunlight radiating behind her as she walked toward him, she looked more ethereal than real.

Blinking a couple of times, Dane looked down at the rough black lava cave floor, then snapped his gaze back to her. The corner of her mouth was still cocked. He saw silent laughter in her large green eyes, and he felt his palms becoming sweaty. His heart raced as she closed the gap between them. He felt like they were two consummate warriors, wary and distrustful and circling one another to try and see the chinks in each other's armor, their Achilles heel, so that one of them might get the upper hand, and be victorious.

Maya felt laughter bubbling up her long, slender throat as she approached York's group. The expressions on their faces made her exuberant. All but York had an awed look as they stared open-mouthed at her and her pilots. The men didn't look angry or challenging. No, they looked all right to her. But Dane York was another matter. Her gaze snapped back to him. Her heart thumped hard in her chest. Her hand tightened momentarily around the black helmet she carried.

He looked older. And more mature. In Maya's eyes, he'd always been a very handsome man, in a rugged sort of way. He had a square face, a stubborn chin that brooked no argument, a long, finely sculpted nose, eyebrows that slashed straight across the forehead, shading his large, intelligent blue eyes. Eyes that used to cut her to ribbons with just one withering look. Well, that was the past. Maya locked fully on to York's challenging, icy gaze. He stood with his arms across his chest, his feet spread apart like a boxer ready to take a coming blow. His full lips had thinned into a single line. Those dark brown eyebrows were bunched into a disapproving scowl. There was nothing friendly or compromising about York. His hair was cut military short, a couple of strands out of place along his wrinkled brow. The dark olive green flight suit outlined his taut body. At six feet tall, he had the broadest set of shoulders Maya had ever seen. York was a man who could carry a lot of loads before he broke.

And that stubborn chin shouted of his inability to change quickly. Flexible he wasn't.

Maya came to a halt. So did her women pilots, who created one solid, unbroken line in front of the contingent of men. She snapped off a crisp salute to him.

York returned her salute.

"Welcome to Black Jaguar Base, Major York."

Dane saw the gleam of laughter lurking in Maya's eyes as she stood toe-to-toe with him. He admired her chutzpah. Maya knew how to get into a man's space real fast. She knew she was tall and powerful. Confidence radiated from her like the sun that had embraced her seconds earlier.

"Thank you, Captain Stevenson. I can't say the welcome was what we'd anticipated." Dane decided to keep things professional between them at all costs. He saw the glint in Maya's eyes deepen. Her lips curled upward—just a little. Her husky voice was pleasant and unruffled.

"Get used to it. Around here, we're on alert twenty-four hours a day, seven days a week."

He nodded and dropped into an at-ease position, his hands behind his back. "The report didn't say that." Maya stood easily, her booted feet slightly apart. The other women pilots were looking his crew over with critical eyes. He felt as if they were all bugs under a microscope.

"The report," Maya said crisply, "was meant to be brief and to the point. My X.O., Lieutenant Klein, here—" she motioned toward Dallas, who stood at her right shoulder "—did warn you of possible altercations with druggies once you entered our airspace. And it happened, unfortunately."

Dane held back a retort. "If you'll get someone to show my men to their quarters and where we can set up our schooling facility, I'd appreciate it, Captain."

All business. Okay, that was fine with Maya. It was better than York taking verbal potshots at her pilots. Turning to Dallas, she said, "Take them to their quarters. Feed them.

And then have Sergeant Paredes take them to our Quonset hut, where we've set up shop for them to teach."

"Yes, ma'am." Dallas smiled hugely at the cluster of men in green flight suits. "Gentlemen? If you'll follow me, I'll give you a quick tour of our base and get you some quarters."

York didn't move as his men left with Dallas. He remained rigidly where he stood. Maya frowned.

"Aren't you going with them?"

"We need to talk, Captain. Somewhere private. Your office, perhaps?"

Smiling suddenly, Maya got it. Okay, York was going to have it out with her in private. *Fine.* She turned to her other pilots. "Let's call it a day, ladies. You all have reports to fill out, plus your collateral duty assignments. Wild Woman, see to it that the crews refuel the Apaches and let's get them on standby. Any problems, see me."

Jess came to attention. "Yes, ma'am!" And she turned on her heel and hurried into the cave with the other copilot at her side.

Turning her head, Maya looked at Dane, the ice between them obvious. The sunlight was suddenly shut out as a thick, cloud slid silently over the Eye. "Well, Major? You ready?" Her voice was a dangerous rasp, a warning that if he thought she was an easy target in private, he was mistaken. She saw York's eyes widened momentarily and then become slits. Maya felt him harness his anger.

"Ready whenever you are, Captain," he said coolly.

Turning, she moved into the cave's murky depths. Within moments, York was at her shoulder, matching her stride, his profile grim and set. Maya could feel the tension within him. As they walked into the maw, the lights overhead illuminated the way, giving the cave a grayish cast with heavy shadows.

"Let me give you a quick idea of our layout, Major," she said, gesturing to the right. "Over there is our HQ. My office and all other collateral offices are located in that two-story building. Just ahead of us is the maintenance area for the helicopters. As soon as they land, we get them inside. Faro Valentino always has his Kamovs snooping around. Luckily, we've got that lava wall between the cave entrance and the jungle out there. Otherwise, I'm sure he'd have come in here a long time ago and tried to use his rockets or missiles on us. The wall prevents that from happening."

York looked back at the landing area. "It's a perfect, natural defense position," he murmured, awe in his tone. "How thick is that rock?"

"Thick enough to stop radar from getting through it." Maya grinned wickedly as she gestured toward it. "We got lucky with this place. On the other side of this inactive volcano is an old mining operation and a shaft that connects us to it. There's no way Faro and his pilots can get access to us. Of course, if we were stupid and left our helicopters out on the landing lip, they might drop a bomb or two, but we don't give them that kind of an opportunity."

Dane looked around. He felt a little of the tension ease between them. Seeing the sudden pride and excitement in Maya's eyes as she talked about her squadron facilities was refreshing to him. So far, she hadn't lobbed any verbal grenades at him. He was waiting, though. There was too much bad blood between them, and he knew she hadn't forgotten a thing he'd said or done to her back in flight school. The depths of her emerald eyes were very readable. Or maybe she was deliberately letting him see her myriad emotions.

"I'm going to look forward to checking out your facility, Captain. Seeing it on paper doesn't do it justice. Seeing it in person...well, frankly, it's overwhelming. Who would ever think you could get a base like this inside a mountain?"

"It took a year for Navy Seabees and a lot of helicopter flights to bring in everything you see here." Maya stopped at the door to the two-story metal building. She took off her gloves and stuffed them into the right thigh pocket of her flight uniform. A number of electric golf carts whizzed around the buildings, coming and going in ceaseless activity. They were the workhorses of the facility.

"And you were here that first year?" Dane found it hard to believe.

She straightened and placed her long, spare fingers over the doorknob, her movements full of grace, like a cat's. "Of course."

He heard the sting in her husky tone. She opened the door and he followed. They climbed quickly up the metal stairs. Looking around, Dane was once more impressed. There was fluorescent lighting in the ivory-painted hallway. The highly polished white tile floor made it even brighter. He saw a number of doors to offices as they walked by—every one of them open. Women dressed in army-green T-shirts and fatigues were busy inside. There were computer monitors, telephones on the desks—just like any other busy squadron HQ. Only this one was situated inside a cave in a mountain. Blown away by the facility, he felt his respect for Maya inch upward.

"In here," she said, and stood aside, gesturing for him to enter the open office.

Dane scowled. "You leave your office door open like this all the time?"

She heard the censure in his tone. "Why not? Who's going to come in here and steal top secret info? One of my people?" She laughed.

"Still," Dane said stubbornly, "it's not a good policy."

Snorting, Maya followed him into the office. She turned and shut the door. The tension between them was there again. Placing her helmet on a nearby table, she shrugged out of her chicken plate and hung it up on a wall hook. Ruffling her hair with her fingers, she moved around her metal desk, which looked like a disaster had hit it, and went to the coffeemaker sitting on a makeshift table behind it.

"Want some coffee?" she asked, without turning around.

Pouring the thick, black brew into a chipped white mug, Maya set it on her desk.

"Yes...I need something to calm my nerves after that attack." Dane stood expectantly behind Maya as she reached for a second white mug and filled it.

Grinning, Maya turned and handed the mug to him. "Cream and sugar are here if you want it." The instant their fingertips touched, Maya wanted to jerk her hand away, but she countered the urge. Smoothly handing the cup to him, she took a seat in her old, creaking chair and leaned back in it, her own mug between her hands.

Dane sipped the coffee. Wrinkling his nose, he muttered, "This is strong."

"So? Around here you have to be or you don't make the grade, Major."

He saw the laughter in her eyes again. There was a thoughtful look on her face. How had Maya grown even more beautiful in four years? Dane sat down on the chair located at one side of her desk. The office was small and cramped. On the wall he saw her flight graduation diplomas. There was a color photo of her father, the general, on her desk, along with another of her silver-haired mother. There was a third photo, of a woman who looked strikingly like Maya and was dressed in a dark green, sleeveless T-shirt, a leather thong with two claws hanging between her breasts. Dane hadn't known Maya had a twin sister.

Family was important to Maya, he realized, even out here in the middle of a godforsaken jungle. He also noticed several spikes of orchids, red with yellow lips, on one edge of her desk—a woman's touch. Color to make the ivory walls and dark metal desk seem less masculine, he supposed. On another wall was a pair of crossed U.S. Army ceremonial swords. He recalled that her nickname was Saber, and he smiled to himself. The swords were a nonverbal reminder of who and what she was.

"That hole you fly through out there is a corker," he muttered as he sipped the coffee.

Chuckling darkly, Maya said, "Yeah, it's an added pucker factor, no doubt." She saw his mouth soften slightly over her joke. One corner lifted. Just barely. Maybe old sourpuss York wasn't going to bust her chops, after all. She remained on guard, however, because he was like a sniping bulldog that would come out of left field and attack her verbally when she least expected it.

"You two flew through it like it was nothing. We inched toward the entrance and then inched our way through. I'm impressed with your ability in such tight quarters."

Maya grinned fully. The cup of coffee felt good in her hands. She wanted to relax a little, but she didn't dare. She felt like raw, exposed nerves with him around. Right now, York's face was losing some of its tension; his broad brow was less wrinkled and the creases around his mouth less deep. But she didn't dare trust that the ease between them would last. "They don't teach that in school, do they?"

She saw him frown.

"We call it threading the Eye of the Needle. If you hear the word, *Eye,* that's what we're referring to. And yes, it's a dangerous maneuver."

"If those clouds are too thick," Dane said, "how can your radar penetrate enough to show you where the entrance is?"

Shrugging, Maya murmured, "We wait until the clouds thin out. My orders to my pilots are not to attempt it if the radar can't scan the opening fully."

"I'm impressed."

"With what? The Eye?"

"No...you. What you've set up here. It's a pretty remarkable facility from what I've seen so far."

Maya didn't let his compliment go too her heart or her head. She saw York struggling to remain distant and polite with her. Well, she was struggling to maintain a professional attitude, too. At least he was trying.

"What's remarkable," Maya told him with seriousness, "is that this is an all-woman operation. It was from the git-go. We have the best flight crews in the world. My pilots can outfly anyone, anywhere and at any time."

Dane opened his mouth and then shut it. The pride in her eyes and in her impassioned, husky voice was unmistakable. "Flying down here would certainly give you skills that most of our other Apache pilots don't have."

"Yeah, there's a real difference between live fire and Kamovs hunting you, and going out to the practice range to shoot at wooden targets that can't shoot back." She laughed derisively.

Dane sipped his coffee. He bit back another acid comment. She was right. Dead right. The glittering look in her eyes excited him. Maya was a hunter of the first order. Like he was.

"I know I'm stuck here for six weeks teaching, but I'd sure as hell like a shot at that Kamov that was chasing me."

"Stuck here?" Maya's voice dripped sarcasm. "Is that how you feel, Major? That you're 'stuck' here with us?"

Damn! Dane closed his eyes momentarily. He'd done it already. He'd spoken before he'd carefully thought over his reply. Opening his hand, he muttered, "Poor choice of words, Captain. My men and I were looking forward to the assignment."

Snorting, Maya stood up, cup in her hands. She glared down at him. "You haven't changed at all, Major. You're just a little smoother around the edges about it, is all. Aren't you?"

Struggling to control his own anger, Dane met her cool, assessing green eyes. His skin prickled beneath her righteous annoyance. "Look, Captain Stevenson, I'm not here to fight with you. We're here to help you fight an enemy, an obviously powerful one. You've got a war going on down here. I wasn't aware of that. Or at least, not the magnitude of it."

Would she believe him? Judging by the way she lifted her chin to an imperious angle, she didn't. At all.

"Let me make one thing *very* clear to you, York." Maya dropped all pretense of military formality. She saw the shock in his eyes over her deliberate use of his last name only. Ordinarily he, as a major, had rank and privilege over her. But not down here. And not ever, as far as she was concerned. "We have a lot of bad history between us. Most of my flight crews don't know about you, and about your reputation of verbally denigrating women who are in the military. Just the women pilots who trained with you at Fort Rucker." Her voice softened, a grating edge to it as she set the mug down and walked slowly around the desk.

"My pilots risk their lives day in and day out. I have only twelve of them. Three fly combat missions every day or night, on a twenty-four-hour duty. Three are on standby at the ready shack. And the other three get a day off that's really not a day off at all. We're shorthanded around here. I've got fifty-four people and that's it. Everyone works twelve-hour shifts, seven days a week. The demands, the responsibilities, are high enough to choke a horse. And every one of those women out there would give her heart, body and soul to me if I asked for it. We operate under wartime conditions at *all* times. There isn't an hour that goes by that my people aren't busting their tails and risking their lives getting necessary things done around here to keep those birds flying."

Her voice lowered to a snarl. "And if you so dare say something like you're 'stuck' here to them, to their faces, I'll be throwing you on board our Apache and sending your butt out of here so fast it'll make even your seasoned head swim." She jabbed her finger into his upturned face. His eyes were nearly colorless and she knew from past experience they only got that way when he was angry. Maya remembered all too well those huge, black pupils set in a pale blue background glaring back at her when she confronted him at the school when he was out of line. "You even *hint* of prejudice toward my pilots or crews and you're out of here. Is that understood?''

Smarting, Dane rose. Maya stood a few feet away, her cheeks flushed, her eyes narrowed with fury, her voice trembling with emotion.

''Why don't you let our past go? That would help one helluva lot,'' he said.

Jerking her chin up, Maya glared at him. ''You started this, I didn't. I'm more than willing to let our past go. But our mutual history is alive and well now, York, from what I can tell. I won't tolerate a *breath* of prejudice from you.''

He controlled his anger. Dane knew her dressing down was warranted. He had no one to blame for his foot-in-mouth this time but himself. Maya had been pleasant with him up to that point. Formal, but at least not angry or nasty like she was being right now. His anger at himself warred with the words he'd had from his colonel; if Maya called his C.O., Dane's career would be over. Looking around, he took some deep breaths to try and settle his frustration.

''Look,'' he rasped, ''let's start all over. All right?'' He held out his hand toward her in a gesture of peace. ''I promise you that my crew is not like me.''

''Thank God.''

''They're just the opposite. They've been looking forward to this assignment.''

''Unlike you.''

Mouth compressing, Dane glared at her. ''You're not going to give me an inch, are you?''

''Not a chance, York. I won't let you think of hurting my people. I know you. My pilots suffered under you just like I did. We have a long, collective memory. And you're the one on the edge of the sword, not us, this time.'' Her nostrils quivered. Tension swirled between them.

''I promise not to allow my mouth to get in the way of any instruction with your pilots and crews.'' Dane held her blazing green eyes. "Is that enough? I'm sorry. Deeply sorry. Or do you want a pound of my flesh, while you're at it?"

Her fury subsided. She sensed York's honest attempt to lessen the tension between them. "You don't have *anything* I want, York. All I expect from you toward my people is *respect.* And if you haven't realized it already, they've more than earned anything you or your men can give them. Like I said, we're on a wartime footing down here. You boys from Fort Rucker 'play' at war, but we're in it up to our hocks every day." Blowing a breath of air between her lips, Maya moved away from him. Why did York have to be such a bastard? And yet, although she hated to admit it, she was powerfully drawn to the army officer. She had to be loco!

Dane waited until her voice ebbed away in the small, cramped room. "You already have our respect," he told her quietly. "I admit I didn't think women could be warriors...but I'm being proved wrong."

Maya walked around her desk and sat down. "You were wrong four years ago, too."

Wincing, Dane set the cup on the edge of her desk. "I think we understand each other, Captain. I'd like to be dismissed so I can get to my men, check out the training facility and get on with why we're down here."

Four years ago, Maya knew, York would not have been so amenable. He'd ridden her ruthlessly and without letting up. Staring at him, she saw that he struggled to be humble in front of her. That must be a new emotion for him—humbleness. He was arrogant before. Maybe he *had* changed.

"Dismissed, Major."

The weariness in her tone told him she wasn't going to forgive or forget. As he walked to the door, he heard her call out to him. "One last thing, Major."

He turned. "Yes?" Maya was studying him like a jaguar might its quarry. Her full lips were compressed with disappointment.

"You got a problem with anything or anyone around my

squadron, you see me about it *first.* Don't talk behind my back, don't manipulate, gossip or think of doing an end run on me and my command here. Got it?"

There was nothing soft about Maya Stevenson, yet he saw the sadness in her eyes, as if she, too, yearned for a truce as badly as he did. Dane placed his hand on the doorknob. He recalled Maya when she'd first come to his school. She'd been fresh, excited, bright and impassioned. Had he snuffed out all those attributes, and was this the result of his handiwork? A no-nonsense woman who could be as brutal as any man in command could be? Well, he had no one to thank for her stance toward him but himself.

"Yes, I've got it," he replied in a deep, dispirited tone.

Maya felt very old and tired. She saw real apology in Dane's eyes and it shook her. The old Dane York would never have admitted fault or apologized, even if he was wrong. "Leave the door open on your way out, Major York. My people have access to me twenty-four hours a day. When you get a schedule set up, bring it to me and I'll look it over. My pilots must continue to fly every day, so you're going to have to work around their duties."

"I understand." Despondency blanketed Dane as he opened the door, turned and walked down the hall. He wanted to say something more to heal the wound he'd just opened up in her. *Damn.*

A number of women looked up as he passed by. He saw the quizzical expressions on their faces. Had they heard the free-for-all in Maya's office? More than likely. This building was not that substantial; was made mostly of corrugated tin and some steel framing to hold it together. Voices would travel well in this complex, he realized glumly.

Maya sat down dejectedly after York left. She leaned back in her chair, gripping the arms and looking up at the ceiling. Her heart was pounding madly in her chest. She wanted to hate York, but that wasn't the main emotion she was feeling. A part of her felt sorry for him. And she wanted to cry. Deep down inside her, Maya had been hoping for a truce between them. She wanted peace, not war. Her life was nothing but combat, and she yearned for peace with him.

Four years ago, Maya had wanted to slug Dane in his arrogant face. Today, just now, she wanted to see some kind of improvement in York's demeanor. And to give him credit, he was trying. That little slip about being stuck here wasn't much, but it had set her off. Judging from the contriteness in his eyes and voice, he was really sorry about it.

"Maybe—" Maya whispered "—maybe you've changed just enough to make this nightmare six weeks tolerable, York. I sure hope so...."

Chapter 5

Maya couldn't wait any longer. She dropped the pen on her desk amid a clutter of papers that desperately needed her attention. She *had* to go down and take a good, close look at the D model Apaches. Glancing at the clock on the wall, she realized it had only been two hours since she'd locked horns with York. Grabbing her black baseball hat off the peg, she settled it on her head and moved out into the hall. Things were curiously quiet. Why? Maya glanced into each office; no one was around. Where was everyone? This was highly unusual.

On the ground floor, Maya pushed opened the door. To her left, the opening to the cave was filled with brilliant sunlight lancing in from the Eye and above the wall as the sun crept higher in the sky. The new D models and the Blackhawk had been brought into the cave complex, at the opposite end from where maintenance was performed on their Apaches. Moving around the end of the building, she grinned and halted. Dropping her hands on her hips, Maya chuckled to herself.

There, surrounding the new helicopters, was nearly the entire squadron. Everyone spoke in excited, animated tones as they looked at the machines, touched them. Her pilots were mingling with the ground crews, and she saw how the new I.P.'s were passionately engaged in conversation, gesturing toward the new D craft, their faces alight with enthusiasm. Some of the worry slid off Maya's shoulders when she saw that the two I.P.s were like little boys with a new toy—only the new toy was a leaner, meaner version of the A model Apaches Maya and her crew flew daily.

Her brows fell. Where was York? She searched the crowd for him. Over fifty people were gathered in a large circle around one chopper. One of the I.P.s, the Texan, squatted near the side of the fuselage, gesturing to all the snakelike coils of wire beneath the panels he held up, proudly showing the insides to the rapt crowd of onlookers.

Maya's heart thumped hard when she spotted York. Her hands settled on her hips as she lifted her chin and laughed softly. Dane York was on his back, on the cave floor, beneath the 30 mm cannon that was suspended beneath the fuselage just below the first cockpit of the D model. Several of her crew chiefs were down on their hands and knees, peering up as he pointed out various parts of the long-nosed machine gun. She watched with interest, close enough to see his expression, but not enough to hear his voice. His square face was alight with enthusiasm. Why, he was even smiling! That caught Maya off guard. York was smiling. What a difference! In flight school at Fort Rucker, he'd never smiled. Not once. She saw Sergeant Nuria Sedano, a Peruvian mechanic, laughing at something he'd said. Another crew chief, Sergeant Lucinda Huisa, was scrunched down on her hands and knees, her eyes narrowed intently, as York continued to extol the changes on this newest model.

"Miracles do happen," Maya muttered. She remained where she was. It was good to see her squadron so enthusiastic about the new helicopters. The other I.P., CWO4 Craig

Barton, was sitting on the lip of the Blackhawk with his own crowd of interested admirers, pointing out details in the interior of the cabin.

Happiness threaded through Maya's heart. It felt good to see her crews eagerly engaged in welcoming the newest helos to their tiny base. Her team worked hard, relentlessly, and she asked everything of them, heart and soul, to keep the operation at peak performance. She wasn't about to wade into the crowd and order them all back to their offices or maintenance areas. No, let them have this small reprieve. Goddess knew, Maya wasn't able to give them much R and R in Agua Caliente, or even better, fly them to Cuzco for a weekend where they could really rest and have a little fun, dancing and drinking at the local clubs. They were a group of young women, nearly all single and in their early twenties. Maya knew that some had boyfriends in Agua Caliente or Cuzco, or back in the States. They signed up for a one-year gig down here, and she understood how tough it was for them to be separated from loved ones for that long. Yet they did it willingly, with a sense of real adventure, knowing the demands and responsibilities before they signed on.

Maya's heart swelled with pride at her crew. She could tell by the looks on the men's faces, that the questions being asked were professional and knowledgeable. Anyone expecting this group to be slow or stupid would be jolted, because some of the sharpest, most intelligent women in the U.S. Army were here in this cave. Maya had literally handpicked her team, all volunteers, during the years the base had been in operation. She was looking for bright, motivated young women who were competitive within themselves—not with others—and who took pride in doing a job right the first time around.

Unable to resist the laughter, the pleasant talk, Maya moved quietly toward the closest group clustered around the D model Apache. She didn't want to be spotted by the men, so she moved at an angle and stayed at the rear of the group.

She saw Jake, the only man in this squadron, standing with his wife, Ana, and listening to the Texas CWO. Her real interest was centered on York, and she eased around the cluster toward the nose of the Apache, where he was still on his back beneath the cannon, explaining the differences between the old and new models to the three attentive crew chiefs.

Dane felt Maya's presence. Oh, it wasn't anything obvious; he just sensed her nearness. Craning his neck to the left, he saw her standing at the rear of the crowd. Her catlike eyes were fixed on him. For a brief moment, his hand froze in midair, then he said to hell with it and went on explaining the technicalities of the helo to the crew chief who was lying on her side and looking up at what he was pointing at. His skin prickled pleasantly. Answering the crew chief as she pointed at the gun where his hand rested, and asked a question, Dane forced himself to pay attention to her and not be distracted by Maya.

Maybe it was the look on Maya's face that made him breathe a little easier. After all, he was still smarting from her angry words of a couple of hours ago. He cast another quick glance at her. She was gone. How had she moved so fast? Where was she? More than once in the last couple of hours, York had heard Maya's loyal squadron describe her as "different." Well, what did that mean? Everyone seemed to tiptoe around the subject. When he asked, they just laughed and said that he would see for himself, and let it go at that. It was clear they loved her, almost idolized her. They seemed to worship the ground she walked on. Dane found that a complete surprise. Usually, a squadron's C.O. was tolerated, never loved.

Where was Maya? Worried that he and his men were somehow doing something wrong, without her permission, he told the crew chiefs he was done. They all moved from out beneath the carriage of the Apache. Dane was the last to leave. As he rolled onto his right side, he saw Maya's black, shining boots. She was standing beside the helicopter now.

Swallowing hard, he realized she was waiting for him. He rolled easily away from the nose and got to his hands and knees. She was standing there, hands on her hips, looking down at him intently.

Rising to his feet, he dusted off his hands. "I thought we'd come over, since there was a crowd already around this helo," he said.

"My people have been waiting for days to see these girls." Maya saw the distrust in his blue eyes. How she wished they could relax around one another. Trust one another. Inwardly, she laughed at her own idealism. York would never give his trust to her. Not until he could honestly accept unconditionally that women were as good as men. That would be the day.

Dane nodded and allowed his hands to rest on his narrow hips. The crew chiefs drifted to the other side of the Apache where the others were, as if sensing Maya and Dane needed to be left alone.

"They're a little excited." He grinned. "I don't blame them. This helicopter is something else. Beyond your wildest dreams come true." He reached forward and patted the black panel with affection. "I think once your pilots get into the training program and see all the differences, the ease in handling, it's going to blow them away. I know it did me."

Seeing the glimmer of sincerity in his eyes, Maya relaxed a little more. "I can tell your I.P.s are excited. It looks like they can't wait to get into teaching mode with my people. I like to see that kind of enthusiasm. It translates positively."

Grin broadening, Dane said, "Oh, you mean Commanche Joe? He lives, eats, breathes and snores in Apache. He's part Indian and that's what we call him. He's one of our best I.P.s. Craig is the other."

Chuckling, Maya nodded and surveyed the chopper with a knowing eye. "One of my pilots, Akiva Redtail, is Native American. Joe should meet her. They probably have a lot in common. What I'm most interested in is that new radar attachment up there, above the rotor. I've been hearing it gives us a huge advantage over the A model."

Just getting to talk on the same footing with Maya about the D model helped lessen Dane's anxiety. Stepping closer to the fuselage, he rested his hand on a panel almost affectionately. Pointing up to the radar dome, he said, "Some people call it a doughnut. Others call it a cheese wheel."

Smiling, Maya studied the circular radar dome that embraced the rotor shaft assembly. "Leave it to the army to call it one thing, and the troops in the field to get down to basics. I like doughnut."

"Then doughnut it will be." He saw the warmth coming to her green eyes, and the tension leaving her mouth. Feeling on safer ground with her, Dane added, "I don't know what you call your Apaches, but the guys...and ladies," he added quickly, "are calling the D model 'Big Rig.'"

"Not Firebird?" Maya mocked with a curl of her lip.

Dane shook his head and gave her a sour look. "You know, that movie really hurt the Apache and the army. It was a joke. No, no one is calling it Firebird."

"That movie was stupid," Maya groused. Moving up to the gunship, she slid her fingers along the flat black skirt that was part of the fuselage. "Big Rig sounds good to me. Strong. I like it."

"The official name for this D model is Longbow."

Shrugging, Maya moved her fingers upward, almost sensing the heart of the new Apache. "Big Rig is good. She's big, bold, and has a magnificent heart beating inside this frame of hers." She gazed up at the rotors that hung unmoving above them.

Just the way Maya slid her long fingers across the smooth metal made Dane's throat tightened. It was as if she were stroking a lover's skin. And the softness in her tone caught him off guard. Her gaze was one of awe combined with warmth. Respect. Finding himself wishing she felt the same way about him startled him even more. Maybe it was the way her fingers moved across the surface of the aircraft. Or maybe it was the look in her eyes. Would she ever give him that kind of look? One of respect and warmth? He found himself craving her approval instead of always earning her scorn. More than anything, Dane realized he had to think before he spoke around her. Somewhere in him, he *needed* Maya's approval. And her respect for him as a pilot—and as a man. A tall order, he realized, not too hopeful that she'd give him an inch on any of those things.

Patting the fuselage gently, Maya turned to him. She saw that he was looking down at the lava floor as if in a quandary, darkness clouding his intelligent blue eyes. His mouth was working, one corner quirked inward, as if he were experiencing pain of some kind. Maya allowed her senses to fully embrace him. It was a skill she'd been taught a long time ago, one of the gifts of being in the Jaguar Clan. If she dropped her walls of defense, if she left herself open and vulnerable, she could pick up on another person's emotions. Unlike Inca, her sister, she couldn't read minds worth a damn, but she could sense and feel the other person accurately.

As she allowed her defenses toward Dane to dissolve, she was surprised and taken aback by what she felt swirling invisibly around him. There was confusion. Desire. A gnawing feeling like an ache entered her heart. Taking a step away from him, her hand still on the Apache, she frowned and sifted through the mire of dark emotions he was caught up within at that moment. He had no idea she could feel him out like this, nor was she ever going to admit to having such a skill. No one but Dallas Klein knew of this particular ability, and Dallas had kept it to herself.

Sorting through his emotions, Maya felt Dane struggling to try and please her. That came as a surprise in itself. She hadn't thought he was going to try at all. She figured he planned to just stick it out for six weeks and get the hell out from beneath her command the moment he could. She had been wrong. Just knowing that made her feel less defensive, but her guard remained up.

The next feeling she encountered was desire. For what? She couldn't quite penetrate the extent of that emotion. Was he feeling desire to leave this place? That would be about right, because he saw this assignment as necessary, but wasn't looking forward to it at all. The last set of emotions—the need for support and nurturing—threw her off balance. Looking at him, no one would ever think Dane York needed anyone at any time. The craggy square face, those frosty, almost flinty blue eyes, the hardness of his expression all countered what she was feeling around him presently.

Gently, Maya withdrew her awareness from around him. When she did, he lifted his head and squarely met her gaze. On some level, he'd sensed her presence within his aura of energy. Smiling to herself, she decided York wasn't so blind, deaf and dumb after all. Certainly, he wasn't in touch consciously with what had just happened; but on a more subliminal, intuitive level, he'd felt her presence. Shutting down her sensing mode, she once again lifted those barriers back into place so that he couldn't take a piece of her. York was not to be trusted, unfortunately.

"So," Maya said, trying to sound relaxed and informal, "I'll bet your wife and kids are going to miss you being gone for the next six weeks on this secret assignment. They probably don't have a clue where you're at, right?" When a person in the military took off on a top-secret assignment, most families never knew where in the world they were being sent, or why. Maya figured that all the emotions of York's that she'd just sensed had to do with missing his family.

"Excuse me?" He frowned.

"Er...your family. You must be missing them?" Maya felt alarmed by the look he gave her. It was one of curiosity and amusement.

Dane saw Maya's unsureness. It was the first time he'd

seen her confidence slip. So, even though she appeared to be like a vengeful warrior goddess, unapproachable and strong, Maya was human after all. That made him breathe a little easier. Maybe…just maybe…they could find a sure footing with one another, where they didn't have to spar all the time. Lifting his hand, he offered her a slight smile of regret. "I don't have family—at least, not a wife and kids. I'm still single."

"Oh…" Maya frowned. So who was he feeling all these emotions for? Certainly, they couldn't be about her. Maya's mind raced with more questions. She instantly rejected some of the answers she came up with, knowing York was incapable of such things. Or was he? Confused, she met his thawing gaze and that cockeyed half smile. His face had lost a lot of its hardness, the mask slowly dissolving. Was it because she'd touched his aura, and he realized she wasn't his enemy, after all, just someone who wanted to be treated with respect? That was too much to hope for.

"Well—" Maya said, lifting her hand from the fuselage "—you looked…sad, maybe like you were missing someone. I thought it might be your family. Six weeks is a long assignment."

Just knowing she was trying to be civil—even thoughtful—toward him made Dane reel. He'd thought Maya incapable of such a response. Not that he deserved any slack from her. No, he'd more than burned the bridges between them a long time ago and had realized that everything that had happened back then was his fault—not hers. "I see. Well…" Dane cleared his throat nervously and thought about what he was going to say this time, instead of just running off at the mouth like he usually did. Looking out the entrance of the cave at the haze sunlight touching the ever-moving clouds, he let the silence build between them.

Turning his head again, Dane met Maya's measuring gaze. He saw the wariness back in her emerald eyes, but her mouth was not a slash. No, her lips were slightly parted. Damn, she had a mouth any man in his right mind would want to kiss.

What the hell was he thinking? Startled over the stray bullet of a thought, Dane found himself scrambling. It was a good thing Maya couldn't read his mind or she'd have decked him right where he stood. Giving her a boyish smile, he said, "Sad. Yeah. I'm sad."

Maya frowned. She saw York trying to be honest with her. "About what? Being here?"

The sarcasm in her low voice wasn't missed by him. To hell with it. He was going to risk it all. He had six weeks here with Maya, under her command, and there was no way in hell he wanted to stay on high guard with her all that time. Looking around, he saw that the crews were well out of earshot.

"I'm sad because..." Dane hunted for the right words. "Because I don't like the tenor between us, Captain. Frankly, I yearn for some peace, but I don't know how to accomplish that. I'm confused. I'm trying to figure out how to be here and not be a pain in the ass all the time to you. I don't want to keep parrying thrusts with you and having you getting hotter than a two-dollar pistol about it."

Her heart pounded with relief. The expression on Dane's face was one of earnestness and desire. So that was what the desire she'd encountered in him moments ago was about. He wanted peace between them. Her surprise that he was not married warred with his other words. Why should she care if York wasn't married? Throwing that question aside, Maya focused on the present problem between them.

"I learned a long time ago, Major, that when there is respect—equal respect—between two people, it makes for a level playing field. And when you have respect, you can begin to build trust. Without respect, there can be no trust."

Dane leaned back against the fuselage, no more than two feet away from where Maya stood. Watching the sunlight strengthen and then wane as the endless clouds drifted in and around the cave entrance, he crossed his arms and thought long and hard about her words. Finally, he glanced at Maya. To his relief, she was not shutting him out. He could tell by the relaxed expression on her beautiful features and the alertness and curiosity burning in her emerald gaze that maybe she wanted to wave a white flag of surrender, too, so that they could get on with what needed to be done around here.

"You're right, of course," he murmured, so that only she could hear him. The echoes of laughter, of people talking, bounced endlessly off the walls of the cave. "I think my men will treat your people with respect. I think you can see that happening already. Sounds more like a party going on in here than a war between the sexes. Don't you think?"

Grinning ruthlessly, Maya said, "Definitely a party atmosphere. It's good to hear people laughing, believe me."

Gauging her from beneath his spiky brown lashes, Dane wanted to say, *What about us? Can you trust me? Can you try?* But he didn't. Her reserve wrapped around her like thick a blanket. Dane knew she wasn't about to drop those massive walls she wore with him. He hadn't proved himself to her—yet. More than anything, he wanted the opportunity to try.

"You know, I'm *really* impressed with your squadron," he said sincerely. "Dallas gave us one hell of a tour. She said you masterminded this whole plan, using the defunct mining operation and shaft on the other side of this mountain as a ruse to hide what's going on in here. I found that incredible."

Maya studied him. She wanted to allow his compliment to wash over her, but she resisted the temptation. York could not be trusted. Not with her or her sensitive emotions, which she hid constantly. Being a base commander meant hiding a lot, carrying a lot, and having no one to cry with, or to tell her own worries and troubles to. She found herself wishing that she could share some of those worries with Dane. More shock rolled through her. What was going on? He was her enemy. The man who had always wanted her to fail, who had tried to destroy her because she was an intelligent and confident woman.

Shaking off her thoughts, she refocused on Dane's words and said, "The Indians of the surrounding villages knew of this place for thousands of years. An old jaguar priestess took me up here to the mining operation. She showed me the lava tube that extended a quarter mile into the mountain. And then we climbed around the mountain to this cave. When I realized that, with some work, we could open up the back of the cave into that lava tube, I knew we could make my vision work." Maya gestured toward the cave's ceiling, wreathed in lights suspended from the lava. "I got a Navy Seabee team down here and they found out that there was only about fifty feet of rock between the cave and the tube." She smiled triumphantly.

"We use the mining area on the other side of the mountain as a cover for our operation. We use civilian helicopters to ferry in all our supplies so they don't raise too much suspicion from the tourist trade in Agua Caliente or around Machu Picchu. In fact, the helicopter service in that little town is our undercover way of getting to and from this base. Our people get R and R every two weeks. They climb into *tourista* clothing and fly out on the civilian helo to Agua Caliente to get a few days of rest and partying."

"It's a brilliant plan," Dane said. "Brilliant."

She arched beneath his roughly spoken compliment. His eyes burned with awe as he regarded her. Maya absorbed the energy, the passion in his statement. She realized reluctantly that she, too, was seeking his approval, whether she wanted to or not. Still, one little compliment was not going to erase their mutual, hellish past.

"This place is inaccessible except by helicopter." Maya eased away from the Apache and began walking toward the lip. Dane followed at her shoulder. "Let's walk out to the Eye. From there, you can see the jungle below."

"Are there villages around this mountain?"

Maya nodded. "Yes, three of them. We're tight with the village leaders. I, uh, well, I share a common heritage with their medicine people, their healers, so I've been able to communicate with them about keeping our presence a secret. Sometimes Faro Valentino will send in a two-man team and start sniffing around the base of this mountain. The villagers know who's local and who isn't. I gave each chief in each village an iridium cell phone so that if they spot strangers, they can alert us."

"And it's always been drug runners?" Dane asked, wiping his brow. The sunlight was hot, the humidity high. He'd rolled up the sleeves on his flight suit to his elbows, but he was still perspiring heavily in the noontime heat.

Approaching the outer wall, with the Eye directly in front of them, Maya said, "Nine times out of ten. Oh, sometimes a young tourist will have followed the Urubamba River from Aqua Caliente, which is twenty miles that way." She pointed. "The chief and his people can always tell a real *tourista* from a wolf in sheep's clothing." She grinned.

"Iridium phones. I'm impressed."

Maya snorted and placed her hand on the black lava, which was welted like water ripples. "I went through hell getting my contact to get me iridium phones, but down here, normal cell phones don't work. The only way we can contact one another is using a GPS—global positioning satellites device—plus an iridium phone."

"You got them in your helos?"

She nodded. "You bet. In all three of them. If we crash, or if we blow an engine or take too big a chunk out of one of our rotors, we have that phone to call to base with."

"That ever happen?"

Grinning, Maya said, "Oh, yeah. You noticed our third Apache at the back of the cave? The dismantled one?"

"Yeah, it looks pretty well cannibalized."

"With good reason." She frowned. "My contacts weren't giving me the necessary budget to fly in replacement parts for my birds. I ended up having to sacrifice one of them to keep the other two flying. One time, Dallas blew an engine during a run for the border after some of Faro's civilian helos, which were carrying coke. She had to land in some heavy jungle terrain. About one-quarter of one rotor was whacked off during landing. So we ended up taking the replacement rotors from the third aircraft. Once that happened, we began taking other necessary parts when I didn't get the money to resupply and outfit my Apaches."

Dane watched the wisps of clouds form and dissipate with incredible rapidity. The sunlight, he was realizing, was a force to reckoned with here. As they stood at the opening of the Eye, he watched a thick wall of clouds form below, just above the dark green jungle, and then move slowly upward to eventually block the view.

"It sounds like you've been doing a helluva lot of juggling over the years to make this base work."

Again Maya saw respect in his eyes. Twice in one day. She was on a roll. Compressing her lips, she muttered, "I'd rather fly, if the truth be known. The paperwork's a real pain."

Chuckling, Dane said, "Spoken like a true squadron commander. I don't know one who wouldn't trade his, er, her desk, for sitting in an Apache and flying instead."

Pleased that he didn't just use "he," Maya gave him a partial smile. "Well, I get plenty of airtime, too. I'm the twelfth pilot around here. I fly every third day, just like everyone else."

"How long are the missions?" Dane knew that keeping a place like this on line and functioning, an incredibly heavy responsibility, would take every scrap of a person's energy and focus. For Maya to also be flying combat missions every third day was an incredible demand on her. Admiration for her crept into him.

"We've developed flight plans based upon Faro Valentino's usual patterns of trying to run for the Bolivian border with his coke. The range can mean a three-hundred-mile flight radius at times. And when he's running, it can mean we're flying until we need to return to base. Once here—" Maya turned and gestured to her right where the fuel depot was located "—my crews can refuel an Apache in ten minutes flat. If they've used ordnance, it's replaced as soon as the refueling is done. And then they're back in the air again, trying to locate and chase down the bad guys."

Shaking his head, Dane said, "I didn't realize that."

"Just wait," Maya said grimly. "I think you and your I.P.s should hang out with us for about three days and get a feel for the demands on our time, our schedule, which is nothing short of chaos usually, before you try and set up a training program for us."

It was a wise request, Dane realized. He watched as a massive cloud closed in on the Eye. In moments, they were surrounded with fog so thick that he could no longer see into the cave complex.

"With these kinds of IFR conditions," he muttered, "you're really riding the edge."

"Tell us about it," Maya chuckled. "The cloud cover around here is constant. My pilots don't take anything for granted, especially visibility. Usually, we're flying on instruments alone, coming and going from this place."

Just as quickly, the cloud dissipated and Dane could once again see the maw of the cave. "This place is like magic," he murmured, looking around at the massive facility. "Now you see it, now you don't. It's phenomenal."

"Yeah," Maya said, laughter in her eyes, "you're right about the magic part."

Dane walked at her shoulder as they moved back into the cave. Sunlight suddenly streamed through the Eye once again, embracing them with radiance and warmth as they went. "I've noticed something," he told her, catching her distrustful gaze. "And if this is personal, just tell me to back off."

Maya went on guard. "What?"

"A number of your crew people have made the same remark about you, and it has me curious."

"Oh?"

He heard the brittleness in her tone. They slowed their pace as they neared the new D model. The rest of the squadron was still on the other side. Dane heard Joe's enthusiastic voice as he continued to explain all the innovations to the engrossed crews.

"Yeah...they all used the same word to describe you."

"What have you been doing? Polling my people about me?"

Dane held up his hands. "Whoa. Easy. We didn't pump anyone for info on you, if that's what you think. No, we've just been talking to them about the D model. They're excited and can't wait to get their hands on it. But every one I talked with mentioned how you'd lobbied the U.S. government to get these new Apaches down here. They clearly think the world of you."

Relaxing slightly, Maya crossed her arms. "They have been excited. And I'm sure my people are bubbling over about these Big Rigs being here." Her curiosity ate at her. She saw the glimmer in York's eyes as he studied her. Maya felt like the tables had been turned, that she was the one under the microscope, not him. So what had her people told him? Uncomfortable, she belligerently returned his stare.

"The people we talked to," Dane said, "all used the same word to describe you—*different*."

Maya's mouth moved slightly and then compressed. "I see."

"It was a compliment," Dane assured her. "Not an insult. I've heard base commanders called a lot of things in my day, but never 'different.'" He cocked his head, a half smile playing across his mouth. "What does that mean? How are they using it in regard to you?"

Shrugging, Maya muttered, "I don't know." Well, she did

know, but she was darned if York was going to find out. Not that anyone except Dallas and Dr. Elizabeth Cornell, their base physician, knew about her other life as a Black Jaguar Clan priestess. No, there were some things better left unsaid. Besides, most of the people under her command were not the least familiar with metaphysics. Gauging Dane, she saw a bit of elfish play in his eyes, as if he were gently teasing her, without malice.

"You know how any squadron is," she said in a bored tone of voice. "Every commander has a personality. I'm sure that's what it's about."

Dane studied her. Maya was ill at ease. She shifted from one booted foot to the other, her arms across her breasts. His intuition, which wasn't great, told him that she was hiding something about herself. Okay, he wouldn't push it. Judging from the look in her narrowed eyes, she wasn't going to say anything more to him about it.

"Yes," he murmured, "that's probably it."

"Captain Stevenson!"

Maya turned, recognizing Private Sandy Wells's high-pitched voice. Sandy, who was her comms—communications—assistant was barely five feet tall, with curly blond hair cut just below her ears and huge blue eyes. As she ran breathlessly toward Maya, she waved a paper above her head.

"Excuse me," Maya told Dane, and turned to meet Sandy.

Sandy came to a halt, breathing hard. "Ma'am, we just got confirmation that two unidentified civilian helicopters are going to be passing right by here in ten minutes!" she said, handing Maya the transmission from the satellite intelligence unit.

Scowling, Maya rapidly read the information. "Faro's at it again," she said.

"I think so, ma'am. Want me to sound the alarm?"

"Yes, Private, do it now."

Running back into the cave, the private headed back to her

comms Quonset hut. A minute later, a clanging bell sounded, echoing eerily throughout the cave.

Maya looked up to see York moving toward her.

"I've gotta go, Major. I'll see you on the return trip. We've got bogeys—more than likely Faro's men. We're going to intercept."

"Wait!" Dane hurried to her side as she walked quickly toward the Apaches at the other end of the apron. "Let me go with you."

She jerked her head toward him. Her eyes became slits. "You?"

"Sure. Why *not* me? Don't you want me to get an understanding of what's going down here? It will help me in assessing what needs to be taught to your pilots."

It made sense, though Maya didn't want him along. But then revenge entered into the equation. Smiling lethally, she said, "Sure, you can be my copilot-gunner, Major. But I'm the commander. Got it?"

Grinning, he broke into a trot at her side, heading toward the Apaches the crews were hurriedly working around. "You're number one." He surprised himself at how easily the words rolled off his tongue.

"Still think you can work an A model's software?" she taunted as she trotted toward her helo. "Or have you forgotten how to do it the old-fashioned way?"

Dane's grin broadened. "I won't embarrass you out there, Captain. That's a promise."

Her heart was beating hard in her chest as she put her foot onto the metal rung to hoist herself upward into the front cockpit. Four years ago, the tables had been turned. She'd had to fly too many hours with York lording it over her from the back seat. Well, now all that was changed. As Maya swung into her seat, she shouted to her crew chief to fetch her helmet from her office and to bring York one that would fit him.

"Never mind, I brought my own," he told her, and

shouted below to one of the other crew people as to where to retrieve his helmet in his quarters. The woman turned and ran into the cave to find it. Time was at a premium. He felt the tempo. Felt the escalating tension. Maya's voice was calm and terse as she spoke to her crew chief. Below, several women hurried to remove the chalks from the Apache landing gear, release the rotor blades from their tie-downs and then pull the machine out onto the lip area, where it could be prepared for takeoff.

Maya was all business. She concentrated solely on what was ahead of her and tried to ignore the fact that York was in her back seat. Settling her helmet on her head, she strapped it on tightly. Jamming the thin black gloves on her hands, she felt her heart pounding erratically with the adrenaline charge. This was for real. Every time they launched, there was a helluva chance they might not return. Faro's men had Kamovs. The sat intel showed two civilian helicopters speeding toward Bolivia. That didn't mean the Kamovs weren't around only that they were waiting...just waiting to jump them. Would York be up to speed? Kamovs had no signature they could detect with their radar. Could she rely on him to spot them if they were around?

How much of her life was she willing to put into his hands? Was the enemy in her cockpit any less dangerous to her than the enemy they were going to try and intercept?

Chapter 6

Dane tried to push his excitement aside. He was going into combat. Finally. There wasn't an Apache pilot alive who didn't thirst for the blood-pounding danger of combat; they lived, ate and breathed for the chance he was going to get right now. The last time he'd seen combat was during the Persian Gulf War, and that was a while ago. Busy cranking up his HUDs and checking them out, he was only peripherally aware of the hurried activity around them. He heard Maya's cool, low voice in his helmet earphones as she talked with her crew chief on the ground. They had been pushed out on the lip, and now the engines were being put on line, one at a time. The shiver that went through the aircraft made him feel good. It fed his mounting excitement.

There were a lot of dangers ahead, too. The warm sunshine streaming through the cockpit canopy, now lowered and locked into place, was making him sweat. The coolness of the air conditioning moved around Dane and reduced the heat within the cabin. Sweat was trickling down the sides of his ribs beneath his flight suit from anticipation. *Combat.* Adrenaline was surging through his bloodstream as he tightened his knee board into place around his right thigh. He grinned lopsidedly. He was glad Maya had let him come along. Now he had a chance to prove himself to her in another way.

The rotor engaged, the engine's whine deepened. The Apache began to shake, a familiar and welcome sensation to Dane. Off to his left, he saw the second Apache warming up, as well. Maya had just snapped off a salute to the crew below. They hurriedly backed away.

"Who's in the second Apache?" he asked her as he punched several codes into the computers that ran the HUDs. A trickle of sweat dripped down his left temple. He reached up with his gloved hand and pushed it away.

"The standby crew," Maya said. "Lieutenant Danielle Gautier. She's on loan from the French Army air wing. Her call sign is Lobo. Her back seat is CWO2 Ellen Canton, Goosey. We call her Luce the Goose because she honks like one when she laughs."

"Roger. Thanks."

"Let's go over our checklist before we hightail it out of here."

"Roger," he said, quickly pulling out the plastic-enclosed cards and resting them on his thigh where he'd placed his knee board. He heard the tension in Maya's tone. His own voice sounded a little tight.

As soon as they were done, Maya said, "Let's rock 'n' roll. Lobo, you and Goosey ready? Over."

Gautier's low, lilting French accent came back. "Roger that, Saber. We're ready. Over."

"Roger. Let's mission launch...." Maya nudged the power up on the Apache. The first order of business was flying through the Eye. As she positioned the gunship, the clouds lifted and she could see the hole clearly. Usually, around noon, the clouds burned off more rapidly with the help of direct sunlight, and it was easier to thread. Applying power and keeping her feet firmly on the yaw pedals, she moved the gunship quickly through the opening. In her helmet, she heard an intake of breath from York. She grinned a little.

"You'll get used to it, Major."

Shaking his head at the ease with which Maya had just negotiated that tight opening, Dane rasped, "I don't think so. You make it look damned easy and I know it's not."

Chuckling, Maya positioned her gunship to one side and waited for Lobo to appear. "I've lost track of how many times I've flown the Eye. It gets easier the more you do it." The second Apache came through quickly.

Dane pulled down the dark visor that would protect the upper half of his face and eyes from the bright sunlight lancing into the cabin. The Apache felt solid and good around him as he typed in the keywords to bring up the identification of local aircraft.

"I'm scanning with radar to try and find those two bogeys," he told her, as he felt the Apache nose down and surge forward.

"Roger," Maya said. She looked around the cloud-cobbled blue sky. "We're climbing above cloud cover first. That will be at around nine or ten thousand feet. Don't get your nose stuck in those HUD screens, Major. You've got to divide your time and attention between them and the Kamovs. They're out there...and it's up to you to find them first before they find us."

"Roger. I hear you loud and clear." Twisting his head, Dane saw the roiling clouds falling away. Maya was pushing the Apache to its limits of speed, over two hundred miles an hour. They were heading in an easterly direction, toward the Bolivian border. Below, the jungle looked like tight little heads of broccoli all crammed together. There was no place to land if they got into trouble. They'd have to drop into the canopy, and that wasn't a pleasant thought.

"You got anything yet?" she demanded.

"No...searching." Dane twisted another knob and

watched the dark green screen intently. "If we had the D model, it would have already picked them up."

"Nice. But it isn't gonna help us right now." Maya continued to scan the airspace around them. Off to her right was Lobo, a mile away. "Sat intel picked up two helos," she told him. "That means we split up and go after them."

"What's their normal avoidance pattern?"

Maya smiled a little, her intent gaze sweeping across her instrument panel. York was asking the right questions. "It differs. Faro Valentino learned a long time ago not to get into a set pattern of flight or time with us. He found out very quickly we're open for business twenty-four hours a day, seven days a week. As soon as you can locate those helos, I can probably tell you more."

"I hear you." He frowned, studying the HUDs. Just the way Maya was flying the Apache made York feel proud of her. She handled the machine deftly and with such silky smoothness that it was hard to tell he was actually in a combat machine. At least right now. Straight flight was one thing, combat flying another.

"Black Jaguar One," Lobo called.

"What've you got, Lobo?" Maya asked.

"We got two Agusta civilian helicopters painted on our HUDs. Looks to me like Faro's running two smaller aircraft into Bolivia this time."

Damn. Had he messed up? Dane quickly scanned again, barely making out something on one HUD—fuzzy outlines at best. He thought it was radar return from some clouds. How could the other Apache crew already have them identified? Smarting beneath his own expectations of finding the bogeys first, he compressed his mouth.

"How could Lobo ID them so fast?" he demanded of Maya.

Dane heard Lobo's musical voice over the earphones on his helmet. "Luce the Goose is used to looking at fuzzy things that float across her HUD, Major. Don't worry, after a while we can ID a cloud from an aircraft no matter how far away or blurred looking it is. It's a real art, believe me.''

Maya grinned. ''Good work, Lobo and Goosey.'' She heard the frustration and embarrassment in Dane's voice. He was in competition with them. It hurt his pride that he hadn't painted the bogeys first. ''Get over it, Major. We have other fish to fry,'' she told him. ''Faro's got quite a mishmash of helicopters in his fleet. Over the past three years, he's bought a lot of different civilian helicopters in an effort to avoid us. The Agusta Lobo is talking about are very similar to the tourist helicopter that is stationed at Agua Caliente. He knows we aren't going to shoot at him until we get a positive visual ID on him. We can't take the chance that we'd be loosing a bunch of rockets into a civilian helicopter and killing all on board. That would become an international incident. We'd get press, political problems from it, and more than likely my base and the operation would be shut down.''

''Visual ID is a must, anyway,'' Dane agreed fervently.

''Roger that. But in Faro's case, it's a high priority. He'd like to see us make this kind of mistake. It would make his life easier if we were outta here.'' Maya swung her gunship in a slight bank. Up ahead, she spotted the two escaping helicopters about four miles ahead of them. The Agusta could never keep up with an Apache speedwise.

''Saber,'' Lobo called. ''It's confirmed ID on them. Italian Agusta A119 Koala.''

''Roger. Let me go in for a confirmation of the numbers on their fuselages before you approach. No use in two Apaches taking the fly-by risk,'' Maya answered.

''Roger.''

Dane saw the helicopters clearly on his HUD now. The screen repeated that they were Agusta helicopters. ''Numbers on their fuselage?''

''Yeah,'' Maya said grimly as she angled the Apache so that there was about half a mile between them and the Agusta. ''You've got a set of binoculars there, on your right side, on top of where we keep the optic eyepiece. I want you to get the numbers, type them into the computer and see what comes up. Do it as soon as possible. Those Kamovs might be around...."

Dane found the binoculars. Maya made it easy for him to see through them by holding the helicopter on a steady flight path. The two Agustas were flying in a militarylike formation. "Are Russians flying those things?" he asked as he quickly typed in the first numbers.

"Probably. Why?"

"They're flying in a damn tight formation for civilian pilots."

Maya nodded. "You're right. It's a good observation. They probably are Soviet mercenaries that Faro hired three years ago. I guess the boys can't get out of military-formation flying." She laughed a little.

"Got the numbers," Dane told her. He put the binoculars aside and watched the screen intently after typing them in. Information regarding the helos popped up in a lighter green color. Pressing his gloved finger against the screen, he said, "Okay, what we have is two unidentified helicopters. The numbers on their fuselages don't jibe with any registered in Peru."

"Did you try Bolivia? Italy? Chile? Colombia and Ecuador?"

"No..." Damn. He'd screwed up again.

"Punch it in. See what comes up."

Quickly he typed the info on the keyboard located near his left knee. Sweat trickled down his wrinkled brow. More data popped up on the screen.

"This is strange. These numbers don't jibe with any country you've mentioned."

"Good."

There was sardonic satisfaction in Maya's low voice, and an edge, too.

Dane looked up and then scanned the cloudless sky around

them. Where would the Kamovs be? "What do you do now?"

"Call them on the radio," Maya said, and she switched channels and made the call to the two helicopters in Spanish, English, Italian and Quechua, the second language of Peru.

Dane was surprised at her grasp of so many foreign languages. But then he reminded himself that Maya was Brazilian and would probably know not only Portuguese, but Spanish as well.

He heard no radio response from the helicopters to any of Maya's queries. "They're not answering us."

"No kidding." She moved her Apache in for a closer look. "They aren't carrying big guns on them, but don't put it past the pilot or copilot to open a window and shoot a firearm at us."

Dane blinked as she brought the Apache within a hundred feet of the first Agusta. He could clearly see both pilots. The one in the right seat, the pilot, was glaring back at them. The man was heavyset, with a broad face and a sneer on his lips.

"I don't think he's happy to see us, do you?"

Maya heard the grim amusement in Dane's voice. Her lips twitched. "No, he's not, and I know who that bastard is. Sasha Karlov. Sweet name for the nasty, mean son of a bitch that he is..." Instantly, Maya pulled the Apache up and to the right, away from the Agusta. "All right, Lobo, you take the one on the left, I'm taking Karlov's helicopter. Let's see if these boys will turn back or if they want to stay and play."

"Roger, Saber."

"The border is only five miles away," Dane warned, pushed deeper into his seat by gravity as Maya took the Apache up and in front of the fleeing helicopters.

"Yeah, I know. Hang on. We're going to play sky chicken with these boys...."

Dane's eyes widened. Maya set the Apache squarely in front of where the Agustas were flying. His mouth dropped opened, but he didn't have time to yell out a warning. The

Agustas hurtled toward them. Gripping the airframe, bracing himself, Dane thought they were going to crash.

At the last moment, the Agustas split off, one to the right and one to the left, into a steep, diving bank toward the jungle eight thousand feet below.

"No you don't...." Maya growled.

Dane was jerked to the right and then to the left. Gravity seized him and slammed him back into the seat. His helmet banged into the side cockpit window. Stunned, he took long seconds to realize what Maya had done with the Apache. She'd banked sharply left, nosed down and was redlining the engines in a screaming dive to catch up with the fleeing Agustas.

"Watch for Kamovs!" she barked at him.

Blinking, Dane tore his gaze from the Augusta they were rapidly approaching. The helicopter began to jump around, as if to try and get rid of them. Looking up, Dane scanned the skies around them.

"Warm up the cannon. I want you to put a couple of shells right across Karlov's broken nose."

Slammed one way and then the other within the narrow confines of the cockpit, Dane had trouble getting to the HUD controls that connected with the cannon beneath the belly of the Apache. As soon as the HUD lit up with it as the main weapon of choice, he quickly got it on line. Watching the crosshairs on the HUD, he began to track the fleeing Agusta.

"Okay, got 'em..."

"Watch for Kamovs, Major! Don't keep your nose stuck in that HUD, dammit! This is when they usually jump us."

Stung, he jerked his head up. Right now, they were leveling out and screaming along over the jungle. Everything was a green blur beneath them. Damn, Maya was close to the trees! Dane tensed. He saw the Agusta make a tight turn around one of the loaf-shaped mountains. Instantly, Maya followed him. She cut so close to the mountain, that Dane sucked in a breath.

"Get ready!"

Yanking his attention back to the HUD, he saw the Agusta was no longer in the crosshairs. The shot would go wide.

"Ready?"

"Roger," he rasped, quickly working the HUD and reconfiguring the software instructions to the cannon.

"Just fire in front of him," she ordered.

"Ready."

"Do it."

There was a slight vibration beneath Maya's seat. She could feel the cannon, located directly beneath her armor-plated seat and platform, shaking away. There were several tracer rounds, bright red, and she followed them as they arced very close to the nose of the Agusta helicopter. She cackled. "Great shot! You've rattled him!"

Dane arched beneath her praise as she brought the Apache up, almost brushing the tops of the trees alongside the mountain as she followed the Agusta, which was now turning away from the Bolivian border.

"Why don't you shoot him out of the sky?"

"Because we don't know for *sure* if this is a civilian helicopter or one of Faro's. I'd know Karlov's wreck of a face anywhere. But what if his other pilot is not working for Faro? What if Faro is playing with the numbers on the fuselage to confuse us? If we shoot them down, it could cause an international incident."

Maya leveled out the Apache and eased back on the throttles until the gunship was in a hover. She watched the copter fleeing back toward the jungle area where she knew Faro had one of his many cocaine loading stations. "We do a lot of hunt and chase, Major. We're not just randomly shooting helicopters out of the sky around here."

"And if they fire at you?" Dane kept looking for Kamovs.

"That's a different story. In the past, years ago, they did that. Well, you shoot at me, and I'm firing back with all the hardware this Apache carries. Faro lost four helicopters in a row due to that little piece of aggression on his part, and then he finally figured out if he stopped his boys from shooting at us, we wouldn't fire back at them, either. So now it's usually a Mexican standoff. Sky chicken. Who will flinch first?'' She chuckled.

''And so he repaints the numbers on the fuselage of his civilian helos to confuse you?''

''Yes.'' Maya turned the Apache back toward their base. Up ahead, she saw Lobo's Apache coming toward them. ''He does the numbers game all the time. He's well aware that unless we have an absolutely positive ID, we aren't going to take him or his helos out of the sky.''

''And you have to let them go into Bolivian airspace?''

Maya heard the frustration in his voice. ''No...we just make it tougher for them to get there, like we did just now. Faro has orders for his cocaine,'' she said, watching as Lobo's Apache came closer. She made a gesture with her hand, signaling the other helo to go back to base. Instantly Lobo raised her gloved hand and moved the gunship forward. Maya positioned her helo three rotor blades' distance from Lobo's, and they flew in formation toward home.

''As I was saying, Faro has orders for his cocaine. By turning his ships back, he's not making his deadlines for drug deliveries. That puts a lot of pressure on him to get it out of Peru. So, next time around, he'll either use bigger civilian aircraft or more of them to try and get some of the orders through to Bolivian airspace.''

''How many helos would he put up at a time?'' Dane asked, keeping his gaze switching between the HUD radar and the sky. Even now he knew they were not safe. Kamovs could sneak up and jump them.

''Oh, he's got a fleet, we estimate, of twelve helicopters of varying types and models from many different countries that he can use. Plus, he's got two Kamovs, which really don't make us happy at all. If we could paint the Kamovs on radar, that would be another thing, but we can't. Chasing civilian helos back from the border is bad enough. Having to chase them and watch for Kamovs is totally another. We've had some close calls this last year, since Faro put those Kamovs in the air." Maya frowned. "We haven't lost a ship or crew yet, but I'm worried about it."

Dane nodded and continued to rubberneck. "I understand...." And he did. He shared her worry. He was drenched in sweat, his flight suit sticking to him. During the chase, his adrenaline had been pumping. He was still tense and jumpy from the encounter. Maya, on the other hand, seemed like an old combat vet. Nothing rattled her much. To her, this had been a cat-and-mouse game, and that was all. Plus she was used to the scenarios, and he was not. Still, Dane admired her coolness in the face of danger.

Within twenty minutes, they were back at the base. This time Maya turned the tables on him.

"You have the controls, Major. Take us through the Eye."

Gulping, he placed his hands around the collective and cyclic. "You like to live dangerously, don't you?"

Maya chuckled. "Always. What else is there in life but risk?"

He focused on the opening. The clouds were thinning and he could see it visually. "Well, this is one helluva risk," he muttered as he eased the Apache up to the Eye.

"Think you ought to train those pilots up at Fort Rucker for this little challenge?" She laughed aloud.

Mouth compressed, he eased the Apache through, his gaze shifting constantly between the rotor length and the sides of the black lava wall crowding in on him. The walls weren't moving of course, but that's how it felt to Dane. Once through the Eye, he saw the crew chief on the right side of the lip indicating with her orange sticks where he was to land the gunship. "This is more than a little challenge," he griped good-naturedly.

Maya smiled and relaxed as York brought them in for a nice, gentle landing. The whine of the engines shut down, and the rotors began to slow. They were home. Looking around, she watched as Lobo followed them through the Eye and came to land a hundred feet away from them. Opening the cockpit frame after the rotors stopped, she felt the fresh, humid air rush in. Taking a deep breath of it, she lifted her hand to her crew and smiled down at them. She was so proud of them, she thought as she looked at them, their expressions full of relief at seeing the flight team return safely.

Climbing out of the front seat, Maya leaped to the ground. She took off her helmet and stuffed her gloves into the right pocket of her flight suit, waiting for York. More than a little curious about how the flight had affected him, she watched as he climbed nimbly down off the fuselage cover to the lava below. His face was sweaty, his eyes almost colorless, the pupils black and large. He looked like the hunter he was, and she smiled to herself.

As he took off the helmet and placed it beneath his left arm, she said, "You didn't do badly for a first time up there."

Dane pushed his fingers through his damp hair and held her assessing gaze. He didn't see any tension or wariness in Maya's features right now. He reminded himself that they'd just been on a combat mission and their adrenaline was still pumping from it. Neither of them was in their usual guarded mode with one another—yet.

"Thanks…I'm still upset I didn't see those birds painted on my HUDs."

Smiling slightly, Maya moved her shoulders to rid them of the accumulated tension. "Don't worry about it. Another week in the back seat with us and you'll know how to read fuzzies on the radar as accurately as Lobo and Goosey did."

Walking with her toward the cave, Dane felt elated. It was the first time Maya had smiled. She had such a beautiful, expressive face. He tried to separate out the combat pilot inside her from her outer beauty. It was impossible. Maya was a complex person and he knew it. More than anything, he found himself wanting to simply stare into those deep, deep, almost fathomless green eyes of hers. She had the kind of eyes a man could lose himself within. It was a disconcerting yearning and he struggled with it.

At HQ, they climbed the stairs together. On the second floor, Maya pointed to an open door near her own.

"In case you don't know it, my head supply clerk, Sergeant Penny Anderson, has assigned this office coming up on your left as yours for the duration of your six weeks with us. If you need anything, ask her. Penny's in the office next to yours."

Dane halted and looked into the small office. It had a dark green metal desk just like Maya's. There were paper, pencils and pens on top of it. And a vase of purple-and-white orchids. A woman's touch.

Maya was standing in the hall, watching him.

"Thanks..." he managed to answer.

"What's wrong?"

"Nothing's wrong." He prickled as her gaze narrowed speculatively on him.

"I can feel it around you."

"What? That women's intuition thing?" Dane closed his eyes. *Damn.* He'd just done it again. When he opened them, he saw the hurt and frustration in her expression. Opening his hand, he muttered, "That came out wrong."

"It always does," Maya grated.

His heart contracted. They were back at square one again. Dane searched for something to say that was not prejudicial sounding. "Look, I'm still edgy from the flight. Not that it's an excuse for what I said, but..."

Maya walked up to him, keeping her voice very low. "In our line of business down here, we need all the help we can get. Now, whether it's from a visual, or HUD, or our gut feeling, we don't like to think of one kind of knowing as being better than any other. And yes, you can bet the farm that we use our intuition just as surely as we'll use our eyes and the instruments in our gunships."

"I hear you," Dane muttered defensively, trying to think of a way to climb out of his mistake.

"You want to know how we knew the Kamovs would attack this morning when you boys came up from Lima?" she asked in a velvet voice.

Dane grimaced. "No, but you're going to tell me anyway. How did you know?"

Maya lifted her chin and held his stormy blue gaze. "The bloodred dawn, that's how." She watched her words sink in. Dane gave her a startled look, one of disbelief. Because of it, Maya wasn't going to cut him one inch of slack.

"That's right, a red dawn. We've found that when the sky is that color, we get Kamovs up our tail rotors. Over time, we can call it with a lot of accuracy. I know in your well-ordered little world it sounds like voodoo. You call it what you want. As you and your other I.P.s ride with us this coming week to find out how we work around here, just keep your minds open, okay?"

He felt heat move up the column of his neck and into his face. Blushing. Of all times for that to happen! Swallowing hard, Dane met and held her glare. "I'm not going to get into a fight with you about intuition, Captain. I'll instruct my other pilots to listen to whatever your pilots have to teach them. Frankly, I don't care how you get your info. We're all in this together, to survive. If a red dawn is a red flag, fine."

Maya took a step back from him and assessed his scowling features. "Good," she murmured. "That's the kind of can-do spirit I want to see from you and your men, Major. There are differences between how we operate down here and what you taught us at Fort Rucker."

He saw a wicked look lingering deep in her eyes. For a moment, Dane thought she was enjoying her power over him. Well, hadn't he lorded his power and control over her at Fort

Rucker? Yes. Smarting beneath her cool gaze, he managed to reply, "We're open to learning new things, Captain."

Flexing her shoulders, Maya stepped aside as a sergeant hurried between them with an apology, on her way to another office. "We're both learning."

Dane watched as she turned on her booted heel and walked purposefully toward her office. Blowing out a breath, he turned and went into his own, shutting the door behind him. The office was small, with no windows. Moving around the desk, he placed his helmet on top of a cabinet and stuffed the gloves into it. There was a polite knock on his door.

"Enter," he growled. Looking up, he saw it was a black-haired woman with dark coppery skin and black, almond-shaped eyes. She looked Indian. Maybe from Peru? Dane wasn't sure. Dressed in baggy green fatigues and a green T-shirt that was stained with sweat under her arms and around her neck, she came to attention.

"Sergeant Paredes, sir. Dr. Elizabeth Cornell requests your presence at her clinic when you get a chance, sir."

"At ease, Sergeant," he murmured. The woman was short and stocky. Dane had no idea who she was. Maybe a mechanic. Wiping his brow, he said, "Tell Dr. Cornell I'll meet her in about thirty minutes. I've got a mission report to fill out first and then I'll be down to see her."

Paredes snapped to attention. "Yes, sir, Major. I'll tell her, sir. Thank you, sir." She saluted.

York snapped off a returning salute. "Dismissed, Sergeant. Thank you."

Paredes nodded, did an about-face and left. The door was left open. He moved around the desk, scowling. He shut the door with finality.

As he turned to go back to the desk, there was another knock. Rolling his eyes, Dane wondered how anyone got anything done around here with these kinds of intrusions constantly occurring. He jerked the door open, a snarl on his lips.

A tall woman stood there, one with blond hair hanging around her shoulders, blue eyes, and a narrow face with a patrician nose. She was in a black flight uniform.

Dane instantly reined in his snarl. This was a pilot. "Yes?"

"Lieutenant Gautier, Major York. Captain Stevenson said you might want this...." She handed him some papers. "Mission report forms."

"Oh...yes. Thanks, Lieutenant..."

She gave him a slight smile as she assessed him. "Just call me Lobo. Around here, we mostly stick to our handles and we aren't very formal."

Standing there, Dane nodded. "Yes...thanks..."

Gautier, who was about five foot eight inches tall, turned gracefully and moved down the hall. He watched her disappear into another office.

Looking at the door, Dane decided to leave it open. Old habits died hard. If he was at Fort Rucker, his office door would be closed. His office was off limits to everyone and everything. A bastion against the rest of the world when he felt the need to withdraw from it and get his act together again. Looking up and down the hall, he saw that every office door was ajar. Even Maya's. Well, he was going to have to adjust or else. "When in Rome, do as the Romans do," he muttered as he turned and went back into his office.

Eyeing the bright purple-and-white spikes of orchids hanging out of a green metal can, Dane stopped and touched one of the flowers. They were real, not some silk flower fake. Looking around at the lifelessness of his office, he began to realize why the orchids were put there. It was a breath of real life. Of nature. One corner of his mouth curved faintly as he dropped the mission report forms on his desk. He knew Maya would sense his consternation over the flowers being put on his desk. At his base at Fort Rucker, he'd never have something like flowers around.

It was a woman's touch, he thought again, as he studied

the full white petals and the rich purple in the center of the orchid. And he was in a woman's world. Shaking his head, he seesawed with the dichotomy. On one hand, Maya knew her business as a combat pilot and squadron commander. Yet the evidence of women's things popped up in the most surprising places. That, and the informality that seemed to pervade her command—a blur between rank and privilege. The way Gautier had treated him—more like an equal, when he was a major and she a lowly lieutenant—had surprised him as well.

He'd heard that women knew how to work as a team a lot better than men did. Maybe that was true. Was it because they didn't keep up walls, the barriers of rank, that this place hummed like a well-ordered beehive? He'd been damned impressed at the short time it took to get those two Apaches off the ground and into the air to chase Faro's helicopters. Shaking his head, Dane sat down on the creaky chair. Maya and this place seemed alien, out of sync with him. He was trying to adjust, but it was hard.

Getting down to the business of penning his flight mission report, Dane decided to stop thinking so much and just let things roll as they might around here. He couldn't afford to be rigid like they were stateside. No, down here, Maya ran her organization differently. Lifting his head, he mused at the word he'd just used: *different.* Maybe that was what her people had meant—that she ran her squadron much more loosely than the military usually did. At least more loosely than they were used to up north.

Sighing, he tried to concentrate on the report in front of him, pulling a pen from the side pocket of the left arm of his flight uniform. What would the next few days bring? Some peace, he hoped...if he could keep his foot out of his mouth long enough.

Chapter 7

The bogey bell clanged gratingly throughout the cave complex. Dane moved from behind his desk and grabbed his helmet from the nearby shelf. He knew Maya had duty today. And he'd been waiting for this opportunity for the last four days, ever since his flight with her. Today she was back on the combat flight roster. Hurrying down the stairs, he ran out toward the lip, where they were pushing out the two Apaches that would intercept. It was late afternoon; the sky was the usual mix of clouds and pale blue. The humidity was high and he was sweating profusely.

The well-trained crews swarmed around the individual gunships, pulling off the rotor tethers as the crew chiefs opened up the cockpits for the pilots, who were running toward them.

Spotting Maya coming from the dispensary, which was located at the rear of the cave complex, Dane slowed until she caught up with him. Since the last flight with her, he'd spent every moment he could in the air, as copilot gunner, on different intercept missions. Maya had given him permission because it would help him set up a realistic training schedule, which would begin next Monday.

"I'm coming with you, if it's all right with you," he said as he jogged at her shoulder.

Maya shrugged and kept up her long stride toward the Apache on the left, nearest the wall. "Fine by me."

Penny handed Maya the sat intel information as she approached the gunship. "They've spotted three helos, Captain. They're forty miles from the border."

"Thanks, Penny." Maya stuffed the printout into her flight suit pocket. Dane had already climbed into the back seat and was busy getting into his harness. Looking to her right, she saw that CWO3 Akiva Redtail, an Apache-Lakota Sioux woman, and her copilot, CWO2 Vickey Mabrey, were already in their gunship and ready to roll. Akiva always wore a bright red scarf around her head, a sign that she was an Apache warrior. In her belt she wore an antique ax and Bowie knife that was given to her when she passed all the demanding tests in her tribe to become a warrior. Maya had allowed her to keep the articles of war on her person not only because she honored Akiva, but because they had been handed down through Akiva's family from her great-great grandmother, who was a warrior and rode with Geronimo.

Climbing into the front seat, Maya automatically went through the motions. In no time, she was lifting off the Apache and threading the Eye of the Needle. This was only the second time she'd flown with Dane since his arrival. She'd heard back from the pilots he'd flown with since, on ten other missions, that he was quickly getting up to speed on the demands of the job. *Good.*

"We're clear, Saber," came Redtail's voice.

"Roger, Chief. Let's rock 'n' roll, ladies...and gentleman."

Dane was busy firing up the HUD radar, searching in the general area that the satellite intel had picked up the helo activity. He heard the irony and amusement in Maya's voice. Since their last head-on confrontation in the hall of HQ, she had left him alone to manage his responsibilities for the training schedule. Sometimes he'd seen her pass in the hall, but she never looked his way or dropped by to talk. No, that steel wall between them was solidly in place.

Mouth compressing, Dane scanned the skies overhead. He had no one to blame but himself. Racking his brain for ways to approach Maya and ask her to trust him was a fool's business. If he'd learned anything in the past four days, it was that she trusted those who proved themselves capable of her trust. Her squadron really did idolize her, he'd discovered. They loved her more like a mother who nurtured them, rather than fearing her as a squadron leader. And there was nothing they wouldn't do for Maya. Yes, the last four days had shown him just how much his own dark prejudice against her, against women in general, was really distorted and inappropriate.

"Got anything on radar yet?" Maya demanded as she pushed the Apache up to ten thousand feet, above the cloud layer.

"No," he murmured. "You got any feelings about this mission?"

Maya chuckled. "Uh-oh, sounds like my pilots have been retraining you on the finer points of using your intuition as radar, too."

He liked the sound of her husky voice. She seemed to have let down her guard. He grinned. "Yeah, you could say that. You sense anything?"

Maya felt him trying to earnestly establish a beachhead of trust with her. She was exhausted by the demands of the squadron, plus having the new I.P.s around and flying combat missions. "I'm too damn tired to sense much of anything right now. How about you?" She looked around, always searching for the lethal Kamovs. In the past four days, since their last attack, the Kamovs seemed to have evaporated from their airspace. That wasn't like them, and Maya was uneasy about it. What was up? What did Faro have up his sleeve?

"I'm not sure it's a feeling," Dane murmured, frowning at the HUDs. He saw a vague outline. That meant it was painting something out there. What, exactly, he wasn't sure. "I've got three bogeys on screen," he stated, giving her the coordinates. Instantly, Maya changed directions, and so did Redtail, who followed two rotor lengths behind her.

"What then?" Maya asked. She felt safe in the cockpit of her Apache, like a child in a mother's arms. She trusted this gunship with her life. Literally.

"I don't know.... I can't explain it...."

"You usually can't define intuition hits that clearly," she said. "You know without knowing."

"Spoken like a true oracle."

Maya laughed outright. It was the first time she'd truly let down around Dane, and it felt good. She heard him chuckling in her headset.

"If I was an oracle, I'd be able to tell you what Faro's up to," she griped unhappily.

"Yeah, Lobo said he's up to no good. He's changing tactics on you—again."

"Yes...and that always makes me nervous."

"I'm scanning for the Kamovs," Dane assured her. All around them rose the lofty mountains, clothed in jungle greenery. Dane was familiar with most of the flight routes now. They'd go due east and intercept somewhere between the lowlands of the jungle and the highlands, which curved steeply up to fourteen thousand feet. Lake Titicaca wasn't that far away, although he had yet to see it. The Bolivian border area was high, arid desert, a no-man's land with harsh conditions.

Just as he lifted his head to scan, he saw something peripherally.

"Wait...."

Twisting his head, he looked again.

"Kamovs!" he barked. "One o'clock high! Break! Break!"

Instantly, Maya peeled off to the left. Redtail sheered to the right. The Apache groaned as she brought the nose up and into a vertical climb, the throttles to the firewall. Jerking her head around, Maya saw the double-rotored Kamovs charging them. Her eyes widened.

"Damn! There's *three* of them!"

Dane sucked in a breath. He saw all three of the black Russian helicopters roaring full speed from behind the mountain where they'd been hiding. They were diving down at them. He and Maya were in trouble. Quickly, he punched up the rockets for launch.

Maya cursed softly and realized that two of the Kamovs were peeling off toward her. Where had Faro gotten a *third* Kamov? Had he bought another one in order to up the ante? The third was after Redtail. Maya was too low. The Kamovs were high. They had the advantage. *Damn!* Sweat stood out on her carved face. Her lips drew back from her teeth as she whipped the Apache around so that they could fire at their oncoming attackers.

"Rockets on line. I've got one painted."

Dane's voice was cool and low. It soothed her. Heart pounding, Maya watched as the second Kamov broke from the first and began to move in for a kill.

"Fire when ready," she snapped.

"Firing."

The white light of the rocket sped from both sides of the Apache. Maya wasted no time watching to see if they hit their target. She had a second Kamov stalking her in earnest. Seeing the winking of gunfire, she knew that he was firing 30 mm cannon shells at them.

Too late!

The front cockpit Plexiglas cracked. It was designed to take a 30 mm hit, but the side panels were not shell resistant. Maya heard the explosion of shattering Plexiglas. She felt a white-hot heat sear her left arm. Several pieces of the canopy slashed against her chest and struck the chicken plate with a thud. The vest had just saved her life.

Jerking the Apache to the right, and moving toward the Kamov, she yelled, "Fire!"

Dane had winced as the shells slammed into the front cockpit and arced above him. Was Maya wounded? He'd heard her groan, but that was all. From the way she was handling the Apache, she didn't seem hurt at all. He quickly thumbed the button. The 30 mm cannon beneath the Apache began thunking out huge rounds at the approaching Kamov. Satisfaction soared through him as Maya held the gunship right on course. The cannon shells were going to find their mark.

In his headset, he heard Redtail yelling excitedly. The crew on the other Apache had their own battle on their hands. Jerking his head around, Dane saw two of the shells impact the right wing of the Kamov. *Good!* Instantly, the helicopter banked to the right, away from them, smoke pouring out of one engine.

Maya rubbernecked around, desperately looking for the other Kamov. It was gone! Breathing hard, she pulled the Apache around to locate Redtail. She was about two miles away. The third Kamov was hightailing it back toward the jungle.

Wind was whipping into the cockpit, through the broken Plexiglas. She saw the shattered, sparkling pieces sprinkled all around her, across her lap and on the floor beneath her feet. And then she saw something else. Blood. Blood was splattered across her instrument panel.

"What the hell..." she muttered. "Take the controls, Dane. I need to check something out. You got the controls?"

Instantly, he placed his hands and feet on them. "I have the controls." He kept searching the sky and twisting around. The Kamovs were gone. They appeared and disappeared like magicians; now you see them, now you don't. Breathing raggedly, he blinked his eyes rapidly. Sweat was stinging them.

He looked up over his console. He could see part of Maya's shattered cockpit. And he could just make out the top of her black helmet. Frowning, he said, "What's wrong? Are you all right?"

Maya felt a vague pain on the inside of her upper left arm. As she lifted her right hand to brush away the Plexiglas, she saw that her uniform had been torn open beneath. Several chunks had been taken out of her chicken plate. Moving her fingers along her chest, she made sure she wasn't injured. She was okay. The wind was making her eyes tear and blur so she couldn't see anything.

"Slow this thing down. I can hardly see up here."

Dane pulled back on the throttles. He saw Redtail coming back to join them. "You want me to hover?"

"No, just head back to base below a hundred miles an hour."

"Roger."

He heard a strange edge in Maya's voice. What was going on? "Are you injured?"

Lifting her left arm, she saw blood pumping out of a deep slash in it. "Damn," she muttered. "I'm bleeding like a stuck hog...."

Frowning, Dane said, "Where? Where are you hit?" His heart began to pound unevenly. They were twenty minutes from base. He resisted the urge to speed up.

"The left arm," Maya muttered. "Cut an artery, I think, by flying Plexiglas. Damn...gotta find something to tie off the area above it...." And she began to search around for something, anything, to wrap around her upper arm. Dizziness assailed her. Maya closed her eyes, then opened them. This couldn't be happening. Of all things...

"There's nothing up there to tie it off with," Dane told her urgently. "Use your right hand and press hard on it, Maya. Use direct pressure, all you have. It'll slow the bleeding down. Can you do that?"

Her fingers became slippery as she tried to squeeze the

opened flesh that was pumping blood. "Yeah...I'm doing that now."

"Are you feeling all right?"

Maya heard the tension in Dane's tone. Leaning her head back, she closed her eyes. "No...I'm not. Call base. Ask the medical team to meet us on the lip. I'm losing blood fast...." And she looked down to realize that it had been pooling below her feet on the deck without her even realizing it. Her heart was pounding in her chest like an overstressed freight train. Her voice sounded weak to her ears, not filled with her usual strong confidence. Was she going to die? *No!* She didn't want to. Trying to press her right hand tighter around her upper arm, she felt coldness creeping into her bones. The wind, although warm and humid, was buffeting her.

"Dane..."

Alarmed, he heard the faraway tone of Maya's voice. It was the first time she'd called him by his first name. He heard an edge of fear in her voice. She was going down. *No! Not her! Not now!*

"I—think...I think I'm going to lose consciousness pretty soon. If I do, I can't hold the pressure on my arm and I'm going to start bleeding out again."

Her voice was growing fainter by the moment. His eyes widened. There was nothing he could do to help her. Frustration ate at him. "Maya, just hold on. Take some deep breaths. Stay awake!"

She heard the raw concern in his voice. Resting her head against the back of her seat, she felt darkness edging her vision. Closing her eyes, she whispered, "Redline this gunship...or I'm not going to make it...."

Those were the last words he heard from her. Instantly, Dane moved the Apache to top speed. He called the base and requested immediate medical standby. As he gave the details of Maya's injury, he knew it was a race against time. She was bleeding out. He knew that if an artery was cut at an angle, in two or three minutes it would close itself off to a bare trickle, and her life would be saved. However, if the artery had been sliced cleanly through, it had no way of closing itself off—and she would bleed out and die. Looking at his watch, he saw they had ten minutes until they landed. Hurry! Hurry! His hands wrapped hard around the controls.

Taking over as flight commander, he radioed Redtail, ordering her back to base as well, as there was no need to put a lone Apache up against the two Kamovs that might still be out hunting them. His mind raced. His heart hurt. Maya was too proud, too beautiful, too brave to die. It couldn't end this way for her. It just couldn't! His mouth compressed into a thin line. As he brought the Apache down to six thousand feet, the sky nearly clear for once, he could see the mountain ahead where their base was located.

"Maya? Maya? Do you hear me? We're almost home. Home. You hear me? We're almost home. You're going to make it. Just hang on. I'll get you help. Just hang on..."

There was no answer.

Son of a bitch! He felt an arcing pain across his chest where his heart thumped wildly. It was frustration mixed with anxiety and something else...something so shadowed and hesitant that he couldn't even name it as he flew the Apache toward the base.

Flying up to the Eye, Dane didn't take a hesitant, slow approach. Instead, he used visual, because the clouds had dissipated, and plunged through the opening, quickly setting the Apache down on the right side of the lip. He could see Dr. Elizabeth Cornell standing near Paredes, her paramedic, and a gurney. Heart pounding unrelentingly, Dane quickly cut the engines.

Without even waiting for the rotors to stop, which was protocol, he unharnessed himself. Shoving the cockpit door open, he climbed out on the side of the helo. The rotation of the rotors was causing a lot of air turbulence. It pounded at him. Gripping the handle to Maya's shattered cockpit canopy, he jerked it open.

Someone else placed a ladder next to where he was crouched and was climbing up it. It was Paredes, her eyes slitted with concern.

Dane gasped as he shoved himself into Maya's tight compartment. Blood was everywhere, on the floor and splattered throughout the cockpit. Maya was unconscious, her head sagging back against the window. Her arms were limp against her form. The left side of her uniform was soaked in blood.

"I'll unharness her," he called to Paredes, who had also climbed up on the fuselage area.

Reaching in, his hands shaking badly, Dane unharnessed Maya. She was a big woman. It was going to take every ounce of his strength to pull her out of that cramped cockpit. Reaching for her helmet, he loosened the chin strap and gently pulled it off her head. Her black hair spilled out across her shoulders and the chest armor. Her face was white. Frightened, Dane handed the helmet to Paredes's outstretched, waiting hands.

Mouth dry, he angled his body so that he faced Maya. Slipping his hands beneath her armpits, he hauled her upward. Grunting, he balanced himself against the airframe and pulled her halfway out of the cockpit. Paredes was there to catch Maya's head as it fell downward.

"I got her!" Paredes said urgently. "We need more hands!" she called to those below.

Another sergeant climbed the ladder. Between the three of them, they were able to pull Maya out of her seat. Dane untangled her feet from around the collective and hoisted the lower half of her body out of the cockpit. Free! She was free. Urgency drummed through him. He looked down. Tears stung his eyes. Every person on the base was standing below. He saw so many hands on either side of the ladder lift upward to receive Maya that it tightened his throat. The fear in their faces, the look in their eyes, touched him deeply as he handed Maya to the awaiting sea of helping hands below.

Wiping his mouth, Dane hunkered down on the fuselage

as Maya was placed quickly on the gurney. He saw Cornell put a tight tourniquet above her left arm, which still had blood pumping out. Issuing orders, Cornell had Paredes push the gurney toward the cave. Once the ladder was clear, Dane jumped down. Looking back, he saw that the rotors were still slowly turning. The blood splattered on the front cockpit was Maya's blood. Cursing softly, he hurried through the dissipating crowd after the gurney.

"Dr. Cornell!" he called, jogging up to her as she walked quickly at the gurney's side.

The red-haired woman gave him a sharp, tight look. "Yes?"

"What are you going to do?"

With a grimace, Cornell managed to get a blood pressure cuff around Maya's limp right arm and pumped it up as they moved into the cave. "I don't know yet...give me a moment...." And she put her stethoscope to her ears and placed it on Maya's arm. Releasing the pressure, she listened as they walked quickly toward the dispensary.

"Eighty over forty," she told Paredes in an unhappy voice.

Dane scowled and watched the paramedic's copper features tighten.

"What's that mean?" he demanded, jogging alongside.

"It's bad. Her blood pressure's too low. If we don't get whole blood into her soon, her heart will cavitate and go into arrest." Cornell looked directly at him for moment. "She'll die."

"Blood? You've got blood on hand here, don't you?" Surely, Dane thought, they would. Especially under the present conditions of daily warfare.

"Of course we do." Elizabeth hurried forward and opened the door to the dispensary. Paredes shoved the gurney inside to a well-lit, white room that was crowded with medical equipment.

Dane slipped in before the door automatically closed. Anxiously, he looked at Maya's slack features. Her once golden skin was washed out now. She looked dead already. Anguish soared through him. He stood helplessly as Paredes quickly followed Cornell's orders to slit away the fabric of her uniform on her injured arm with a pair of scissors. He saw the doctor take scissors to the other arm and slit it from wrist to shoulder. In moments, they had an IV fluids going into her right arm.

Dane moved closer to get a look at the injury. It was a gash about two inches long, and he could see the artery was now dripping only slightly, thanks to the tourniquet.

''It had to be a piece of Plexiglas from the shattered cockpit that cut into her,'' he told the doctor. He saw Cornell's face. She looked grim as she reached for a series of dressings.

''Doctor,'' Paredes said, ''what's her blood type? I can go get the whole blood to give to her.''

Cornell hissed, ''Dammit, I just realized we don't have her blood type here, Paredes.''

Paredes paled. She halted halfway to the refrigeration unit where the blood was kept. ''But...''

Cornell quickly cleaned the wound and threw the bloody dressings down at her feet. She worked like a madwoman.

Dane frowned. He looked at Paredes, whose mouth had fallen open. And then he jerked a glance at the doctor, still working feverishly over Maya.

''What are you talking about, Doctor? You just told me you keep blood on hand here.''

Cornell grimaced. ''Major, what you don't realize—'' she swabbed Maya's left arm with antiseptic ''—is that we're on a very limited budget. Maya handles what supplies we get in here. She opted to spend the money for O-type blood, the one that is most common, the one that nearly all our pilots have, instead of keeping any of her type on hand, instead.''

Running his fingers through his hair, he approached the gurney, his eyes slits. ''You're telling me the type she needs you don't have?'' His voice had risen in disbelief. Shock.

"That's right, Major. Dammit! Paredes, take her BP again."

"Yes, ma'am!" Paredes quickly moved between Dane and the gurney.

"Eighty over thirty-nine."

"We're gonna lose her...." Cornell whispered. "Dammit to hell!"

"What blood type do you need?" Dane demanded.

Cornell's eyes were awash with tears. "AB positive, Major. It's not the kind of blood you find just anywhere. It would have cost too much to get it and keep it here, and Maya knew that. She took a risk. She wanted the O on hand for the bulk of her pilots, in case they got injured."

Stunned, Dane stood looking down at Maya. Her lips were colorless, her skin leaching out even more. His throat ached. She took a risk. That's what Maya had done. She'd taken a calculated risk, thinking that she would not be the one to get hit or need blood. The looks on the two women's faces made him feel their anguish.

"I've got good news for you, Doctor," he told her quietly as he rolled up the sleeve of his uniform. "I'm AB positive. You can use my blood."

Cornell's head shot up. Her eyes widened. "You *are?*" Her voice echoed around the room.

"Yes!" Paredes shouted triumphantly, her eyes shining with hope. She quickly ran and got the supplies for a blood transfusion from a cabinet.

Dane grinned. "Maya is gonna be pissed off as hell about it, but right now, I'm her knight in shining armor coming to the rescue. Where do you want me to sit, Doctor? You can take as much as you need."

Paredes quickly swabbed down his left arm and placed the needle into one of his large veins. She was smiling ear-to-ear.

Cornell pulled another gurney next to Maya's. "Lie down on this, Major. Quickly. There's no time left...."

Dane did as he was instructed. Paredes moved like lightning, making the IV tube connection into Maya's right arm. Relief flowed through him. The universe worked in strange and mysterious ways, he thought, as Paredes handed him a rubber ball to squeeze from time to time, to keep the blood flowing out of his body and into Maya's. Finally, he'd found a way to connect with her. He wasn't at all sure she was going to be happy about it. Watching as his dark red blood flowed through the tubing and into Maya's receiving arm, he grinned lopsidedly. Cornell was listening intently to Maya's heart after removing the chicken plate. Her brows were furrowed, her eyes half-closed. Her lips were tight.

Paredes hooked Maya up to a blood pressure gauge that was suspended on the wall behind her head. Both medical people watched it raptly.

"Ninety over fifty!" Paredes whispered. She clenched her fist and yelled, "Yes!"

Dane scowled. "What does that mean, Sergeant?"

Paredes glowed, her teeth white against her coppery skin. "It means that her blood pressure is rising, sir. It means your blood is making the difference."

"It means," Cornell whispered unsteadily, as she placed her arm on Maya's shoulder, "that you're saving her life. Literally. She's lost over two pints of blood, Major. I'm going to take about one and half out of you. Normally, we take only a pint."

"Take what you need!" he repeated fervently.

Cornell shook her head. "Depending upon how Maya's blood pressure responds, I may take more—or less—I don't know yet." She watched the monitors fluctuating above Maya's head.

"I'm not going to die with two pints gone," Dane said.

"No, but you'll definitely feel like a ton of bricks hit you for a good two weeks, until your body can make enough to bring you back to your own healthy levels and needs," Cornell warned.

"I can handle it," he assured her with a grin. His heart soared. Maya's life was going to be saved! Dane couldn't recall when he'd ever felt as good about anything as this. Ever.

Cornell smiled hesitantly, her hand moving in a motherly fashion across Maya's shoulder. "We're treading on dangerous ground here, Major. Maya, judging from her blood pressure, lost closer to three pints of blood. I have to balance it out between you." She began to sew the artery back together, with Paredes handing her the needle and thread. "This is a game of balance, Major. I can't take too much from you, or you'll have problems. And I've got to give Maya enough to recover without having to worry about her going into cardiac arrest. I don't have any AB positive whole blood as backup if you go down on me."

A warmth moved through Dane as he lay there watching them work on Maya's left arm. He was beginning to feel the effects of blood loss from the transfusion. It must have been how Maya felt in the cockpit. Closing his eyes, Dane kept squeezing the ball every few seconds. Maya could have died. She almost had. His heart twinged with anguish. She was too beautiful. Too bold and brave to die. If anyone should live, it should be her, he thought as he placed his free arm across his eyes.

Just remembering the crowd of women surrounding the Apache, their arms stretched high to receive Maya and pass her down the line made his throat tighten again. There was something so special about her that instilled people to surround her and protect her. Hell, even he had. What was it? What was that difference? He tried to figure it out as he lay there, his senses tumbling.

"We need to get ahold of Inca," Paredes said to the doctor. "She can help us."

"Maya's sister? The healer?" Cornell asked.

"Yes, ma'am. When we're done here, can I run over to comms and try to raise her?"

"She's in Brazil."

"I know that, ma'am, but maybe they can fly her over here? You know, she touches someone and they heal up."

Dane frowned, listening to the intensely whispered conversation. He lifted his arm from across his eyes, twisted his head and looked at them.

"What are you talking about?"

Cornell continued to sew the ends of the artery together. "Maya has a fraternal twin sister who is a healer in Brazil. I can tell by the look on your face, Major, that you're a little surprised by our conversation. Inca can lay her hands on a person and heal them. Right now, I could use everything possible, to get Maya stabilized. My bet is she's lost three pints of blood. We're putting only one and a half or maybe two back into her. If Inca can help, we're going to explore that possibility, too."

Stunned, Dane stared at them. "A healer?"

Paredes smiled gamely. "Major, this isn't like other bases you've been at. We practice voodoo, too."

"Paredes!" Cornell said sharply.

"Well, I'm just teasing, Major. It's not voodoo, really. The Captain's sister is well known down here for her healing abilities. She's known as the jaguar goddess by just about everyone."

With a shake of his head, Dane covered his eyes with his arm again. "You're right," he muttered, "this is one hell of a strange place."

"Angel, when I'm done here, get to comms. Make the call."

"Yes, ma'am." Paredes glowed with excitement as she handed the doctor a sponge.

Feeling a little floaty, Dane took in a deep breath. Tiredness was beginning to creep through him.

"Ninety over sixty," Paredes crowed triumphantly. "It's working, Major. Your blood is stabilizing her real well."

Dane nodded. "Good, Sergeant. I'm glad." And he was.

The adrenaline he had felt was beginning to ebb away, leaving him feeling shaky in the aftermath. The urgency was still with him, though. Maya wasn't out of the woods yet, according to Cornell. More than anything, he wanted Maya to live. As he lay there, his heart ached with that same feeling he'd felt before, in the cockpit, after Maya had started losing consciousness.

Frowning, Dane focused on the feeling. When he thought he could put a name to the emotion, he instantly recoiled from it. No...it couldn't be. He couldn't feel that way about Maya. Or could he? His mouth compressed in a slash against the possibility. How could he have these kinds of raw, needy feelings toward a woman who hated the very earth he walked upon? He felt a strong caring feeling flowing toward her, a need to hold her in his arms, kiss her and breathe his life back into her. The thoughts were absolutely shocking to Dane, and yet here they were, alive, vibrant and clamoring to be acted upon.

Great, he wanted her as a woman to his man. He craved to feel Maya's arms around him. He wondered what it would be like to feel the softness and womanly strength of her lips against his mouth. Would the heat in her eyes translate to another kind of vibrant heat that could only come from within her? His need of Maya on that level gnawed at him relentlessly. Maybe because he was weakening from blood loss in the transfusion, he was a little more vulnerable to his buried thoughts and feelings toward her.

Confusion spun around in him. Dane felt light-headed. His raw emotions were bubbling to the surface, and they had his full attention. There was no way he could fall in love with Maya. Or have feelings of love toward her. Could he? *How* could he? Nothing made sense to Dane. Not right now. He blamed his present state on the urgency of his emotions. It was just the possibility of losing Maya at the base, on this mission, which was so important. That was all. It had to be all.

Chapter 8

The first thing Maya felt as she dragged herself out of the darkness was pain. Pain throbbing in her left arm. She heard women's voices, low and whispering. Her shorting-out consciousness then became aware of the warmth of a hand on her right shoulder. What had happened? Blinking, she squinted as she opened her eyes.

"Ah, she's awake."

It was Captain Dove Rivera's soft, melodic voice.

Opening her eyes, Maya saw Dr. Cornell and Angel bending over her.

"Do I look like a bug under a microscope?" she demanded in a rusty voice.

Dove Rivera, who sat on a stool next to her bed, lifted her hand from Maya's shoulder and grinned hugely. Her flashing smile filled the room as she gazed down at Maya.

"Welcome back from the Threshold, Maya."

Barely lifting her head, Maya looked around. "I'm in our hospital. Why?"

Elizabeth placed her hands in the pockets of her white coat.

Her stethoscope hung around her neck. "Because you almost croaked on us, that's why, Maya. Do you remember what happened about two hours ago?"

Closing her eyes, her mouth dry, Maya whispered, "Oh damn...we got nailed by a Kamov...." And then her lashes lifted and worry filled her voice. "Dane? Is he okay? I mean...Major York? Did he get hit, too?"

Chuckling, Paredes hoisted her thumb toward the door at the other end of their four-bed hospital section, which was part of the clinic. "Well, he got hit all right. But he's okay." She traded an amused look with the doctor.

Maya felt incredibly weak. "Then...he's okay...." She had been alarmed that he might have gotten hurt, too.

Elizabeth placed her hand on Maya's left shoulder and squeezed it gently. "You received a deep cut to the under side of your left arm. It sliced your brachial artery wide open. You tried to stop the bleeding and eventually, because of blood loss, you fell unconscious. Major York flew you home."

Dove tittered. "You shoulda seen him come barreling through the Eye, Maya. I mean, that man's tail was on fire. He didn't creep through like he'd been doing before." She slapped her knee and giggled. "It wasn't funny at the time, but it is now. We were all waiting for you on the lip." She gestured toward Elizabeth and Angel. "I mean, that guy came through the Eye like it wasn't there. Even *we* were impressed. He's got guts when he needs them."

Closing her eyes, Maya remembered vague bits of the Kamov attack. "Then why is he hurt?" She heard the collective laugh of the women who surrounded her bed. In each of her arms were IVs feeding her nutrients.

"Because," Elizabeth said quietly and seriously, "he literally saved your life."

Opening her eyes to slits, Maya whispered, "He did a good job of flying us home."

"Oh," Dove said, her thick black, brows arching, "he did

a little more than that.'' Her black eyes gleamed with amusement as she traded smiles with her compatriots once more.

''I don't think you're going to like what I have to tell you,'' Elizabeth said, ''but Major York gave you a blood transfusion of AB positive. We had none on hand, as you well know.'' Elizabeth frowned. ''And you were dumping on us, Maya. I figure you've lost three pints of blood. You shouldn't have even have made it back here. When we got you into the dispensary, your blood pressure was falling through the floor. Major York was hovering over you like a mother hen. When he found out we didn't have AB positive on hand, he told us he was.'' She smiled softly. ''The guy is okay, Maya. He started rolling up his sleeve and asking where he could sit so you could get enough blood into you before you went into cardiac arrest.''

Stunned, Maya stared up at the doctor. ''He—Dane—I mean, Major York—he—you've got to be kidding me!'' His blood in her body. The explosion of shock rippled through Maya. She saw the serious set of Elizabeth's narrow face. At thirty-five, Elizabeth was one of the oldest women on the base. And her heart was one of the largest.

''What was it he said?'' Angel said, laughing. ''That when you woke up and found out you had his redneck blood in your body, that you wouldn't be very happy about it?''

''That's what he said,'' Elizabeth murmured. She smoothed the blue gown Maya wore in a motherly fashion. ''We've got other things in motion, too. I had Angel go to comms and contact your sister, Inca. We just got word that she's being flown out from Manaus on a Perseus jet to Cuzco. As soon as she gets here—'' Elizabeth looked at her watch ''—which should be about five hours from now, Dove is going to take the civilian helo from the mining side into Cuzco to pick her up at the airport. She'll then fly her out here.'' She gently tapped Maya's shoulder. ''You're still not out of the woods, Maya. We've got another flight in at the Good Samaritan Hospital in Lima right now, and we're picking up four pints of AB positive blood. You need more, and I'm afraid Major York is really weakened from giving you two pints of his own blood. As soon as Dallas arrives back here with it, we're pumping both of you to normal levels to get you on safer ground. Until then, you are to just lie here and rest. You're going nowhere.'' Her voice had turned grim.

Blown away by the news, Maya stared up at the doctor. ''I still can't believe this—*he* gave his blood to *me?*''

Sliding off the stool, Dove laughed. Though she was half Spanish, half Q'uero Indian, Dove, who stood a little over five foot five inches tall, was built solidly like her Q'uero ancestors, the original Incas. ''Now you got redneck blood in you, too, Maya. Just think—blood of the guy you hated the most, the one who almost did all of us in back at Fort Rucker, is in your veins now. Isn't that something?'' She picked up her helmet and placed it under her left arm. ''I'm on standby, so I gotta get out of here. I just wanted to be here when you came around. You've got fifty other people who are wanting to see you, too.''

''Dove, spread the word that Maya is awake and stable.''

''I will,'' she told the doctor as she headed toward the swinging doors at the end of the small hospital unit. At the doors, she halted. ''Oh. Major York has been asking about you. He wants to see you. Do you want to see him? He's just outside in the dispensary, lying down. The man keeps asking about you every five minutes.''

Frowning, Maya whispered, ''Sure…I'll see him….'' And her heart fluttered with a strange, new emotion.

Angel and Elizabeth left her bedside. ''We'll give you two some time alone,'' Elizabeth counseled. She wagged her finger in Maya's face. ''But if he upsets you, or you want him to leave, just tell him that. I don't want you stressed. Not right now, okay?''

Compressing her dry lips, Maya nodded weakly. ''Doc, I'm in no shape to fight or spar with anyone. I just want to thank him. It's the least I can do.''

Pleased, Elizabeth said, "Good for you. Angel will come and check on you every half hour. The buzzer is located near your right hand. Push it and we'll be here in a heartbeat, okay?"

"Yes...thank you...all of you..."

The ward became quiet after they left. It was a small room with two beds on either side. Maya had helped create this small hospital section, but this was the first time in three years she'd been in it. There were windows located on the side that faced the opening to the cave. Everything was painted white, and white cotton curtains hung at the rectangular windows, which allowed feeble light to enter the area.

She was propped up slightly in bed, she realized. Her arm ached dully, and looking down at it, she saw it was wrapped in several bandages. The water sitting on the bedstand nearby looked awfully good. Trying to reach for it, she found, to her consternation, that she was so weak it took every effort to drag her hand across her lap toward it.

Lying back, exhausted, Maya closed her eyes. Dane York had saved her life. His blood was in her body. A lot of it. Emotions roiled within her. How could someone who hated her as much as he did do something like this for her? Confused, Maya didn't have much time to work through her feelings. She heard the door open quietly and then close. Turning her head, she forced her eyes open. Through her thick, black lashes, she saw Dane York, still in his black flight uniform, his left sleeve rolled up above his elbow, come walking into the unit. Her heart skipped a beat.

Dane looked washed out. No longer did he walk with that vital step she'd come to know so well. His face was haggard, and there were shadows lurking beneath his large blue eyes. Warmth moved through her unexpectedly as she met and held his welcoming gaze. There was a slight, hesitant smile on his mouth. His eyes were alive with anxiety and worry in their depths. For who? Her? Maya found it hard to think of Dane York as someone who really cared what happened to her. All of her old assumptions exploded suddenly. As he reached the rail of her bed and looked down at her, Maya realized that for the first time she was seeing him without his armor in place. Right now, his face was so very readable. His mouth, usually so harshly set, no longer turned in at the corners. No, if anything, he had an incredible expression of care that radiated straight through her to her heart.

"I didn't hear any hysterical screaming coming from here when you found out you have some of my blood," he teased, his voice husky with emotion. How badly he wanted to reach out and touch Maya. She looked wan, her once golden flesh leached out. Her black hair lay in thick ebony strands around her face and gowned shoulders. Her lips were slightly parted. The look in her eyes was one of confusion, warmth and something else he couldn't easily decipher.

To hell with it. Facing her, Dane reached over and gently moved his hand across the crown of her head, barely grazing her hair. A look of shock registered in her dull green eyes at his gesture of unspoken concern and care. Dane removed his hand. He realized he shouldn't have tried making contact with her. His heart ached.

Tiny tingles radiated across Maya's scalp where he'd skimmed her hair. His touch was so unexpected that she was speechless for a moment. The anxiety in his face was unmistakable. He cared for *her*. Blinking, she opened her mouth to speak. Only a croak came out.

"Sounds like you need some water?" he teased and, reaching over, he poured some in a glass and held it out to her. Dane wanted to do something—anything—to show how much he was concerned for Maya. Surprise and confusion were alive in her eyes as she stared up at him when he patiently offered her the glass.

"I—I'm weak… Can you…can you help me get it to my mouth? I'm dying of thirst."

She'd asked for his help. His heart soared. A slight, self-conscious grin pulled at one corner of his mouth. "Yeah, hold on. Let me situate myself so I can get you into enough of a sitting position to drink it without wearing it...." He set the glass down and moved toward her head. He was looking forward to contact with her once again. Maybe touch was all he had to communicate to Maya that he wasn't the bastard he'd been four years earlier. Leaning over her, Dane slid his arm beneath her neck and shoulders and eased her upward. Maya didn't protest or struggle. She didn't try and fight him or move away from his supportive embrace. Again his heart soared.

"Here," he murmured, bringing the glass to her cracked, dry lips, "drink all you want." As he pressed the rim of the glass to her mouth, he saw her try to raise her hand, but fail. Alarmed at her weakness, Dane realized that although Maya was alive, she was far from well.

Sucking noisily, Maya drank the entire contents of the glass. Dane's arm felt strong and reassuring around her. When she asked for more, he chuckled.

"Good sign. Anytime someone wants water or food, they're going to live." He poured her another glass and then eased her up into his arms again.

Maya absorbed his care. Right now, she was feeling very weak and out of control. The second glass of water sated her. Leaning her head against his strong, capable shoulder, she whispered, "Thanks..."

Dane didn't want to release her, but he knew he had to. Easing Maya onto the bed, he put the glass aside. Fussing with the pillows under her head, he gazed down at Maya. How beautiful she looked. And how in need of care she was right now.

"There. Better?"

Maya nodded once and closed her eyes. "Yeah...better. Thanks." All sorts of warm ripples were moving throughout her neck and shoulders where he'd held her. A part of her wondered why they had this ongoing battle between them at all.

Dane pulled up the stool and sat down, his arm resting on the rail as he faced Maya. The hum of constant activity outside the room could be heard. He felt like a beggar being given the chance to simply absorb her beauty, her strength and bravery as he sat there in the silence of the room.

"You know," he began awkwardly, in a halting, low tone, "I was so scared out there. I didn't realize when the Kamov started firing at us that your cockpit would shatter. I felt frustrated, Maya. I couldn't reach you or help you." He saw her eyes barely open, her pupils large and black and centered on him. Without thinking, Dane reached out and settled his hand over hers, which lay across her stomach on top of the covers. "I don't know what I expected out of that combat situation. When you turned the gunship to meet the Kamov head-on, I was surprised." He grinned a little, his fingers moving to enclose her cool hand. "You were already wounded. I don't know if you knew it at that time or not, but you turned and faced him." Shaking his head, he whispered, "You're the gutsiest person I know."

The admiration, the respect in his low, husky voice riffled through Maya. It was healing. They were words she had wanted to hear from him for so long. And just the warm, quiet strength of his hand over hers fed her and made her feel less confused. As her eyes widened, Maya realized that Dane was no longer wearing his military mask with her. No, he was just a man. A gentle, quiet man who had moved through her heart and soul like a warm breeze over a cold winter landscape.

Dane removed his hand. He knew he was taking a terrible risk by touching Maya a second time. Yet his intuition gnawed at him to keep contact with her. He saw much of the confusion leave her eyes as he'd placed his hand over hers for that precious moment.

"I—uh, don't remember much…at least, not now," Maya began with an effort. "I couldn't believe there were three Kamovs." Her brows knitted. "Dane…he's got three of those gunships now. That's bad news for us. He must have bought another one.'' Closing her eyes, Maya whispered emotionally, ''That's going to up the ante. My pilots are really going to be targets now. We can't paint the Kamovs, dammit.''

''Hey,'' he soothed as he leaned forward and once more grazed the crown of her head, ''don't even buy into that stuff right now.'' Maya barely opened her eyes, and he saw tears glimmering in the depths of them. His heart contracted. Sliding off the stool, Dane leaned over the rail. Framing her face with his hands, he said quietly, ''Listen to me for once, will you? We've got two D models sitting out there. They're more than a match for the Kamovs. Just as soon as we can get your pilots retrained in them, you're going to have *four* aircraft that can combat anything Faro's got to throw against us out there. Okay?''

All her fears rose to the surface. Maya fought the heat of the tears in her eyes. When Dane gently framed her face, a sob worked its way up her slender throat. Mouth moving, she fought not to cry. How incredibly gentle he was with her. How sensitive to her needs right now. As his hands left her face, her tears drifted down her cheeks. He was smiling down at her, his eyes burning with a tenderness she'd never seen before. Reaching out, Dane carefully removed the trail of tears with his thumbs. His touch was so fleeting, and Maya found herself starved for more of whatever he was feeding her right now. Maybe it was her present medical condition that made her excruciatingly vulnerable to him. She wasn't sure.

''I shouldn't be crying...I can't let my people see me cry....'' And she compressed her lips.

Dane settled back on the chair and gripped her hand within his. ''Listen, you run a squadron, Maya, and I'm sure you've shed a lot of tears in private for your people already. I know you have.'' He gave her a tender look while squeezing her hand. ''Behind closed doors, where no one can see you cry.''

Her fingers closed shyly about his. Dane's heart soared with euphoria. His gut feeling that she needed to be touched, to be held, had been correct, after all. For once he was doing something right by Maya—something good, not combative or argumentative. She was not erecting those walls against him, either. If anything, moment by moment, Maya was becoming wonderfully human with him. It was such an incredible gift that Dane was afraid he'd somehow blow it and ruin the tender, healing warmth that swirled invisibly between them.

Sniffing, Maya closed her eyes. "Your hand feels good, Dane. I'm feeling a little wimpy right now...."

He sat there realizing how much bravery it took for Maya to admit that to him. She'd never given him an inch before, not ever. Patting her hand gently, he rasped unsteadily, "A brush with death always makes us see the world a little more clearly. We begin to value what's really important—and what isn't."

Drowning beneath his warm blue gaze, Maya felt a new strength flowing from him into her. "You're right," she whispered. She understood on a deeper level that he was healing her with his heart. The look in Dane's eyes was one she had never anticipated. It was the look of a man who cared for his woman. She wasn't any stranger to a look like that. How could he even *like* her? None of this made any sense to her. Not at all.

"You saved my life, Dane. I want to thank you—"

"Shhh," he whispered. "I think, right now, Maya, you need to sleep. You've got dark rings under your eyes and they're getting darker by the minute."

Her mouth quirked as she stared up at him. He had that slight, boyish smile now, his head cocked, his eyes a stormy blue as he gazed down at her. How handsome Dane was. How strong. How caring. The nurturing feeling coming from him was undeniable.

"Like you don't?" she managed to retort in a croak.

His grin widened. "We have the time," he told her huskily. Releasing her hand, he eased off the stool. Pulling the covers up a little, to tuck her in, he held Maya's green gaze as it followed his every move. "I didn't lose three pints of blood," he told her lightly. "You did. I'm going to let you sleep. The next time you wake up, that AB blood ought to be here from Lima."

Nodding, Maya whispered, "You're right...."

"If you want me to come back to visit you and make a pest out of myself, let Angel or Dr. Cornell know, okay?"

She saw the hesitancy in Dane's eyes and heard it in his voice as he stood there, one hand on the railing. "You saved my life. I think I owe you something."

Dane shook his head and sobered. "Maya, you owe me *nothing.* You hear me? After what I did to you...to all the women pilots at Fort Rucker...if I can atone just a little by giving you some of my blood, that doesn't justify me thinking you want me around you. It doesn't make up for all the pain I caused you, not by a long shot. I don't expect anything from you." He grimaced. "I'm just trying to help instead of hurting you, this time around...."

She felt his pain within her heart. Tiredness was making her feel very sleepy. How badly Maya wanted to lift her hand and place it over his, but she was too weak to even do that. "Listen," she murmured, exhausted, "we need to talk... later...when we're both feeling better. Okay?"

Nodding, Dane said, "You let me know when, sweetheart. I'll be hanging around like a bad cold." He froze momentarily when he realized the endearment had slipped out of his mouth. Instantly, his gaze settled on Maya. He thought she'd be outraged.

Sweetheart. The word rolled off his tongue like honey. Maya absorbed the warmth behind it. She lapped it up like the starving jaguar that she was. Before she could answer, she heard him walking away. As the door opened and closed, she fell into a deep, healing sleep. Her last thoughts were that when her sister arrived, she would ask Inca to not only heal her, but to heal Dane as well. He deserved it.

Dane jerked awake. He'd been sleeping on one of the gurneys in the dispensary. What time was it? Looking down at his watch, he realized he had slept at least six hours. Hearing voices, he sat up and rubbed his face. When he realized they were coming from the hospital section, he slid off the gurney. Was Maya okay?

Dizziness struck him. Dr. Cornell had warned him that he wasn't going to feel very lively for a while. The blood had arrived from Lima much earlier, and he'd gotten a transfusion of two pints of AB blood and was now medically stable. Maya had been given another pint, so that she was now back at the level she should be.

It was 0300. Rubbing his face, exhaustion eating at him, Dane stumbled drowsily toward the doors. Pushing them open, he saw Dr. Cornell standing with another woman. Halting, Dane stared openmouthed for a moment.

The woman, who was dressed in jungle fatigues, black boots and a sleeveless green T-shirt, turned toward him as he entered. Her willow-green eyes assessed him. He felt as if someone had just scorched him with a flamethrower. Standing there, Dane realized with a jolt that this was Inca, Maya's fraternal twin. Their looks were remarkably similar, and yet he saw the dissimilarity, too. Inca was as tall as Maya, but she was small boned, like a slender bird.

"Come in," Elizabeth invited in a warm voice. "We were just going to come and get you, Major York."

Maya, who was sitting up in bed, leaned forward between the two women. She held out her right hand toward him. "Dane. Come over. Meet my sister, Inca. Inca, this is Dane York, the guy who saved my life."

Feeling as though he were breaking in on a party that he'd not been invited to formally, Dane moved hesitantly. "Inca, it's a pleasure to meet you." He held out his hand in her direction as he approached her. Those willow-green eyes scanned him. Once more, Dane felt heat rock through him. Who was this woman? She was a healer, whatever that meant.

Inca slid her roughened hand into his. "You have saved my sister's life. I am grateful." She gripped his hand solidly.

Surprised at her strength, Dane gazed past Inca to Maya. She looked surprisingly well. There was color back in her face. And her eyes glowed with life again. Even more, he realized she was sitting up on her own in the bed. No longer was she weak as a newborn kitten, as he'd seen her hours earlier.

Releasing Inca's hand, he stood there marveling at Maya's change in condition. "That extra blood really worked," he said to Dr. Cornell, impressed.

Maya grinned wickedly at him. "The blood transfusion helped," she told him in a conspiratorial tone, "but look at what Inca just did for me. She healed me." Holding up her left arm, no longer swathed in bandages, Maya pointed to a slight pink scar where the Plexiglas had cut into her arm.

Inca stepped aside and allowed the army officer to move to Maya's bedside to get a closer look at her arm.

"Look," Maya urged him, and raised her arm so that Dane could observe where the wound had once been. "Isn't that something? Inca is so good at what she does."

Disbelievingly, Dane stared at the slight scar. Reaching out, he gently ran his fingers across her arm where the injury had once been. "Impossible," he breathed. "I saw this less than twelve hours ago. That wound was deep...."

Inca's husky laughter filled the room. "You were right, my sister. He does not want to believe that the power of touch can heal another."

Maya lowered her arm and smiled patiently at Dane. He looked confused. And tired. Her heart went out to him. "If you want, Inca will perform a healing on you, too."

Elizabeth stepped aside and brought the stool up for Dane

to sit on. "If you do, Major, you'd better sit down before you fall down." She smiled over at Inca, who stood near the end of Maya's bed. "Inca's well known for her healing abilities, and people who have experienced it say that it's like lightning striking them. Do you want to sit?"

Dane hesitated.

Maya saw it. "Let him think about it, Elizabeth."

Studying Inca, Dane said, "I don't know that I believe in such a thing."

Inca's lips stretched knowingly. "I have no desire to push myself upon you, Major. I heal only when asked to do so. If you do not want a healing, you do not have to have one."

Again, Dane stared at Maya's newly healed arm. It was impossible that it should look like that. Yet she was clearly more alert, her eyes sparkling once more, and she had that slight, careless smile on her full lips that he had hungered to see.

"Don't be bullheaded about this, Dane," Maya said. "Come, sit down. Just let my sister put her hands on you. I promise you'll feel a lot better than you look right now."

Her cajoling made him sit tentatively on the stool. "I guess it can't hurt anything," he muttered uneasily.

Elizabeth chuckled. "Major, you're in South America now, where magic meets reality every single day of the year. I'm a Harvard-trained physician and I can assure you, when I came down here three years ago I hadn't a clue as to what really goes on around here. This place—" she looked around, giving him a slight smile "—is an incredible place of mystery, magic and real life all rolled into one. You can't take your *norte americano* ideas and force them to work down here." She turned to Inca and regarded her warmly. "Inca is a jaguar priestess. She has been trained to heal. To help. Her works in the villages of Brazil are legendary. They call her the jaguar goddess over there, and with good reason." Elizabeth's forest-green eyes sparkled. "I've seen Inca in action before, so I'm not surprised at what she's done for Maya or her wound. If you really want to understand South America, Major, I would suggest you release your rigid ideas and just go with the flow here.''

''Okay...I'm convinced....'' Dane gave Maya a wry look. ''I'll do this because I trust you.''

Trust. Maya's heart fluttered as he spoke that word to her. She nodded and met his serious look with sincerity. ''Trust is earned...and I entrusted myself to you and you didn't let me down. You saved my life. Let Inca work on you. I promise you will feel better afterward.''

Nodding, Dane took a deep breath and settled himself on the stool. Looking up at Inca, who had a very serious expression on her face, he said, ''Okay, Inca, I'm ready. Fire away.''

Inca's mouth barely hitched into a smile. She moved forward and stood behind him, her hands coming to rest on his broad shoulders.

''Very well, Major. You have asked. Close your eyes, take a deep breath and release it. They will do the rest....''

Dane expected nothing. Yet, the moment he released that breath from within him, he felt Inca's hands become like hot brands against his skin. He felt the startling heat flow out of her hands, and within seconds he felt as if he were being consumed in searing flames. Sweat popped out on his forehead. He took in another jerky breath. A deep one. An explosion of colors popped like Fourth of July fireworks behind his eyelids. In seconds, he felt heat. And then, moments later, a cooling breeze moved down through the top of his head and swept all the way down to his feet. The rainbow colors ceased. What he saw next startled him even more: the face of a yellow jaguar with black spots staring back at him. And then the vision was gone as quickly as it had appeared.

''There,'' Inca said, satisfaction in her voice as she lifted her hands away from him. ''It is done. The Mother Goddess has healed you.''

Dane slowly opened his eyes. He felt a new sense of vibrancy, of energy, throbbing through him, like a fountain pulsing with renewed life. He saw Inca move to the other side of the bed and place her hand over Maya's. The sisterly love between them was undeniable. They were both grinning like there was a joke between them, but he didn't know what the punch line was.

Elizabeth came up and placed a steadying hand on his shoulder. "How do you feel, Major?"

Dane sat there for a moment, unsure. Inca laughed huskily. He heard Maya laugh with her. Blinking several times, he looked up at the doctor. "Fine...great...like I just got an incredible kick of energy into me...."

Maya heard the awe in his tone and saw it in his eyes. She squeezed Inca's long, roughened hand. "Thank you...and thank them, too...."

Nodding, Inca said, "I think it is time both of you go to sleep. You each need your rest. Come dawn tomorrow, you will feel good once more."

Maya smiled up at her sister. "Can you stay a little while? I know you have a lot going on in Brazil right now."

"I will stay a day," she said. "But then I must go. My husband misses me. And I miss him."

Maya nodded. How she wished that she could find a man like Roan Storm Walker, who was Inca's partner. She had met him several times, and always she was impressed with his quiet, strong demeanor. Together, he and Inca were working in Brazil to protect the Indians from the miners and those who would cut down the rain forest.

"Good," Maya whispered, releasing her hand. "Because I want to spend at least a little while with you...to catch up on gossip and that sort of thing."

Inca raised one thin, black eyebrow. Her gaze settled on the army officer. "My sister, I think what would be best for your healing was if you were to spend some time with the major, too."

Stunned, Dane got up. "No," he replied, his partial laugh

strained, "I don't think Captain Stevenson wants to spend any more time with me than she has to, Inca." Dane tried to avoid the shocked expression on Maya's face as he lifted his hand in farewell. "I'm going to hit the rack. Thanks, Inca." He held his hand out to her and shook hers warmly. "I'll see all of you later. Good night..."

Chapter 9

"I have wonderful news, my sister," Inca said after Dane left, and the hospital was quiet once more. She reached out and gripped Maya's hands, which rested on her blanketed lap.

Anything was better than having to respond to Inca's statement about her seeing more of Dane York. Still, Maya felt guilt eat at her over the reply Dane had made before he left. Why couldn't she have been a little more sensitive to him? A little more kind, rather than lying here staring at him after Inca's unexpected suggestion? Discarding her morose thoughts, she turned toward Inca and saw joy burning in her sister's eyes. She placed her hand over Inca's long, strong fingers. "What? Tell me. I could use some good news." She laughed a little unsteadily.

"Well," Inca whispered huskily, "when I received word that you were badly injured, I was upset. I talked it over with Roan. I decided to try and teleport and not wait to fly by airplane from Brazil to Peru." She wrinkled her nose and laughed demurely. "Now, I know members of the Black Jaguar Clan have teleporting as their specialty, and others of the Jaguar Clan must work at it for a long time before they learn the skill, *if* they do."

"You've done it before," Maya said, searching her memory. "You teleported into Peru when Mike Houston's wife, Ann, was in trouble. Right?"

"Yes, that was the one and only time I was able to do it successfully." Inca released her hand and pulled the leather thong from around her neck. A jaguar claw was suspended from the end of it. "When I met Ann, I gave her one of my two jaguar claws. I told her if she ever needed me, to call me, and I would be there." She tucked the claw beneath her dark green T-shirt again. Reaching out, she captured Maya's hand once more, her eyes gleaming with excitement.

"It worked! I was so surprised. But I was happy, too, because if I could not have been there, Ann would have died before Michael could have reached her himself."

"It was very brave of you," Maya murmured, knowing the story well. "And I know Mike Houston is forever grateful to you."

Inca nodded and licked her lower lip. "Listen, there is more!" Eagerly, she leaned forward. "Roan agreed I should try to teleport. Well, you know how you must be feeling in a very peaceful and harmonious place in order to attempt it?"

Rolling her eyes, Maya said, "No kidding. Ninety percent of the time when I try to do it, I'm not in a state of harmony. I can't control my emotional state that well to make it happen, so don't feel bad."

"How true," Inca murmured wryly. "I felt that, to reach you, I could do it, Maya. Roan supported my decision. I went into our meditation room, sat down and closed my eyes. I began to do the breathing exercise that we were taught, when suddenly Grandmother Alaria materialized in the room!" Her voice was filled with awe. "Can you imagine my surprise when she appeared? This is the first time she has ever visited me like that."

Maya's brows rose. "Wow. Yeah, that's extreme all right. Why did she appear to you? What was going down?"

Gripping Maya's hands, Inca grinned broadly. "She told me that I could not teleport to you. That I must take the airplane instead. I was shocked. I asked why. I told her how seriously wounded you were. Grandmother raised her hand and gave me that look she gives us...."

Maya laughed weakly. "Yeah, the 'look.' I know it well."

"She said that you were going to be all right. She had gazed into the future and seen that you would live. And," Inca's voice wobbled slightly as she added, "she said I could not teleport because I was with child! And when one is pregnant, one cannot teleport or it could harm the babies."

Maya gasped. She saw the joy dancing in Inca's willow-green eyes. "Babies? You're pregnant?"

Inca gave her a proud look. "Twins, Maya. Grandmother Alaria said I was carrying twins."

Shocked, Maya sat there, her eyes widening.

Inca moved her hand tenderly to caress her abdomen. "She said our mother's side always had twins, and that we carry this heritage within us." Her eyes shone. "And they are fraternal—one boy and one girl, Grandmother Alaria said."

"Oh, this is *wonderful* news, Inca!" Maya placed her arms around her sister's shoulders and hugged her as hard as she could. They sat there and held one another, laughing and crying together.

Eventually, Maya eased away. She wiped her eyes, sniffed then found a box of tissues and pulled some out, handing them to her sister, who was still sniffling. They blew their noses together and wiped their eyes. Maya's grin was uneven.

"Hey, this makes me an *aunt twice over!* How about that?"

Laughing, Inca blotted her eyes self-consciously. "Yes. You will be an aunt." Reaching out, she gripped Maya's hand. "Do you realize what this means? It means that these babies I carry will have a *family,* Maya. They will know who their mother and father are, who their aunt is...." Inca pressed her hand against her trembling lower lip and stared at her twin. Tears spilled down her cheeks.

"Oh, Inca..." Maya whispered. Leaning over, she pulled Inca into her arms and just held her. She knew all too well the pain of abandonment that Inca's early loss of their parents had caused her. Maya knew that in a way, she had been the lucky one; she had been adopted two weeks after their parents had been murdered, by the colonel and his wife at the American embassy in São Paulo. Inca, on the other hand, had been passed from jaguar priestess to priest, all her life, until she was sixteen years old, when she'd gone to the Village of the Clouds to begin her metaphysical training in the Jaguar Clan.

Pressing a kiss to Inca's hair, Maya squeezed her eyes shut. Hot tears jammed into them. She heard the relief, the pain and the joy in Inca's weeping. All she could do was hold her sister, rock her gently and let her cry. There was such beautiful strength and caring in Inca. And at the same time, such a bleeding wound in her heart from the trauma of being abandoned and not knowing that she had any family at all. Inca had searched all her life for family. And when she'd gotten kicked out of the Village of the Clouds for making a bad decision, she had lost the only close relations she'd known. It had devastated her.

Hurting for her past pain, Maya pressed her cheek against Inca's hair and gently ran her hand slowly up and down her long, strong back. Murmuring words of comfort, she felt grateful that she had her foster family, who loved her, as she loved them. Understanding how much the twins meant to Inca, and to her husband, Roan, Maya knew that this would help Inca heal even more since their marriage. Smiling through her tears, Maya whispered, "You're twice blessed, Inca. I'm so happy for you and Roan. These little babies you carry are gonna be the luckiest kids alive. You'll spoil them rotten. You'll be such a great mother...."

Inca pulled out of her arms and used her hands to wipe the tears from her face. Her eyes were red rimmed, but she was smiling. After blowing her nose, she took several more tissues to blot her eyes. "Grandmother Alaria said I was two months along. I did not realize it. I had missed two moons, but I thought it was because of all the stress we were under."

Maya moved several damp strands of black hair away from Inca's cheek. "How wonderful. I'm so happy for you. Does Roan know yet?"

Inca smiled. "Yes, I told him right away. He picked me up, Maya, and he twirled me around in a circle until we were both so dizzy we fell on the floor. We laughed. We held one another. And we cried. But they were tears of joy, not pain."

Maya leaned back against the pillows. She felt exhausted and knew it was because of the power of Inca's healing. She held her sister's damp, happy gaze. "I can't think of two people more deserving than you and Roan."

"He is going to fly me to his home in North America. I will meet his family. I am excited but scared. I do not know what they will think of me."

"They'll see you as part of their family," Maya murmured soothingly as she reached out and patted Inca's hand. "Don't worry. I'm sure they're going to be as happy as you are about your babies." She grinned a little. "So a girl and a boy? Is that what Grandmother Alaria told you?"

Nodding, Inca put another tissue in the pile collecting on Maya's bedcover. "Yes, she is positive of this." Her lips curved softly. "And I have been in contact with their spirits already, Maya. It is wonderful. They are so excited about coming into the world through me. They are very strong spirits. Spirits with a purpose."

"Hmm, I don't doubt that. Look at you, how strong and mission oriented you are."

Laughing, Inca said, "As if you are not?"

"Guilty as charged."

Looking around the small hospital room, Inca whispered, "When I touched you, to allow the healing energies to come through to you, I felt great loneliness in you, my sister."

Frowning, Maya nodded. She avoided Inca's gaze, resting thoughtfully upon her. Maya knew that during a healing, all aspects of a person—their thoughts, their pain, their joy, their past and present—were available for the healer to perceive. "Yeah, I feel a little alone, I guess."

Inca slid off the bed and straightened her T-shirt. Her gaze never left Maya. "You feel very alone, my sister. Why?"

One corner of Maya's mouth quirked. "It comes with the territory here, Inca. As a squadron commander with fifty-some people under my care, I get a little worried about them, their safety, especially with Faro Valentino's Kamovs out there. That's what got me into this mess—a third Kamov came out of nowhere and nailed me and Dane. We were lucky it didn't blow us out of the sky."

"Sometimes, when a person must carry such heavy loads, having a partner helps," Inca murmured, coming back to the bed and placing her hand on Maya's slumped shoulder.

"A partner?" Maya said. "You can't share a squadron command position, Inca. I have Dallas, and she's a great X.O."

"No," Inca replied, gripping her by the shoulder and giving her a small shake, "I am talking about a partner who can hold you, as you just held me as I cried in your arms. A man who can complete you. Give you a harbor of safety when you are feeling very vulnerable and naked to the world around you."

Maya stared up at Inca. Even though her twin didn't have the schooling or the worldliness that she did, the wisdom in her eyes touched Maya to her soul. She felt a little frightened by how much Inca saw in her, and yet Maya knew she was safe with her sister.

"Even now, I feel your fearful response, my sister."

"Yeah...well, for twenty-five-plus years I've gone on alone in an emotional sense, Inca. Somewhere in myself, before I found out the truth about us, that you were my sister—I felt alone. Alone in a way that most people don't have a clue about." Scowling, Maya whispered, "Just having you around, being able to talk to you, contact you, has helped me a lot, whether you know it or not." She gave her a lopsided smile, tears coming yet again to her eyes.

Inca nodded, her own eyes gentle with understanding. "Our love as sisters is one thing, Maya. I talk of another love. The kind that Roan and I share."

"Oh...that..." Maya rolled her eyes. "Forget it."

"What? That you could love a man? That he would support you, care for you, hold you when you felt so alone and burdened?"

"Inca, you're naive. I know you mean well, but you know the rules of the Black Jaguar Clan. We're here to do the dirty work. We're the dark underbelly of the Jaguar Clan." She looked around and gestured. "This cave, this squadron, is what I do best. This is my mission. It doesn't leave me *any* time for a private life. I'll never be big on marriage, kids and family. In a sense, I'm a big mother hen to fifty-some people. I handle people problems twenty-four hours a day. I have no *time* for something like that, Inca."

"So," she whispered, "who holds you when you feel like crying?"

Wincing, Maya avoided Inca's probing look. "You might be naive, but you aren't dumb," she muttered.

Moving quietly to the window, Inca pushed the white curtain aside and watched the activity within the cave for a long moment before she turned again. When she did, she saw Maya frowning, working hard to keep her emotions at bay.

"When I placed my hands on Dane, he had a similar feeling in him."

Maya snapped her head up and looked across the aisle to where Inca was standing. Her sister had placed her hands on her hips and stood watching her from the shadows. "There are a lot of lonely people around," Maya muttered defensively. "So what?"

"He cares for you, Maya."

Snorting, she dragged in a deep breath and said, "I'm sure it's out of guilt over the way he treated me and the other women pilots who had the misfortune to be studying under him."

Shaking her head, Inca slowly moved from the shadows into the light, halting near the end of Maya's bed. Picking at the coverlet, she murmured, "No, his turmoil is not about guilt. I know the difference between those emotions. He is lonely like you. He is a man with many responsibilities, who carries as many burdens on his shoulders as you do. Perhaps, if you find time in the coming days as you rest and recuperate from this trauma you have endured, you might spend some time with him."

"Oh, and do what? Talk about the weather?" Maya moved uncomfortably. She wanted to get up, get dressed and get back to work. However, Dr. Cornell had ordered bed rest for the next two days. Tomorrow, one way or another, Maya intended to work half a day at her office, whether the doctor approved it or not. She was off the flight-duty roster for a full week. That put an added strain on the pilots who had to keep flying, which bothered Maya greatly.

Inca laughed softly. "Ah, I see you trying to evade me, my sister. No, you do not need to talk of the weather with him. He is a man of deep convictions, of goodness. Perhaps you can explore those things with him?"

"Look, I owe him my life," Maya muttered darkly, "isn't that enough? I think what he did for me more than rights the wrongs from the past, as far as I'm concerned."

"That is good—you are willing to forgive. That is a start." Inca smiled again. "I felt him, Maya. I felt his heart. I grazed his spirit. He has his weaknesses, but do we not all have them?"

Maya gave Inca a strange, unsettled look. "What are you trying to do? Just because you're pregnant and going to be a mommy, do you think you can be a matchmaker, too?"

Inca raised her brows. "The words you use, I do not know them all." She opened her hands guilelessly. "What is 'matchmaker'?"

"Humph."

Laughing, Inca moved to Maya's shoulder. She reached out and smoothed her dark hair into place around her neck and shoulder.

"If I didn't know better, Inca, I'd think you're trying to tell me that Dane York likes me or some such hooey."

"Me?"

"Yeah, you. And don't give me that completely innocent look. We're twins, remember? We can read each other like an open book."

Chuckling, Inca folded her hands together and kept on smiling. "I know how stubborn you are. I am the same. I am asking you to see Dane differently than you have been seeing him."

"Dammit," Maya exclaimed softly, giving Inca an uncomfortable look, "he's prejudiced against women!"

"And you are equally prejudiced against men."

Stunned, Maya stared at Inca, the silence swirling between them. Her sister was grim faced now, her willow-green eyes narrowed. Inca was not teasing. She meant it. Averting her gaze, Maya looked down at the covers, the floor, the doors at the other end of the facility. Working her mouth, she finally turned back and met Inca's eyes.

"You're right."

Reaching over, Inca patted her tightly clasped hands. "If you have the wisdom and humility to acknowledge your own weakness, as he does, then there is hope."

"Dammit, Inca, I didn't need to hear that from you."

"What? The hope or the prejudice?" Inca tilted her head and studied Maya's scowling features. "You are like two jaguars. You both have the same spots, the same color of coat. Sometimes—'' she lifted her hands expressively ''—when one meets someone who is just like them, they fight it—fight the other person, because what they see in them they see in themselves. But they will never admit it, of course.''

''That's called projection,'' Maya growled. ''A psychological term.''

''Oh. Well, am I not correct?''

''Yes, dammit, you are.''

''I would think you would be happy, realizing this weakness you both share.''

''It's complicated, Inca. I know you see the world very simply. I don't. I can't. You don't live out in the real world like I do. It's a helluva lot more complex a situation, believe me. Dane York is like a Gordian knot to me and my world…my life. Recently, it's gotten even murkier, so I'm feeling damned vulnerable toward him right now. I don't know whether he's a good guy or a bad guy. He used to be nothing but bad in my book.''

Sighing, Inca whispered, ''My sister, none of us are either all bad or good. You know that from your training. Why do you not apply what you know to him? I could feel the wounding in you that he created. And when I touched him, felt him, I felt his desire to heal this wound between you.'' She tapped Maya's hands. ''You must forgive and move on now. He is trying very hard to please you. To get you to forgive him. He *is* trying, Maya.''

''Okay, okay.'' Maya made an irritated gesture with her hand. ''I hear you.''

''Part of the Black Jaguar Clan schooling is to learn to forgive. Those born into the clan are learning through their wounding. You have an opportunity here, my loving sister. Why do you think the Great Mother Goddess set up what happened to you? I feel that if you had not resisted Dane's offer to find peace and forgiveness between you in the first place, it would not have come to this—this injury to yourself." Inca shrugged. "Sometimes, when we become too stubborn, too set in our ways, something traumatic must happen in order to allow a door to swing open. When it does, you can choose to walk through it or not with the other person involved." She smiled unevenly, tears glimmering in her eyes. "I do not think it an accident that his blood now moves through your body. He is a part of you, yes? And you cannot war against someone whose blood is part of you, can you?"

"I hear you, Inca." Maya whispered unhappily. "I don't like it, but I hear you. And I know you're right. I also understand why I'm in the Black Jaguar Clan. I'm not so evolved, spiritually, as you are. I'm still learning some of the basics, like not taking revenge, feeling hatred and stuff like that." Maya lifted her head and met Inca's softened gaze, now filled with tender compassion for her. "And I'm not so stupid as to realize, symbolically, what happened between me and him. It's just...a shock, that's all. I feel...right now...like the world's closing in on me. I've got three Kamov's to worry about. I have this training for the D model to get underway. I have Dane's old prejudice to fight in myself every time I lay eyes on him. There's just so much going on right now. I feel so damned raw and vulnerable...."

"My sister," Inca whispered gently, "we all undergo such tests, and you are in a test right now. You have gone through them many times before. All I am saying is do not make Dane your enemy while he is here. If you can forgive him, you forgive yourself. Your prejudice toward men is no less wounding as his is against women. Somehow, you must let all that go. Somehow, you must drop your armor and allow who you are, your vulnerable, good side, to show itself to him."

"Yeah, right, and he'll gut me right where I stand."

Inca shook her head. "You are wrong. You must trust me on this, Maya."

Giving her a dark look, Maya rasped, "Dammit, this is

hard, Inca!'' Looking around, she muttered, ''There are days when I want to say to hell with this whole thing. There are days when I don't want to know what I know, metaphysically speaking. I just wish I was like every other blind, deaf and dumb human being down here.'' Maya clenched her fist, her voice turning raw with anger. ''I just want to walk away from the mission at times. Away from being in the Black Jaguar Clan. I get sick of it! I get sick of the responsibility, and knowing I'm damn well going to pay for whatever choices I make, right or wrong, because of my knowing.'' Her voice cracked. ''Right now, it's just too much. Don't spew metaphysical pabulum at me, Inca. I can't handle one more stone on the load I'm carrying on these shoulders, all right?''

Nodding, Inca slid her arm around Maya's tense shoulders and hugged her for a long, long time. When she finally released her, she whispered, ''Sometimes our greatest enemy can become our greatest ally.''

Dane was sitting at his office desk the next morning, working on the fine points of the training schedule that would be initiated shortly. Again and again he resisted calling in at the dispensary to ask Dr. Cornell how Maya was doing. Earlier this morning, Inca had left. He'd been pleasantly surprised when she'd dropped by his office to tell him goodbye. She had shared the news with him that she was pregnant with twins. The look in her eyes made him smile self-consciously. Inca was so open, so available emotionally compared to Maya, that he'd reeled when she'd shared the good news with him. She didn't treat him coldly, or as if he were an unwelcome stranger. Just the opposite. She had gifted him with several sprays of orchids, yellow with red lips, and told him to give some of them to Maya when she got back to her office duties.

Inca's eyes had been sparkling, and Dane could almost feel as if there was some underlying reason for her giving him the orchids, but he didn't know what it was.

Inca had suggested that he visit Maya at the dispensary that morning. He muttered that he might, if he could get the schedule completed, but he made no specific promise. The way Inca regarded him, with those thoughtful, compassionate eyes of hers, made his heart contract with pain and need—for Maya.

Trying to shake off thoughts of the early morning meeting, Dane rested his hand against his brow and studied the complex schedule before him. This was a helluva undertaking, and it wasn't easy trying to fit training time for the pilots in between the missions they flew daily against Faro Valentino's aircraft.

There was a soft knock at his opened door. Dane lifted his head. It was Maya. She was standing there hesitantly, her hand on the doorjamb, looking at him with an unsure expression. Instantly, he was on his feet, his chair nearly tipping over. He caught it, straightening self-consciously beneath her gaze.

"I thought you were supposed to be in the hospital," he blurted, rubbing his hands down the sides of his thighs. Her eyes were soft looking and so was her mouth. She was dressed in her usual black flight uniform, which surprised him. Dane knew that the doctor had grounded Maya for a week, and she couldn't fly. The shadowy smudges beneath her glorious emerald eyes told him that her recovery was by no means a hundred percent.

"I was," she said wryly.

"Does Dr. Cornell know you've escaped the dispensary?"

Maya grinned a little. "No, but she'll find out soon enough when she goes to check on me during her rounds."

"I see...."

"I'm like a horse in harness. You can't put me out to pasture too long or I get bored and antsy."

"Yeah, I know that one, too."

"Are you feeling okay?" Maya asked. Dane looked almost

normal, but not quite. His flesh was still not back to its usual color, and there were hints of shadows beneath his eyes.

"I'm fine...fine. And you?"

"I'm okay.... Feeling a little tired, is all." Motioning toward his desk, Maya asked, "Do you mind if I drop by for a visit...for just a moment?"

"Why, er, no...no, not at all. Let me get you a chair." He quickly moved from behind his desk and brought the only other chair to the center of his small office for her.

Maya's heart opened automatically. She saw a red flush staining Dane's cheeks. He was obviously rattled by her unexpected appearance. She had never come to his office since he'd arrived. Swallowing hard, she made her way to the chair and sat down.

"Thank you..."

Stunned by her friendly behavior, Dane didn't know what to think. His head swam with questions. Had Inca's healing done this to her? Or had the trauma of Maya's injury? Maybe she was just unguarded for the moment, but would return to her normal armored state shortly. He thought the latter, and yet he didn't try to erect his own armor to protect himself from whatever she might say to him.

"Coffee? I have coffee." He pointed to the machine behind his desk. Nervousness thrummed through him. Dane saw the uneasiness in Maya's eyes now. She was nervous, too. He could tell by the way she kept shifting around on the chair. Yet she was hurting and he knew it. Oh, it was nothing obvious, but he could sense it—by intuition, he guessed. Moving toward the coffeemaker, he raised a second cup toward her.

"Yes, I'd like some."

"It's strong," he warned.

"I need a strong cup of coffee," Maya said. "Put a little cream and sugar in it, will you?"

His hand shook as he poured coffee into the white, chipped ceramic cup. Laughing a little to ease the tension over her sudden, unexpected appearance, he said, "Now that you're being funded by Perseus, maybe the supply officer can get you in some decent coffee mugs. These have seen better days."

Maya laughed weakly. "Yeah, you're right." She watched as he carefully spooned sugar and creamer into the coffee. She saw his hand tremble. Maya had never seen Dane like this before. And then she realized that Inca's healing had probably opened him up, just as it had her. In her eyes, Dane was like a little boy trying hard to please her, to get her approval, even over such a small thing as a cup of coffee. Her heart opened more.

As he brought the cup to her and their fingers touched, she felt warmth flow up into her hand and wrist from their contact. She saw his eyes grow a smoky blue. She'd seen that look once before, when he'd visited her shortly after she became conscious. It made her feel safe. And cared for. This time, she didn't try and fight that energy sensation flowing from him. No, this time, she allowed it and, if she were honest with herself, welcomed it.

"Thanks," she whispered, taking the cup. Pressing it to her lips, she took a sip. He was standing there expectantly. "It's fine, Dane. Go sit down."

He grinned a little and nodded. "Okay."

Maya watched him take his seat. "You working on the schedule?"

Nodding again, he said, "Yeah, and I'm afraid you aren't going to like what I've come up with. But I'm damned if I can fine-tune it any more than I have because of the heavy-duty circumstances your squadron operates under." Dane gave her a worried look.

Maya sat with her legs crossed, the cup balanced on her lap between her hands. Did she know how beautiful she looked with her long, black hair curling around her shoulders, showing off that slender neck of hers? He thought not. Maya wore no makeup. She didn't need to. When he saw her fine, thin brows knit, his mouth quirked.

"I know you've been working nonstop on it when you weren't flying missions," Maya said, trying to defuse the worry and anxiety she saw in his blue eyes. "What's the problem?"

With a shrug, Dane dropped the pencil on the schedule and leaned back in his creaking chair. "You aren't going to be happy about this, but based upon how many flights your pilots are making daily, I have no choice."

Hearing the grim tone in his voice, Maya said, "Give me the bad news, then."

His heart shrank. Trying to steel himself against the reaction he knew was coming, Dane eased the chair down and set his elbows on the desk, staring directly across it at her. "We have a six-week training program. I know when we came here I said we'd stay for that amount of time. But given the number of flights, the demands on your people and the fact you're shorthanded, I don't have any choice."

"Choice? In what?"

Grimly, Dane looked down at the schedule. "According to my best estimates, Captain, it's going to take three times as long as anticipated to train all your people."

Maya sat there digesting his quietly spoken comment. She saw the worry in Dane's narrowed eyes. She felt his anxiety over her possible response to his statement. Compressing her lips, she said, "Okay…instead of you being here six weeks, we're looking at an extended training-in period of…eighteen weeks. Is that right?"

Dane marveled at the continued softness in her tone. Maya's eyes held no anger, only interest. Shocked that she hadn't come out of the chair or started to make angry comments, he sat there dumbfounded for a moment. "Er, yes…eighteen weeks."

"I see."

Dane held her gaze. Silence filled the void between them.

She sipped her coffee almost gratefully. Sitting up, Dane said, "And you're okay with that?" He tried to keep the disbelief out of his tone.

Shrugging, Maya said, "I wanted you to assess our flight demands against your training schedule, Dane. You did that. If that's what you've come up with, then I'm fine with it. What's wrong? You look like you just got hit by a freight train."

Blinking once, Dane opened his mouth and then closed it. Maya was giving him a wry look, a smile barely touching her full lips. No anger. No accusations. No…nothing. "Maybe I have been," he admitted in a hushed tone, followed by a nervous laugh. How badly he wanted to just stare at Maya. How badly he ached to have just a normal, human-to-human conversation with her. She looked hauntingly vulnerable right now. Scratching his head, Dane muttered, "I just thought you might be upset that we'd be here a lot longer than you wanted us here, was all. I know we're not all that welcome…well, *I'm* not welcome. The rest of my men aren't like me."

"Honest to a fault," Maya murmured. After sipping the coffee, she set the cup on the front of his desk. "Look, Dane…may I call you by your first name?"

He nodded. "Of course!" He tried to keep the shock out of his voice and face.

"My sister just gave me a good talking to," she admitted, amusement in her tone. "Inca's made me realize that I'm part and parcel of our ongoing problem."

Looking at her quizzically, Dane said, "I don't understand, Captain."

"Call me Maya, if you want." She slowly rose and stood before him. He was looking at her in utter shock—maybe because she was trying to be friendly. Or because she had called him by his first name. Unsure, and equally nervous, Maya opened her hand toward him. "We've both had a lot of water go under the bridge, from where I stand. You were prejudiced against women gunship pilots. Well—'' Maya grimaced ''—I was equally prejudiced against men. The pot calling the kettle black. I know...'' She hesitated. ''I know since you've arrived here you've been trying to bury the hatchet between us, and I haven't let you. Well, that's all changing as of now.'' Maya's voice deepened with barely held emotion. ''You didn't have to give your blood to me. I know that. Inca made me realize a lot of things this morning. I was just as blindly prejudiced against you as you were against us. I'm calling a halt to it, Dane. I want peace between us. Can you live with that?''

Chapter 10

"Maya?"

Dane's voice feathered across her. She felt his large, strong hand move gently across her shoulders.

"Ummph..."

"Come on, you need to get some sleep...."

Barely lifting her head off her crossed arms, which were resting on her desk, Maya forced her eyes open. She felt Dane lean over her, his lips very close to her ear. His moist breath flowed over her temple and brow. Strands of her hair tickled her nose as she looked up at him.

"What...what time is it?" she mumbled, sitting up and rubbing her face wearily.

"Too late," he growled. Easing her out of the chair, Dane pointed her toward the cot in the corner of her office. "Come on..."

Maya had lost count of how many times Dane had found her working late in her office. For the past three weeks, ever since their truce, he was like a big guard dog, always looking out for her, taking care of her in small but meaningful ways.

Right now, Maya appreciated his thoughtfulness as she felt him grip her upper arm, guiding her around the desk and to the cot.

Once she got there, she started to lie down.

"Take your boots off."

"Ohhh...I sleep with them on all the time, Dane."

"Not with me around. Come on. Just sit up and stick out your right foot."

Maya watched as he crouched down in front of her, his hand slipping around the heel of the boot she offered. Sleep warped her sense of time, and when she awakened she was always vulnerable. Somehow Dane knew that, because he always spoke to her in a soft, low tone. Appreciating him even more, Maya whispered, "You don't have to keep doing this, you know. I've been sleeping on this cot for three years straight."

Dane eased the boot off and set it aside. "Give me the other one."

Maya did so. Pushing the hair away from her face, she said, "What are *you* doing up so late?"

"Making sure *you* get some decent sleep under your belt."

Wrinkling her nose, Maya felt the boot slip off. "It's enough that *I'm* sleep deprived. Don't take on any of my bad habits."

Chuckling, Dane straightened. His heart contracted with joy as he watched Maya ease onto the cot and settle on her left side, as she always did. Picking up the blanket from the foot of the cot, he unfolded it and drew it across her form. Her dark hair pooled around her shoulders as she bent her legs up near her body, one hand beneath her cheek. Did Maya know how excruciatingly beautiful she really was? Dane didn't think so. One day, he wanted to tell her that. He spread the blanket over her shoulders, tucking her in.

"Good night, fairy tale princess," he whispered. He lifted his hand and stroked her hair. It was the thing he most looked forward to—touching Maya like this. Instantly, he saw the tension around her mouth ease. Her lips parted. She was already asleep.

Dane leaned over Maya and watched the soft rise and fall of her breasts. He'd made an exhilarating discovery three weeks ago when he'd awakened her after she'd fallen asleep while working on the mission reports and flight data. In her drowsy state, Maya was vulnerable. She seemed to *want* his touch, his nurturing as he helped her from the desk to the cot to catch three or four hours of badly needed sleep. The strain and tension was thick around the base since the third Kamov had showed up in Faro's arsenal. Dane had noticed as he'd take off her boots, pull the cover over her and simply stroke her hair, that all of that tension around Maya would dissolve. Would melt away, just like that.

Smiling tenderly down at her as she slept, Dane realized it was a backhanded compliment that Maya would relax with him so near to her. Her thick, black lashes lay against her golden skin. Her breathing was soft and rhythmic. Dane could see her sinking into a deep, deep slumber. Straightening, he shook his head. He didn't know how Maya managed to keep going on so little sleep. Dallas assured him that this wasn't normal, that Maya usually got six to eight hours. She felt it was due to the worry Maya had for her pilots, with the third Kamov being around. Dane couldn't argue with the X.O.'s logic.

Moving to the door, he closed it partially to stop the flood of light into her quiet office. Outside, the echoing sounds of two crews loading ordnance on the Apaches could be heard faintly. Living in a cave, Dane was discovering, had certain repercussions. Everything echoed. A wrench dropped on the lava floor, a person talking near the outer wall—everything reverberated back through the massive cavern.

Instead of leaving Maya's office, Dane glanced over his shoulder again. Something pulled him to stay. Hell, he needed sleep himself. He had taken on the responsibility of getting Maya away from her desk and to her cot because Dr.

Cornell had mentioned to him shortly after Maya had come back to work that she wasn't getting enough sleep. The doctor was worried and so was he. Scowling, he looked around the shadowy office. On Maya's desk were the yellow-and-red orchids that he'd given her. Orchids stayed in bloom a long time, he discovered—four to six weeks. And Maya had appreciated the spikes of orchids he'd given her. It was a daily reminder to him that she was allowing him to remain in her life, to get closer to her.

A sudden idea came to him. The corners of his mouth lifted and he nodded. Yeah, that was a helluva good plan. He'd see Dr. Cornell about it in the morning, and then spring it on Maya, if the doctor gave her approval.

Dane left her office and walked quietly down the hall toward the exit. He wondered how Maya would react to his creative inspiration.

"Maya, I'm officially ordering you to take forty-eight hours of R and R," Elizabeth Cornell told her sternly.

"What?" Maya sat on her cot, pulling on her boots. It was 0700 and she had overslept. Elizabeth stood before her in her dark green fatigues and white coat, her hands in the pockets, an authoritative look on her face.

"You heard me." Elizabeth tried to look severe, but it didn't quite come off as Maya stared at her, a half smile on her face. "And to make sure you do, I've ordered Major York to fly you to Cuzco. I had comms make you reservations at the Libertador Hotel." She shook her finger at Maya, who paused in the middle of putting on her boots and sat there, thighs apart, her hands resting between them. "The major is going to be your bodyguard of sorts. He'll fly you there in our civilian helo and fly you back. Got it?"

Maya laughed and pulled on the second boot. "Liz, you can't be serious!"

"Oh, she's dead serious," Dane said, coming into the office unannounced.

Looking up when she heard his low, modulated tone, Maya sat back and stared at him. He was dressed in a pair of jeans, hiking boots, a short-sleeved white shirt and a blue-and-yellow Saint Louis Rams baseball cap. The bill was pulled down so that it shadowed his narrowed eyes as they locked with her widening gaze.

"So," Dane told her smoothly, moving around Elizabeth, who was now looking quite pleased with herself and her prescription, "put these on." He tossed Maya some civilian clothes. "You need a shower, but I won't hold that against you. You'll get one at the hotel. It's only a thirty-minute hop from here."

Stunned, Maya picked up the clothes, which consisted of a pair of green nylon slacks and a short-sleeved, pink tank top. Dane handed her her hiking boots.

"Put these on, too," he told her briskly.

"But—"

"No buts," Elizabeth said darkly, a threat in her tone. "You're sleep deprived, Maya. And if you don't have the good sense to get the rest you need, then I, as flight surgeon, will ensure you do."

Dane stood there, a silly grin on his face, his hands draped casually across his hips as he looked at the doctor and then at Maya's nonplussed expression. "I think the doc's right, Maya." He looked at his watch. "Meet me down below in ten minutes. I know it doesn't take you long to change."

Frowning, Maya looked from one to the other. "You two are in cahoots on this. I can tell."

Elizabeth smiled triumphantly and traded a fond look with Dane. "You have two friends who care deeply about you, Maya. Listen to them for once, will you? It's not going to hurt anything if you leave this base for forty-eight hours. You'll be in constant contact, anyway. Dane, here, is just going to make sure you get the shut-eye you need."

"Yes, ma'am," Dane murmured to the doctor. "If I have

to put a padlock on her room at that five-star hotel and bring her room service, it will be done. You can roger that."

Giving them both a dirty look, Maya muttered, "Okay, okay...I know when I'm outgunned. Get out of here. Let me change my clothes in peace."

Someone knocked softly at her hotel room door. Maya made several muffled sounds of protest and slowly lifted her head from the feather pillow. It was dark in her room, but sunlight filtered in around the edges of the draperies. What time was it?

The knock came again. "Just a moment..." Maya called sleepily, and forced the covers off her. As she sat up, she felt the dregs of sleep still pulling at her. Stumbling to the door, she fumbled for the knob. Opening it, she squinted in the bright light coming from the hall, holding up her hand to protect her eyes.

Dane smiled. Maya was dressed in a wrinkled, pale pink cotton nightgown that fell to her knees. Her hair was in utter disarray. When she dropped her hand, he saw the puffiness beneath her eyes. "You've slept for eighteen hours. I thought I might wake you and get some food in you."

"Uhhh..." Maya frowned, looked down and then back up at him. Dane was dressed in a bright red polo shirt, tan chinos and his hiking boots. He looked devastatingly handsome. "What? Eighteen hours? You've got to be kidding!" She looked at the aviator's watch on her wrist, and was stunned to find out it was 8:00 a.m.

Dane saw several tourists coming down the hall toward them, speaking German. He didn't think Maya would want to be seen in her nightgown by strangers. "Let me come in for a sec," he coaxed. "Company's comin' down the hall." And he eased her back into her room and closed the door quietly behind him.

"Eighteen hours?" Her voice was thick and scratchy.

Maya looked at the watch again. "I don't believe it…." She stumbled off toward the bathroom.

Dane smiled sympathetically and pulled up the covers on the bed, then sat down. Picking up the phone, he ordered breakfast for both of them. It wasn't long before Maya came back. Her eyes were barely open, and they were still puffy. She was holding her hand against her brow as she walked toward him. He got off the bed and moved aside.

"I can't believe this…eighteen hours. I feel like I've been hit by a Mack truck." Maya sat down on the edge of the bed.

"You needed the sleep," Dane told her. Going to the bathroom, he found her hairbrush on the counter. Coming back, he followed his intuition and settled down next to her.

"Turn around," he told her, and guided Maya so that she sat with her back toward him. "This is something I've been wanting to do for a long time…." And he took the brush and began to pull it through the silky, thick strands of her hair.

Maya made a purring sound as he eased the brush across her scalp. The sensation was delicious. Surprising. And wonderful. Without thinking, she leaned back, and was glad when Dane allowed her to relax against him. He continued to draw the brush gently through her hair. When he was done, Maya allowed herself the luxury of simply being held by him. Pressing her head against his neck, she sighed.

"That was wonderful…thank you…."

Dane's heart was pounding. "You deserve a little care," he told her, his voice husky. He wanted to take Maya into his arms, press her back on the bed and kiss her until they melted into one another. Placing a choke chain on those desires, Dane absorbed the feel of having her tall, graceful form resting against him.

Maya's lips parted. With every moment that passed, she entrusted herself more and more to Dane and his strong, caring arms. How long had she wanted this to happen? Ever since she'd made peace with him over their past. He smelled of lime, probably from his shaving cream. Smiling a little, Maya absorbed his strength and the way he pressed his jaw against her hair.

"I never knew..." Maya whispered, her eyes closing.

"Knew what?" Dane held himself in check, fearful of doing something to scare Maya out of his arms. She was a woman who demanded respect, and he knew that if he overstepped the boundaries, she'd fly away like a startled dove. The sound of her voice was soft and faraway, as if she were still half-asleep.

"That a man could be so caring..."

"Even a man like me, eh?"

Maya laughed softly. "Especially you. I would never have guessed...."

Dane closed his eyes. He felt like a starving wolf having Maya in his arms. If she could read his mind, he was sure she'd run screaming away from him. His heart was pounding. His lower body was in a tortured knot of boiling heat and need. How badly he wanted to kiss her. Just kiss her. What would Maya's lips feel like? How many times had he thought about kissing her?

"I'm full of surprises," he joked softly.

"So am I."

"You? Naw. You're pretty predicable," he teased and smiled. Taking a risk, Dane pressed a small kiss on the top of her head.

Maya felt his mouth come to rest upon her hair. A delicious sensation, an awakening, flowed through her. She felt him laugh. The feeling flowed through her warmly. When he tightened his arms around her briefly, Maya felt incredibly safe. No one had ever given her that sense of safety before. Dane was a natural-born leader, and he had confidence to burn. In the past three weeks, since looking at him differently, Maya realized that Inca had been right: they were more alike than she'd ever realized. He'd worked hard to keep that connection with her. And she'd reciprocated.

It was loco, Maya decided—crazy magic. Somehow, the intense healing Inca had given them had opened up their hearts and their eyes, and now they saw one another differently. Better. More provocatively. Maya stirred in Dane's arms, her eyes still closed. Inhaling the male scent of him, she followed her own primal instincts. Shifting in his arms, she lifted her face to him and looked into Dane's hooded eyes. They were a smoky blue color.

For once, Maya wanted to leave her heritage behind. Just this one time, she wanted to resist past lessons learned, and pretend they'd never happened. For once she wanted to simply enjoy this man, explore him and feel the sense of connection that he was offering her. Maya saw the surprise in his eyes as she turned and lifted her lips to his. Surprise turned to raw desire and his black pupils grew large and intense with longing—for her. She felt his hands upon her arms, pulling her more deeply into his embrace. Her breasts pressed against his chest. With her breath hitching as his head came closer, closer, Maya shut her eyes and eased forward. She'd never wanted anything more than she wanted this moment with Dane.

As he closed his mouth across Maya's, a deep shudder went through Dane. Her lips were soft and tentative. Feeling her hesitancy, he placed massive control over his raging desire.

At first he was surprised. His mind churned despite the fire arcing through his body. Maya was vulnerable, and she was sending out a feeler of trust. Maybe, like him, she was a little afraid of the intimacy that the kiss she offered him signaled. Just knowing that gave Dane the patience to move his mouth tenderly across her lips, to let her know that he, too, was shy for the very same reasons.

Maya moaned softly as his mouth grazed hers with unexpected tenderness. Never in her wildest imaginings would she have thought Dane capable of this kind of sensitivity. Sliding her hand across his chest, she wrapped her fingers around the nape of his neck, wanting more of him. He'd shown that he could take her fear, her hesitancy, in stride. He wasn't about to blunder in.

Just knowing that he was attuned to her needs made Maya hunger for more of him. How could she have not realized that Dane was different from other men? Different in the most wonderful of ways? Lost in the glowing heat spreading throughout her belly, she felt his mouth cajole hers. He teethed her lower lip gently, wordlessly asking her to participate. His breath was ragged and moist across her cheek and nose. Maya felt the sandpapery quality of his face against hers. As he fitted his mouth fully against hers and rocked her lips open, Maya surrendered herself to him.

Easing his fingers through Maya's thick, luxurious hair, and framing her face with his hands, Dane kissed her deeply and thoroughly. She was at once wet, responsive, yielding and bold with him. There was a courageous quality to Maya. Even if she was still afraid, she was trusting him—despite their stained past. Inhaling her soft, sleepy scent, feeling her hair swirling silkily against his jaw, he eased his mouth from hers. Opening his eyes, their lips now barely touching, he looked down into her drowzy emerald gaze. The desire in her eyes, the sunlit gold flecks in them, called to him. Dane felt Maya's hand move across his shoulder to pull him forward so that he could ease back onto the bed, with him on top of her.

Just then, there was a sharp knock at the door.

"Room service."

Maya jumped.

Dane tensed.

She laughed softly as she released him. "Real life intrudes."

He gave her an apologetic grin and reluctantly stood up to

answer the door. "I thought what we were sharing was real life, too."

Maya smiled. "It's a dream."

Tipping the waiter, he took the tray into the room himself and set it on the round table located at the window, which overlooked Cuzco. Dane felt his body aching without relief. He wanted Maya, he didn't want food. Hearing her move around, Dane decided to stash those hopes away for another time and place. As he pulled the lids off the two plates filled with breakfast food, he saw Maya come to the table. She had her pink robe on, the color matching the high blush in her cheeks. Her hair was pleasantly mussed, and her mouth looked well kissed—by him.

"Coffee?" he asked as he sat down opposite her.

Maya nodded and placed the white linen napkin in her lap. Her heart was pounding. She could still taste Dane on her lips. Giving him a wry look as he handed her the china cup filled with coffee, she said, "I didn't mean to kiss you...but I'm not sorry I did, either."

Pouring himself coffee, Dane gave her an amused look. "Don't be looking for an apology from me."

Maya ate in silence. Her mind churned. Her heart somersaulted. There was something so strong, so good in Dane that she sat there feeling like an idiot. Inca had seen it. Why hadn't she herself detected it a long time ago? He was a strong, capable man, a man with feelings. He had an incredible sensitivity, an ability to know her, what she wanted and needed, without her ever saying a word to him. Maya knew how unusual that was in a man. Paying attention to her scrambled eggs and slathering her toast with strawberry jam, Maya knew the answer. She had been projecting all her own stuff onto him so she couldn't see who Dane York really was.

"What do you want to do today?" Dane asked lightly as he spooned eggs into his mouth.

With a slight, embarrassed laugh, Maya said, "Well, after

sleeping eighteen hours straight, I think I ought to get off my duff, don't you?" She tilted her head and caught his amused expression. "How about if I show you Cuzco? If you love architecture or history, this is the place to be."

"I like both," Dane said. What he really wanted to do was get up and drag Maya over to the bed to finish the delicious exploration they'd started earlier. Dane knew that it was Maya's call to make. Besides, they needed to get to know one another better. He didn't just idly hop into a woman's bed for the hell of it. No, there had to be a lot more between them than just raw sex and desire.

"Good," Maya murmured between bites. "Let me take a bath and get dressed, after I make a pig of myself here with all this great food, and then we'll play *tourista.*"

Chuckling, Dane agreed. "I've got the most beautiful guide in the world. My day won't go wrong no matter what we do."

"So, your dad was an army helicopter pilot, too?" Maya asked. They sat at El Trucha, one of the five-star restaurants in Cuzco. After a day of touring the beautiful old Catholic cathedrals that graced the central Plaza del Sol, they'd settled on this seafood restaurant as their farewell to the city.

Dane cut into the tender pink flesh of the filleted trout on his white china plate. El Trucha was quiet, the service excellent, the booths very private. "Yeah, he was a career man. He retired after thirty years."

Maya tried the tasty yellow potatoes, a delicacy of Peru. "And your mom? What did she do? Was she a career army wife?" She smiled at him in the low light, enjoying the intimacy that had remained with them all day long. Sometimes Dane would touch her hand or shoulder, but he never made another attempt to kiss her. The day had been wonderful for Maya. She had never enjoyed anyone's company as much as she did his.

Frowning, Dane stopped eating. "No...she didn't like the idea of staying home and being a mother to me...."

Hearing the pain, Maya stopped eating and looked up, seeing the hurt in his hooded blue gaze. "Did they divorce?"

"Yes." Dane tried to concentrate on the moment, not his painful past. Maya had changed into a sleek black dress with a boat neck and a pale pink bolero jacket. She had bought it this afternoon at one of the many shops around Plaza de Armas, the main plaza in Cuzco. Her hair was caught up in a French twist, a pale pink orchid with a red lip entwined in the strands. It made her look delicious and so very exquisite. Pink shell earrings and a necklace adorned her ears and slender throat. He had bought them for her. And she'd accepted the gift like an excited child. But as she sat waiting for his reply, he knew he owed her the truth.

"My mother was a lot like you," Dane said, placing the flatware aside and picking up his glass of white wine. "She was headstrong, independent. She shot from the hip and didn't like staying home to do housework."

Maya smiled a little. "I don't know of a woman alive who likes doing housework, do you?"

"No, but she could have at least hung around to help raise me. She left us when I was twelve. She told my father that she just wasn't happy being a housewife."

Blotting her lips, Maya heard raw pain in his low voice. She could see that by talking about it, Dane had lost his appetite. "So, you've been alone for a long time, too."

Her words sunk into him. "Alone? I had my dad, but he was away a lot of the time. I had a baby-sitter until I was thirteen, and then I was on my own."

"Did your mother have visitation rights?"

"Yeah...but she moved away, and then my father got transferred, and it was impossible for her to travel two thousand miles to see me. You know how it is when you're a military brat."

Setting her plate aside, Maya thanked the waiter when he

came over and whisked it away. Turning her attention back to Dane, she whispered, "I do know. One camp after another somewhere in the world, moving every two years whether you liked it or not." She smiled bravely. "I learned a lot of German and French when my father was moved around."

"I did, too, but so what?" Dane shrugged and handed his half-eaten plate of food to the waiter. "I swore that when I went into the army, I wasn't going to raise a kid the way I was raised."

"Does that translate into 'I'm not going to marry a headstrong, independent woman who might run off and abandon me again'?"

Dane stared at her across the table. The low lighting emphasized the clean lines of her face. Maya's eyes were warm with compassion. "Probably."

"No wonder," she mused softly, "you saw your mother in me. We're alike, from the sound of it. Only, I don't abandon people."

His mouth twitched. "Yes, you two were a lot alike. She's dead now. Got killed by a drunk driver coming out for my high school graduation."

Maya's heart squeezed with sympathy. "I'm sorry. It sounds like she tried to stay in touch with you?"

"Oh, sure, by letters, phone calls once a week, usually. And sometimes she'd visit when we were stateside, but it didn't help."

"You felt she didn't love you enough to stay and raise you, right?"

"Ouch." Dane scratched his head and gave her a long, intent look. "You're pretty savvy about seeing straight through people, aren't you?"

"One of my better qualities," Maya laughed. "And you know as well as I do how that skill comes in handy when you're a squadron commander trying to make fifty-some people work as a team, going in one direction, all at the same time."

He laughed with her. A lot of the weight from the past seemed to dissolve from his shoulders. Maya's eyes were half-closed, and filled with desire—for him. Dane knew now what that look meant. If only they had time...but they did not.

"What about you, Maya? Why aren't you married? You're beautiful, bright and successful. There's got to be men standing in line waiting for you after this assignment." Dane hoped not, but he wasn't a fool.

Now it was Maya's turn to laugh. The sound was husky and filled with derision. "Most men, when they see me coming, run the other way, screaming." Shaking her head, she sipped the wine. "I scare men, Dane, in case you didn't already know that. They aren't ready to deal on an equal basis with a woman like myself."

"I'm learning to...."

Her lips pulled upward. "I can't decide why you towed the mark with me. And no, you never flinched or backed down from me. I respected you for that—despite our past troubles with one another. You were never scared of me, either."

"I was raised with a mother very much like you in personality. Just because you're strong and confident doesn't mean you aren't feminine. I think, looking back on it, that my father married her because he was so taken with her individuality and charisma."

"It takes a real man to deal with a woman like that," Maya said. "And frankly, I just haven't met that many."

"Mike Houston? Morgan Trayhern?"

"Yes, they qualify. But they're a rare species, you've got to admit."

"So," Dane murmured, "you've got your personal life on hold until..."

Grimacing, Maya finished off the rest of the wine and set the glass aside. "I don't have a personal life. The reason I'm here is to do what I'm doing now."

"But that doesn't mean you can't have a personal life." Dane gave her a quizzical look. Her eyes look troubled, and she wouldn't meet his gaze.

"There's a lot you don't know about me, Dane, and I'm sitting here trying to decide whether or not to level with you about it. I owe you the truth. In my line of work, what I want personally has to come second, not first. I'm dedicated to this mission. It's my life."

He ran a finger aimlessly across the linen tablecloth as he considered her words. "Is this where 'different' comes into play?"

Sitting back, Maya regarded him in the building silence. "Let me tell you a story, Dane. When I was twenty-one, I fell in love with a warrant officer who flew the Apache. I kept a...secret from him until it was too late, and we were completely involved with one another. My secret eventually was revealed. And when it was, he was shocked—and scared. He never came back. I lost him. I was devastated, of course. I had been warned that my uniqueness would cause a lot of pain. My teacher warned me that most people would never accept me—all of me." Maya shrugged painfully and set the napkin on the table. Dane's eyes glittered with intense interest. "Well, I'm not going to make that mistake twice. I learned a lot from that affair. I swore never to enter into any kind of a relationship with a man unless he knew up front the truth about me."

"Okay...so what's the truth that will make me run the other way?"

One corner of her mouth lifted. Dane was trying to tease her into relaxing. The look on his face was placid. Could he accept the truth? Maya didn't think so. "It's not that easy.... The truth, that is..."

"You're a highly complex person," Dane murmured. "It's a large part of what makes you charismatic, I think." And desirable to him, but he didn't say that. He saw the fear and indecision banked in Maya's dark green eyes. She licked her lower lip—and that meant she was genuinely nervous, he knew. "Complex people are fascinating to me," Dane continued. "You never lose interest in someone who's complicated. At least, I don't." Nothing she could tell him would scare Dane off, but he was piqued by the intrigue she presented.

"Don't be so sure," Maya warned, her brows dipping. Opening her hands, she said, "I was orphaned at birth. I was then adopted two weeks later by my foster parents. When I was seven years old, I began to have a dream every night. This very old woman, very regal looking, her face very kind, would visit me. This went on for years. I never told anyone about it because she asked me not to. Her name was Grandmother Alaria, Dane. And she's a real person, not just a figment of my imagination."

"Okay," he murmured. "How did you find out that she was alive?"

"When I was seventeen, I went down to Brazil with my mother, who loved the country. Grandmother Alaria met me in São Paulo. I was blown away when she appeared to me in the flesh. She'd told me that we'd meet there and I didn't really believe it. But when she showed up, everything changed."

"She had the capacity to talk to you in your dreams at night?"

"Yes, she did. Still does. She's a very powerful woman."

Dane placed his elbows on the table and rested his chin on his closed hands as he studied Maya's shadowed face. "Okay, you've hooked me and now I'm interested. Go on."

"I'm going to cut to the chase. I found out that my real parents had been murdered by a drug lord in Brazil. And that they were members of the Jaguar Clan, a worldwide mystical community of people who have metaphysical skills and who work for the greater good of humanity and Mother Earth. There are two branches—the Jaguar Clan and the Black Jaguar Clan. Inca, my sister, belongs to the first. I'm of the Black Jaguar Clan."

"I see. So how does this help you? What does it do for you?"

Maya could see Dane earnestly trying to understand it all. Opening her hands, she said, "Grandmother Alaria had trained me via dream work to develop a certain skill that all Black Jaguar Clan members possess."

"Which is?"

Maya pointed to the small crystal salt shaker with a silver cap on it. "See that?"

"Yes."

"Just watch it." She folded her hands, closed her eyes and took a long, deep breath.

Dane felt a shift in energy around them. It was nothing obvious, just different. One moment the salt shaker was in front of him. The next, it had disappeared. He blinked. Moving his hand forward, he frowned. Looking up, he saw Maya open her eyes and stare at him, unblinking.

"The salt shaker..." he began, looking around for it.

"You won't find it, Dane."

Frowning, he said, "Why not?"

"Because I teleported it over there." And she pointed to the window. The salt shaker sat on the sill.

Dane looked at her, his chin raising slightly. And then he stared at the salt shaker. "What did you do? Is it a magic trick? Sleight of hand or something?"

Maya shook her head gravely. "Watch the salt shaker." She closed her eyes and took another deep breath.

Staring hard at it, Dane saw it suddenly dissolve in front of him. He gasped. Jerking a look at Maya, he saw that she was just opening her eyes.

"What the hell..."

"Look, Dane." She pointed to the table between them.

He looked down at where she was pointing. There was the salt shaker. Scratching his head, he picked it up. It was real.

And it was back on the table. Giving her a wary look, he said, "All right, maybe you had a second salt shaker in your hand, hidden, and put it on the table while I was looking over there at the windowsill."

Maya smiled weakly. "If that was so, why isn't the salt shaker still on the sill?"

Stymied, Dane shrugged. He looked hard at her. "What is going on here? What did you do?"

Leaning forward, Maya kept her voice low as she answered. "It's called teleportation. It is the ability to move an object, any object, from point A to point B."

"But…that's physics…that's changing molecular structures from one form to another—and then back again."

"Yes, it is. And I can do it, Dane. I've got the training to do it, and it comes genetically to me because of my heritage with the Black Jaguar Clan."

Taking a ragged breath, Dane looked at Maya for a long time without speaking. "This is voodoo."

"No, it's metaphysics. There's a big difference. What I did, old Tibetan lamas could do. It's noted in their writings. Same with the teachers of India. This is nothing new. It's just new to you, is all."

"You could have made me disappear?" He said it partly in jest, but he studied her intently.

With a slight laugh, Maya said, "Look, Dane, don't get too serious about this little gift—or should I say curse—of mine. The key is that I've got to be in a very harmonious, balanced state to engage it." Maya rolled her eyes. "And my life in the squadron is anything but harmonious, emotionally speaking. Ninety percent of the time I can't do it."

"I see…and this is what your people know about you?"

"They don't know anything about this, or my life as a Jaguar Clan member. I'm telling you because you deserve to know up front, before anything else happens one way or another between us."

His mouth quirked. "But your people kept using the word

different. If they don't know who you really are, why do they call you that?''

''Because I also have a pretty good sixth sense. When I'm well rested and 'on,' I can feel the Kamovs around—even the direction they're coming from, before we visually spot them. I've gained notoriety for that over the past three years.''

Nodding, Dane said, ''You've thrown me for a loop, Maya. But from what I've seen, you're terribly human just like the rest of us.''

Her grin widened. ''I am. Probably more so.''

''And that's why Inca has healing ability? Her genetic heritage is from the Jaguar Clan, too?''

''Exactly.'' Maya was pleased with his insight. Although Dane looked shaken, he didn't look scared. ''The most important thing you want to remember is that we're mission driven. Black Jaguar Clan members do the dirty work. We engage the bad guys, face-to-face. The other branch does a lot of healing work for the planet, and for people. We just tear up real estate when necessary.'' Maya laughed derisively.

''You're the soldiers on the front lines. They're the academic part of it.''

''Yes, you got it.''

''Okay...I think I can handle all of this...'' Dane met her guarded gaze.

''There's one more thing,'' Maya told him, and she patted the lounge seat beside her. Their booth was in a horseshoe shape, and she gestured for him to come and sit next to her.

''Take off my jacket,'' she instructed him when he'd done so, and she turned her back toward him.

Maya made sure no one was around. The walls of the booth were high and hid them from prying eyes. She felt Dane's hands on her jacket, and she closed her eyes, knowing that this would scare him off. No one had been able to handle the rest of her secret life. No one.

As the jacket slid off her arms, Dane noticed a dark shape on her left shoulder blade. He took the jacket and put it aside.

"What am I supposed to see?"

"That crescent moon symbol on my left shoulder," she said.

"The tattoo?" He didn't think anything of it. In the low lighting, he saw the curved mark she'd mentioned, but it wasn't any big deal to him.

Maya twisted to look at him over her shoulder. "It's not a tattoo, Dane. Touch it." She held her breath.

He ran his fingertips across her creamy, smooth skin, until they encountered the crescent moon. Instantly, he moved them back and forth several times.

"What is this? Did you paste it on or something? I don't understand."

She heard the frustration in his voice—and the curiosity. "That is the symbol for anyone in the clan. A Black Jaguar has black jaguar fur. I received this when I was initiated into the clan, at age eighteen. It appears there afterward. It doesn't hurt and it's not a brand. It's our way of telling our own kind."

Dane picked at the edges of it with his fingernails, thinking it must be taped on. It was not. Running his hand across her shoulder one more time, he said, "I don't understand how it got there." He was more interested in it than frightened of it. He wanted to figure out *how* it got there, not the fact it was there.

Maya took her jacket and slid it over her shoulders again. "It's a mystery how it got there, Dane. But it's there forever. It won't go away."

Raising his brows, he said, "Interesting...really interesting. Now you've got me going on how it could have happened," He smiled at her.

"All this doesn't scare you?"

"No, why should it? It's an anomaly. Something to be studied and answered."

"Spoken like a true scientist," Maya murmured in disbelief. "You're not scared?"

"No. Perplexed, maybe…fascinated with this skill of yours, the teleportation…but scared, no."

"Every other man I've shown this to has run like hell, Dane York."

He caught and held her amused stare. "Well, I'm not every other man, am I?"

Chapter 11

"Uh-oh," Maya murmured from behind her desk as Dane walked in, "you're a man on a mission. I can tell by the look on your face." She met and held his warm gaze. Instantly, her body responded. So did her heart. He stood, hands on his hips, and gave her a wicked smile.

"You're perceptive, Captain. You ready for the scheduled reconnaisance mission?"

Scribbling on several sets of orders before her, Maya muttered, "Almost..." She forced herself to return to the business at hand. Where had the last two months flown? Since she had boldly initiated kissing Dane at the hotel, her whole world was slowly reordering itself. Not that Dane had pushed her about their burgeoning relationship, or crowded her in any way. No, he wisely had stood back and let her come to him, when she felt ready, when she felt sure of herself with him.

Glancing up, Maya melted beneath his hooded perusal. "Stop looking at me that way, Major. You're blowing my concentration."

His mouth quirked as he leaned against the doorjamb. "Can't help it. You're easy on the eyes." It was another busy day at the base. People hurried to and from their offices. Everyone was always in a hurry around here, but after two months, Dane knew why. They were on a wartime footing.

Maya rose and neatly stacked the papers into her out basket for her assistant to pick up and distribute. Her heart was skittering. Today was the day. They'd planned this little work-play outing for a month. Grabbing her helmet off a peg on the wall, she picked up her chicken plate and moved around the desk.

"Let's saddle up. I'm hungry!"

"So am I, and it isn't for food," he murmured as she moved in front of him and out the door.

Maya laughed throatily. She stopped at her X.O.'s office, poked her head in and told Dallas, "We're going now. You got the controls."

Dallas smiled and looked up from the stacks of paper on her desk. "Okay. Take it easy out there."

"We will. Be back in about three hours."

"Roger. Bye..."

Once out of the building, Maya smiled at Dane. "You got the picnic basket packed in the cargo bay of the Cobra?"

His smile was playful. "Oh, yeah. Got a bottle of really fine sirah wine, and I had Patrick, from the India Feliz, make us a picnic lunch that will put anything I could have put together to shame."

Maya dangled her helmet in her left hand as she walked. All around her, the noontime crews were busy. The Apaches were up and patroling. Off to her right, she saw a number of other pilots working with Craig and Joe over the finer points of the D model. The mechanics were schooling the squadrons on software installation. The sun was bright, the humidity exceedingly high. Wiping her brow, Maya said, "We're in for thunderstorms today. Big time."

Dane saw that the crew had just finished refueling the

Cobra. "Yeah, the meteorologist said that it's real unstable where we're going to do our mapping and surveying work."

As they walked out of the cave, sunlight embraced them momentarily before the white, twisting wisps of clouds closed in once again. "Nothing new for this time of year," Maya assured him. Halting at the Cobra, which like the choppers was painted black, she said, "You be the pilot and I'll do the chart work."

Dane nodded. "Fine by me," He climbed in and took the righthand seat in the cockpit.

"What's this?" Maya asked as she stepped up into the Cobra. She saw that the picnic basket he'd mentioned had been carefully boxed to keep it from rolling around in the wide cargo bay. Blankets, pillows and a checked red-and-white tablecloth were strapped to the rear panel.

Dane twisted in the seat as he strapped in. "Oh, those. Comfort things."

Chuckling, Maya slid the door shut, then bent over and climbed into the cockpit. Unlike the Apache helicopter, the Cobra had a tandem seat, where the pilots sat next to one another. "Looks like you thought of everything," she teased, easing the helmet onto her head.

"I think I have," Dane said, going through his checklist once he got his own helmet on. Outside, the crew chief waited for them to start up the Cobra's engine and engage the rotor.

"Wait till you see this little waterfall and meadow we're going to sneak off to," Maya said, flipping several switches and turning the radio knob to a specific frequency. She placed the map between them and slid it into a holder on her seat for easy access once they lifted off.

"Did you put in your flight plan where we'd be going?" Dane asked.

"Absolutely."

"So, the whole base knows we're going off to have a picnic?" Dane asked wryly, lifting his finger and making a circular motion to the crew chief, who stood to one side of the Cobra's nose.

Maya chuckled. ''Probably. I've completed my checklist. You ready to go?''

''Roger.'' He engaged the engine.

The Cobra shook and came to life. It was an old model saved from the closing days of the Vietnam War. Dane had had the chance to fly the relic a number of times, and looked forward to doing so once more. Today they were going to check some areas to see if new trails were being cut into the jungle. This kind of recon mission took place routinely. Faro Valentino never used the same trails more than two or three times to transport his cocaine over the border. He varied his routes, always constructing new ones. Knowing where they were helped Maya know where to run her missions in order to intercept Faro's supply lines.

More than anything, Dane looked forward to this quality time with Maya. Since their kiss at the hotel, his life had changed remarkably. Any lingering shreds of their past disharmony had dissolved. Yet the last two months had been a special hell for him. At the base, there wasn't time or place for him to talk to Maya on a personal level. He came to realize just how busy she was. Everyone wanted her attention. And as squadron commander, her work was never done. To try and steal a kiss was nearly impossible. They had agreed to keep their relationship, whatever it would become, separate from their duties, at the base. But for Dane it was hell.

As he took the Cobra out the Eye and headed north toward their target area, about seventy miles away, he smiled to himself. Glancing over, he saw Maya placing the plastic-enclosed chart across her thighs. She had a grease pencil in hand and was already beginning to concentrate on the job ahead. Work first, then play, Dane told himself. All around him, he saw rising turrets of cumulonimbus clouds forming massively above the jungle. As they sped toward the new area to be charted, he eyed the thickening thunderheads. The Cobra was not equipped to fly through a thunderstorm, where the winds could toss them around like a flea in a tornado.

Dane was damned if thunderstorms in the area were going to stop him from reaching that nice little picnic area known as Landing Zone Echo. He'd discovered that the LZ was a place many of the pilots and crew flew to for a little R and R. It was a low-threat area, as it was off the beaten trail from Faro's cocaine production and Kamov patrols. The waterfall wasn't big, but the pool below it was great for swimming, and there was a nice grassy spot nearby. The beauty of the place couldn't be rivaled. Dane had discovered it through Wild Woman, who had pointed it out one day when they were flying the Apache D. That had got him thinking and scheming on how to get Maya away from the base, to give them some badly needed time alone.

As he flew, the shiver of the Cobra felt good around him. The shaking and shuddering were part of this intrepid aircraft that had seen so much war duty. Even now, Maya used the Cobra for many things, as a medical air ambulance as well as to carry weapons, food and other needed supplies. It was a real workhorse with a multiple mission purpose. The new Blackhawk was replacing it, but the Cobra was still used.

Glancing left, Dane saw Maya working on the map. They flew at five thousand feet, high enough above the jungle to spot any new trail systems being hacked into it. The forest was so thick and lush that it was almost impenetrable. Over the years, the Quechua villagers had cut a maze of trails through it with their axes and machetes. No one could get through that dense growth without such tools.

The air was becoming increasingly bumpy because of the building thermals. Dane grimaced. From the looks of the dark clouds along the horizon, they were going to be rained out. Damn, he didn't want that to happen. He wanted this time with Maya. He had so many questions for her, so many things he wanted to listen to her talk about and share with him. He hungered for it.

He dreamed of her every night, of loving her fully. What would it be like to love Maya? To undress her? To make her one with him? His body automatically tightened at those heated thoughts. And where was his heart in all of this? Over the past two months, Dane had had to be ruthlessly honest with himself.

Maya wasn't a woman to catch, conquer and then walk away from. He'd never do that to her—or to himself. He'd had a lot of time to accept her other life as a Jaguar Clan member. On the surface, Maya appeared to be just as human as anyone else at the base, except for her charisma, that power that radiated from her like sunlight. Everyone responded to it. Hell, he did, too. And yet Maya seemed supremely unaware of it. What drove her, Dane had discovered, was her mission—the legacy of her clan, which ran in her blood. Now he understood why she'd fought so hard to get this base set up.

In the few conversations they'd had during these rare moments when they were alone, he'd explored her connection with that ongoing mission. Maya didn't care about upward mobility in the army. She would be happy being here for twenty or thirty years, doing exactly the same thing. It was then that Dane realized the seriousness of her commitment to slowing the drug trade and helping the world become a better place. Maya was driven. She had a vision. Could her life include a personal relationship? Dane wasn't sure. And what did he want out of this?

"Looks like rain ahead," Maya murmured. She glanced over at Dane. His profile was strong and clean. Feeling the warmth building in her lower body, she met and held his gaze for a moment. "But somehow, I don't think rain is going to detour you from your target or mission."

"You got that right." Dane frowned. "You okay with a picnic inside the Cobra?"

Smiling, Maya lifted the binoculars and scanned the jungle ahead for new trails. "Sure. Let's go for it."

"Helluva day for a picnic," Dane groused as he slipped out of the harness. The rotors were slowly coming to a halt. Outside, it was pouring rain. The sharp pinging sound against the skin of the chopper reverberated through the cabin. Lightning zigzagged across the jungle above them. Easing out of the seat, he moved into the rear cabin. Maya followed him.

"Spread the blankets on the deck," Maya suggested with amusement. "We're going to enjoy our time together no matter if the rain gods are dancing on our head or not." She smiled at him as she took the picnic basket out of the box.

Within minutes, they were comfortable, chicken sandwiches in hand as they sipped the ruby wine. Maya leaned against the rear bulkhead, her legs spread out before her. Dane sat next to her, his elbow occasionally brushing hers. The thunder caromed around them and the rain intensified. She gazed through the cockpit windows at the blurred landscape outside. They had landed in a small clearing. To their left was the waterfall.

"This storm will pass," she murmured.

He leaned back, tipped his head to the left and smiled at her. She had released her hair so that it flowed around her shoulders. The look in her eyes was one of invitation. Maya was so easy to read. Dane corrected himself; she was easy to read when she allowed him to read her.

"The storm between us did," he murmured, finishing off the sandwich.

Laughing, Maya said, "I'd say it was more than a little storm." Gusts of wind rocked the Cobra slightly. The rain was beginning to slacken off. She wiped her hands on the pink linen napkin that Patrick had provided with his five-star feast. Reaching for a slice of potato covered with cheese and bacon, Maya felt a frisson of fear. In another month, Dane and his crew would be gone. She frowned.

"What's the matter?"

"Oh...nothing..."

Dane sipped his wine and watched her enjoy the potatoes. Peru was famous for having more than two hundred varieties of potatoes, thanks to the Incas. Potatoes had been a staple for the empire and still were in Peru. "You're mulling over something," he murmured. "I can feel it."

She leaned back and settled against his left shoulder, wanting to feel his closeness. "You're getting a little too good at reading me."

"Does that bother you?"

Shrugging, Maya sipped the last of her wine and set the glass back in the picnic basket near their feet. "No...it's just that I'm not used to a man knowing how I feel about something, is all." Her eyes sparkled. "I'll get over it."

Placing his own wineglass in the basket, he lifted his arm and brought her into his embrace. Maya came like a purring cat into the circle of his arms. Smiling, Dane leaned back as she settled against him. As she rested her head on his shoulder and wrapped her left arm around his waist, Dane sighed. "*This* is what I've missed. You."

Closing her eyes, Maya allowed the sound of the splattering rain to soothe her fractious state. "Feels good, doesn't it?"

"Yeah, it's kinda nice to be able to put my arms around you without worrying that someone might see us." He chuckled indulgently. Pressing a kiss to her hair, he added, "I feel like a kid in the back seat of a car. Don't you?"

Giggling, Maya pressed her hand to her lips. "Yes. Exactly."

"Sometimes there's no other place to meet your favorite girl but in your old beat-up car," he mused. Looking around, he said, "In our case, it's a beat-up, antique Cobra helicopter."

"Are we dyed-in-the-wool helicopter pilots or what?"

He laughed deeply, along with Maya. Squeezing her, he

felt the fullness of her breasts beneath her flight suit. She felt good and strong and vibrant in his arms. Inhaling her fragrance, he smiled wistfully. "I don't care where I am, as long as I'm with you."

His words feathered across Maya. She closed her eyes, content to be held and to hear the soothing thud of his heart against her ear. "You kinda grow on a person, you know?"

Opening one eye, he angled his head and looked down into her smiling face. Her emerald eyes were wide and drowsy looking. "Like mold?" he teased.

Hitting him playfully on the shoulder, Maya said, "No, not mold."

Catching her hand, Dane placed a warm kiss on it. "What then? Am I like a lousy head cold that just won't go away? Comes back again and again?"

"You certainly have a low opinion of yourself, Major. Mold. A cold. Why couldn't you see yourself as sunshine for an orchid? Rain for Pachamama, Mother Earth?"

He kept her hand and pressed it against his heart. "Very sensual. I like that."

Quirking her lips, she retorted, "Just like a man to pick a disease, or something else yucky."

"I'd rather be rain for the orchid," Dane decided nonchalantly, a smile playing across his mouth.

"Well," Maya grumped, "we sure got the rain." And she pointed at the cockpit windows.

Dane eased her onto her back against the thick blankets spread across the deck. There was plenty of room for two people to stretch out and be comfortable in the Cobra. He saw surprise and then pleasure flare in Maya's gaze as he lay beside her, his arm beneath her neck.

"You're like an orchid, you know," he whispered as he leaned down. "Mysterious, beautiful, exotic..." And he captured her lips beneath his.

Maya's world melted instantly. How much she'd looked forward to kissing Dane once again. Sliding her hands up his shoulders, she pulled him toward her. Wanting to feel the strength of his body against her own, she savored his hot, exploratory kiss. As he eased away from her mouth, she saw his stormy blue eyes watch her intently. Moving her fingertips upward to caress his hard jawline, she whispered, "I want you. All of you..."

Nodding, Dane eased himself into a sitting position. "I know..." And he began to undress.

Maya heard the boom of thunder. The Cobra shook slightly. More wind pounded against its sides. There might be a storm surrounding them, but the storm inside her was building, making her needy and bold. She saw the lazy smile, the confidence burning in Dane's eyes. This time, there was no uncertainty in his expression. Only the look of a man who was going to claim his woman—her. Excitement thrummed through Maya as she eased out of her black uniform. She never wore a bra with it, so as she slid the fabric off her shoulders, she saw his gaze narrow upon her.

Thick strands of hair fell across her exposed breasts. Dane quickly took his uniform off and pushed it aside. He was naked as he got to his knees and helped Maya slide her feet out of the legs of her flight suit. She wore nothing at all beneath the uniform. Smiling a little, he met and held her bold, heated look. How long he'd waited for this—for her. Everything was right as he lay down at her side and she languidly stretched out before him. Maya was more catlike grace than human to his mind and senses. Her eyes were slightly tilted, sultry looking as she moved toward him to make full contact.

The moment her breasts grazed his darkly haired chest, he groaned. Dane took her deeply into his arms, crushing his hips against hers. Maya was soft, yet strong in womanly ways. Her mouth was hot, searching and hungry against his. Breath shallow, he drank of her offering, and tasted the sweet tartness of the wine on her lips. His heart sang. It opened wide like an orchid blooming. Never had he wanted to please anyone more than her. Her leg wrapped around his and locked him tightly against her. Smiling against her lips, he decided he liked Maya's boldness.

As his hand skimmed her left shoulder, it passed across the crescent moon symbol of her clan. Sliding his fingers down the deep curve of her spine, Dane felt himself spiraling like a hawk on a column of heat and need, eager to fulfill himself within her, to join her and connect with her on the deepest, most intimate levels that a man could with a woman. Maya was just as courageous in loving him as she was in flying her gunship against great odds and danger. She was risking herself once more, not in battle, but on the human frontier of intimacy with him. As he met her searching mouth, he kissed her hard and pressed her against the blankets. With his knee, he gently nudged open her long, firm thighs. His heart was thudding like thunder in his chest. The soft moan that rose in her slender throat as he leaned down and captured the hardened peak of her nipple made him sing with joy. The growling sound, the way her fingers dug frantically into his shoulders as he suckled her, made him soar on wings of happiness. More than anything, he wanted to give Maya pleasure.

Breath hitching momentarily, Maya waited impatiently as Dane moved across her. The feral gleam in his eyes made her raw with need. As his hips moved downward, she lifted hers to meet him. The moment he slid into her slick, heated confines, Maya's eyelids shuttered closed. Something primal, so necessary to her life and heart, rolled rhythmically through her. She gripped his shoulders as he thrust deeply into her. A moan of raw hunger tore from her lips. Arching upward, she invited him into her.

Their bodies were slick and moved with an ageless rhythm. As his mouth captured hers, Maya drowned in the sensations, the taste of him as a man, and dug her fingers more deeply into his tense shoulders. Every movement was escalating her pleasure. She saw his lips draw away from his teeth, and felt an explosion deep within her at that moment.

The heat was lavalike, hurling her into a dark oblivion of incredible pleasure and wavelike rhythm. Lost in his arms, the strength of him as a male, his touch and taste, Maya surrendered herself to him in every way possible. An arcing heat raced through her. It made her freeze momentarily, her pleasure so sharp and deep that she gasped with surprise and joy. Hearing him groan, his head pressed against hers, she moved her hips to increase the pleasure for him as well.

Moments strung together like heartbeats. As the tidal wave of heat receded within her, Maya felt Dane sink heavily against her. Smiling softly, she slid her arms around his back and kissed his cheek. They were both panting raggedly. Dane eased himself off her, onto his elbows, and looked down at her. His eyes were a stormy blue, the pupils huge and black with satisfaction. She shared a tremulous smile with him and slid her fingers up across his face and into his damp hair, her body glowing hotly in the aftermath. Words were useless. When he moved in her, she moaned a little and arched in response.

"You are so beautiful," Dane rasped as he leaned down and grazed her parted lips with his own. "Bold, beautiful and courageous."

His words made her feel good. His face was damp, and Maya wiped the perspiration away with her fingers. "You were wonderful," she managed to murmur.

Dane absorbed her trembling words. Maya's voice was husky with satiation. He saw she was fulfilled. So was he. Moving several damp strands of hair away from her temple, he said, "If I'd only known then what I know now about you..."

Maya shook her head, her dark hair spilling away from her shoulders. "Don't go there, Dane."

It was chilly in the cabin, and Dane eased off of her and then leaned down and pulled one of the blankets up and over them. Bringing Maya into his arms, he welcomed her warmth against him, her hand sliding around his torso to draw them even closer.

Lying with her head in the crook of his arm, Maya closed her eyes, a smile lingering on her well-kissed lips. Gazing down at her, Dane ran his fingers slowly through her hair. "I don't know how I could have been so stupid," he murmured. "I really blew it with you back at Fort Rucker."

Barely opening her eyes, Maya looked up at him. She saw the pain in his gaze and the way his mouth was set. "The time wasn't right, Dane, that's all."

The rain was lessening dramatically now. Dane could see slats of sunlight filtering weakly through the storm clouds, which were now moving away from them. "I guess not," he admitted gravely. Combing his fingers through the thick silk of Maya's hair, he held her drowsy green gaze, which was filled with flecks of gold. "Do you know how happy it makes me to see you smile? To kiss you and know that everything's right in the world again? To touch you and be in heaven on earth?"

She nodded and slid her hand up across his arm and shoulder. "Ever since I first kissed you, my world has been a lot better than it used to be, too." Maya saw male pride gleaming in his eyes and liked the way his mouth curved upward. Dane deserved to know how much happiness he brought to her.

Moving his finger along her hairline near her temple, he followed the sweet curve of her jaw. "I've only got one more month down here." His brows moved downward as he studied the slender line of her neck and how it fit beautifully in her shoulder. "Before our truce, I could hardly wait to leave. Now...every day is going to be like a gift. You're a gift to me, Maya... Do you realize that?" He moved his gaze to her emerald eyes, which widened in response to his honesty. "I've never met a woman like you before. And I find myself being very selfish, wanting you all to myself, though I know that can't be."

"Would it help you to know that I'm feeling very frustrated that I don't have the time alone that I want with you?"

Giving her a tender smile, Dane whispered, "I don't know what to do, sweet woman of mine. I want to stretch thirty days into years."

Nodding, Maya said, "I know what you mean...." Did she have the courage to tell Dane how much she liked him? Maya was afraid to say "love" because that word scared her. If she loved Dane, that would change her life. She had her mission; that came first. All other things must come second...or third....

Grazing her lips with his mouth, Dane rasped, "I'm going to make every minute count with you when we get back. I know we can't show any affection for one another out in public, but I'm going to start closing that office door of yours every now and again...for just a few minutes...."

Maya drowned in the promise of his mouth. His lips were searching, tender and exploratory. Maya moved her arms around his shoulders, realizing she'd never felt happier—and never more afraid. Did Dane love her? What was that look in his eyes? Maya had been unable to decipher it. Or was it her imagination? No. Because she was extraordinarily sensitive, she could feel Dane on all levels.

And if he did love her, did she love him? The answer came as a resounding warmth that flowed through her opened heart when he molded his mouth against hers. His breath was moist, his kiss capturing.

Maya felt his other hand range down along her shoulder and gently cup her breast. She leaned into him, wanting him to touch her even more. They were so well matched to one another. Her mind was shorting out. Her body was singing as he grazed her nipple with his lips. What if she did love Dane? The thought scared Maya. The only other time she had loved, the man had backed off because of her secret life.

Well, her other life didn't bother Dane at all. He accepted her at face value. It mattered not one whit about her Black Jaguar heritage. Dane was brave and accepting in ways Maya knew would never happen again in her life. Why had this happened now? How could she split herself between her mission and her need for him? In turmoil, she shoved all her doubts and needs aside and concentrated on Dane, on him touching her and making her moan with pleasure once again.

The world, the pressures, the responsibilities all melted away from Maya. When Dane eased her on top of him so that she straddled his hips, she smiled down at him and placed her hands upon his massive, darkly haired chest. He met her catlike smile with a primal look of his own. She arched as he moved into her. More than anything, Maya realized in that moment that they were made for one another. He was her equal, and she was his. And the respect they had for one another was as solid as Mother Earth herself. Dane owned her heart. He touched her soul. And he completed her as no one had ever done in her life.

Chapter 12

Maya jerked awake, a scream jammed in her throat. She sat up, her breath choppy and ragged. *No! Oh, no!* Closing her eyes, she leaned forward, rubbing her hands roughly across her face to help her wake up. It was a nightmare. Just a nightmare...or was it? The sounds of the cave complex filtered into her office, where she sat on the cot. She'd fallen asleep around 0300, after Dane had come in and forced her to leave her desk and the mission plans she was working on.

Sitting there trembling, Maya felt a trickle of sweat between her breasts. Running her hands through her thick hair to tame it into place, Maya looked around the quiet office. Glancing down at her watch, she saw it was 0600. Time to get up. She had a mission scheduled with Cam Anderson in the Cobra at 0630. A new trail had been spotted fifty miles to the north, and they had to go in and look at it closely this morning.

The nightmare still hung darkly around her. Making herself some coffee, Maya heard booted feet in the hallway outside. Turning, she saw Dane open the door to her office. He had recently shaved, but she saw telltale gray shadows beneath his blue eyes. As he met and held her gaze, Maya nodded.

"I'm up. I'm not coherent yet...but I'm up."

Dane saw the puffiness beneath her glorious emerald eyes. Her hair was still in mild disarray around her shoulders as she made her very necessary coffee.

"You look shaken," he observed as he came in and shut the door quietly behind him. "What's wrong?" Indeed, she looked pale as hell. He saw fear lurking in Maya's eyes as she turned away, her lips compressing into a line that he'd come to recognize as irritation.

"Oh," Maya muttered defensively, "I had a nightmare, was all...." She felt Dane come to a halt near her, and she absorbed his quiet, strong masculine energy. Somehow, just having Dane nearby always steadied Maya when she got into emotional maelstroms like this one. She flipped the switch on the coffeemaker. "There...coffee in three minutes."

Dane pulled out the chair for her to sit on. "Need a brush?"

She gave him a disgruntled look. "That bad, huh?"

Chuckling, he went to the locker near the cot and opened it. Maya kept her cosmetic kit in there, and he pulled it out for her. The past month, this had become an anticipated routine between them. Dane tried to keep the anguish he felt in his heart at bay as he brought the colorful cloth bag containing her toiletries over to her desk. In two days, he and his crew were scheduled to fly back to Fort Rucker, Alabama. It was the *last* thing he wanted to do.

Reaching for the brush, Maya quickly pulled it through her tangled hair. She saw that cockeyed smile on Dane's mouth as he stood in front of the desk observing her with that warm look in his blue eyes. "Thanks..." she murmured grumpily.

Dane sat on the edge of the desk. "You don't normally have nightmares," he stated as he took pleasure in her running the brush through her dark, glinting hair. "What was it about?"

Shrugging, she said, "Oh…nothing…"

"Don't pull that on me, Maya."

She glared at him and then put the brush down and picked up the comb. "It was my guardian."

"Your guardian?"

"Yes, every clan member has a spirit guardian." She saw the puzzlement in his eyes and explained, "They're like a guardian angel. Does that compute a little better for you and your reality?"

His brows raised. "Yeah, I get it now."

"Only," Maya said in a husky tone, "our spirit guides aren't just ethereal, as most people think of guardian angels. They can literally appear into our third dimension." She pointed to the desk. "And if they materialize, they are *real*—as solid as this is. They aren't a figment of anyone's imagination."

"What's the purpose in their materializing?"

Maya looked at him for a moment. In the last month, she'd told him more and more about her secret life. Dane was always fascinated by it, never put off, and certainly never afraid of it or her. He was an amazing person. And she loved him. How badly Maya wanted to say those words to him, but he was leaving shortly. And they hadn't talked about that, either. Both were putting it off. She knew why: she was afraid to admit she'd fallen in love with him, and was unsure how that would upset the well-ordered worlds they revolved within. Maya knew she would not leave her base or her mission. And she knew how much Dane's army career meant to him. She would never expect him to resign his commission and come back down here to live with her.

"They can materialize for a lot of reasons," she murmured as she combed her hair into place. "Sometimes my guardian comes in on his own, without me asking for him. A priestess always gets a male jaguar, and a priest, a female one. That way, the energy is balanced." She put the comb down and saw to her relief that the coffee was ready. Picking up the pot, she poured two cups. "I don't allow my guardian to materialize around here. It would scare the living hell out of my people. Sometimes, when I go into Agua Caliente on a flight, I'll go down to the Urubamba River and let him materialize there, out of sight of everyone. He loves the water, so I'll walk along the shore while he wades and tries to catch trout." Maya smiled softly and, turning, handed Dane the cup.

"And what are they for?" Dane asked, sipping the coffee. He watched as Maya sat down, placed her hands around the mug and slowly drank, pleasure in her expression.

"Protection, help, support and guidance."

"Like—" he searched his mind "—a big guard dog?"

She grinned slightly. "If I was in serious trouble, yeah, my jag would appear. He'd kill to protect me."

"That's good to know," Dane murmured. "I guess he doesn't consider me a threat or I'd have been so much dog meat a long time ago."

Maya chuckled. "Our guides sense a person's intent. And no, he's not going to bother you."

"Good to know." Dane met her smile. "So, what about this nightmare of yours? What was it about?"

Maya hesitated. She didn't want to worry Dane. "Oh…it was nothing…."

"Want me to repeat the question?" Dane nailed her with a direct look that told Maya he truly wanted to know.

Pursing her lips, she sat back in the squeaky chair, the mug between her hands, and looked up at the wall. "My black jag was fighting darkness. Not the kind of night darkness you know. This darkness…well, it was evil. It's the heavy energy that some people accumulate around themselves, like Faro Valentino has around him. *That* kind of energy."

"Okay…" Dane murmured. "What happened?"

Shrugging, Maya muttered, "My jag got overwhelmed

with fire, explosions, gunfire and thick, black smoke. That's when I woke up. It scared me a little.''

Dane studied her. Maya was clearly more than a little upset by the nightmare. ''Do your dreams come true?''

''Yes.''

''That's great,'' he said in a worried voice. ''Do you know what it was about? Where it happened?''

''No, nothing...just an explosion, fire, and a lot of thick, choking black smoke. I saw my black jag appear and I saw him fighting the smoke. Our guides are very powerful, Dane, but even they have limits on what they can and cannot do, just like us.'' Maya slanted a glance at him. ''Well, I gotta get going. I have to meet Cam down on the lip in about fifteen minutes.''

''Oh, that trail recon mission?'' he asked, easing off the desk.

''Yeah. By the book. It will be an easy flight, thank Goddess. I'm not up for a demanding mission in a D model today.''

Dane grinned and set his empty mug on her desk as she rose. ''Well, you're all now official graduates of the new Apaches. Your pilots were the easiest we've ever trained in on it.''

Maya rummaged around in the locker for a fresh, clean uniform. She'd take a quick shower and then get down to the lip. ''Thanks...I think it's because we're in combat mode already.''

''No argument from me. I'll see you down there,'' Dane said. He wanted to go over and kiss Maya, but he saw she was already into the mission. He saw it in her darkened eyes.

''Fine...see you there....''

''Let's go down for a closer look,'' Maya ordered Cam, who was flying the Cobra. Below them stretched the green jungle for as far as the eye could see. Clouds were swirling just above the trees with sunlight poking through in splotchy patterns.

Out of the cockpit window, Maya sighted the new trail. It looked like it was being hacked out at a good rate of speed, judging by how far they'd penetrated the area. The Cobra banked, and Maya held on to the map across her lap, the grease pencil poised in her right hand. Slats of sunlight shot through the broken cloud layer, temporarily blinding her. She pulled down the dark visor that fitted over the upper half of her face.

Cam craned her neck. "You want treetop level, Maya?"

Grinning, Maya said, "Not quite. Let's keep the skids clean on this trip, shall we?" She saw Cam grin broadly. A wisp of red hair stuck out from beneath her helmet near her shoulder. Her forest-green eyes were alive with mirth. Cam had once put a skid into a tree on another such trip, and she'd garnered the nickname Tree Trimmer as a result of the near accident.

Maya looked down at the trail. She could see newly hacked trees and brush pushed aside. There was no one around that she could spot, but that didn't mean there weren't people down there. They would be hiding from them. Faro would often threaten the Quechua men of a nearby village to work on a new trail or else he would start shooting the women and children.

"Look out!"

Cam's cry filled her ears. Maya jerked her head up. She saw a Kamov come barreling through the clouds, its 30 mm cannon blasting away—right at them. *Damn!*

Maya felt the Cobra lurch. Cam had no room to bank or escape. If she tried, she'd slam the helicopter into the trees. Maya opened her mouth to cry out a warning. She saw the tracers from the cannon moving upward. They were going to be hit!

The first explosion came above and behind them—right into the rotor assembly cuff. Maya automatically winced. Her hands went for her collective and cyclic. Cam tried to steady the wounded helicopter. Impossible!

Smoke poured into the cockpit. Coughing violently, Maya felt the entire gunship groan and began to sink. They were going to crash! Hanging on, unable to see because of the thick, greasy smoke in the cabin, Maya shoved the window open. Air! They had to have air or they'd die! Only briefly did she recall her nightmare. This was it.

The screech of treetops digging into the sinking Cobra's skin began. Everything tipped upside down for Maya. She heard the engine scream and begin to race wildly out of control. The blades began snapping like sheet metal being ripped apart. Automatically, she raised her arms over her face. Above them, she heard the heavy, punctuating rotor blades of the Kamov, gloating over its kill.

The last thing Maya saw was a huge tree limb slamming into the side of the cockpit, lunging at them like a spear as the Cobra tumbled in slow motion toward the jungle floor.

"Well, well..." Faro Valentino leaned over and tapped the shoulder of the woman in the black uniform. "Wake up! Wake up, bitch!"

Maya heard a man's voice, very far away, echoing in her hurting head. She heard laughter. Male laughter. Struggling to come out to consciousness, she dragged her eyes open. The man who met her gaze made her recoil. Faro Valentino, his face narrow, his dark brown eyes alight with triumph, stared back at her from close range. The smile on his thin lips increased.

"Ahh, she's awake, *hombres,*" he crowed. His lips lifted away from his even white teeth. "And if I'm not mistaken, you are the very infamous Capitano Maya Stevenson. No?"

Maya listened to him berate her in Spanish. She was lying on the ground, on her back. Her head ached. Nearby she saw what was left of the Cobra, partly on the ground and partly suspended from some trees, still burning. The billowing black smoke was rising skyward in a dark, ugly column. Where was Cam? Maya struggled to a sitting position. Faro backed away from her and stood looking her over. He was dressed in a short-sleeved, white silk shirt and tan pants, and had a smug smile on his face. Three men, armed with weapons, moved in, the barrels aimed down at her.

"Where's my—"

"Gone," Faro snarled. "Before we could get here, she took off. I have my men looking for her right now." He shrugged elegantly. "We'll find her." His eyes gleamed. "But we have you, Captain. You know, you're very infamous around here. You've really hurt my cocaine trade. I'm not a happy man, *señorita.*"

Glaring up at him, Maya tried to divide her awareness between Faro and her own condition. Was she hurt? Her head ached abominably. Looking down, she saw that there was a rip in her flight suit on her left leg, but that was all. Feeling bruised and shaken, Maya realized she hadn't been seriously hurt. What about Cam? What had happened to her? Maya narrowed her gaze on Faro, who was smiling like the jackal he was. The delight on his face made her nauseous.

"My pilot got away?" she demanded, her voice hoarse.

"*Sí, señorita.* Unfortunately, we got here about five minutes after the crash. My Russian pilot, Sasha Karlov, called me on the radio of my sport-utility vehicle," He pointed to a black SUV nearby. "We got here as soon as we could. We found you here, lying on the ground. Your pilot was nowhere to be seen, but we spotted her tracks." His smile increased. "We'll find her. She won't be able to get through that wall of jungle by herself."

Maybe, maybe not, Maya thought. She eyed the heavily armed drug soldiers. They came from a number of countries, judging by the various shades of their skin. All wore military tiger fatigues of gray and black. Their eyes were merciless, as if they'd just as soon shoot her than look at her. Some of the guards wore bandoleers of ammunition across their chests. All had machetes at their sides, as well as pistols. Any thought of her trying to escape dissolved—at least for now.

They were watching her closely. The pistol she carried under her left arm had been removed from its holster. She was alone. And she was at Faro's mercy.

"Get up, Captain Stevenson. You're coming with me." He bowed slightly and gestured gallantly toward the black vehicle.

Maya slowly got to her feet. Dizziness assailed her. She was still wearing her helmet. Taking it off, she felt a trickle of moisture near her left temple. Frowning, she took off her Nomex gloves and touched the area with her fingertips. When she looked at them, she saw they were smeared with blood. No wonder she was dizzy and her head hurt. It was then she noticed that her dark visor had been shattered. Realizing she was lucky her eye hadn't been put out, Maya was glad to sustain a cut over her temple, instead.

"Come," Faro cajoled in a soft voice. "My physician, Dr. Alejandro Lazaro, will clean you up." His voice deepened with satisfaction. "I want you well, Captain. There's a hunt we must take part in. You must be well enough to participate."

Maya moved slowly. The tallest soldier jerked her helmet out of her hand. She glared at him but kept moving forward. At the vehicle, they placed handcuffs on her wrists before they shoved her into the rear seat. Faro sat up front. A big man with a thick brown beard drove. On either side of her were armed soldiers. There was no escape. Her heart was beating wildly in her chest as the vehicle lurched around in a semicircle and headed back down a dirt road. Yellow dust rose in its wake.

Her mind spun. Pain kept jabbing intermittently at her temple. She had to think. *Think!* Faro would kill her, Maya knew. It was just a question of when and how. Well, this was her death spiral dance come to a close. They had now met and confronted one another. That was the warning in the nightmare she'd had earlier, Maya realized.

Closing her eyes, she took in a deep, ragged breath. Dane. She loved him! Oh, why hadn't she told him that? She couldn't even imagine how he must feel about her, but she knew he'd move heaven and earth to find her once he knew they'd been shot down. The only way her squadron would be able to find her was if they saw the smoke rising on the horizon. One of the Apache crews could spot it, and she knew they would. Once they realized it was the downed Cobra, Dane would institute some kind of search for her and Cam, Maya knew.

Faro lit a cigarette and turned around, his arm resting on the butter-yellow leather seat. He regarded her for a long time through the curling smoke. "You know, I'm looking forward to this little contest, Captain. They say you're the best helicopter pilot around. Well, we're going to find out what you're really made of." And he grinned.

"What are you talking about?" Maya growled. She hated Faro. She couldn't help it. He had shot Inca and almost killed her. If it hadn't been for her intervention, Inca would be dead. It was then that Maya had sworn ongoing vengeance against Faro. She knew he hated her as well. She could see it in his dark, crafty eyes. His light brown hair was long, almost shoulder length, coifed and carefully set in place, she was sure, with a lot of hair spray. His nails were manicured and his hands long and expressive. To all appearances, Faro was a very rich, handsome man, about five foot ten inches in height. He wore a heavy gold chain with a crucifix around his throat, the cross exposed where his shirt lay open to reveal part of his upper chest.

Chuckling, Faro took a long, pleasurable drag on his cigarette and blew the smoke toward the roof of the vehicle. "You'll see, Captain. I think it will be a very fitting and just end to you. I've been planning this day for a long, long time. And now you're mine."

Maya clenched her teeth. It would do no good to snarl back at Faro. She would wait for her chance and make a break for it.

Her head ached. Pain skittered into her left temple, and she closed her eyes momentarily. Any thought of teleporting out of this situation was useless. With the pain in her head so severe, Maya knew she couldn't gather and hold the necessary energy to even attempt it.

She'd probably sustained a mild concussion from the crash, because she felt nauseous. Furthermore, her hatred of Faro, for what he'd tried to do to Inca, was roiling in her like a savage jaguar just begging to be loosed upon him. She knew her jaguar guardian was around, but she could barely feel his invisible presence. This was not the time or place to ask him to materialize. No, at the right time, she'd ask for his help. Her thoughts raced back to Dane. What would he do when he found out they'd been shot down?

Hot tears jammed into Maya's closed eyes. She loved Dane. Why hadn't she admitted it to him? Why? Maya knew she was scared of commitment—that was why. Now, bitterly, she realized her folly. More than likely, she was going to die, and Dane would never know…never know that she loved him, ached for him and wanted him as part of her every breathing moment.

Dane was in the back seat of an Apache D model when he received the news that Black Jaguar One had been shot down by a Kamov. Instantly, the pilot, Jessica Merrill—Wild Woman—brought the gunship over in a hard, right bank, redlined the engines and headed toward the crash site. Dane fought emotions that warred with his focus on the HUDs in front of him. Kamovs were around; he and Wild Woman had already chased one back from the border, along with a civilian helicopter that was carrying cocaine. Throat tightening, Dane blinked his eyes a couple of times. Maya and Cam. They were down. Were they alive? He had no way of knowing until the other Apache gunship, Jaguar Three, could hang around the site and try to look for them with its infrared equipment.

"I'm sorry, Major," Jess said, her voice choked. "I know you and Maya...well...we all know how you feel about each other. I'm sorry...really sorry about what's happened...." She gave a sob.

Dane wanted to cry himself. He wanted to scream. Rubbing his compressed mouth with the back of his gloved hand, he rasped, "They're alive. I know they're alive...." He didn't know *how* he knew it; he simply did. Living with Maya for the last three months, he'd learned to trust his intuition without questioning it.

Just then, the radio crackled.

"Black Jaguar Two, this is Three, over."

Dane instantly recognized Akiva Redtail's strained voice. "This is Three. What can you report, Chief?" he asked, his voice hard and emotionless.

"Gunslinger, we have *no* sign of bodies. No sign of anyone on IR. We can see from our vantage point, two hundred feet above the wreckage, that there are tire tracks leading away from it. Do you want us to follow them? Over."

Relief shattered through Dane, though he was far from elated. What if both Maya and Cam had burned up in the flames, unable to cut free and bail out of the Cobra? The IR would not show that—it would only show heat from a living person or animal. He'd just have to wait and see.

"Roger that, Chief. We'll be there in—" he looked at his watch and quickly calculated the distance "—twenty minutes, over."

"Roger, Gunslinger. We're on their trail. Out."

"Beware of Kamovs," Dane warned darkly. "Over and out."

Maya's nightmare came back to him. He sat there and digested the terror he'd seen in her eyes earlier this morning. Why hadn't they both taken the warning more seriously?

Shaking his head, he muttered, "Dammit." Rapidly scanning his HUDs, he knew the Kamovs had smelled blood today. They'd just blown the Cobra out of the sky. He could feel their triumph, sensed they were scanning for him and Jessica, too. They were hungry and wanted another kill. Dane could feel the bloodthirsty energy of the Kamovs, out there hunting for them in earnest. No, he couldn't let his emotions unravel over Maya, over her possible death. If he did, he would put him and Jessica at risk, and he was damned if the Kamovs were going to take a second gunship today.

"Major," Jess said, clearing her throat and trying to deal with her emotions, "we have an S.O.P. for a downed gunship. Do you want to put it into motion?"

S.O.P. was standard operating procedure, a plan. Dane said, "Yes. Call Dallas back at the base and ask her to institute it. Thank you." He wasn't thinking clearly. *Damn!* All he could think about, all he could see in front of him, was Maya's strong, proud face, her eyes gleaming with laughter, her lips curved in that wry, teasing way that always enticed him. Why hadn't he kissed her goodbye this morning at the office? He'd wanted to. He always wanted to kiss her during stolen moments, and that's all they ever had at the base. Stolen moments. Trying to balance their growing love for one another against the needs and demands of the base and its personnel was hell. And the base and its operation always came first—as it had this morning.

Jamming one fingertip beneath his helmet, he wiped away the sweat, feeling afraid. Scanning the equipment, he lifted his head and eyed the sky around them. It was a hot, humid day, the clouds rising in puffs and turrets, threatening eventual thunderstorms later. Where was Maya? Was she all right? Was Cam with her? Were they wounded? Dying? His mouth grew dry. Frustration thrummed through him. The Apache shook around him as they sped toward the dark column of smoke he could see now across the green carpet of jungle.

Sitting there, his mind racing, Dane regretted a lot. He regretted that he'd never been honest enough with Maya to tell her that he loved her. He'd been afraid. Why? Why hadn't he told her? Closing his eyes for a second, Dane cursed softly to himself. He knew that to admit love would mean he had to make life-altering decisions. Well, what was more important right now to him? His army career or Maya? Opening his eyes, he glared out at the green canopy below. The last three months had been more beautiful, more happy, than any other time in his life that he could ever recall. And he knew it was because of Maya, his loving her and opening up to her, them sharing their lives with one another.

"What a damned fool you've been, York."

"Sir?"

"Uh…nothing, Jess. Just muttering to myself."

He scowled and scanned. The column of smoke looked like a dark scar slashed across the pale blue sky. His heart contracted as they angled in toward it. Eyes narrowing, Dane swept the screen, which could detect heat, and quickly scanned the burning pyre of the Cobra, which hung nose down among several trees it had chopped up as it crashed. Most of the gunship had already burned up. The mangled metal of the cabin and tail had survived, but that was all. The heat of the fire showed up on the HUD, a bright apple-green color. Moving the IR scanner, Dane felt his heart thundering in his chest. If there was a body around, the IR would find it.

"Anything?" Jess asked stiffly.

He heard the tension and worry in her tone as she moved the Apache over the crash site. "No…nothing…" Dane switched to the television camera. Instantly, the HUDs showed the wreckage as clearly as if they were literally standing there in front of it. His mouth quirked. "A bad crash."

"Yes, sir," Jess whispered.

"Take us up about three hundred feet. I want to sweep a broader area with IR."

"Yes, sir."

Instantly, the Apache rose. Dane increased the range of the IR. Nothing. No heat... A moment later he saw heat signatures show up on the HUD, but it was either monkeys or birds, nothing large enough to be a human being...

"Wait!" Dane almost shouted. Anxiously, he studied the HUD. There! Yes! He saw a human being moving slowly through the jungle about five miles away from the crash site. Who? It was a solitary figure....

"I got a fix," he told Jess excitedly, and gave her the coordinates. Instantly, Jess brought the Apache up and headed in that direction.

Within a minute they were on top of the heat signature. Dane saw the human form on the screen—a light green against the dark background of the HUD screen. The jungle was too thick to try and use the television camera to see who it was. Whoever it was, he or she had stopped and was waving an arm wildly up at them.

"It's gotta be one of ours," Jess said excitedly.

"I hope...." Dane rasped. He looked up. "See that break in the canopy to your left? Move the gunship over it. See if this person will follow us to that opening."

His heart rose as he saw the figure turn and work its way slowly toward where the gunship now hovered just above the canopy. The rotors were kicking up a lot of flying debris, leaves knocked off the tops of the trees by the powerful blades. Dane saw a small opening between two trees. He steadied his binoculars over the edge of the cockpit and trained them downward. His mouth grew even drier. Who was it? Cam? Maya? A villager? Hands tightening around the binoculars, he waited, breath suspended.

"It's Cam!" he called out. She was down below, still in her uniform and helmet, her arm raised and waving at them. Dane saw the blood smeared across her tense face. Her uniform was ripped in several places. But she was alive. The look on her face was one of relief, tears and anguish.

"Call in the Blackhawk for rescue," he ordered Jess.
"You bet!"

Back at the base, Dane waited impatiently as the Blackhawk landed, with Cam aboard. They'd performed a sling rescue by lowering a harness on a cable down to her. She'd put on the harness and they'd lifted her up and out of the jungle. Dane had hung around for the rescue, guarding Cam and the Blackhawk, for fear of another Kamov attack. None came. From the Blackhawk, Cam had got on the radio and told the bad news about Maya's capture. At this point, Dane could do nothing more. Now that they were back at the base, the team was able to question Cam further and form a rescue plan for Maya. Dane couldn't wait to talk to Cam, to find out what had happened. As the Blackhawk landed on the lip, he jogged toward it. The door slid open after the rotors slowed. He saw Cam, her red hair in disarray around her shoulders, as she climbed out. She saw him and headed directly toward him, the wind whipping around them.

Ducking beneath the blades, Cam reached toward Dane's offered hand. "Major, I'm sorry...so sorry...." she said brokenly. Releasing his hand, she stood, her eyes filled with tears. "We got nailed by a Kamov. He brought us down with cannon fire. It threw us into the canopy. I never lost consciousness. As we tumbled down toward the ground, Maya got hit in the head by a tree branch shattering the cockpit. It knocked her out."

Cam wiped her eyes with a trembling hand. Blood had dried across her face and jawline. "Once we stopped tumbling, the cockpit filled with smoke. I screamed at Maya, but she didn't answer me. I got unharnessed and fell on top of her, because of the way the Cobra was sitting on its nose and side. I managed to get her out of the burning gunship, sir. She fell about ten feet to the ground. I jumped out and pulled her away from the helo, in case it exploded."

Dane stood there watching her face contort. Cam shakily

ran her hand through her tangled hair. "I heard trucks coming. I tried to get Maya to come to, but she was unconscious. I didn't see any other wounds on her, sir. The side of her helmet was dented where that limb slammed into the side of her head. The helmet saved her from worse injury, but she was out cold. I saw two vehicles hightailing it down the road toward us. I knew they were druggies."

Gulping, Cam, said in a broken voice, "I had a decision to make, Major. I couldn't carry Maya into that jungle with me. It was impossible. I decided to try and escape, to get back here to get us help." Cam closed her eyes and pressed her hands to her face. "I feel like I abandoned Maya, but I know I did the only thing I could do. I'm sorry...just so sorry...."

Dane reached out and placed his hand on her shoulder. "You made the right decision, Cam. If you'll tried to carry Maya into that jungle, the druggies would have captured both of you. It's all right...let's get you to the dispensary. Come on...we'll figure out what to do next after you get taken care of. Come on...."

Chapter 13

"Are you ready to meet your fate, Captain Stevenson?"

Maya sat on a stool as Dr. Alejandro Lazaro finished stitching up the cut she'd sustained during the crash. Her left temple ached, and pain kept jabbing into her left eye. The doctor, a thin, balding man, with a well-trimmed gray beard, stepped away. Faro stood in the doorway of his villa, where he'd brought her. The ride from the crash site, on a series of back roads, had taken over an hour. The villa, unseen from the air because it had been built below the thick canopy of trees, was small and functional.

"Let's get on with it, Faro." She had been stripped of her chicken plate and helmet. Sitting on the wooden stool, Maya felt Faro's intense inspection. His mouth curved indulgently. Anyone who did not know of him would think him a rich Peruvian from Lima. He leaned languidly against the doorjamb, his arms crossed against his chest. It was noon, and Maya could smell the odor of spicy food wafting into the small medical facility.

"So, Doctor, is she ready for her last flight?"

Lazaro peeled off his latex gloves and dropped them into a small basket near the table. "*Sí,* she is, *patron.*"

Eyes narrowing, Maya watched the two armed guards standing near Faro. She'd been waiting for an opportunity to escape, but none had come yet. And with her concussion, she often experienced sudden stabs of dizziness that almost made her fall to the right. If she was going to try and escape, she couldn't have that happening or she'd get nowhere.

"Come, Captain. One last sumptuous meal." He gestured for her to get up and follow him.

Maya eased suspiciously off the stool. The guards lowered the barrels of their guns—at her—as she crossed the red-tiled expanse. Faro chuckled and moved into the spacious, sunlit dining room, where he sat down at the end of a long, rectangular table. There was a five-tiered chandelier hanging above it. Floor-to-ceiling windows on one wall showed off brilliant bougainvillea in bright red, fuschia and orange colors against the dark green foilage around the villa. Beyond that was the thick, dark jungle. No wonder they'd never found this villa!

Two maids, dressed in black dresses with starched white caps and aprons, waited anxiously to serve them. It would just be her and Faro dining, apparently.

"Sit there," he ordered Maya congenially, and pointed to the other end of the table. "You must eat well. It is your last meal."

Maya pulled out the heavily carved, straight-backed mahogany chair and sat down on its burgundy cushion. Faro was smiling like a jaguar who knew he had his quarry. At either end of the bright yellow dining room, guards took their stations on the thick cream carpet. Again, she'd have no opportunity to escape.

The first maid hurried to her and placed a bowl of fragrant vegetable soup before her. It was a creamy yellow color, with slivers of almonds and shreds of orange cheese floating in it.

Genially, Faro dug into his soup and delicately picked up a piece of bread and slowly tore it apart. He dipped it judiciously into his soup with two fingers. "You know," he began in a jovial tone, "you have no idea how long I have envisioned you sitting here, eating with me. Eating your last meal." He waved a piece of bread around to emphasize his words. "You have been my nemesis, Captain Stevenson. Until you moved into your base to stop me, it was very easy to get my cocaine out of Peru and around the world." He sipped the soup noisily and then chewed on the bread, his eyes never leaving her.

Maya ate, though her stomach was tight with tension. She knew that to have any hope of escape, she'd have to have nourishment. Eating was the last thing she wanted to do right now, but it was necessary.

Her mind spun with options. Questions. Fear. Opportunity. What was Dane doing? Did they know by now that she and Cam had been shot down? They must know. Dallas would initiate the S.O.P. for rescue. Would they ever find her? No, Maya didn't think so.

Her head was aching. The pain would increase and then lull. When it worsened, she'd be struck with the dizziness that made her want to fall to the right. *Think!* She had to think. No one at the base, other than Dane, knew about her guardian. It hurt to think of even contacting him mentally, because it took a lot of mind focus and concentration to do so. With the pain and dizziness, Maya found it impossible at the moment.

"Even if you get rid of me, you're not getting rid of our commitment to stop you, Valentino."

Chuckling, Faro shrugged. "Ah, but if you cut off the head of the snake, the body will gradually die, no?"

"No." Maya glared at him and continued to eat. Once the soup was gone, the maid quickly whisked the bowl away. A green salad with croutons was set before her. Maya's stomach rebelled. A sudden wave of nausea made her push it aside. It was instantly taken away. Reaching for the glass of water, she drank deeply from it.

Faro studied her and then ordered his soup to be taken away as well. The small maid, a Q'uero Indian, moved in and took it instantly. Her eyes were full of fear. She set the salad before Faro. He politely thanked her and poured the raspberry vinaigrette over it.

"You know, your twin sister has been a real thorn in my brother's side in Brazil," he told her in a soft, dangerous tone. "And you helped put my brother in prison. That is unforgivable." He stabbed his fork into the fresh salad as if stabbing a living thing. "I thought I'd killed her that night at the compound." He lifted his head and stared down at Maya. "But for whatever reason...she lived."

"Your brother deserves prison, Faro. So do you. We're not as easy to kill as you might think," Maya snarled. Her anger and hatred rose, cleansing away the pain and dizziness momentarily. "And I swore I'd get you for trying to kill her."

"Ah, blood vengeance. Good. Good. Well, that's something I can certainly understand." Faro broke off another piece of bread. Slathering it with butter, he murmured, "We had no idea the two of you were related. Inca hasn't been seen by many people, and never allows her photograph to be taken. And, of course, you...well, I had never seen you except in your gunship, so we didn't put two and two together...until recently. When we did, I told my brother you must both die."

Maya said nothing. A plate filled with vegetables and a huge piece of steaming beef was placed in front of her. This was typical Peruvian fare. They ate only twice a day, and when they did, consumed a generous amount of food. Yellow potatoes, orange carrots and other vegetables surrounded the beef. Maya forced herself to begin to eat.

"You know, there are other drug lords, one from Colombia and one from Ecuador, who are joining forces with me." He gave her a pleased look as he finished his salad. "With our combined money, we are purchasing more Russian military aircraft. Pretty soon, you are going to be outgunned down here. Even with the addition of those new D model Apaches we've been seeing of late.''

''So the back door to Bolivia is *that* important?''

''*Sí,* it is. That is why you must die, Captain.'' He patted his lips gently with the white linen napkin and nodded his thanks as the maid placed the main course in front of him. ''I have good news for you. My men were unable to find the other pilot who flew with you. Perhaps she is out in the jungle right now, dying. As soon as we're done, I'm taking you to our heliport,'' he informed her. He sliced into the beef with short, precise strokes, like a surgeon performing an operation. ''I'm going to be sporting about this, Captain. I'll give you a helicopter to fly.''

The news that Cam had at least escaped Faro's men made Maya's heart soar. And at the mention of the copter, she snapped her head up. Her eyes narrowed on him. ''To fly?'' she asked.

''Of course. I will give you a sporting chance to escape.''

She chewed on the potato, not tasting it, and watched him warily. ''You're going to let me fly away?''

He chuckled indulgently. ''Well, not exactly. I will have my three Kamovs up in the air to make sure you fly *El Cañón de Muerte,* the Canyon of Death, where I will 'hunt' you down.''

Stunned, Maya sat back. The Canyon of Death. Yes, she knew it well. It was located in Bolivia, the top rim at fourteen thousand feet. The canyon was nearly a mile deep, and resembled the Grand Canyon in some respects, with narrow confines, yellow and ochre walls, and in places, white speckled granite. The canyon was forty miles long. And it twisted and writhed like a snake that had been attacked. The walls of the canyon were narrow, and with one wrong move, a helicopter pilot could crash into the rock and die. Furthermore, the winds up through the dry canyon could be wicked and untrustworthy. Especially around noon, when the radiant heat made thermals rise from the earth.

"You see," Faro told her genially, "I am going to give you a sporting chance to survive this little man...er...woman hunt, Captain. I will be in my favorite helicopter, a Russian Hind. I will have a Kamov stationed at either end of the canyon, and one above it. You will start at the north end and try to fly to the south end of it. If you get there, before I find and shoot you down, then you win. On the other hand, if I catch you first, well...too bad...."

"What kind of helo are you being so generous with?" she demanded darkly.

He gave her a pleased smile and cut up his potato into precise, small bits. "You're very perceptive, Captain Stevenson. I expected that of you, you know? I'm giving you a Vietnam era Huey—a Slick, I think, is how you refer to it?"

A Slick? Maya's mind raced. That was a medical helicopter, a workhorse helo from the Vietnam days. It carried no ordnance and no weapons. Her mouth tightened. "I see," she whispered, "you're in an armed Hind and I'm in a Slick with no way to protect myself."

He grinned hugely and popped a slice of carrot into his mouth. "Ah, you see. Yes, well, you *are* the hunted one, after all, Captain. And judging from your legendary flight skills, I felt that just giving you an unarmed helicopter against my Hind would be fair enough. No?"

"You bastard."

His smile fell. He glared at her. "Such table manners, Captain. Didn't they teach you better in *Norteamérica?*"

"Go to hell."

He grinned ferociously and ate more of the food. "No, Captain, *you* are the one who is going to hell. As soon as we're done with your final meal, I'll take you to the canyon by helicopter. Our aircraft are waiting for us there, as I speak. You will have a three-minute head start and then I will take off after you. If you try to escape or leave the canyon, the

Kamov will shoot you down. The canyon is half a mile deep; 2500 feet. You can fly up to seventeen thousand feet, but that is your limit. You can choose to fly through the canyons or above it with this altitude restriction. Frankly, the slick wasn't made for 14,000 feet, much less anything higher, so my suggestion is you fly within the canyon. But that is up to you. If you go above the altitude I've restricted you to, then my Kamov will be happy to send a rocket into your Slick.''

Maya didn't believe for one minute that Faro would give her a three-minute head start. Still, the idea that he was giving her a helicopter at all provided a glimmer of hope. The Slick was unarmed. It was slow and bulky compared to the Cobra, which was a true gunship. Plus, the high altitude would be very hard on the bird. Faro was right: even at 14,000 feet the helo would labor mightily. It lessened her chance of survival. And the Russian Hind was a huge monster, with a lot of power and enough armament to match the Apache arsenal. Her mind spun. She knew the canyon well. Wondering if Faro knew that, Maya said, ''What made you choose that canyon?''

''It's risky. It's dangerous to fly in. I fly it all the time.'' He placed his flatware on the table and held up his long, expressive hands. ''It is where I hone my skills, Captain. I know it like the back of my hands, literally.''

She nodded and pushed the plate aside. Maya understood very clearly that if she made it to the south end of the Canyon of Death, the Kamov at the end would shoot her down. There was no way Faro was going to let her escape. And she was sure that the orbiting Kamov above the canyon would have his radar targeted on her Slick at all times.

''What happens if I win, Valentino?''

He erupted into mirthful laughter. ''Oh, you won't, Captain!''

''But if I do?'' Maya whispered. ''Are you going to let me fly free?''

Patting his lips, his eyes sparkling with vast amusement, Faro said, "I am a Spanish gentleman, Captain. Of course, I'll let you go. If I'm down, then more than likely I'll be dead." His lips curved away from his perfect white teeth. "But how you could possibly take me down is a mystery to me. I am the one with rockets on board my helicopter—not you. All you can do is act like a rabbit—running, hiding, ducking and dodging. Your only way to 'win' is to run, not confront. No, I'm not worried about losing our little hunt."

Of course he wasn't. Maya wiped her lips with the linen napkin. "Then let's get saddled up, Valentino, because if you think this is going to be easy, you've got another think coming."

Dane straightened up. Four pilots huddled around the map in the small room and talked in low tones. Rubbing his neck, he listened to them discuss possible search patterns to locate Maya's whereabouts. Cam was there, despite her injuries. She had a broken right arm, now in a cast and sling. These pilots knew the area well, and he had to defer to them.

His heart ached. Where was Maya? Did Faro Valentino have her? His gut said yes. A cold chill worked up his back and he turned away. Opening the door, Dane moved out into the well-lit hall of HQ. It was quiet. The whole base was in shock over Maya's disappearance. He saw it in every woman's face. He felt the thickness of shock rolling through the fortress even though no one said anything. In some women's eyes, he saw tears. Others had sat down and cried outright. Still others had a grim look of determination on their faces. It was clear they were angry. So was he.

Rubbing his eyes tiredly, Dane looked at his watch. It was 1300. The crash had occurred at 0700. It felt like the day was going to stretch out forever, with no resolution. Standing in the empty hall, he looked toward the exit, a good hundred feet away.

Was he seeing things? He blinked. No, it was

there…again…. What was it? He frowned and narrowed his vision toward the end of the hall and the exit door.

A grayish cloud seemed to be hanging there. It would disappear, then reappear moments later. Scratching his head, Dane watched it, perplexed. Was stress over Maya's disappearance making him see things? Again the cloud dissipated into nothingness, then came back. He could almost see a shape….

His mouth fell open. He took a step back and gasped as the cloud darkened. This time he saw four black legs appear out of the churning grayness. Stunned, he watched as the apparition became more solid. Tensing, he saw a black jaguar materialize out of the grayish cloud. It stood there, huge yellow eyes with tiny black pupils staring directly at him.

Gulping, Dane wondered once more if he was seeing things. His mind churned and raced. What the hell was he seeing?

And then the truth suddenly slammed into him: it was Maya's guardian! The black jaguar! Dane sucked in a breath of air. He watched the cat as it stood there, its tail twitching languidly from side to side. It was watching him intently. A sudden sense washed over Dane, as if it a powerful ocean wave had deluged him. The jaguar wanted him to follow it!

That was crazy! Was he going insane because of his worry for Maya? Was he making this up? Dane turned to see if anyone else was in the hall. It was empty and quiet. He started to turn toward the door and call to the other pilots to come and look at the cat—to see if they saw it, too.

The moment he started to turn, he felt an even more powerful message slam into him: he should get into his helicopter and follow the jaguar.

It was so crazy. Dane stared at the cat again. The black jaguar stared back. And then the cat turned and lifted the front of its body, placing its paws against the door. The door opened. Dane gasped. He saw the jaguar leap out and down the stairs. Shaken, Dane trotted down the hall and pushed the door open. Peering down the concrete steps, he saw the black jaguar on the stairs leading to the first floor. It was looking up at him expectedly.

All the conversations Maya had had with him flooded back to Dane. He now recalled that if she was in danger, she could send the jaguar for help. Yes! That was it! She was sending her guide to him to get help!

"Stay there!" he shouted to the jaguar. "I'll be back in a moment! Don't move!" And he spun around on his heel and ran down the hall.

Dane knew he probably looked insane as he ran into the room and told them to saddle up, to get every available Apache into the air and follow him. He didn't tell them *how* he knew where Maya would be, only, that he knew.

The women pilots all stared at him, but Dallas leaped to her feet.

"Maya's contacted you, hasn't she?" she exclaimed, and looked around at the other pilots. "I was hoping she'd contact someone. Okay, ladies, let's saddle up." She looked up at Dane. "Major? I'm assuming you'll lead the squadron?"

Dane nodded. "Yes." As he turned and trotted down the hall, he wondered if the black jaguar would still be there. He'd feel like a fool if it wasn't. Shoving open the door, he saw the cat standing expectantly, waiting for him. Relief sheeted through him. The cat leaped down the stairwell, and Dane quickly followed.

He wondered if the people in the complex would run in fear as the jaguar pushed open the last door that lead out of HQ and into the cave itself. As he raced down the stairs, the rest of pilots not far behind, Dane was breathing raggedly. His heart pounded with fear and with hope. Maya had sent her jaguar to him. It had worked. Right now, he didn't care to know how it worked, only that it had. As he hurried out the door, he saw the jaguar running toward the closest D model Apache. To his surprise, no one seemed to see the animal. How could they *not* see him? The big cat was plain as day to him.

As he strapped in, with Jessica as his copilot and gunner, Dane wondered how the jaguar would lead them to Maya. The cat couldn't fly, yet stood expectantly on the cave lip, the white wisps of clouds sometimes swirling around and yet never making him disappear from Dane's view. Within minutes, the Apaches were ready for flight, their combined punctuation of rotors echoing throughout the complex. All four Apaches were going up. Was it a wild-goose chase? Was this all part of his fevered imagination? Because of his desperate desire to find Maya? Dane wasn't sure. As he eased the Apache off the lip, he saw the jaguar suddenly make a leap through the Eye.

It was airborne! Dane decided he was crazy and delusional. But none of them had any idea of where to look for Maya. The crash site had been scoured, with no luck. The set of tire imprints disappeared into the jungle. All he could do was trust.

As he flew the Apache through the Eye, he saw between the noonday clouds wreathing the mountaintops, the dark outline of the jaguar up ahead of them.

"You know where we're going?" Jess asked.

"Kind of..." Dane answered evasively, keeping his eyes on the jaguar, which ran easily in front of them, almost half a mile ahead.

"I got something on radar," Jess murmured, "but the signature is unidentified. Right out in front of us. About half a mile. Do you see it, Major?"

Dane was shaken. The jaguar—or its energy, was showing up on their radar! He wiped his mouth. With a tremor in his voice, he rasped, "Yeah, I see it. Can *you* see anything just ahead of us?"

"Uh...no sir, I don't see a *thing*." Jess added a moment later, puzzlement in her voice, "But something *is* being painted on our radar..."

"Okay, no problem. Punch into the computer that it's friendly."

"Yes, sir..."

"Just keep watching for Kamovs."

"Yes, sir."

So, the jaguar could be picked up on radar. Dane looked down at his own HUDs and sure enough, there was a fuzzy apple-green ball of light on his display. It didn't look like a jaguar, though, just a fuzzy oval ball. He felt a little better knowing that Wild Woman saw something. He felt a little less crazy. If the other pilots knew that he was following Maya's spirit guide, they'd think him certifiable. Yet, when Dane checked where they were going, he realized it was straight for the Bolivian border. What if he was wrong? What if he *was* crazy? Dane was torn. He was a nononsense aviator—nuts and bolts. He didn't believe in stuff like this. Or hadn't until Maya came along. She made the invisible and impossible a part of her living, breathing existence. She accepted the possibility of the unknown. He'd never believed in magic. Not until just recently.

Narrowing his eyes, Dane watched the jaguar bound through the sky at full speed, its stride long and rhythmic as it ran. His heart ached. Maya? What of her? How was she? *Where* was she? Was the jaguar leading them to her? The pain of losing her was too much to contemplate. Dane kept himself busy flying the powerful Apache toward some unknown destination in front of them. And yet, as he flew, he somehow was in touch with Maya on a much deeper level. As he kept the gunship steady with his hands and feet, he felt her. He felt her in his heart, in his head, as a part of his spirit. She was dynamic. Unquenchable. A warrior. A lover. His best friend. And the woman he wanted to spend the rest of his life with. Dane found himself praying for her life, praying for a second chance with Maya. If only...if only she could survive. If only...

Maya sat in the Huey helicopter as it warmed up. The blades were kicking up massive amounts of yellow dust around it. Faro had given her her helmet back, but not her chicken plate. She was without any kind of protection. As she sat in the right seat of the old, olive drab Slick, she watched the gauges. Her heart fell when she saw that she had barely enough fuel on board to make it to the other end of the canyon. There was no way Faro was planning on her surviving this hunt.

Looking up, she saw the Russian Hind, a much larger gunship loaded with rockets on its stubby wings, warming up. Faro was at the controls, and a Russian pilot with him in the copilot's seat. She wondered if Faro was really going to be flying it, or his hired gun, who sure as hell had a lot more experience with the Hind. Faro couldn't be trusted, Maya decided. She cinched up the straps on her shoulders and made sure the lap belt was as tight as she could get it. There was no way in hell, she decided, as she looked out the dusty cockpit windows at the canyon before her, that she was going down without a fight. What Faro didn't know was that she knew this canyon as intimately as she knew herself. And that was her one advantage. She routinely flew all her pilots up here to learn how to fly in tight quarters, deal with uneven winds and gusts.

Above her, she saw a double-bladed Kamov Black Shark moving into position at eighteen thousand feet. It would follow her progress all the way down the canyon. The other two Kamovs were already in place. Her scalp prickled. She stopped for a moment and lifted her head. Feeling her jaguar touch her aching mind, Maya smiled a little. *Good.* Her guide had made contact with Dane. Because of her head injury and the intermittent pain and dizziness, sending her guardian for help had been the only thing left open to her to do. Would Dane follow her jaguar? Would he believe enough in what he saw to act? Maya wasn't sure. But it was her only hope. And it was a long shot. If Dane didn't believe what his eyes saw, if he didn't listen to the urgency of the jaguar's message, she was as good as dead.

A guard outside the Slick made a motion for her to take off. In her headset, she heard Faro's voice.

"Captain, take off. I'm giving you a three-minute head start."

Yeah, right. Maya pressed the mouthpiece against her lips. "Today is a good day to die, Valentino."

His laughter filled her headset. "Yes, a good day for you to die, Captain. You're the quarry. I'm the hunter. Take off!"

Maya tried turning the radio dial to another frequency, but nothing happened. Faro had rigged the radio so he could talk to her, but that was all. There was no way she could send a message to Dane or the other pilots. Faro had foreseen that possibility. Heart pumping hard, Maya eased her hands around the cyclic and collective. The Slick shuddered as she upped the speed to take off. It had been a long time since she'd flown the antique aircraft. In her late teens, she had flown one with her father. She had been taught how to fly in a Slick, so it was fitting she would find herself back in one at a time like this. As Maya lifted off, the jagged, ochre walls of the canyon in front of her, she prayed that the machine was truly airworthy. Glancing down at her watch, she mentally memorized the hands. She had a three-minute head start. Gaining more altitude and leveling off at a thousand feet, Maya tilted the nose forward and headed into the mouth of the Canyon of Death.

The sky was a bright, uncontested blue. The sun was high. Her heart was banging savagely in her chest. Wrestling with the surge of adrenaline through her, Maya used it to her advantage and became supersensitive to her surroundings. She watched the jagged spires of the canyon walls carefully. The Huey shook as it encountered gusting winds when she rounded the first, snaking curve of the canyon. She glanced down at her watch.

One minute.

She had to get moving. Feeling blind without the advanced avionics that were always available to her in an Apache, Maya realized she would not be able to see the Hind stalking her. Only if she risked turning in midair to look behind her, or jinxing around so the tail rotor didn't obstruct her vision, would she be able to see it.

The Hind, in contrast, was full of avionics and would easily locate her.

The Huey shook as she moved it sleekly around the second curve. The granite was yellowed by dust that clung to the canyon walls. Maya was tense, her breath coming in shallow gulps. At fifteen thousand feet the copter labored mightily, for this wasn't an altitude it was used to flying at. Air was thin and the rotor blades were gasping for all the cushioning they could find.

One minute, thirty seconds.

Maya didn't trust Faro. At the next turn, she brought the Slick up and turned just enough to see if he was behind her yet. She saw nothing. But then, the curves were so many and frequent that it would be hard to see another aircraft approaching. Below, Maya saw the sand and rock along the floor of the canyon. Only a few hardy green bushes stubbornly clung to life in the canyon. Compressing her lips, she moved the Slick on and pushed the throttles to the firewall. Her mind raced. What would Faro do? Would he follow her through the canyon or just pop up above it, locate her and fire rockets at her? That's what she'd do if she were in his place. But Faro had this love of hunting. He might snake through the narrow canyon as part of the test, because of this mano-a-mano thing that South American men clung to like a shell of armor around them. In her case, that was good. It gave her a slim chance.

Smiling to herself, Maya bet that he'd take the canyon route. The Hind wasn't the most graceful or quick of the Russian gunships. No, it was a huge behemoth that was actually better suited for wide-open spaces and not the tightness of Muerte. On that point, Maya knew the Slick was a helluva lot better equipped to zig and zag between the curves. Above, she saw the Kamov moving along at eighteen thousand feet, its avionics trained on her.

Two minutes.

Again, Maya halted. Here and there in the canyon were nooks and crannies just wide enough to hide behind to wait and watch. The walls of the canyon sometimes jutted out in a slice of thin rock, and she chose one of them to hover near as she turned to check what was coming.

Her heart dropped.

There was the Hind! It was moving bulkily around the last curve, about half a mile behind her. Faro had cheated! Maya cursed softly and turned the Slick toward the south. Now he would stalk her. She redlined her aircraft. The helicopter groaned and shuddered. She could see the shadow of it against the yellow sand and rock below. The ship shook around her. Up ahead was a long S curve. Maya took a hard right and the Slick literally leaned on its right side as she skimmed as close to the wall as she could. The Hind might fire at her, but the rocket could confuse the thin partition of rock with her signature and hit the wall instead, if the pilot didn't set the rocket correctly.

Gravity pushed her into the seat as she worked the Slick out of the hard right turn. The walls shot past her in a blur. She was breathing raggedly, her eyes narrowed as she snapped a hard left yaw. Instantly, the Slick banked hard. The rotor tips almost struck the overhang of granite. Too much! Instantly, Maya corrected, just a little. The Slick steadied and flew along the wall, the rotor blades inches away from the granite outcropping.

She heard a thundering roar erupt behind her. *Damn!* The Slick lurched forward from the shock wave caused by the explosion of a rocket nearby. Correcting the fleeing helicopter, Maya hit the right yaw peddle once more as the wall raced up at her. Faro had missed her! Jerking a look to her right, Maya saw huge clouds of yellow dust rising into the air where she'd flown seconds before. The Hind burst through the wall of dust, hot on the trail of her laboring aircraft.

Faro was closing in on her. She had to think! She had to do something! The Huey was groaning from the hard, demanding flying. Maya wrenched the collective to the right, and then hard left. The walls raced up at her. The winds were inconstant. They pummeled the Huey one moment and eased off the next. Having to juggle the aircraft in that kind of a wind made it even more dangerous to fly this unforgiving canyon.

Another explosion! This time directly in front of her, to the right. Maya cried out as she saw a huge deluge of dirt, debris and rocks hurtling directly down at her. Wrenching the Slick up, she hit the left yaw peddle and climbed up and out of the canyon. The helicopter strained. Panels popped and groaned in protest. The engine screamed like a wounded banshee. She knew by flying above the canyon rim she was as good as dead. It would be easy for the Hind to paint her on radar and fire a rocket at her. *No way!*

As soon as she'd avoided the cloud of debris caused by the explosion, Maya shoved the nose of the Huey straight back down into the canyon. She heard a hiss. Jerking a look off to her left, she saw a rocket speed by, narrowly missing her. Sobbing for breath, she jammed the Slick back down into the gorge. The S turns were tight. She worked the Slick hard and forced it to bend tightly to the right, then to the left. She was flying so low that the rotors of her aircraft were kicking up huge clouds of sand in her wake. It was one way to stop the Hind—to throw sand in its face, literally, and cloud her escape. Radar could paint her less easily through thick dust, Maya knew. She needed every edge she could get.

A buzzer went off. Her eyes snapped to the instruments. The engine was overheating! She saw the needle slowly starting to move up toward the red portion of the gauge. *Damn!* Fifty percent of her fuel was gone. She'd managed to get halfway through Muerte. Suddenly, Maya had an idea. It was a long shot, but it was probably the only chance she had. Mouth compressed, she kept the Slick at full throttle. She could feel the Hind stalking her in earnest. The game was almost over.

Chapter 14

Maya knew of one place in Muerte that might save her from a fiery death. *Maybe.* She sped toward that point, which was a wall partition that stuck out, literally, like a sore thumb, jutting into the canyon. This was the narrowest part of the entire gorge, and as she slid through it, she turned the Slick hard right. Bringing the helicopter around, she hid behind the wall in a hover and waited. Breathing hard, sweat running down into her eyes, she sat tensely, her hands gripping the controls. The Huey was hovering and shaking all around her. Her grip was so tight that her knuckles were white.

Wait...just wait....

The seconds ticked by.

Maya closed her eyes and tried to be patient. Her only chance was the moment when the Hind slowed down to carefully maneuver between the wall of the canyon and the partition causing the constriction. She had to time her attack just right. The Slick had runners instead of wheels on its undercarriage. They were long and slender rods, made of heavy, impact-resistant tubular metal. She was going to try and time it so that as the Hind came crawling past her, she would ram the Slick forward. With the tip of one of the skids, she would jam into the tail rotor assembly of the Hind. If she could manage such a delicate assault, she might destroy the Hind's tail rotor and the chopper would lose control and crash.

It was a horrible risk and Maya knew it. The Slick shuddered around her. When would the Hind show itself? She jerked a look above her. Off to her right, at eighteen thousand feet, the Kamov hovered. Would he warn Faro what she was doing? Even if they told him she was hiding behind the wall, Maya knew none of them would guess her lethal intent. And the timing was critical. If she couldn't do it right, then the Slick would slam full throttle into the Hind itself and they'd all die in a fiery explosion.

Her last thoughts before she saw the nose of the Hind inching from behind the wall, was that she loved Dane. Her only regret was she had never told him that. Gripping the controls hard, Maya waited one more second as the first half of the Hind appeared. She saw Faro's face turned toward her. He was grinning. He had been told by the pilot in the Kamov that she was hiding there. No matter. Lips lifting away from her teeth, she tensed. Maya rammed the Slick forward. The machine groaned. The engines screamed. The temperature needle shot into the danger zone.

Just as the Hind flew from behind the partition, Maya lurched the Slick into a slight right turn. She dipped the nose and aimed the skid right at the tail rotor assembly of the Hind. Bracing herself, she sucked in a breath of air. The Slick shuddered. Her neck snapped back. She heard the grating scream of metal being torn apart. As she slammed back into the seat, the harness cut deeply into her shoulders. The Hind shuddered drunkenly. An explosion occurred in the tail rotor, and then Maya felt the Slick being pulled into the Hind. *No!* She jammed the left yaw peddle and wrenched her aircraft away from the Hind. More metal snapped. The Slick labored. The rotors of the Hind were dangerously close. Maya cringed and pulled away as she saw the Hind suddenly moving upward toward her. *No!*

Yanking at the controls, she realized her skid had jammed into the Hind's rotor and was now stuck there. She felt the Slick sinking along with the heavier aircraft. *No! Oh, dammit!* She had to get free! *Free!*

Hissing a curse, Maya powered up. The mangled skid pulled free. They were falling! She was fifty feet from the ground. Out of the corner of her eye, Maya saw the Hind suddenly nose up. Its rotors bit savagely into the wall of the canyon. Rock, dirt and dust exploded in all directions. She worked the pedals wildly to keep her own ship from crashing. The Hind slammed into the wall, out of control. A huge explosion of black-red-and-orange flames and smoke erupted all around her.

Maya let out a yell as she hauled the Slick to the left, away from the explosion. She was too close! She knew the shock wave from the holocaust would knock the Slick out of her control. The ground was coming up fast! She braced herself. Her breath jammed in her throat. Eyes bulging, she called on every flying skill she'd ever learned to turn away from the fire vomiting in her direction. If she could just get the nose turned...

The wave from the explosion, hot and searing, struck the wounded Slick. Maya cried out and tried to hold her aircraft steady. She was going to crash! The ground came up swiftly. Jerking the nose up, Maya felt heat searing into the cabin. For a moment she was completely enveloped by a fireball from hell itself. Her skin burned. Shutting her eyes, she clung to the controls and stopped breathing. To breathe meant to drag the fire and heat into her lungs, and she knew it would kill her.

Within seconds, the fireball from the destroyed Hind moved past her. Opening her eyes, she gasped. The ground was still racing up at her. The rotors of the Slick slammed into the sand and rock at an angle. The blades snapped off.

Lethal chunks became flying shrapnel that could take off a person's head. Maya threw up her hands to protect her face. The Slick's nose dug into the sand. The cockpit canopy snapped. Plexiglas exploded inward across her body. The harnesses bit savagely into her flesh. The ship dug its nose in and the tail rotor flipped upward.

A cry was torn from Maya's throat. She felt the machine turning, cartwheeling. But not for long. Maya knew the floor of the canyon was nearby.

At the sound of screeching metal, Maya knew the tail of the ship had flipped into the unforgiving granite wall. Would the helicopter burst into flame? She hoped not. With so little fuel on board, the chances were unlikely. Just let her stay conscious! Maya heard the ship groan, and felt it begin to buckle around her. The ochre wall loomed before her widening eyes. She felt the metal around her booted feet caving inward. Instantly, Maya lifted her legs. The last thing she needed was to be trapped by the torn metal, one of her feet sheared off in the impact.

Within seconds, it was over. Dust made her cough and gag. The Slick settled in a corner of the canyon, metal shrieking and groaning. Fumbling for the harness release, Maya managed to jerk it open. She fell heavily between the seats, her eyes blurred from the dust blowing around her. Blindly, she made for the light she saw at the rear of the cabin. *Escape!* She had to escape. She knew the Kamov would be coming in to finish her off.

Maya tumbled out of the Slick and onto the sand, landing on her hands and feet. The roar of the Hind burning fifty feet away, the continuing explosions, hurt her ears. A black, greasy column of smoke rose around her. Maya realized it was her escape route. She knew the Kamov couldn't paint her through that thick, roiling smoke. Struggling to her feet, she dug the toes of her boots into the sand and sprinted drunkenly toward the Hind. They couldn't locate her, with all that heat. Let them think she'd died in the crash, and they'd leave. Then and only then would she have a chance of getting away.

Gasping for breath, Maya flattened herself against the scorched, blackened sand twenty feet from the burning Hind. She looked up through the smoke, looking fearfully for the Kamov. A startled cry broke from her lips as she saw the Russian craft that had been targeting her suddenly explode in a red-orange ball of fire. Metal and debris rained down upon her. The canyon echoed with clanging metallic sounds. Puffs of dust exploded everywhere as the sheared-off metal struck the rocks.

Within a minute, she saw an Apache D model coming in low over the canyon, right toward her. The canyon reverberated with the thick, heavy beat of its rotors.

A sob of relief broke from Maya's lips. She got to her feet and ran hard, away from the Hind so that the pilots could spot her. Lifting her arms, she waved wildly to catch their attention. Just ahead, Maya saw an area where the Apache could land, and she ran toward it. Sobbing with relief, she realized that her jaguar spirit had gotten in touch with Dane and that he had followed him here, to the Canyon of Death. Hot tears blurred her vision as she ran unsteadily toward the landing spot. She watched as the Apache crew detected her and came in for a landing. Gasping for breath, Maya leaned against the wall, her hands on her knees. She was safe. *Safe.* She'd managed to survive Faro and their death spiral dance. There could only be one survivor in the spiral—and it was her.

As Maya turned away, protecting her eyes from the flying sand and dust as the Apache landed, she suddenly felt weak. Within moments, her knees buckled. Crumbling on the sand, Maya sat back on her heels, sobbing. She didn't care who saw her crying. Life was precious. She loved Dane.

As the Apache landed, Maya tried to see who the pilot was. It was impossible, the dust was so thick. Protecting her eyes with her hands, she waited. When she looked up again, she saw Dane running toward her. He was dressed in a black flight suit, without his helmet. His face was grim, his eyes alive with anguish.

"Maya!" he called out to her. His voice was lost in the sounds of the Hind burning nearby.

"Dane!" Her own voice broke. Maya knew she couldn't stand. The relief at her life being spared had totaled her in a way she'd never expected. Opening her arms, she called to him as he skidded to a halt in front of her.

"Maya!" Dane fell to his knees and gripped her by her shoulders. Her face was bloody. Her uniform was scorched and several strands of hair that had worked their way from beneath the helmet she wore were burned. Her eyes were glazed, and she was clearly in shock. Maya sagged forward into his open arms. He groaned and pulled her hard against him and held her. Just held her. She was shaking like a scared child. He began to talk to her, soothe her and let her know she was safe.

Anxiously, Dane moved his hand down her back and shoulders, searching for wounds. Lifting his head, his saw the crumpled Slick off to one side. What was going on? What had happened? He pulled away and looked into her wet face.

"Are you hurt?" he yelled above the roar of the fire from the Hind.

"No...no...I'm fine...oh, Dane, I love you!" Maya sobbed, holding his narrowed blue gaze. She saw the strength in his face and the sudden fierce tenderness enter his glacial gaze. His mouth softened. She felt his hands come up as he gently removed the helmet from her head. Her black hair tumbled around her shoulders.

Easing his fingers through her hair, he held Maya captive by framing her damp face. Leaning forward, he said, "And I love the hell out of you, too. Just take it easy. You've been through a lot. I've got the Blackhawk coming. Angel's on board. It should land in a few minutes. We'll get you back to base and you'll be okay."

Maya nodded and leaned forward. She pressed a trembling kiss against his mouth. Never had she wanted contact with Dane more than in this moment. Maya wanted to convince herself that she was alive and that he was here, with her. Dane kissed her hard in return. His mouth was hot and seeking against her lips. As he broke the kiss, he smiled down at her and tenderly caressed her cheek. Maya felt shaky. Out of control. Sagging back on her heels, she gripped his hands in hers.

"Cam? How is Cam? Did you find her? Is she okay?"

"Yeah, she's fine. We rescued her earlier. A broken arm is all."

Closing her eyes, Maya whispered, "Thank Goddess. I was so scared for her...I didn't know what'd happened."

Dane took in a ragged breath. Joy surged through him. Maya was alive! He tried to gather his spinning thoughts and fight the wave of emotion that nearly overwhelmed him. In the distance, beyond the Apache, he saw the Blackhawk coming in for a landing. As its rotors stopped turning and the dust and pummeling wind died away, Dane stood and then brought Maya up into his arms. Her legs were rubbery. He patiently held on to her as she struggled to get her strength back. She was still crying. Hell, his eyes were wet, too. He grinned boyishly as he looked at her, his arm around her shoulders to steady her.

"I followed your jaguar."

She sighed and surrendered to his superior strength. Just having Dane's arm around her made Maya feel safe from the hell of the last hour. "I'm so glad. I was afraid you wouldn't...."

"It didn't leave me much choice." Dane laughed out of relief. The Blackhawk's door opened and he eased her forward. "Can you make it?"

Giving him a wry look, Maya said, "One step at a time." Looking up worriedly, she asked, "What about the Kamovs? There were three of them."

"Gone," Dane told her with satisfaction. "It was a turkey shoot. They were otherwise occupied when we painted them on radar. They didn't know what hit them."

Relief shuddered through Maya as they walked around the stationary Apache. She lifted her hand to Jessica, who remained on board, handling all the controls. No gunship could be left without a pilot on board during a wartime situation. The look on the woman's face was one of joy. "They were making sure I stayed in the canyon as the Hind stalked me," she told him.

Dane turned and looked at the burning gunship. "You took it down, didn't you."

Maya grinned a little and wiped tears from her cheeks. "Yeah, you might say that. Not that my method is in any flight training manual."

With a shake of his head, Dane realized he'd never met a woman as resourceful or courageous as Maya. As he held her and walked her toward the waiting Blackhawk, Angel stood outside the door, tense and expectant. Because Maya was able to walk under her own power, Angel would remain on the aircraft. Under the circumstances, no one knew if Faro had other gunships around.

"When we get back to the base, you can tell us all about it," he assured Maya.

She gave him a hooded look, some of her old strength returning now that the shock was wearing off. "You know what I want, Major?"

He grinned. "Name it and it's yours."

"You and a hotel room in Cuzco. I've got some things to say to you and I'm not going to wait any longer. I've learned my lesson."

Tears came to Maya's eyes as she left the Blackhawk where it was parked on the lip. On her left, Dane had his grip on her arm to steady her. To her right Parades, otherwise known as the Angel of Death, was grinning broadly. Maya's legs still felt wobbly beneath her, but she was determined to walk back into the base complex under her own power, despite the dizziness that assailed her.

The men and women of the base surrounded her. They cheered and cried out her name. Some jumped up and down. Others hugged one another. Many cried. Maya grinned unevenly and raised her right hand to all of them. She understood her role as leader and squadron commander, but until just now she hadn't realized on an emotional level just how much she as a person meant to those who worked under her command. Many reached out to touch her hand, to welcome her back. When she glanced over at Dane, he was smiling widely.

And when the ranks of the crowd parted and Cam came forward, her eyes awash with tears, her arm in a sling, Maya threw her arms around the other pilot and held her and sobbed.

Dane stood back and watched. A tremendous cheer went up, resonating throughout the cave as Maya embraced her pilot and friend. The expressions of joy, of relief, were everywhere. Selfconsciously, Dane wiped his own eyes. At the edge of the crowd he spotted Joe and Craig. To his surprise, there wasn't a dry eye in the house. Dane knew that a returning male pilot would never do what Maya was doing—or what her people were doing—crying, hugging and cheering for all they were worth. He was humbled by the strength and softness that women possessed.

As Maya released Cam, she whispered, "It's all right, Cam. You did the right thing. You couldn't have carried me into that jungle. You and I both know that." She smiled through her tears and touched Cam's sagging shoulder. "Don't be hard on yourself. If only one of us could escape, that was better than both of us being caught."

Nodding sadly, Cam whispered brokenly, "I feel so guilty, Maya...for leaving you there with them. So guilty..."

Giving her a gentle hug, Maya said, "We'll talk more later, okay?"

Sniffing, Cam whispered, "Sure...you get to the dispensary. You're looking pretty bad."

Laughing, Maya lifted her head and met the damp, proud gazes of her squadron, who were surrounding her in what felt like an almost a maternal gesture of respect. She saw Dane come up, his awareness that she was once again in her role as commander of the base, not just the woman he loved, evident in his eyes. Giving him a tender look, she stepped away from Cam into the crowd of women around her.

"I understand," she said in a clear, strong voice that quieted everyone, "that you moved heaven and earth to find us. Thank you." Maya met each person's gaze. They were smiling and clapping their hands. "We scored a big victory today. Faro Valentino is dead. We've bagged four of his gunships." Maya gave a whoop and plunged her fist skyward. "Thanks to all of you! Now, let's get back to work. In the coming week, we're gonna do some heavy celebrating!"

The crowd cheered raucously, the sounds echoing and reechoing throughout the cave. Maya felt dizziness assail her and she automatically put out her hand in search of Dane's steadying one. She wasn't disappointed as he grasped it, then gripped her upper arm. She grinned up at him as the crowd continued to cheer and yell victoriously.

"Come on," he urged, "I think Liz wants to check you over."

Weariness stalked Maya. She knew she was still living on the last of her adrenaline charge. The crowd parted, allowing them to go to the rear of the complex, toward the dispensary. Angel opened the door to it and Maya walked in with Dane at her side. Elizabeth Cornell was waiting for her.

The silence was welcoming as Maya sat on the edge of the gurney. While Angel took her blood pressure and Elizabeth fussed over her, Dane stood back, his arms across his chest, just holding her gaze, that cockeyed grin on his handsome features. In the Blackhawk, she had lain on the gurney while Angel attended her. Dane had remained at her feet, and she'd told him everything that had happened. Wild Woman had flown the Apache home by herself.

Maya was still glad that Dane was nearby. Right now, she felt emotionally shredded by the last twelve hours.

Later, Elizabeth ordered her to her quarters—not headquarters—to rest. Maya agreed. The doctor had placed a dressing on her left temple over the laceration and told her she had a mild concussion. There were some first and second degree burns on her neck and hands from the explosion of the Hind, but that was all.

Dane accompanied her to her quarters, a tiny room with a bunk, a locker and a makeshift cabinet, in the Quonset hut reserved for the officers near the dispensary. Plywood walls gave the pilots and other officers a little privacy in what was basically a dormitory. Right now, the place was deserted, and Maya was glad. She went straight to the shower at the end of the hall and washed the dirt, sweat, blood and fear off her. Dressing in a pair of jeans and a bright red tank top, she padded barefoot back to her room.

Dane was sitting on the edge of the bed, waiting for her. "You look like a drowned rat," he teased, getting up and gesturing for her to come and sit down.

Touching her damp hair, Maya said, "I didn't get it too dry."

Dane picked up one of the folded towels on the dresser. "I'll do it for you. Come and sit down," he coaxed. There were dark shadows beneath her eyes. Maya was in shock and he knew it. When she sat down and turned her back to him, he eased the soft green towel across her damp, dark strands. Gently, he began to squeeze the towel against them. Just the small act of doing this helped her relax. He felt her shiver.

"Cold?"

"N-no...just coming down, Dane...."

He sat down and continued to gently dry her hair. "How are you feeling?"

"Right now, I'm scared," she admitted hoarsely. "I keep reliving that flight down the canyon and wondering what possessed me to think I could survive it at all." Maya shook her head. Clasping her hands in her lap, she absorbed his touch. How badly she needed Dane's closeness right now. Just hearing his deep voice soothed the raggedness she was feeling.

"That's what makes the difference," he told her quietly as he finished his work. "Warriors focus above and beyond the fray. If they didn't have the confidence to think they could survive, they wouldn't try." He got up, retrieved the comb and brush from her dresser and sat back down. Picking up a lock of her hair, he eased the comb through it. "And you believed in yourself, your skills. You knew the canyon, and that was enough."

His words fell like soothing rain on her inner turmoil. Maya's scalp tingled pleasantly as Dane continued to comb her hair until it lay in dark waves around her head. "Right now, I feel like a scared little girl."

Hearing the tremble in her voice, Dane put the comb and brush aside, turned her around and framed her beautiful face with his hands. Looking deep into her emotion-filled gaze, he saw tears in the depths of her eyes. Maya's lower lip trembled. "I love you," he rasped, his fingers tightening momentarily on her firm, warm flesh. "You're so very, very brave. One in a million, Maya. I don't know how you did it—how you escaped Faro like that. I'm just blown away. I'm sure I couldn't have done it. He'd have knocked me out of the sky in a hurry."

Dane gave her a slight smile. She tried to smile in return and slid her hands along his forearms. Her touch was warm and inviting. Dane knew it wasn't time to love her fully, man to woman. It was a time to hold her. Maya needed to be held.

"Come here, sweetheart," he whispered, and pulled her into his arms.

With a soft moan, Maya sank into his embrace. She nuzzled her brow against the strong column of his neck and slid her hands around his torso. Having Dane's arms around her, holding her against him, was exactly what she needed. A ragged sigh broke from her lips and she closed her eyes. In every way, she surrendered to Dane because right now he was strong and she was weak. Wasn't that what love was about? When one partner was weak, the stronger one could stand and hold the other until he or she was able to stand on her own once again? *Yes.* She inhaled the male scent of him. The solid thud of his heart against hers provided stability when she felt so wildly out of control emotionally.

"I came so close to death out there," Maya admitted in a whisper. Dane stroked her shoulder and back. "And the one thing I regretted, Dane, was that I hadn't told you how I felt about you. I mean...really felt about you." The words came out with her tears. "I sat in that Slick thinking I hadn't told you I loved you. And I knew I was going to die. And that was the one regret I had—that you wouldn't ever know. I felt so terrible about that. I was mad at myself, at my own cowardice in not telling you."

Dane rocked her gently in his arms as she sobbed. Pressing his cheek against her damp hair, he rasped, "Well, I wasn't any better about it than you. I'm equally guilty, Maya. I was on patrol when the call came in that you were down. My first thought was that I hadn't told you I loved you. And I was so sorry...so sorry. I prayed for a chance to get to tell you that."

Sniffing, Maya raised her hand and wiped the tears from her eyes. She eased out of his arms just enough to look up at him. Dane's eyes were burning with tenderness for her.

"I didn't tell you because I didn't know how it could work," she confessed rawly. "I'm not going to leave here, Dane. This is my life. My work." She scowled and swallowed hard. "And I know how much the army means to you. You get your rank and retirement in twenty years. I had no right to ask you to give up those things, either." She opened her hands, her voice cracking. "So, I didn't tell you how I really felt. I didn't see how it could work, so I kept it to myself."

Dane nodded grimly and pulled Maya back into his arms. She sank against him. "I know," he admitted. "But this last couple of hours has made me rethink a lot of things, Maya. I realized what was really important to me." He looked down at her, at her face glistening with spent tears and the shadowy darkness in her half-closed eyes. Just the fact that she could be weak, could come to him and ask for his strength, his care, made him feel powerful and good. Maya was a strong, confident woman, but she also knew how to surrender to her emotions, and to trust him. More than anything, Dane was glad that she had given him her trust.

"I don't know how it can work," Maya said brokenly as she slid her hand up across his chest. "I—just don't...."

"Listen, you're really tired. Come on, I want you to curl up here on your bed and sleep. That's what you really need now—to sleep off the shock."

"I wish you could lie with me."

Dane laughed gently. "Makes two of us, but I don't think it would go down very well here at the base. Tongues would wag."

Maya felt him squeeze her, and she clung to him for a moment before he eased her out of his arms. Dane was right: she needed to sleep off the shock. As he got up and moved her feet to the bed, she lay down, watching him as he took the blanket, opened it and spread it across her. Then she reached out and touched his hand.

"You're such a mother hen."

Leaning down, he pressed a kiss to her damp cheek. "Yes, I am, with you," he whispered. Stroking her drying hair, Dane whispered fiercely, "Now, get some sleep. That's an order. Dallas is handling all your duties for now."

Maya felt the exhaustion pulling her eyes closed. "And

you? What are you going to be doing?'' She knew that in less than two days, Dane was scheduled to leave. Her heart broke at that thought.

Chuckling, Dane straightened and looked around the tiny room, which was shrouded in gray light. ''Oh, I've got a bunch of details to attend to. I'll drop by later and see how you're doing, okay?''

''You'd better.''

His smile increased. ''Yes, ma'am.''

Chapter 15

Maya felt strong, warm fingers moving slowly across her shoulder and down her blanketed back. Moaning, she barely opened her eyes, clinging to sleep. Someone was sitting on the edge of her bunk. In the low light of the small lamp on the nearby dresser, she saw Dane leaning over, a worried look on his shadowed face.

"Uhhh...what time is it?"

Dane brushed several strands of dark hair away from Maya's drowsy looking face. The white dressing where she'd sustained the cut during the crash was exposed, reminding him once more how close he'd come to losing her earlier today. "Hi, sleepyhead," he murmured. Looking at his watch, he said, "It's 2100 hours. Liz thought I should come in and wake you up. You've slept deep and hard since returning to base. She's worried about your concussion and wanted to make sure you hadn't gone into a coma."

Groaning, Maya turned over onto her back, her hand moving to her brow. "I feel like I'm coming out of a coma," she muttered thickly. In the dimness, Dane's face was sharply etched, accentuating his quiet strength. His eyes burned with that familiar tender flame that wrenched her heart every time he looked at her that way. He caressed her cheek, longing in his expression.

"You look so beautiful when you wake up," Dane mused quietly. Normal noises of the base operation were muted at the moment, with many of the pilots and crews in their rooms for the evening hours. The sounds of doors opening and closing, the murmur of women's voices, filtered through to Maya's room. Nothing was completely private in such a setting.

Maya drowned in Dane's hooded look and pressed her cheek against the open palm of his hand. Sleep was gradually releasing its hold on her. "Do you know how good it is to say I love you?"

Nodding, Dane watched the play of light and dark across her high cheekbones and smooth forehead. "I'm grateful we can say it to one another, face-to-face." Maya was so brave. So incredibly courageous. Dane now understood why her troops were so loyal to her. She was truly a woman's role model of mythic proportions.

Maya eased up into a sitting position with a protesting groan. She'd slept in her clothes, and her hair tumbled in an unruly mass across her shoulders. Rubbing her face, and trying to wipe the sleep from her eyes, she felt Dane get up and leave her side. Her heart cried out. All she wanted right now was his presence, his strength, his love. Dropping her hands, she watched as he moved to the dresser. He picked up a tray of food from the mess hall and brought it over to her.

"Liz said you should try and eat something," he told her as he placed it across her lap. "The head cook made your favorite meal—lamb."

The fragrant, herbed odors drifted toward her nostrils. Maya looked down at the aluminum tray, which was stacked with food. The sumptuous meal included small, tasty lamb chops, thick brown gravy, potatoes and carrots. Dane handed her the flatware.

"Where'd she get lamb? That's not on the food requisition form."

Chuckling, Dane sat down near the end of her bunk and simply watched her. Absorbing Maya's presence was like absorbing sunlight into his starving heart. "Dallas asked Akiva to take the civilian helo down to Agua Caliente. They got some from Patrick, the chef at India Feliz Restaurant and brought it back for you. A kind of we're-glad-you're-alive dinner."

Touched by her people's thoughtfulness, Maya heard her stomach grumble. She hadn't eaten since…since she'd had that meal with Faro Valentino. Giving Dane a wry look, she said, "They shouldn't have…."

Dane watched her cut into the lamb chop with enthusiasm. "They love you. Why wouldn't they go out of their way to do something to show that to you? To celebrate your return?" Maya had the most beautiful, well-shaped hands he'd ever seen. There was nothing not to love about her. His body tightened with need of her. Dane wanted to seal the bond of love between them, but this was not the time or place to do it.

Maya chewed thoughtfully on the fragrant lamb. "I don't know about love, Dane. I know they respect me."

His mouth curved in a smile. "You know, under ordinary circumstances, I'd say you were right, but you've built something here that defies the usual laws of gravity in the army's universe. Did you see the looks on those women's faces after you landed and walked out of that Blackhawk under your own power? And the cheers? The smiles of relief that you were alive?" Shaking his head, Dane whispered, "No, Maya, they love you. Liz was telling me that while we were off searching for you this place was like a tomb. She said every woman here was depressed and anxious. They were really worried about you and Cam."

He could see more life coming back to Maya's dark green eyes as she ate with pleasure, her glazed look disappearing. She'd managed to sleep off the shock. Relief flowed through Dane.

"We're a tight group here," she agreed. Cutting into the potatoes and carrots, Maya felt her hunger being sated. "And it's happened over time, because of the threat of death that hangs over us daily."

"Combat troops are the tightest group in the world," Dane agreed. He saw color flooding back to Maya's cheeks. Her eyes were beginning to lose that exhausted look. She ate voraciously—like the jaguar she was. Smiling to himself, he said, "And no one but me saw your black jaguar. Do you know that? It led me to you. I thought I was seeing things at first until it pushed open the exit door at HQ. That's when I knew it wasn't my imagination."

Maya lifted her head and grinned a little. "I wish I could have been here to see the look on your face." She chuckled softly. Handing him the tray, she said, "I'm done. Thanks."

Dane picked up the tray and sat it back on the dresser. Handing her a cup of coffee he'd also brought from the mess hall, he sat back down and watched her sip it with relish. "So, how do you explain that I could see it and no one else could?"

Maya set the cup in her lap, her hands wrapped around it. Silence stretched gently between them. "When you love someone, Dane, it's easy to send a spirit guide to ask for his help," she finally answered.

"I see…I think."

Clearing her throat, Maya said, "What are we going to do, Dane? I love you. I don't know when it happened—or how—but it did." She licked her bottom lip and frowned as she watched his shadowed face grow serious. "I don't know how love grew out of our mutual dislike of one another. I can't explain it." Maya laughed a little, obviously embarrassed. "Another one of life's mysteries, I suppose." Then she looked directly at him. "What are we going to do? I never told you how I really felt because you were leaving, flying back north. I know how much your career means to you. And I know how much this place—" she looked around the room, her voice softening "—means to me. I can't leave here. I don't want to leave here. This is my life. My mission." Mouth quirking with pain, Maya added in a low tone, "And I know you feel equally strong about your career. I would never ask you to leave it. So I don't know what we're going to do, now that our hands have been forced by this event."

Dane picked at a small thread on the light blue coverlet. He heard the unsureness in Maya's voice. And the yearning—for him. It sent a delicious sensation from his heart to his lower body. Even now he wanted her in every possible way. Could any man tame Maya? No, not ever. She was wild and primal. She was a woman of the next century, one who was confident in herself and her femininity in ways very few other women were right now. Maya was truly a prototype for women of the future, who would one day follow in her footsteps. There always had to be a catalyst, one unique individual who cracked the collective reality so that everyone else could see new possibilities, with new eyes. New vision. The combination was dazzling to him, testing and challenging.

And yet Dane knew without a doubt that they were equals. She was someone he could be forever involved with, never bored with, always challenged by, to grow and become a better man than he had been in the past.

"Well..." he murmured. "I didn't tell you I loved you, for the same reasons." He slanted her a glance, his mouth pulled into a wry smile. "And no, I knew you would never leave this base, Maya. Your heart and soul are here."

Reaching out, Maya slid her fingers over his, which rested on his thigh. "You understand that now."

Nodding, Dane looked around the dimly lit room. "Yeah, I get it—now. I don't pretend to understand the magic of you, of this place, or your Jaguar Clan relations. I only know that these things are a part of you and that they have become very real to me as a result. I can't explain it, Maya. I probably never will, but that's not going to stop me from loving you, or wanting you...." Dane squeezed her fingers gently.

Sipping the last of the coffee, Maya leaned down and placed the mug on the wooden floor next to the bunk. She saw the angst in Dane's eyes, and the sadness and hope in them, too. Pushing the covers aside, she slid down and wrapped her arms around him, resting her head against his broad shoulder. "So, what are we going to do? How are we going to handle the love that we tried so hard to hide from one another?"

Dane absorbed the warmth and soft firmness of her body as she leaned against his side. Clasping her hands as she slid them around his waist, he smiled a little. "I'm leaving with my team tomorrow morning," he told her in a low tone. "And I've got a few ideas, Maya, but I've got to present them to my commanding officer at Fort Rucker." He squeezed her long, sculpted fingers, enjoying the way her cheek was pressed against his shoulder. Her breath was moist against the column of his neck.

"Ideas?"

"Yeah...but I don't want to say what they are just yet...."

Puzzled, Maya lifted her head and looked at him. When Dane turned and met her gaze, she melted beneath his burning blue appraisal. "Dane, I'll settle for anything we can have. If that means me flying north to see you when I can pull free of the base and the demands here, I will. Or vice versa. I'm not willing to let go of what we have."

Her lips were bare inches from his. Dane eased away so that he could turn her around to face him. "I'm a lot more selfish than you," he told her quietly as he framed her face with his hands. "I'm not willing to settle for seeing each other every three or four months for a few hours, or maybe a day in some hotel somewhere." He searched her eyes, which were now glimmering with tears. "In the last three months I fell in love with you, sweet woman, and I'm damned if I'm going to lose you." Leaning down, Dane captured her trembling lips with his. Maya was on the verge of crying and so was he. His heart was splintering at the thought of having to leave her tomorrow morning. Dane had come to rely on Maya's presence, her strength, her womanly wisdom and her magical, catalytic effect on his everyday life.

Maya choked back a sob. Dane was leaving. He wasn't sure when he'd return. As his strong mouth grazed her lips, she moaned. Lifting her arms, she slid them around his capable shoulders and pressed herself wantonly against him. She wasn't disappointed. His arms brought her close, squeezing the breath from her as he captured her lips and rocked them open. As his breath moved into her body, she drank him in hungrily and tried to absorb every sensation. Just the way his mouth molded to hers, gently and tenderly moved against her, made tears form and fall from her thick, black lashes. Maya felt their hot trails down her cheeks. As the tears dripped into the corners of her mouth and became part of the heated kiss, she tasted their saltiness. And so did he.

Gently, Dane broke their long, searching kiss. Both of them were breathing raggedly. He saw the burning desire in Maya's half-closed eyes as she looked at him in the throbbing silence. His heart was pounding in his chest. Ranging his hands across her shoulders and arms, he managed a one-cornered smile. "I'll be back," he promised her huskily. "I'll be back...."

Maya hadn't known how much love could hurt. As she stood out on the lip near the refueling tanks and equipment, her arms across her breasts, she sighed raggedly. The noontime sun was beginning to burn away the clouds around the base. Crews were getting ready to send off the two D models for routine flight coverage of the area. Since Faro had died, the shipments of cocaine had ceased. There were no more

Kamovs to watch for. There were no more games of hide-and-seek.

Moving restlessly around the area, Maya rubbed her chest above her heart. Dane had been gone for two weeks. Two of the longest, worst weeks of her life.

Dressed in her usual black uniform and boots, her hair loose about her shoulders, Maya scowled as she walked, hands behind her back, toward the cave entrance. It was then that she picked up the sound of an approaching helicopter coming toward the Eye. Frowning, she turned. Who could that be? All her helos were on the lip. She noticed that the crews preparing the D models for flight also stopped their duties to look.

Maya's mind spun with options. Possibilities. The sound was definitely that of a D model Apache. What was going down? Nearly everyone in the cave complex was now watching the Eye with open curiosity. Within moments, in a swirl of clouds, the Apache D model came flying confidently through the opening. The rotor wash blasted Maya, because she was closest to it. Shielding her face, she watched as the helicopter came in for a landing. Who was flying it? She had no knowledge of plans for another gunship to fly into her base today. Frowning, she walked quickly toward it. In the cockpit, the two pilots began to unhitch their respective harnesses. The engines were shut down and the rotors began to move slower and slower.

Maya stayed out of reach of the blades, stationing herself on the side where the pilots would emerge. A shaft of sunlight slanted toward her, and she shaded her eyes to see who they were. Again she wondered why there was radio silence. Whoever they were, they should have contacted her to get permission to land here. As the blades stopped, the front cockpit door opened and the pilot turned in her direction, she gasped. It was Dane! He had the biggest grin on his face as he lifted his hand and waved down at her.

Her heart sped up. Maya gaped. Dane was here! The second cockpit opened and Joe Calhoun stepped out. He, too, was grinning for all he was worth. As soon as the blades stopped turning, Maya ordered her crew to put the chocks beneath the wheels and to tether the blades. The flight crew moved with ballet precision to make the Apache safe for the pilots to disembark.

Once the blades stopped turning, Maya moved forward. She saw Dane ease out of the cockpit, climb along the fuselage and step down from the ladder. As he turned, he took off his helmet and set it on the frame of the helicopter. Running his fingers thorough his hair, he turned and opened his arms to her. Maya didn't care who saw them. Everyone on the base knew of their love for one another, even though she'd tried to keep it a secret.

"Maya!" Dane moved forward, his arms wide. He saw the joy and the questions in her eyes as she ran to him. Not giving a damn who saw them, he laughed and took the full weight of her body as she threw herself into his embrace.

"Hi, stranger," he greeted her with a laugh. Holding Maya, he twirled her around and finally allowed her feet to touch the ground. Her dark hair swirled around her as he pulled her against him and captured her smiling lips beneath his own. The world rocked to a halt. Dane heard Joe's big, Texas laugh, heard people cheering and calling their names, but nothing else mattered in that moment but Maya. Her mouth was warm and eagerly welcoming. He held her against him, felt her breath coming into his starving lungs and heart. She tasted of coffee, of the natural sweetness of herself as a woman. Her moan reverberated through him and he smiled against her mouth.

"I love the hell out of you," Dane rasped against her wet, soft lips. He looked deep into her glistening eyes.

Maya breathed raggedly as she met and held his ice-blue, burning gaze. She felt Dane's hands range tenderly across her waist and up to her shoulders. Smiling breathlessly, she whispered unsteadily, "Welcome home, darling. I've missed you so much…so much…."

Her words cascaded over him and fed his starving heart. Easing her away, Dane looked up to see the assembled women crowding around them. The expressions on their faces made him smile. He called to many of them by name and lifted his hand in greeting.

Maya heard her people shouting a welcome. She turned beneath Dane's protective arm and looked around. The joy and delight mirrored on the faces of her crew was something to behold. They seemed to glow collectively—happy for her and Dane, she realized humbly. Managing a smile of her own, Maya thanked them and then ordered them back to the business at hand. They clapped, yelled and shouted, and then dispersed to their individual duties.

Maya gave Dane a dirty look. "You could have at least let us know you were coming."

Chuckling indulgently, Dane released her. He took off his Nomex gloves and stuffed them in the pocket of his uniform. Joe ambled over. "Nice to see you again, Captain," he greeted, her, shaking Maya's hand.

"Hi, Joe. Welcome back to Black Jaguar Base."

Joe looked around. "Is Akiva here?"

Dane traded a knowing look with Maya. Maya grinned a little.

"She's got the flu, Joe. She's over in the officers' quarters, on orders to rest. But I'll bet she'll be happy to see you. Why don't you go over for a visit? I'm sure she'll feel a lot better real fast when she hears you're here."

Joe blushed good-naturedly and tucked his helmet under his left arm. "Thank you, Captain. I think I'll pay her a call right now." He hurried into the cave.

Maya stood there and gave Dane a wicked, teasing look. "Why are you back here with *another* Apache, Major?"

Dane grinned back. He took her hand. "Come on, let's go

to your office. I've got some things in motion that you need to approve."

Maya sat behind her desk, her eyes wide as Dane finished explaining his plan. Before her were orders that had been cut and were awaiting her signature. She shook her head. "I don't believe this," she whispered, touching them tentatively.

Dane sat on the edge of her desk, relaxed and at ease. The door to her office was closed for once. He wanted this conversation conducted in private. Maya's eyes gleamed with excitement. He felt it. And he wanted to capture that excitement within him, as well. Two weeks without her vital energy, her sense of humor, her unique perspective on the world, had carved a groove of loneliness so deep within him that he knew he could never be without Maya in his life again.

"Well? What do you think? Will it work? Will your women pilots go for it?"

Rubbing her brow, Maya said, "This is all so much, Dane. So much! I mean, before, we were the black sheep of the army. They were more than happy to see us shoved away to South America. We were out of sight, out of mind."

"Well," he murmured, pleased, "that's all changed."

Giving him a stunned look, Maya said, "This is…wonderful…more than I dared ever hope for my people. They're such good pilots and crews…."

"Thank Morgan Trayhern," Dane told her seriously, pointing at the orders. "When I left here, I flew into Fort Rucker and got him on the phone. I shared my ideas with him."

"And he went to bat for us." Shaking her head in amazement, Maya whispered, "This is just incredible, Dane. I'm in shock…."

He reached out and grazed her cheek. "Good shock, I hope?"

Giving him a tender look, Maya said, "The best kind. Now

you can stay down here with me. That's what I like most about it.''

Dane grinned wolfishly. ''Believe me, sweetheart, I was racking my brain as to how to have my cake and eat it, too.''

Reaching for the orders, Maya lifted them and read them again. ''The army is agreeing to take some of my women pilots for I.P.—instructor pilot—duty along the Mexican border, to teach other Apache pilots night maneuvers against enemy aircraft. They'll start interdiction of flights originating out of Mexico, headed for the U.S.A. And the army will be sending replacement pilots down here for combat training, both male and female. There's even an opening for two of my pilots at Fort Rucker, to instruct on the finer points of combat flying.''

''Yes. What I see happening down here, Maya, is far-reaching. Your base provides an excellent opportunity for advanced combat training for our best Apache pilots. We don't get to train for combat except when there's a war going on, and then it's too late. All we do now is shoot down cardboard or wooden targets that can't shoot back. My being down here showed me that this environment, although dangerous, is also a way to finely hone our best pilots in real combat conditions.'' He laughed derisively. ''Just having them fly through the Eye will make them better pilots.''

Laughing with him, Maya set the orders on her desk. ''This means my officers can have a career now. They're not at a dead end by being down here.''

''No, just the opposite. Because of their three years of combat flying, they are in a prime position to turn around and teach others, to redefine our combat training even more. All their knowledge and experience is going to be tapped, Maya. Thanks to you holding on to your vision of this place and the mission you undertook.'' Dane regarded her proudly. Pulling a small box out of the pocket of his olive-green flight uniform, he said, ''And here's the army's way of supporting you....''

Taking the box, Maya opened it. She gasped. Inside was a set of gold major's leaves. Jerking a look up at Dane, she said, "Is this real? Am I going to be a major?"

He smiled down at her as she delicately touched the round gold oak leaves that denoted she was now a major in the army. "Yes. More than deserved," Dane murmured. "And it should have been done a long time ago. Your mother and father are going to fly down to Fort Rucker, where there's going to be a ceremony for you seven days from now. Your dad is going to pin them on your shoulders. And I'm going to be there to see it happen." His mouth curved in a proud smile.

Tears flooded into Maya's eyes. "This is all too much, Dane...too much...." She put the box with the metal insignias aside. "The best of this is you get to stay down here and continue to train formally as an I.P."

"Yes," Dane said, easing off the edge of the desk and coming around to her. He pulled Maya up and into his arms. Their hips met and her arms slid around his waist as he studied her in the warm silence. "And judging from the sat intel that Morgan has picked up, it looks like the Colombian drug lord Manuel Navarro, and his Ecuadorian counterpart, Hector Osoro, are going to come in here shortly and pick up where Faro Valentino left off. Morgan's collected proof that Navarro has just sent an order to Russia to buy more of those Kamovs we just took out a couple of weeks ago. He's going to rebuild the fleet and challenge you again."

Her heart squeezing in fear, Maya said, "I knew it wouldn't last long...the peace here, I mean." She looked up into Dane's strong, quiet face. Her heart blossomed with such a fierce love for him.

"The peace won't last long," he agreed. "But Joe is here, and he's going to be my righthand man, to help set up our advanced combat school here at the base." He leaned down and found her lips. Kissing her softly, he whispered, "And right now, as I speak, Major Stevenson, that Bell helicopter is being readied for us to fly to Cuzco.'' He lifted his head, his eyes glimmering. ''Interested in taking me up on a nice, four-day R and R in the city? I've got the best room at the Libertador Hotel reserved for us. The champagne is being chilled as I speak. The whirlpool is being heated. The bathrobes are being laid out for us. Fresh flowers...''

Laughing softly, Maya embraced him hard. ''Yes, I am. We deserve this little break, Major York. Don't you think?''

His laughter joined hers. Maya drowned in the joy she found in his eyes—joy that they were going to be together. Somehow, Dane had made it happen. As she kissed him hard and swiftly on his smiling mouth, Maya wanted nothing more than that precious time alone with him. They had more than earned it.

''Strawberries, chocolate and champagne,'' Maya sighed as she languished in the hot, bubbling water of the whirlpool in their suite at the hotel. ''This is heaven....'' Sipping the golden liquid, she felt Dane's arm around her. Both naked, they allowed the heat of the water to draw out the tiredness of the last few months and reinvigorate them. He lifted a strawberry that had been dipped in chocolate to her mouth.

The look in his eyes was feral, one of a hunter, as Maya took the tidbit in her mouth and then sipped her champagne. Outside the window was the city of Cuzco. The afternoon sun slanted against the barren brown mountains that surrounded the second largest city in Peru. The drapes, gold brocade, swathed the huge window so that it looked like a guilt-framed picture of the city she loved so much.

Moving away, Dane drank the rest of his champagne and set the glass on the dark blue carpet that surrounded the octagonal whirlpool. Their room was sumptuous, with gilded furniture from the period of the Sun King. The bed was huge, with a flowing canopy of gold brocade, plus midnight blue and gauzy white veils of fabric flowing from each of the four white-and-gold carved posts.

He saw Maya smiling at him as he turned and stood up. Her eyes were half-closed with desire in their depths—for him. It made him feel good and strong as he offered his hand to her. As her fingers slid into his, he surprised her and lifted her into his arms. The water splashed around them as she gasped and threw her arms around his slick, wet shoulders.

"Dane!"

Laughing deeply, he carried her up out of the bubbling tub of hot water to the bed. Maya didn't have enough playfulness in her life, he'd discovered long ago. Well, that was going to change with him around. Her laughter was music to his ears. If he wasn't good at much else, he did know how to play. And he was going to teach her. Depositing her wet body on the brocade bedspread, he slid down beside her and pinned her hands just above her head. Her laughter dissolved as he leaned over and caressed her smiling lips. Moaning, she pressed her body urgently against his. Moving his hand down her sleek, firm waist and hip, he brought her fully against him.

"We're getting everything wet," Maya whispered as she placed kiss after kiss along his jaw and the column of his neck.

"So what? We're paying enough for it." Dane eased his knee between her thighs. Her body was strong and warm and sleek against his. They were like two warriors of equal power and skill. Relishing her womanly strength, her boldness and inventiveness as she ran her tongue along his collarbone, Dane closed his eyes.

Giggling, Maya arched as his hand moved around her hip and she felt him press himself against the juncture of her thighs. "You're so cavalier, Major...." she whispered, easing her head back as she felt him press insistently against her dampness. Oh, how long she'd looked forward to this intimacy, this playfulness with Dane. He made her laugh. He made her feel so free, like a child again in many ways. Sliding her fingers along the sculpted muscles of his arms and shoulders, she sighed raggedly. Opening her thighs to him, she felt him thrust deeply into her.

The pleasure shimmered hotly within her belly. An arc of heat throbbed upward. Surrendering to him, Maya lay on her back with him moving commandingly above her. With a smile on her lips and her eyes closed, she arched, sliding her hands down his narrow hips. The moment his lips brushed the tip of her hardened nipple, her mind exploded. She could no longer think, only feel, and then feel some more.

The world and all its troubles vanished, dissolving in the heat of their mutual desire. As he caught and captured her lips with a growl, Maya drank hungrily from his own. The droplets of water helped them move slickly against each other as he thrust deeply and rhythmically into her. Each throbbing pulse created a lavalike heat that pooled through her. She tasted the strawberries on his lips, inhaled the male odor that was his alone, and thrilled to the way his hard, muscled body moved in such joyful rhythm with hers. Where he was hard, she was soft. And where she was pressed wantonly against him, there was such a smooth give and take that Maya felt they had been made for one another, like lost puzzle pieces finally fitted together to complete a beautiful picture.

As her body exploded with the gift of his love, she arched and moaned. His arms came around her shoulders and he gripped her to him, thrusting deeply to prolong the wonderful, sunlit sensations that rippled like waves from the core of her body outward. Seconds later, Maya felt him tense. His growl was male. Dominating. He gripped her even tighter and she clung to him, her face pressed against the column of his neck, lost in the sweet, hot haze of their mutual love for one another.

Moments spun into golden sunlight and silvered moonlight for Maya afterward. She felt Dane move off her and draw her fully against him, dragging the fluffy coverlet across them. Lying in the crook of his arm, Maya barely opened her eyes, a smile lingering on her lips. He was gazing down at her, his blue eyes thoughtful as he eased his fingers through her damp hair.

"I love you, Maya."

The words fell tenderly across her. The deep, husky quality of Dane's voice touched her wildly thudding heart. She reached up and caressed his recently shaved jaw. "I'll love you until I draw my last breath, darling."

"I know you will," he answered. And he did. Maya's commitment was total, encompassing her heart and soul. There was nothing tentative about her loyalty to those around her, Dane knew. "There might be times when we fight like hell, but we'll argue constructively, above the belt." He rubbed a silken strand of her hair between his thumb and index finger. "We're strong people. We know our own minds. But we also hold one another's hearts."

Smiling tenderly at him, Maya rested her hand against his cheek. "I trust you with my life, darling. I have for a long time. And you've never let me down." And he hadn't. Even in her worst moments when she'd known she was going to die, Dane had been flying toward her to try and save her. "You're so heroic in my eyes."

He traced her arched brow with his fingertip. Her eyes were emerald, with sunlight dappling their depths as they clung to his. "Not compared to you," he rasped. "You've got such a brave, brave heart in this loving body of yours.... I just hope I can always see what I see in your eyes now, Maya."

"You will. It takes a real man to admit he was wrong, and then right the wrong, like you did between us."

Grimacing, Dane sighed and said, "Yes, and I'm sorry I did that to you...to the other women...."

"That's past now," she whispered. "We've all forgiven you." She grinned. "After you took off the prejudicial armor, look at the man who was behind it. I fell in love with him!"

He chuckled. "A far better Dane York than the old one,

that's for sure.'' Easing his arm from beneath her, he turned over and opened the small drawer in the bedstand.

Maya looked up. ''What are you doing?'' She missed his warmth, his maleness, against her. When he turned back to her, he presented her with a small, gold covered case. ''What's this?'' Maya murmured, setting it down between them on the damp coverlet.

''Why don't you open it and find out.'' Dane's heart raced with anticipation. Maya rose up on her elbow and fiddled with the latch, her brow knitted in concentration. She looked beautiful lying naked, stretched out like a sated jaguar, next to him. His breath hitched as she opened the lid. Her eyes widened beautifully.

''Dane!''

He looked down at the solitaire emerald ring set in gold. ''Do you like it?''

Gasping, Maya eased it from the box. The light glistened through the small solitaire emerald as she held it in her fingers. Her gaze snapped up to his. ''Oh! It's beautiful!'' She looked up at him. ''An engagement ring? For me?''

Laughing fully, he said matter-of-factly, ''Well, yes...I didn't have any other woman in mind.''

Maya sat up, the coverlet pooling around her hips and long legs. ''This is so beautiful! Where...when...?'' She gave him a helpless look. Dane was grinning like a fox.

''Blame Dallas. I asked her who the best jeweler in Cuzco was. I told her what I wanted for you, and she gave me the name of the store. Dallas knew your ring size, so I was all set.''

''And she knew about this all along?''

''Yep. She knows how to keep a secret, too.'' Dane met Maya's wide, stunned eyes. ''Well? Do you like it? I tried to match the color of the stone with the color of your eyes. Did I succeed?''

Staring down at the ring, Maya felt a lump forming in her throat. ''Yes, yes, it's the color of my eyes.'' She was touched beyond words, knowing that emeralds were expensive. And this one was as clear as could be. An emerald of this quality would cost far more than any diamond would.

"It's yours," Dane told her in a low, unsteady tone. "My promise to you, Maya. It's an engagement ring, but it can mean anything you want it to, between us. I'm not trying to rush you toward marriage. The ring is my commitment to you. To us. I want every day we have left to be spent together."

Tears jammed Maya's eyes as she handed him the ring. "Here," she said brokenly, "put it on me?" And she held out her hand.

Sitting up, Dane slid his fingers around hers. In that moment, as he eased the ring onto her left hand, love for Maya welled up through him as never before. Holding her hand in his, he lifted his other palm and slid it along her clean jawline. His own tears blurred her beautiful face for a moment as he spoke. "I'll love you forever, Maya. Forever."

Epilogue

"Take my hand," Maya urged Dane, excitement in her voice. They stood together in the cloud-shrouded Temple of Balance on top of Machu Picchu, the ruins of one of the most famous architectural wonders ever built by the Incas. Even though the entire complex atop this ten-thousand-foot, jungle-shrouded mountain had been abandoned in the 1500s, those who knew better still used the ley lines—complex flow lines of invisible energy that had been purposely directed through the temples—to this day.

As they stood on the grassy expanse of what had been an old courtyard in the temple, Maya drew in a deep breath, happiness threading through her. Machu Picchu appeared as an ancient temple site to the thousands of tourists who came here, but there was much more to it than met the eye. She had been trained to know where the ley lines of energy intersected one another. Where they crossed, a doorway into another dimension existed. It could be accessed by someone who knew how to do it, opened for transport purposes.

Dane stepped toward Maya. He slid his hand into hers.

They were dressed in civilian attire because of the nature of their visit to Agua Caliente. Inca was giving birth to her twins at the Village of the Clouds. Dane had been with Maya, in their bed at their small house on the mining side of the mountain, near the base, when she'd suddenly sat up out of a dead sleep. He'd awakened instantly, and what he saw stunned him. At the foot of their bed stood a woman who looked like a holographic image. When Dane heard her speak, cold chills had worked up his spine. Maya knew her, however. She was Grandmother Alaria, the head elder from the Village of the Clouds. And she had come to tell Maya that her sister was in labor, and to come as soon as she—and Dane—could.

Dane had sat there staring, his mouth open. Oh, he'd heard from Maya of visitations like this, but he'd never experienced one before. They'd hurriedly gotten out of bed and dressed. Maya had transferred base operations to her executive officer, and they'd taken the civilian helicopter to Agua Caliente, at the base of Machu Picchu.

Dane wondered how they were going to reach the village of the Clouds, the mysterious headquarters of the Jaguar Clan. They had taken a bus up from the small Peruvian town to the temple structure atop the green-clothed mountain. This was not his first time up to the ruins. Once before, Maya had taken him up here and given him a full day's tour of the magnificent remains. She had told him then that there was another way to access the Village of the Clouds, but that it was known only to Jaguar Clan members. She'd patiently explained about ley lines, and how the Incas had knowingly gathered, directed and brought them together atop this complex. As much as Dane wanted to grasp her knowledge of metaphysics and the mountain, it was still just a head trip for him—until this morning.

Now, as he looked around the green, grassy area, the Temple of Balance behind them, he saw before them a huge hole—an old underground entrance. Archeologists at the turn of the twentieth century had discovered that a tunnel system had been dug around the entire complex. They hadn't known what it was for. But Maya did. The entrance had been blocked by a huge boulder to discourage the many tourists from even thinking about trying to go down into the tunnel to explore it out of curiosity.

Dane smiled at Maya. Her hair was mussed by the inconstant wind that moved up the steep slope of the mountain and then blew across the ruins on top. It was 0800, and few tourists were up and about at this time of morning.

"See that tunnel?" she asked him in a low tone as she pointed at it.

"Yeah. It's blocked. Is that where we're going?" He still had it in his mind that somehow the tunnel would take them to this mysterious village where Maya had trained.

"Yes. It doesn't matter if it's blocked or not, Dane. The energy door is still present even if you can't see it or feel it."

He raised his brows. "I feel something...like a pull or tug toward the tunnel?"

She smiled a little. "Bingo." She hitched her thumb across her shoulder. "The Temple of Balance is the opening for us to teleport to the village. You see that beautiful *apu*—mountain—in the distance behind us?"

He half turned. There was a tall, snow-covered mountain at least thirty miles away from them. "Yes."

"That's Apu Mandor. You see that huge black stone slab on the western perimeter of the temple? It's called the Pachamama stone, and the Incas carved out the top of it to conform exactly with Apu Mandor's major features."

There was a huge slab of black granite that was about the length of a car and roughly ten feet high. The stone had been hewn to resemble Mandor's mountainous outline almost exactly, Dane realized upon closer inspection. Then it had been raised and set upright. In front of the stone was a square courtyard of dry, packed earth. On either side were stone structures with thatched roofs, standing two terraces below.

Maya had told him that she would sometimes come to this temple to receive a healing, and that the energy was four-directional. Beyond the tunnel entrance, she'd explained, far out across the Valley, was Apu San Juan, another huge snow-covered summit somewhere beyond their view. Between the two massive *apus* and the Pachamama stone was a powerful, transformative energy link. The two small temples in the courtyard represented right and left, or female and male, energy. The Pachamama stone was the neutral source that brought the right and left together and made it into one androgynous flow of energy. It was then linked to the two mighty mountain spirits. Combined, it created an energy door for teleportation purposes. Only Jaguar Clan members, and the Q'uero people who were trained from birth in the old Incan religion, knew about and used it.

Dane didn't pretend to understand the energy dynamics as Maya had painstakingly explained them to him. But even he could feel the pull of energy upon his body. It wasn't his imagination. He was always trying to figure out Maya's magical world, which defied his third-dimensional, reality-based logic, but he hadn't succeeded yet. Over time, he came to simply accept that he didn't know a whole lot about the unseen world that she was so comfortable living in. That never stopped him from loving her. It simply added a unique and fascinating element. Dane was never bored with Maya around.

"You ready?" she asked as she turned and fully faced the tunnel opening.

"Yeah. You sure this is gonna work? I don't understand how we can physically move from this place to somewhere else. What's at work here? Quantum physics?"

He saw Maya roll her eyes in exasperation at him. They'd had many spirited discussions about teleportation.

"I don't know *how* it works, Dane. I only know that it *does*. I accept it on blind-faith knowing and trust."

His mouth hitching upward in a teasing grin, he said, "I don't have to believe it will work in order for it to work?"

Chuckling, Maya shook her head. "No, because your disbelief and questioning is offset by my belief and intent." Her eyes sparkled wickedly. "And what I *know* will more than make up for your questioning. My intent is like a laser compared to the mild skepticism you have about this little trip. Intent, strong intent, will get the job done. So just sit back, relax and enjoy the ride."

Smiling, he said, "What do I do?" Dane saw the excitement in Maya's features and knew it had to do with the birthing of her sister's babies. She could hardly wait to see Inca and the new infants. Neither Maya nor Dane was sure that they'd arrive in time for the births, but they were going to try.

"Bend your knees slightly. Then close your eyes and take a couple of good, deep breaths into your lungs. I'll do the rest."

Dane trusted Maya with his life. In the seven months since he'd returned to the base, their love had done nothing but grow, transform and become more beautiful. As he closed his eyes and took in the deep breaths of air, he felt a warm, shivering sensation enter his booted feet. The warmth moved quickly up through him. Suddenly he heard a pop and felt an undeniable sense of movement, but it was barely discernible.

"Open your eyes," Maya said.

When Dane opened his eyes, he was standing in the middle of the hard-packed dirt plaza of a village. It looked like any other Q'uero village he'd seen before, except for one thing. Looking around, Dane saw people of all colors, of all races and nationalities. Many were dressed in clothes befitting their culture. Blinking, he gave Maya a puzzled look.

"Is this it? The Village of the Clouds?"

She grinned. It had been an easy teleportation and it left her energized, as it should, in the wake of the event. "Yes, this is the Village of the Clouds. Welcome to my other home. It's yours now, too. Come on, follow me." Her voice rose in excitement. "Inca and Roan will be at the birthing hut."

Dane kept ahold of her hand. He felt mildly dizzy, but the sensation quickly evaporated as he walked. "How did you get us here? What, exactly, did you do?"

She chuckled, her stride long as she passed several huts. "I spent over a decade learning how to do this, Dane. I just hooked us up with the energy that's there on Machu Picchu, at that portal we stood in front of. Once I engaged it, we were allowed entrance, and here we are."

Dogs and children were playing here and there. A number of people were gathered around one of the cooking pots in the center of the village. The plaza was square in design, and around the circle were many different-sized huts.

Mystified, Dane eyed the mighty Andes, their snow-covered peaks blue in color, rising off to one side of the busy, productive village. A roll of huge white clouds seemed to revolve slowly, all along the boundary where the plowed fields of the village met the steep slopes of the mountains. Turning his attention back to Maya, who was almost running now, he quickened his own stride. It had been more than seven months since Maya had seen Inca, and he knew she was anxious to be with her sister again, especially on such a wonderful occasion.

As they came to a long, rectangular thatched hut, Maya slowed. An old woman, very tall and proud, wearing a long, pink, flowing robe, her silver hair caught up on top of her head with white-and-purple orchids tucked in the strands, walked out to meet them. Maya released Dane's hand and threw her arms around the woman. Dane stood back and nodded deferentially. It was the same woman he'd seen yesterday night at the foot of their bed.

"Grandmother Alaria!" Maya whispered as she hugged her gently. "It's so good to see you again."

Alaria laughed softly and kissed Maya on her flushed

cheeks. "Welcome, my child." She turned her attention to Dane, who stood there uncertain. "And you are the man who holds Maya's heart." She extended her long, frail-looking hand to him. "Welcome, Dane York. We're glad to have you among us."

Dane slid his hand into Alaria's. He was surprised at the strength of her returning grip, for she seemed almost ethereal, not quite of this world. He could perceive a distinct glow around her, which he'd also seen last night. There was laughter and warmth in her eyes as she met and held his gaze.

"It's good to see you again, my son. Welcome to our humble village."

"Thank you, Grandmother."

Her eyes danced with amusement. "You have many questions," she said.

Dane nodded. He looked over at Maya and grinned sickly. "Yes, ma'am, I guess I do."

"Perhaps, later, I may answer some of them for you?"

"I'd like that. Yes." As he said the words, he felt a shocking jolt come down through his head and pass through him. Shaken, he felt momentarily dizzy from the experience. Blinking, he saw Alaria smile knowingly up at him. What had happened? Dane wasn't sure. Was it Grandmother Alaria? The kindness in her eyes made him realize that whatever had happened was not harmful to him.

"You are a good man, Dane. One of honor." She released his hand and returned her attention to Maya, who was shedding her backpack and placing it against the outer wall of the hut. "Come, both of you. Inca has just birthed and welcomed the twins into the world. Roan is with her and all went well."

"Thank Goddess," Maya whispered fervently as she followed Alaria into the light, airy hut. "I was so worried...." Reaching out, Maya grabbed Dane's hand and gave him a triumphant grin. "Come on!"

He caught her infectious enthusiasm and followed her into the hut. There were windows everywhere. The day was warm, around seventy-five degrees, he would guess, and the sun was shining through the tropical canopy that surrounded the village on three sides. The scent of orchids was wonderful as he followed them down a hall to a room on the left. Entering it, Dane saw Inca with a baby in each of her arms, her face glowing with joy. The man who sat with her, Roan Storm Walker, looked more relieved at the moment than anything else. He was touching his daughter's small, perfectly formed hand with obvious awe. The infants were swaddled in pale pink blankets woven of soft alpaca wool.

"Ohh," Maya whispered softly as she knelt near Inca's pallet. "How beautiful they are, Inca!" Maya placed one hand on her sister's shoulder in welcome and gave her a gentle hug. Then she reached out and delicately touched each baby's dark hair.

Alaria smiled and stood off to one side. "Roan, I'd like you to meet Dane York. Dane, this is Roan. Inca's husband."

Roan eased to his feet and came around the end of the pallet. Gripping Dane's hand, he said, "I'm glad you and Maya could make it. Take a seat. You'll have to wait your turn to hold little Kayla Alaria and Michael Adair Storm Walker."

Grinning, Dane took a seat on one of the three-legged stools in the room and fondly watched as Maya knelt at Inca's side and cooed lovingly over the first infant. Kayla had thick black hair, like her parents, Dane observed. She was golden-skinned like Inca, and looked like she might have green eyes like her, too. Roan knelt at his wife's side, his arm around her shoulder, a look of pride and love burning in his eyes. He was staring down at the little babies as if they were a miracle. Well, weren't they? Dane watched as Maya's facade as a squadron commander melted away. Right now, she was a woman who loved babies. The aunt to the new children brought into the world with obvious love from those who now surrounded her.

Inca lifted her head and smiled at Dane. "I am glad you came."

"Thanks, Inca. I'm glad to be a part of this, too." And he was. Inca's eyes were warm with emotion. Her hair was damp, the dark strands falling nearly to her waist. Wearing a loose white shift, one shoulder pulled down, she held her daughter gently against her as she suckled noisily and strongly at her breast.

Alaria laughed. "Kayla and Michael have their family here, now."

Roan took his son into his arms while Kayla fed. Michael Storm Walker had black hair and his father's deep blue eyes.

Tears welled up in Maya's eyes as she sat back on her heels and met Inca's willow-green gaze. Reaching out, she slid her hand against her twin's cheek. "Family. You hear that? We're family. Isn't this wonderful, Inca? Finally, we've come full circle. We lost our parents. We lost our way, we thought. But we didn't. Not really. All along, there was a larger, hidden plan for us. But we didn't know it at the time. All we could do was trust and carry on." Tears glimmered in her eyes, and she saw Inca's own lips tremble. "And look at the outcome...."

Sniffing, Inca whispered, "I know...I cannot believe it, Maya. Everything in our lives is so good right now. We passed through our own dark tunnel. We passed the tests that were thrown at us." Inca gazed down lovingly at her daughter. A bead of breast milk formed at the corner of her tiny bud-shaped mouth. Roan leaned over and gently removed it with his finger. She smiled into her husband's face and they held one another's gaze for a long time. Then Inca reached out and tenderly touched her son's flushed cheek as he slept in her husband's massive arms.

Maya sniffed and dug into the pocket of her pants. She withdrew a bright red pouch and carefully opened it while Inca watched. "I think," Maya murmured as she pulled out a necklace with Peruvian blue opals and cougar claws on it, "that this necklace Roan gave to you, and you gave to me, should return to the twins here? You could have it refashioned into two medicine pieces. One for each?"

Smiling softly, Inca took the necklace into her hands. "That is a wonderful gift," she exclaimed. Carefully she draped the necklace, which was much too large for the babies to wear yet, across her pink alpaca blanket. The blue-green gems seemed to glow.

Inca looked up at Roan. "Does this feel right to you? To pass this necklace from your family to your son and daughter?"

Roan gave Maya a grateful look. "Yes," he murmured, "it's a wonderful gift back to us all. Thank you, Maya."

"Hey, your medicine necklace helped save my tail," she told them, grinning. "I figured I'd used up one of its nine lives in the process, and your children should enjoy the protection of it now." Patting Inca's hand, she said, "I feel good that it's going home, with you. It belongs in your part of the family tree."

Gripping her hand, Inca whispered, "Thank you...."

Maya leaned forward and kissed her damp cheek. Then, sniffing, she turned. She held out her hand toward Dane. "Come here, trade places with me. You've got to see Kayla. She's so beautiful!" And she pushed herself to her feet.

Dane gave her an unsure look. "Hey, I'm not exactly a parent type," he said as he slowly knelt down beside Inca.

"You do not have to be to look at a baby or touch her tiny hand."

Giving Inca a nervous smile, Dane turned his attention to the first newborn. Soon he was mesmerized by the baby's little hand, waving energetically from side to side as she noisily fed. "Her fingers are so perfectly formed," he said in a low tone. "It's just amazing, isn't it?" He reached out, and the moment his finger made contact with Kayla's hand, her tiny fingers wrapped strongly around his. "Oh," Dane exclaimed, "she's strong!" And then Roan transferred his son carefully to Dane's awaiting arms. He handled the precious cargo carefully. The babies looked similar, and yet each had slightly different features. Dane rocked the baby gently and grinned uneasily. They laughed. Roan patted him on the shoulder to reassure him that he was doing just fine.

Maya stood back, all smiles. Grandmother Alaria had tucked her hands into the long sleeves of her robe and was standing there, her face serene and pleased. Looking around at Inca, with her dark hair loose and shining; Roan in his short-sleeved, plaid shirt and jeans; and Dane, who seemed hypnotized by little Michael, Maya realized there were no dry eyes in the birthing room. A baby broke down barriers in everyone, she thought, warmth flowing through her heart as it throbbed with joy.

There was a movement at the door, and Maya turned. She saw Mike Houston, dressed in a white, long-sleeved shirt with the cuffs rolled up, tan chinos and hiking boots. He was smiling as he placed his hands on the doorjamb and looked in at all of them. Maya heard Inca cry out his name, saw her lift her hand toward him. Mike nodded to Maya and then to Alaria.

"Hi, gang," he called. "Hey, I hear a little girl and boy were just born."

Dane got up and moved to Maya's side as Mike came over. He shook Dane's hand and then Roan's. Then he lowered himself to his knees, at Inca's side. "Come here, Little Sister," he said, calling her the endearment he'd given her ever since they'd been bound by blood in a ceremony long ago. "Let me hold you...." And he placed his arm around her and gave her a long, gentle embrace. Inca sobbed and slid her arm across Mike's massive shoulders as he hugged her.

"Mike!" she wept. "I am so glad you could come! I wanted you here, to be with us...."

"Hey, what's this?" Mike laughed as he pressed a kiss to Inca's hair. "Tears? You should be jumping up and down for joy. Look at what you did. She's pretty, Inca. Just beautiful. You did good, girl."

Self-consciously wiping the tears from her eyes, Inca smiled bravely up at Mike. "Even now you joke and tease me."

Chuckling, Mike ran his hand lovingly across Inca's head. He gave Roan a wink. "Hey, I'm just built that way, Little Sister. Everything looks like it went well. You feeling all right?" He gave her a searching look.

Inca responded with a trembling smile. "Yes...even after eight hours of labor." She gazed up at her husband and reached out and squeezed his hand. "I could not have done it without Roan."

Mike nodded. "I'm sure. Well, hey, this little squirt is awful pretty. She looks just like you, Inca." And he touched Kayla's pudgy, rosy cheek. Then, he rose and went over to Dane. Opening his arms, he took Inca and Roan's son into his arms, pride in his eyes as he studied the sleeping baby boy. His voice turned scratchy as he regarded them. "Thanks for calling him Michael. That's a helluva compliment," he said and he grinned unevenly, tears coming to his eyes.

Inca sniffed and smiled at Roan, and then shifted her tearful gaze back to her blood brother. "I swore a long time ago if I were ever allowed to have a son, he would be named in your honor."

Mike leaned down and placed a kiss on the baby's thick, black hair. "Well," he said, his voice strained with emotion. "This son of yours will always have my heart, Little Sister. Thank you...both of you, for this honor." He gazed tenderly down at his namesake and rocked him gently.

Standing back, Maya slipped beneath Dane's arm. He always knew when she needed to be held. Giving her a warm look he saw Maya wipe tears from her own eyes. Dane knew how much Mike meant to Inca. He was her blood brother and they were so very close, like family.

"Think you'd ever want one or two of these little critters?'' Dane asked, pressing a kiss to Maya's temple. He saw her smile and raise her gaze to his. There was such happiness in her emerald eyes.

''Maybe…some day. Not now, though….''

Nodding, Dane understood. Just seeing Roan and Inca together, Roan's arm around Inca's shoulders as she nursed their baby girl, made him love Maya even more fiercely. Someday, when she realized that her mission could be fulfilled by others who would come and do a tour of duty at her base, Maya might connect into her mothering side. Right now, she used her nurturing skills to mother her squadron, instead. Smiling to himself, Dane could see them having one or two children. He'd like the opportunity to try and be a good father, to work with Maya to help their children grow up healthy and happy. Coming from a broken home, he knew what to do to help a child feel safe and secure. And he knew that because Maya had been a foster child adopted by very loving people, she had an awful lot of love to shower on any child she might have.

Dane knew enough of Inca's background, the pain, the abandonment and loss, to know that little Kayla and Michael would heal many of the deep wounds left within her soul. And the way Roan cared for his wife moved Dane deeply. Roan was a big man, rough-hewn, but his touch was tender and obviously filled with complete love toward Inca. Looking at himself in reflection, Dane could see some similarities between him and Roan. As much as Inca was the introvert, the shy one, the one who hid from much of life and civilization except for the small world she'd carved out in the Amazon jungle, Maya had taken an opposite path. She was out there—extroverted, confident, assertive and combative when she needed to be. Not that Inca wasn't a warrior, because she was, in her own way. Still, the softness of Inca's features told Dane that Kayla and Michael, along with Roan's love and support, would help her bind the last of her open wounds from the past. They had a very bright, hopeful future together.

Mike kissed Kayla on the noggin, gave Inca a kiss on the cheek and then handed Roan back his sleeping son. He excused himself. "I need to talk to Maya and Dane for a moment. I'll be back in a little while."

Inca nodded. "Do not be long, my brother?"

Mike nodded. Reaching down, he tousled her hair a little. "Not long," he promised her. He got to his feet and moved over to Maya and Dane. He turned his back toward Inca and Roan, his voice lowered. "I hate to be a wet blanket on such a happy occasion, but if you two have a moment, I need to talk to you about some stuff that's stirring."

Rolling her eyes, Maya muttered, "Even here, we can't get away from the heavy energy."

Mike hitched one shoulder and gave her a wicked look. "The world doesn't stop turning just because we're here. You know better than that."

Frowning, Maya nodded. "Okay, let's go over to the main kettle on the plaza to grab something to eat. I'm starving to death." She didn't want to discuss things in front of Inca that might upset her right now. Inca deserved the happiness of the moment. She didn't need to hear about another combat mission that Mike had more than likely cooked up, judging from the look in his eyes. Inca's life had been one of constant war. Right now, Maya wanted her to enjoy the peace and harmony that she so richly deserved with the birth of her twins and with Roan at her side. Nothing should upset this precious moment for her.

"Inca, Roan, we're gonna grab a bite to eat. We'll be back in a little while," Maya said lightly.

Inca lifted her head, her eyes showing instant worry. "You will come back? Can you stay a little while longer?"

Maya nodded. "Dane and I are planning on spending at least two days here with you." She saw instant relief in Inca's moist eyes. More than anything, after giving birth to her babies, Inca wanted her family nearby, Maya knew. When she turned and looked at Grandmother Alaria, Maya could tell the older woman was aware that something was up.

Quietly leaving the birthing hut, Maya walked on one side of Mike Houston, Dane on the other. There were several logs in the center of the plaza that had been cut in half and positioned in a square around the black tripod and kettle. A fortifying cereal known as *kiwicha* bubbled in the pot over the coals of the dying fire. Maya picked up some wooden bowls from a nearby table. Going to the kettle, she spooned healthy portions into each. They all sat down with their food at the table.

Pouring some honey onto her cereal, Maya took one of the many clean wooden spoons held in a large, rough-hewn cup. "Okay, Mike, you've got that look in your eyes. What's comin' down?"

Dane sat next to Maya. Houston sat across from them, his expression becoming serious. Pouring some honey into his own bowl, he stirred it slowly.

"You ever heard of a Mexican drug lord by the name of Javier Rios?"

Maya nodded and chewed on the grainy-textured cereal. "He's one of the main kingpins in Mexico for drug runnin' from there into the U.S. and Canada. A mean son of a bitch who'd rather fire first and ask questions later."

"Yep, same one," Mike said. He poured some water from a pitcher into his wooden cup. Offering some to them, he filled two more cups. "Morgan has been contacted by the U.S. Border Patrol. They're asking for his and the army's help in putting Apaches along the Mexico-U.S. border. The pilots of drug-carrying planes are flying into the States undetected, and the border patrol doesn't have the facilities to stop the air shipments. Rios knows this. He's got enough money to hire U.S. pilots who are looking to pick up an easy ten grand to fly a couple hundred kilos to dealers in major cities.''

Dane quirked his lips. ''So they want Apaches along the border to pick them up on radar as they fly from Mexico into U.S. airspace. And then what? What do you want them to do? Fire on them?''

''I wish. They deserve it,'' Mike growled, taking a deep draft from his glass. Setting it down, he wiped his mouth with the back of his hand. ''The Apaches are to do interdiction duty from San Diego, California, through Del Rio, Texas. The army is going to provide a certain number of Apaches to fly between point A and B every night with their radar turned toward Mexico. Any flight they pick up that's not got a flight plan is suspect. They are authorized to initiate a second Apache, which will meet the intruder flight carrying the drugs and force it down at the nearest available airport.''

''So, no shooting them out of the sky?'' Maya said. She scraped her bowl and finished off the last of the tasty cereal.

''No. The Apaches are to identify, interdict and ground 'em, that's all.''

''So, where does Maya come into all this?'' Dane queried.

Mike put his empty bowl aside. ''I need three of your savviest pilots, Maya. Women who are used to cowboying around, know drug dealers, can smell 'em coming a mile away and aren't afraid of a little confrontation. There's actually three missions being planned. Two are border patrol related and the third is an undercover one. I also need one to help coordinate the border patrol with the U.S. Army contingent. She will be responsible for setting up a plan of action and coordinating this whole ball of wax—successfully. The others will go to San Diego and work with the agents at the other end.'' He smiled at her. ''You got a pilot like that?''

''I'm thinking of one in particular,'' Maya said. ''Chief Warrant Officer Akiva Redtail. She's trim—an Apache and Lakota woman warrior. She's got that sixth sense you're wanting. She's been with us for three years and she knows the ropes."

"Is she aggressive?"

Dane chuckled. "Tell me one Apache pilot who isn't? It's bred into them, Mike. I've flown with Akiva and she puts new meaning into the word 'Apache.' She can teach us a lot about aggressive interdiction."

A grin softened the hard line of Mike's mouth. His gaze remained on Maya. "Well?"

"You need three of my pilots," Maya began, thinking out loud. "First of all, I know Rios. I've tangled with him before." She frowned and tapped the wooden table with her fingers. "Will Mexico give us permission to fly in their airspace?"

"Yes."

"How far from the border?"

"They haven't given us a distance yet. That's still on the negotiating table right now."

Leaning forward, Maya gave him a cutting look. "You know as well as I do that bribery of high Mexican government and police officials by drug lords is rampant. What you really need is permission to work without many people knowing what the plan will be, if you want success."

"Okay," Mike said, "tell me what you're thinking."

Giving Dane a knowing look, Maya said, "Interview my pilots—Akiva Redtail and Lieutenant Dallas Klein should be on the list. Dallas is my X.O.—executive officer—and you're going to need someone of her capabilities, her familiarity with mission planning, to coordinate this whole thing tactically. Akiva will be good to go on Mexican airspace interior work, hunting down some of Rios's aircraft on their home turf. Or maybe that undercover mission."

Nodding, Houston murmured, "Okay, you got my attention. I'll take this info back to Morgan and he can contact the responsible parties about it."

"Sounds good to me," Maya said.

"They won't mind these TAD assignments?"

She grinned. "Not if I know my women. They like to be where the action is, and right now it's pretty quiet, for once, down in our sector. Until those other two drug lords take over Valentino's turf, it should be pretty peaceful—almost boring—at the base."

Dane placed his arm around her shoulders and smiled over at her. "I like the peace and quiet."

Mike eased off his chair. "I've got to get going. I'll be in touch with you by satcom, Maya. Thanks for your help. Morgan will be sending down someone to interview your volunteer pilots very shortly. So, stand by."

"I'll look for info on these three up-and-coming missions, Mike. Thanks for thinking of us." She watched as Mike moved back to the birthing hut to say goodbye to Inca. Sighing, she rested her cheek against Dane's shoulder. "Just when I think it's finally going to quiet down, something else pops up."

Kissing her wrinkled brow, he whispered, "I know. The only thing we can count on is change."

"Isn't *that* the truth." Maya slid her arm around his waist and kissed the hard line of his jaw.

"Your base is going to become a real international hub for Apache pilots," Dane told her proudly. "We have two from the Netherlands scheduled to come in a month from now. And other countries that have bought Apaches from Boeing are standing in line fighting to get orders to Black Jaguar Base. Everyone wants real-time combat experience and this is the place to get it."

"Once an outcast, now the darling of the military elite," Maya chuckled. "Talk about the twists and turns of life."

Dane squeezed her gently. "Well, life is really all about those little babies in Inca's and Roan's arms. We're doing this for them, for their generation. If we can keep the heat on, if we can make these drug lords pay in their own backyard, maybe we'll make enough of a difference. Maybe their children will see real peace in their lifetime.''

Maya saw the worry and the determination in Dane's eyes. She sat up and turned to him. Sliding her hands around his jaw, she whispered, ''One heart, one mind. We're a good team, darling.'' The emerald ring glinted on her left hand. ''Why don't we sew up the loose ends on our relationship and make them permanent?'' She saw his eyes flare with surprise. Maya had never talked of marriage since he'd given her the engagement ring.

Taken aback, Dane stared at her momentarily. Slipping his hand over one of hers, he brought it to his lips and kissed the back of it gently. ''You're serious?''

Her eyes filled with laughter. With tenderness. ''Very. You ready to make the leap? To go from single to married, Major York?''

The corners of his mouth quirked. Drowning in the green depths of her sunlit eyes, Dane rasped, ''Yeah, if you are, Major Stevenson.'' And he grinned broadly at her.

Maya looked up toward the birthing hut. ''I'd like Grandmother Alaria to marry us, Dane. I know our families would like a wedding, too. We can marry here, and then have a second ceremony at your father's home in Texas, can't we? And my mom and dad can join us there as well.'' She searched his pensive features.

His blue eyes were warm with love—for her. ''Why not? Will that make us twice as married?'' he chuckled.

She joined his laughter. ''Humor...no matter what the circumstance.''

''That's one of the many things you love about me.''

Maya's lips curved. ''You're so sure of yourself, Dane York.''

''Another reason you love me.''

''Yes.''

''And my unflagging confidence.''

''That, too.''

He preened a little and squared his shoulders a tad more as he held her warm emerald gaze.

"They broke the mold when they made you, York."

Dane gave her a very proud look, one eyebrow moving upward. "Thank you."

Maya broke into a grin. "You're so full of yourself, York."

"Yeah, I know it." Laughter rumbled from his chest.

Sitting there in Dane's arms, Maya surrendered to his strength and tenderness. Closing her eyes, she rested her brow against his jaw as he held and rocked her. Dane was one of a kind and so was she. Jaguars mated for life. And she wanted him as her mate. Forever.

* * * * *

Chapter 1

Sarah gasped as a giant of a man walked into her camp. She hadn't even heard his approach. Out of instinct, she swung her rifle into firing position.

"Hold it!" she ordered. "Don't move or I'll shoot!" He'd crouched into combat stance.

Frightened and confused, Sarah tried to control her chattering teeth. "Who are you?" she croaked, and she saw his intent gaze soften. Her heart pounded beneath his cursory inspection. The hard line of his mouth relaxed slightly.

"Ranger Harding, U.S. Forest Service," Wolf answered the shivering woman. "You can put the gun down." He set his own beside a tree to show his peaceful intent. She seemed to be trapped beneath a tree, Wolf saw. She certainly posed no threat to him. She was covered with mud, and exhaustion was evident in her strained features. Still she stood out like a yellow buttercup, he thought, her blond hair contrasting brightly with the lush green of the surrounding trees.

"Ranger?" Sarah said challengingly. "You'd better prove

it, mister, or I'll blow your head off before you come a step closer.''

Wolf was nonplussed by her angry response. She appeared to be serious. He looked down at his olive-green gabardine uniform. ''I've got a badge underneath this,'' he offered, slowly moving his hand to open his jacket and show it to her.

''Don't move!'' Sarah stiffened, and the gun's barrel wavered. Black dots swam in front of her eyes. Did that mean she was going to faint? She couldn't—not yet!

Wolf scowled. ''How am I going to prove to you who I am, then?'' How could something so tiny and bedraggled be so completely distrusting? But very real fear showed in her huge blue eyes, forcing Wolf to respect her anxiety, whatever its cause.

''You could have a gun under that jacket,'' she said.

One corner of Wolf's mouth quirked into a bare semblance of a smile. ''Lady, where I come from we hide guns in a lot of places, but under the jacket's a little too obvious.''

Sarah stared at him hard. Maybe it was the faint curve at one corner of his mouth that made her want to believe him. How could she trust this man? Sarah had learned the hard way that she couldn't afford to trust anyone—even the people she loved most had abandoned her in one way or another. No, she could depend only on herself. She had no choice.

''Move slowly, mister. Show me your badge—real slowly. I'm a crack shot.''

Wolf suspected she was in a lot of pain—possibly in shock. She was extremely pale. Wolf's protective nature reacted strongly. On the team in South America, he'd been the leader and paramedic, and now his caring instincts were aroused in spite of the unnecessary game she was playing with him. ''I'll bet you are,'' he said, easing the jacket aside to reveal the silver badge above his left breast pocket.

''Your credentials,'' the woman bit out. ''A badge means

nothing. I could go to Anaconda and buy one at a surplus store if I wanted."

Hollows showed beneath her delicate cheekbones and Wolf could see darkness stalking her eyes. He was certain she was in shock, and going deeper by the minute. How long had she been trapped here? "Look, you are in no shape to be playing this silly game. From the looks of things, you're hurt."

The rifle wavered badly in Sarah's hands. "You could kill me. I'm so tired, and my legs are numb. I can't get myself free," she muttered, more to herself than him.

"I'm not going to hurt you," Wolf told her soothingly. "Put the rifle down," he urged, "and I'll come over and help you."

"I'll put it down, but not out of my reach." So much of her wanted to give in, to rest...Sarah ached to believe what she thought she saw in the man's eyes. Was he really a ranger or one of Summer's men playing a trick on her? She had no choice. She had to let him help her. Reluctantly, she put the rifle down in the mud beside her.

Then she looked up at the ruggedly handsome man who could be her savior—or her enemy...